MAGEBORN:

THE ARCHMAGE UNBOUND

BY
MICHAEL G. MANNING

Cover by Amalia Chitulescu

Map Artwork by Maxime Plasse

Illustrations by Michael G. Manning

Copyright 2011 by Michael G. Manning

First Edition May 2012

Second Edition March 2018

All rights reserved.

ISBN: 9781943481224

Printed in the United States of America

Dedication

I would like to dedicate this book to my family. They provide a lot of inspiration for me, in particular my wife, who often serves as a role model for some of the feistier female characters in the novels. I'd also like to thank my proof-readers. Their input made this a more enjoyable reading experience for all of us. You know who you are.

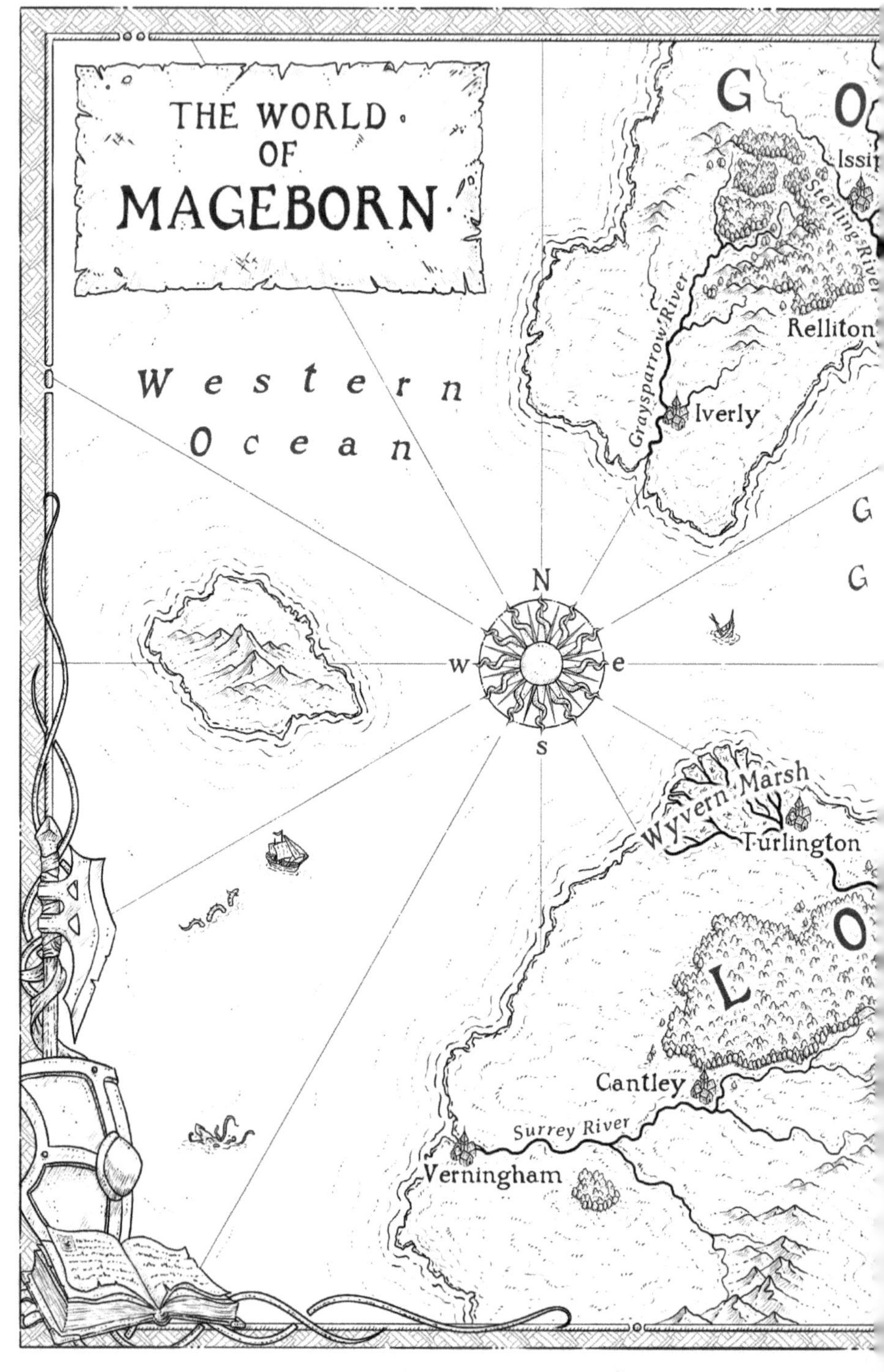

THE WORLD
OF
MAGEBORN

Western Ocean

N
W   e
S

Graysparrow River
Sterling River
Issi
Relliton
Iverly
G
G
G
Wyvern Marsh
Turlington
Cantley
Surrey River
Verningham
L O

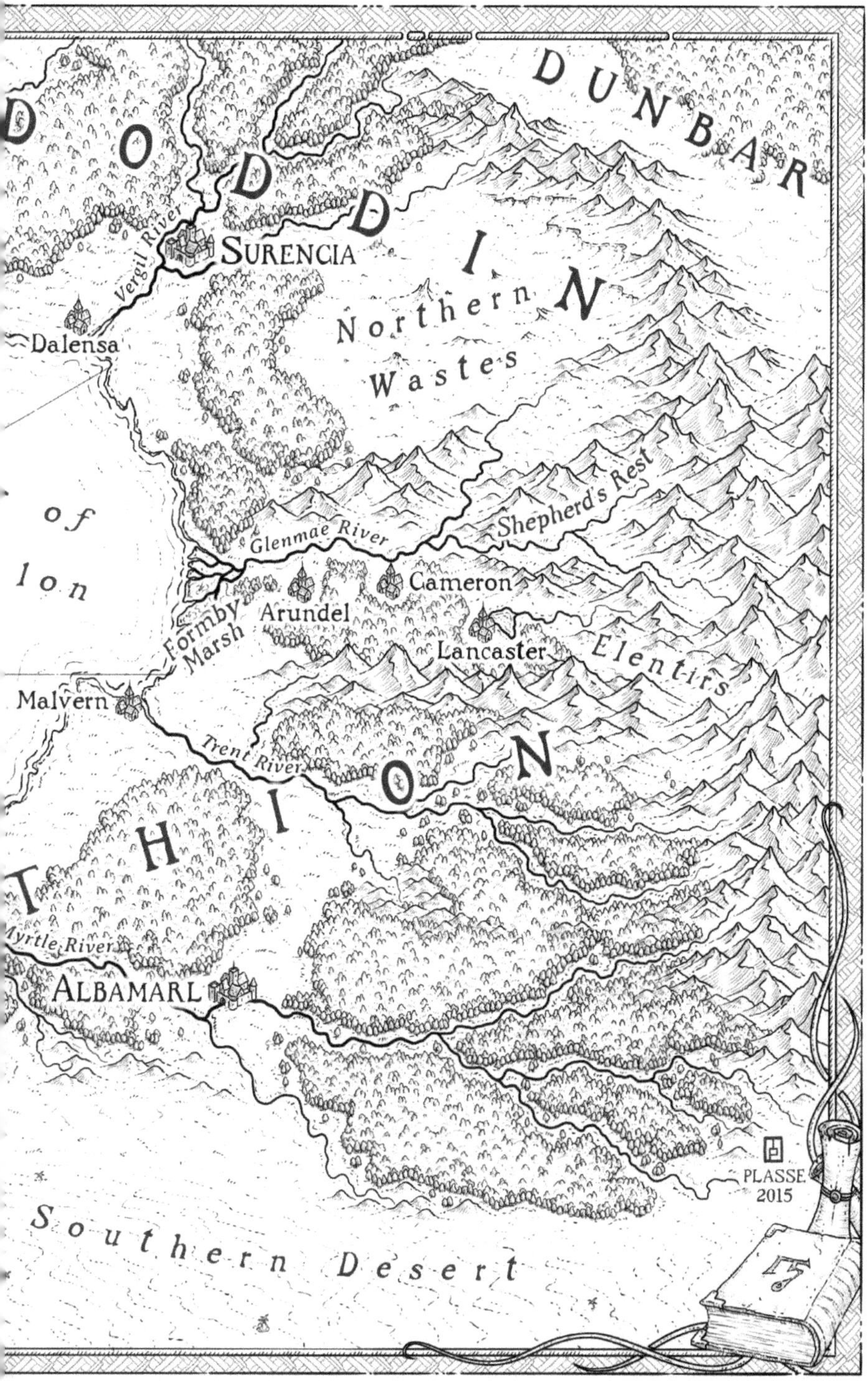

DUNBAR
DODDIN
Vergil River
SURENCIA
Dalensa
Northern
Wastes
of
Ion
Glenmae River
Shepherd's Rest
Cameron
Arundel
Formby
Marsh
Lancaster
Elentirs
Malvern
Trent River
THION
Myrtle River
ALBAMARL
PLASSE.
2015
Southern Desert

CHAPTER 1

I walked carefully down the stone stairway leading to the lower parts of Lancaster. Although I had spent considerable time in the castle during my younger days I had never dared venture into these places before.

James Lancaster was well known as a fair and equitable lord; consequently the dungeon of Castle Lancaster had seen little use during his lifetime, aside from the occasional thief. Recently the war with Gododdin had changed things, but not as one might expect. There had been no prisoners in that war, I had seen to that. The memories of that war were still fresh and I frequently woke trembling at night, though I rarely remembered the dreams that disturbed my slumber.

Today I had come to remedy one of the problems that had been held over from that war. One of my allies, a man I had come to consider a friend, had turned against me near the end. It was no simple betrayal though, Cyhan had had his reasons. Considered from a different perspective it might be said that I had betrayed him, rather than the reverse. The warrior locked up here had acted according to his honor and the trust given to him by the King, a king who had already declared me an outlaw. In fact, the more one looked at the situation the less Cyhan deserved the cell he was currently locked within.

None of these thoughts were new; I had mulled them over almost daily since the end of the battle outside Castle Cameron. I should have come sooner, but a thousand more urgent matters had kept me away and when I did have the rare free moment I procrastinated. This was not a conversation I looked forward to.

I stood now outside a heavy wooden door and with my mind I could sense the other man waiting within. He had heard me coming long before I reached the door, but that was no surprise. Being almost completely empty the dungeon was very quiet, and every sound seemed magnified. I had come alone, though James had urged me to bring several guards with me. The last time I had faced Cyhan he had been hell bent on sending me to an early grave.

I had declined the offer of guards. I wanted to talk to him alone. Besides, if he did attempt violence I doubted guards would be much help. The veteran fighter was quite possibly the most skilled and dangerous warrior I had ever met. If I couldn't stop him the guards would just be additional casualties. I would have brought someone like Dorian with me if I had thought it might come to that.

Taking a deep breath I removed the bar and with a thought and a word unlocked the door. I hadn't brought the key, but locks were rarely an impediment for me anyway. The smell within was anything but pleasant. The man I had come to see was sitting at the far side of the room and he watched me intently as I stepped into the room but made no move to rise.

I looked him over carefully. Cyhan appeared ragged but in good health. James had made sure he was provided with clean water and decent food. His hair was unkempt but I could tell he had been doing his best to wash himself occasionally. A man such as Cyhan wouldn't let himself fall into despair. "You look like shit," I told him casually. Normally I like to start conversations with a compliment, but none had come to mind.

His face crinkled for a moment, an expression almost like humor passing quietly over his features, but it was gone before I could be sure. He declined to respond.

"I am here to settle things between us," I added.

"You must have set a date then," Cyhan ventured.

I almost asked him 'for what' before I realized he meant for his execution. "I don't plan to execute you," I replied.

"Then you're a fool."

"I wonder that you never became a councilor to the king, your charm is wasted as a warrior," I answered sarcastically. "I came to offer you some choices."

"Forget it. I have done as I swore to do. My choices were my own, and unlike some, I have kept my oaths." His gaze was piercing as he said this. It was a deliberate attempt to goad me into anger.

"The last time you used that one on me I lost my temper. Don't waste your time with that tactic," I said. Actually the last time he had called my mother a 'failure' and I had tried to attack him. Too many things had happened over the past few months for me to lose my cool over petty insults.

"At least you're learning," he responded. "Still, I will not change my stance. Your only choice is to kill me."

"*I* will decide what my choices are," I said calmly, "and you will listen to what I have to say before you make your own choice."

He didn't waste words by bothering to answer. Instead he stood up, a slow careful motion that carried a subtle hint of menace. I watched him intently but continued talking, "The king sent me a message the other day." I could see that I had the older warrior's attention and his body language conveyed a sense of interest.

"And?" he asked.

"He wants to meet… secretly. He didn't state his reasons, but I expect he wants to find a way out of our awkward political situation," I elaborated.

"He wants you dead. Your victory here created as many problems for him as it solved," Cyhan replied.

"I didn't think you still cared." My remark was sarcastic but my intuition told me that it might not fall far from the truth.

"I think you will be the undoing of mankind and I swore to put an end to you if the bond were broken." He paused for a moment before adding, "Still, if things were otherwise, I would gladly call you 'friend'."

I almost choked. That was as close to an emotional confession as I had ever witnessed coming from the stalwart trainer. I covered my shock with a short laugh. "You never fail to surprise me. Honestly, I'm starting to think you'd try to kill your own mother if she were in my position."

He gave me an even stare that answered the question better than any amount of words could have done. As unsettling as that thought was, at least he was consistent. I went on, "Do you honestly think I'm still going mad? It has been over a month since the bond was broken."

"How would I know? Madness can take many forms. Are you still hearing the voices?" he asked. I could hear an honest curiosity in his voice.

"Certainly… I hear them constantly now. I've become quite used to it. It isn't nearly so unsettling once you realize what the voices represent," I said calmly. In truth I could hear the deep thrumming of the earth below us even now, and the air brought a quiet murmur I had come to associate with the wind. The world itself was alive, and I could hear it whispering softly to me with a thousand voices. Now that I understood what I was hearing it wasn't nearly as frightening as it had initially seemed.

A shadow passed over Cyhan's face as I spoke and he turned away. "Tell me… what do they represent?" His voice was even but my senses easily picked up the growing tension in his body.

"The world is alive and those who have the right sort of ears can hear it speaking. That's all," I said.

"You say that and still expect me to believe you are not mad?"

"The wizards before the sundering didn't have the bond. Some of them could hear the voice of the earth… and they could call upon it for aid. Moira Centyr didn't defeat Balinthor with mere wizardry," I answered.

"Lies! Did some dark spirit whisper these things to you, to convince you your madness was power?" Cyhan turned to glare at me and his face was lit with anger.

"No. I read them, in a book of history written not long after the sundering itself. My father's house has an extensive library well protected from revisionist priests and politicians."

"What is that supposed to mean?"

"Exactly what it sounds like… whether you choose to believe it… or not, is entirely up to you," I said calmly.

"I couldn't possibly believe that," he said.

"Of course you can't. In order to accept that you would have to face the possibility that much of what you were taught is a lie, that the very truths that you based your oath upon, that you have lived your life for… were false."

"You're wasting your time," the older man growled under his breath.

"Answer one question for me. If you believed me… if most of what you had been taught was shown to be false… what would you do then?" I asked.

Cyhan paused for a moment and I could see him giving it serious thought. Something approaching sadness settled in his eyes for a moment before he answered, "I would fulfill my oath."

"What folly! What meaning does honor have if it does not serve reason?" I exclaimed.

His face was deadly serious when he replied, "Honor is all I have and it means nothing if I could change my oaths at a whim."

"It is worse than nothing if it doesn't answer to a man's conscience!" I spat out. For all my reserve the resolute warrior in front of me had finally managed to rouse my ire. Not that my anger had any discernible effect. "I can't believe I thought you might possibly listen to reason." Turning away from him I stepped back into the corridor. "Come on," I said, gesturing for him to follow, "it's time for you to leave."

He stepped out into the hallway behind me. "You really are a fool," he muttered.

I didn't bother to look back at him, "Don't push your luck." With my extra senses I could see him looking around as he followed me up and out of the dungeon; even now he was looking for opportunities… whether they were for escape or murder I didn't want to know. I led him through the castle halls and eventually we emerged into the sunlight of the castle yard.

"Where are we going?" he asked.

"The stables," I replied, not bothering to explain further. A few minutes later we reached the stable and I told the groom to fetch my horse. I had ridden to Lancaster that day, rather than use the teleport circle.

Cyhan raised an eyebrow as I handed him the reins, "What sort of game is this?" he asked. I could almost hear the unspoken 'boy' at the end of his sentence. At some point during the war with Gododdin he had stopped adding that to his sentences when he spoke to me, but some habits are hard to break.

"The king wants me to meet him at a small village named 'Tilbrook' in two weeks' time," I said. "I need to send him a reply and I'm short on messengers. I figure returning you to his majesty's service will serve that purpose and get you out of my hair."

"You want me to tell him you'll be there to put your head in the noose?"

"I don't intend to go. Tell his majesty I will meet him in his chambers within a day or two of your arrival," I said.

"I doubt that he'll welcome that message. If you intend to sneak into the royal palace it might be wise not to warn him you're coming," he suggested.

"For a man that wants me dead you're remarkably full of advice," I responded. "By warning him in advance I'll be able to give him three messages at once. The first being that I can come and go at will, whether he is forewarned or not, and second that I am a civilized man… otherwise we would already be looking for a new king." I stopped there.

"What is the third message?"

I smiled. "That's for the king's ears alone; otherwise there'd be no purpose for our private chat."

Cyhan mounted the horse and looked down at me. I could see a dozen possible responses flickering across his features, but in the end he left with a simple statement, "I regret our next meeting Mordecai." The calm confidence in those words sent a chill down my spine but I shrugged it off. I hadn't come this far by giving in to fear. I watched him ride for long minutes with my eyes and I continued to follow his progress with my arcane senses even after the trees had obscured him from view.

Since Penny and I had broken the bond my 'magesight' had returned to its previous acuity. If I focused my attention I could sense things slightly more than a mile away. If I was following a particular person or thing I could stretch that limit even further, to something approaching a mile and a half. As far as I could tell, that was the limit of my 'wizardly' senses, but I was beginning to learn that there were other ways to experience the world.

Cyhan and the horse I had given him were passing beyond my normal limit now, and still they seemed to be headed in the proper direction, south, toward the capital. I decided to test my newer abilities and took a deep breath, stilling my mind and listening quietly to the voices that surrounded me. As usual the first sensation was one of confusion, much like walking into a crowded room filled with a hundred different conversations. The key was to relax and listen, 'til you could locate the sound of a familiar voice and begin to make sense of their conversation. This time I had a particular voice in mind and I focused on the susurrations of the wind. Over the past month I had discovered that the wind is a capricious and chaotic entity, at times soft and gentle it could turn wild with little notice. I felt my mind expanding as I followed its random eddies and currents until I was swept out into an ever larger sky filled with scattered clouds and warm sunshine. As my world expanded I struggled to keep part of my attention upon the terrain near Lancaster, and one particular rider on a road not too far from the castle.

He was still heading south, though I wasn't sure why I cared anymore. For some reason I had yet to comprehend, the wider I spread my awareness the less I cared about the particulars. The real skill lay in balancing the knowledge of the carefree wind against the well-defined questions of my all too limited human mind. If I opened myself too much I would forget my reasons for looking and be swept away in daydreams of swaying trees and rushing clouds, not enough and I wouldn't be able to find the information I wanted.

I stood there, transfixed for what may have been an hour, or a full day… time no longer seemed relevant. I had watched the tiny rider and his mount pass beyond the border of Lancaster but they no longer interested me. What really fascinated me now were the great currents of air that drove the clouds to the south and east. I could feel myself spreading ever further as the sun poured through me, illuminating the earth below and casting dappled shadows from the clouds upon the ground…

"Mordecai!" Someone was shouting into my ear again. The voice seemed familiar. I blinked, which was a strange sensation for I couldn't recall having something periodically blocking my vision like this before. Something stood before me, a strange creature with soft filaments of reddish gold streaming around it… what was that called again? *Hair I think, that's what I used to call it,* I thought to myself. She was also waving her appendages at me… *She? What does that mean?* I wondered.

At last my fragmented thoughts began to come together and I realized that Ariadne Lancaster was standing in front of me, waving her hands in my face to get my attention. "Mordecai! Can you hear me? Look at me!" she said, sounding alarmed. Things snapped into focus at last, and my eyes locked onto hers.

"Ariadne?" I said stupidly. "What's wrong?" Ariadne was my best friend Marcus Lancaster's younger sister. Although she was a few years younger than us she had developed into a stunning beauty, much like her mother. Red gold hair framed a pixie's face that was currently marred by a look of concern.

"I should be the one asking that question," she replied. "You've been standing in the yard out here all afternoon. I came out to talk to you earlier but you seemed entranced so I left you alone."

"All afternoon…" I mumbled. I was still having a little trouble getting my mind wrapped around the meaning of the words.

"Yes, all afternoon. When I came back to check on you just now I got a bit worried, you were sort of transparent and you looked as though you might start to float away. I started yelling to get your attention and I tried to grab your shoulder but I couldn't get a hold on you. My hand went right through you." She paused and slapped my arm. "You seem perfectly solid now, though. What were you doing?"

"I'm not sure," I said idly. "I was monitoring Cyhan's progress out of Lancaster… I think."

"You're not sure? It took me several minutes just to get your attention; you were looking straight through me as though I wasn't even there. Were you able to tell if he went the right direction?" she asked. The wind had died down and her hair was lying calmly across her shoulders now.

"I'm sure of that. He went south, heading toward Albamarl. If he's planning to double back he went an awfully long way before changing directions." A stray thought passed through my mind, *her hair looked better with the wind in it.* A sudden playful gust picked a lock of hair up and tossed it about. *Did I do that?* I wondered but I couldn't be sure. I hadn't used my power; the wind seemed to move of its own accord.

"Focus, Mordecai." Ariadne snapped her fingers in front of my face. "Your eyes were drifting away again. Am I going to have to talk to Penny about you?"

"No I'm fine," I lied. "I'm just trying to get used to some of my abilities." In truth I really wasn't certain. "What did you want to talk to me about… before I frightened you?" I forcefully drew my mind in on itself and began walking toward the main keep.

Ariadne kept pace with me as she responded, "I wanted to ask you about Marcus. How has he been?"

Her brother hadn't returned to Lancaster after the end of our battle with Gododdin's army. His goddess had refused to heal Penny when she was mortally wounded, ostensibly because Penny and I had broken the bond that shielded my mind. That refusal had led Marc to reject her and the resulting void within him had left him despondent and a bit lost. He had been staying with me at Castle Cameron since then but I hadn't been able to draw him out much. Naturally his parents and siblings were worried about him.

"He's about the same," I replied. "I convinced him to have a few drinks with me and Dorian the other day but he wasn't very jovial."

Her brows pinched together in an expression of concern. "I wish he would come home for a while. Maybe I could talk some sense into him."

I sincerely doubted having his younger sister nagging at him would help, but I didn't dare tell her that, instead I used my considerable powers of misdirection to rephrase my thoughts. "I don't think having your father lecturing him would help much right now." I do seem to be gaining some wisdom as time goes on.

"You're probably right," she agreed. "Will you be staying for dinner or returning home right away?"

I honestly hadn't given it much thought. My focus had been entirely on how to handle Cyhan when I rode out that morning. I was pretty sure Penelope expected me home for dinner that evening, though. "I hadn't planned on staying this late actually. But if you like, we could have dinner here tomorrow evening. I'm sure Dorian would like an excuse to visit his mother as well." Dorian was living with us in Washbrook now, serving as my seneschal and master at arms.

"Is Rose still staying with you? If so, you should extend the invitation to her as well," Ariadne added, giving me an impish grin. She seemed to like Rose Hightower; she had looked up to her as a young girl. I suspected she had some ulterior motive, though. I didn't doubt that she was plotting to fix Rose and Dorian up together. Penny had similar ideas, though I wasn't sure I approved of their meddling, as far as I could tell the two of them would be just fine if everyone left them alone.

"I wouldn't dream of leaving her out," I answered politely. Our steps had brought us to the building James had had constructed to hold the teleportation circles I created in Lancaster. "I will have to say good-bye, I need to return. I didn't expect to spend so much time standing in the courtyard."

"Give Penelope my regards. I do hope you can both visit for dinner tomorrow," she replied.

"I can't imagine anything that would keep us from the invitation," I said with a smile, and then with a thought and a word I teleported back to Castle Cameron.

CHAPTER 2

The hall was empty when I stepped out of the alcove in Castle Cameron. I felt a bit relieved actually. Lately I had been besieged by various people needing me to make decisions about this and that. The castle itself had survived our recent war with little damage, aside from the one wall that was breached. Repairs there were proceeding rapidly and soon enough I would have the workmen starting on a new outer wall to encircle the rest of the rapidly growing town of Washbrook.

With some luck I might be able to reach my workshop without encountering anyone needing me to make pressing decisions. I had taken over my father's smithy and expanded it to suit my needs. I doubted I would ever become a master smith as he had been, but I did frequently work with metal and the forge was quite handy when I needed it. There might have been a few sentimental reasons as well, but I tried not to dwell on those.

I waved at Cecil Draper as I left the main door of the keep and headed across the yard. My luck didn't hold though, Cecil left his post and ran up to me before I could get ten steps toward the smithy. "My lord! Sir Dorian asked me to let you know he was looking for you."

I stopped and gave him a gracious smile, "And where would my friend be presently?" I really wasn't in the mood to deal with Dorian just then but I always tried to be polite in dealing with the people who supported, and were dependent, upon me.

"He said he would be at the tavern my lord," Cecil replied quickly. I nodded and changed direction. The tavern he was referring to was operated and maintained by Joe McDaniel, a good friend of Dorian's and also the head of our town militia now. After things had quieted down I had given him the house Penny and I had lived in (before the castle was completed) and he had made great strides in having it remodeled into a serviceable tavern.

I spotted the large wooden sign soon enough, gaily painted with a large pig covered in mud. The artistic rendering had been inspired by my first meeting with the Baron of Arundel, on which occasion I had slathered myself with mud to better make a good impression. Taverns traditionally had simple names that could be depicted with pictures since many people couldn't read. This one had the words, 'The Muddy Pig' written carefully under the picture. It was a bit embarrassing that they had chosen my meeting with Arundel to use for the name of the tavern but hopefully people would soon forget the meaning behind the name.

I stepped through the doorway and let my eyes adjust to the somewhat dimmer interior; it was twilight outside and the lamps inside hadn't been lit yet. The evening crowd had barely begun to gather so I didn't have too much trouble spotting Dorian sitting at the end of the bar. "Ho, Dorian!" I shouted to catch his attention. "Cecil said you were looking for me?"

My large friend's head turned as he heard my voice and his eyes lit upon me. "Mort! Glad you're back. How did it go?"

Naturally he was referring to my visit with Cyhan. "I let him go and he told me I was a fool," I said, summing up my previous conversation for him.

Dorian snorted, "You are, and a stubborn one at that. I still think it's a mistake."

"Only time will tell my friend, surely you didn't want me just so you could nag about a mistake already made?" I hid my impatience poorly.

"In a hurry to get back to work again? Sit down, you can spare a few minutes. Have a drink." He waved at Joe who had been listening intently and the older man went to draw a tankard for me. "It's about Marc," he added.

"Ariadne was asking about him as well," I told him.

"She's right to be worried, he isn't getting any better."

"He's just depressed. He'll snap out of it eventually. He seemed alright when we were together the other night," I said.

"That's the only time, when he's with us, and drunk… we can't do that every day," Dorian answered. It was odd to hear him urging sobriety, since reaching his majority Dorian had shown a great fondness for drinking.

"Where is he today? I notice you're sitting here alone," I remarked pointedly.

"Joe asked me to come by this morning and take him back to his room. He passed out a little before noon," he replied.

"Point taken," I said, grimacing. "He hasn't done that before has he?"

Dorian sighed, "It hardly matters. It's almost random, he starts drinking whenever he wakes up, and usually that's in the afternoon. You'd know this if you paid more attention." I could hear a tone of rebuke in his voice.

"Look I'm sorry Dorian, I've just been busy. There's so much to do…," I told him, hoping he would understand.

"Yeah I know. There always is, but you have to make some time for your friends. What have you been working on anyway? Every free minute you have, you sneak off to the smithy."

I was glad he had turned the conversation to a more positive topic. "Actually I was thinking of having you come over and look at it. I could use a second opinion," I answered smiling. Of everyone living in the area, Dorian was the first I wanted to see this new project. I took a long draught, trying to finish my beer quickly. "Now would be an excellent time, you should come see," I said rising to my feet.

"Always in a hurry aren't you?" Dorian took a long breath and then finished his mug. "Alright, let's see what monstrosity you've cooked up this time!" He rose and followed me to the door.

When we finally reached the smithy I spent a moment and a word to light the work area. I had installed several enchanted globes around the perimeter of the room for lighting. I could have made do by conjuring light myself each time but I had been experimenting again. These simple glass globes could be lit by anyone, provided that they knew the proper command word. I had initially created them with Penny in mind, but now that they were finished I was considering making more for our rooms in the castle. They might be useful for lighting the streets of Washbrook too, but I doubted I'd have time to start mass producing them.

"Those are really nice!" Dorian said looking at the enchanted glass.

"No not the lights… I made those weeks ago," I told him. "This is something I think you will *really* appreciate." I moved over to one of the long workbenches set along the wall. The top of it was covered with a large canvas drop cloth, concealing what lay beneath it. Dorian looked over my shoulder curiously. "You remember how I enchanted your armor?" I said, reminding him.

"Of course, the damn stuff still hasn't started rusting," he remarked.

"This is like that… only better." I drew the cloth back, revealing a beautiful set of armor. Unlike most of the armor currently in the keep this was actual plate armor, crafted from carefully shaped and articulated steel plates. Armor of this type was still extremely rare in Lothion, and usually reserved for the very wealthy. Technically I was currently one of the wealthiest nobles in Lothion, but given my outlaw status I really had no way to spend my money, or even access it, since most of it was still in the Royal Bank. But I hadn't bought this armor; I had carefully crafted it over a period of two weeks.

"Holy… Mort where did you get this?!" Dorian exclaimed. I found myself pleased with his shock and surprise.

"I made it," I said modestly.

"Seriously… where did you get it?" he repeated. Even as he implied that I had lied about the source, he ran his hands over the greaves, marveling at the lovely maroon lacquer that had been applied there. The breastplate and vambraces were similarly adorned with matching patterns, highlighted by gilding around the edges and a golden hawk in the center of the breastplate.

"I made it Dorian. Look at the colors and the design," I replied.

Recognition lit his face as he realized that the colors and design matched the Cameron arms. "It looks like your livery! How? You couldn't have bought this."

I was beginning to get exasperated with his continuing disbelief, "One more time… I made it."

"Even your father couldn't have made something like this!" he exclaimed. A look of embarrassment crossed his face as he realized what he had said. My father had died a few months prior, right before our battle with the army of Gododdin.

I gave him an even stare, "If he'd ever put his mind to armor crafting, I don't doubt but that he could have done so."

"Sorry Mort, I wasn't thinking. I just meant… well your father was much more skilled with metal and he never produced anything like this. How did you?" Dorian's hands were still examining the armor.

I didn't have the heart to get angry. Dorian and I had been friends most of our lives, and I wasn't the only one to have lost his father. Instead I took up a small piece of scrap metal. "I have a lot of advantages my father didn't have." I set the metal in the cold ashes of the forge and heated it with a word and my power. Within a minute it was glowing brightly, close to the melting point.

"Normally I use the forge for heating the metal, but since it isn't lit at the moment it would take too long to show you," I continued. *"Na'Pyrren Ingak mai Lathos,"* I intoned softly, blowing on my palms, and then I reached into the forge and pulled out the fiercely glowing piece of metal… with my bare hands.

Dorian flinched visibly when he saw me touch the metal with my naked skin, but he kept his tongue. If I didn't know better, I'd think that he was getting more used to casual displays of magic. "Is that really necessary?" he asked. "There are plenty of tongs for that here."

"The spell isn't just so I can pick the metal up without being burned," I replied and then I began kneading the metal with my fingers, as if it were a piece of very stiff clay. I had imbued my hands with an unnatural degree of strength and hardness, for even as hot as it was the iron would have been impossible to mold without using a hammer and anvil. I shaped the metal into a rod by rolling it between my hands, reheating it as necessary, and then I bent it into a circle, joining the ends with a simple lap weld. It only took me a couple of minutes since I was able to shape the metal quickly with my bare hands.

"Why did you set it in the forge if you were just going to use magic to heat it?" Dorian asked.

"Habit… and I didn't want to burn the workbench or risk damaging the anvil," I said as I twisted the hot metal into a spiral.

Dorian watched the glowing orange iron in my hands with fascinated eyes. "What is that supposed to be?"

"Nothing," I replied, "I was just making a point. Using magic I can shape metal almost like a potter shapes clay. It makes a lot of things vastly easier when you don't have to use a hammer and tongs to do everything."

"You always had clever hands," Dorian remarked, "but somehow I thought you'd be doing something more productive than sitting around here creating new forms of art."

"Oh ye of little faith," I intoned solemnly, "that's what this *is*." I gestured at the armor still quietly gleaming on the worktable.

"Something like that would take one of the king's finest armorers half a year to make," Dorian stated, yet his face was full of doubt.

"I'm not going to try and convince you. Hold still for a moment." I walked past him and picked something up from the table behind him.

Dorian's head twisted to follow me. "Wait a minute there Mort! Don't be doing anything strange now!"

I laughed inwardly. Have I mentioned that my friends trust me implicitly? "Relax! I'm not going to use any magic on you." I bent over and reached for his ankle but my fearless friend sidestepped with an almost comical hop.

"What's that?" he asked nervously.

"A tape-measure… hold very still or it might strangle you," I remarked sarcastically. Taking another step I began measuring him carefully. After a moment he relaxed, although we did have an awkward moment with the 'inseam' measurement. I won't go into that, though.

"I'm still patiently awaiting your full explanation, are you planning to make another set of armor like that for me?" Dorian asked. Although he hid it well I could almost hear the secret desire in his voice. What warrior wouldn't want a set of armor such as was lying there on the bench in front of him?

"Not exactly," I said mysteriously. I knew the vague answer would drive him crazy but I couldn't help but draw things out. "I copied one of the sets we stole from the king when we liberated my goods from his warehouse, but now that I've finished with it I think it could be improved."

"How so?"

"Well, to begin with the enchantments I add give an exceptional amount of strength and integrity to the metal, so I think I can redesign some of the joints and remove some of the extra pieces they used to guard the underarms, the inside of the elbows et cetera." I pointed to the wings that flared out past the piece of metal that guarded the elbow.

"You mean the couter?" Dorian asked, pointing to the articulated metal joint. I guessed that must be its proper name.

"Yes, the elbow and knee couters particularly," I answered excitedly. I was glad to finally know the actual name for them.

"The ones at the knee are called poleyns," he chuckled as he corrected me. It wasn't often Dorian got the upper hand when it came to intellectual knowledge, but he knew the warrior's craft far better than I did. Of course he was raised to it. "You shouldn't get rid of the wings on them," he added seriously.

"But they aren't necessary," I insisted. "The chainmail in those places will be strong enough to prevent any weapon from piercing the wearer there."

Dorian sighed. "Mordecai, you are so smart that sometimes I forget how ignorant you can be. Those wings aren't to prevent a cut or stab. What do you think a man wearing this sort of armor fears most?" He paused to give me a chance to answer but I wasn't playing his game so I waited him out. Eventually he continued, "He fears the mace and the axe. Those wings are to keep a crushing blow from destroying his knee or elbow."

"Oh…" I replied intelligently. "Does the same thing apply here?" I pointed to the round disks that were mounted below the pauldrons that protected the shoulders.

"Besagews," Dorian supplied. "They're called besagews… and yes the same reasoning holds true there, they protect the underarm."

"You make do without them in your current armor," I argued.

"My chain hauberk protects me from cuts and arrows; it does nothing to prevent broken bones. That's the very reason they started designing 'this' sort of armor," he replied.

Dorian's knowledge was clearly superior to my own in this regard so I drew out my carefully done plans for the next set of armor and showed them to him. I began showing him my proposed changes to the design and after several hours he had talked me out of most of them. If my father had still been alive he would have laughed and told me that I should have consulted an expert in the beginning, but then I had always been one to make mistakes first and *then* learn from them.

We grew so engrossed in our discussion that the hours flew by and we were both late for dinner. As usual there never seemed to be enough hours in the day. When we entered the great hall, the conversation there dimmed for a moment as a hush fell over the assembled folk. That had bothered me at first but I had begun to get used to it. Now I merely nodded at everyone and made my way to my seat at the high table.

I stopped beside my chair and glanced at the food already set before it on the table. I could almost feel Penelope's eyes burning a hole through me as I gave her an apologetic look. "My dear lady wife," I said loudly, making sure my voice was loud enough to carry, "I hope I didn't worry you." I turned and addressed the room, "Please everyone… eat!" I tried to make my tone amiable to reassure them. It seemed to work as the conversations around the room started up and everyone relaxed and began eating again. I had learned a lot watching how James Lancaster dealt with his people, but inwardly I still felt awkward.

Penny leaned toward me after I had sat down, "You're getting better at that but it is still embarrassing when I have to start without knowing when you're going to show up." Her voice was pitched low enough that no one would overhear us and I could tell by her inflection that she was only mildly annoyed.

"Sorry," I said sincerely.

"Just send me a note if you're going to be late so I don't have people standing around waiting for you before we just decide to eat anyway," she replied. Since taking on the mantle of lady of the castle she had become markedly more demure and courteous… at least in public. I let my eyes wander over her, taking in the modest dress she wore. It was complemented by the sapphire earrings and necklace that she wore. Her attire was tasteful without being extravagant and I could not help but admire her beauty. Penny's eyes met mine and she spoke again, "Stop staring… you'll set people to talking."

I grinned at her, "Let them talk. I'm married to the most beautiful woman in the world. It would be more unusual if I didn't stare now and then." I didn't bother to keep my voice low either.

She blushed and gave me a look that told me I'd pay for embarrassing her, but it was a pleasant look. "What were you doing that was so important it kept you and Dorian from coming to dinner on time?" she said, changing the subject deftly. "Lady Rose was most disappointed when he wasn't here at the start."

Rose Hightower happened to be sitting next to her when she said that and she shot Penny a warning glance. "I was merely concerned," she said, dabbing at her lips with a hand towel.

Dorian spoke up then, "Forgive me for worrying you lady, I was merely educating my good friend the Count as to the particulars of the armorer's craft." As usual he seemed completely oblivious. I was beginning to doubt he would ever realize his love wasn't unrequited… then again perhaps he kept himself in the dark on purpose. If he ever admitted to himself that she felt as he did he might be forced to do something about it. That was probably a more terrifying possibility for him than facing the army of Gododdin had been.

"Armorer's craft?" Rose said, lifting one eyebrow in an artful expression of surprise. "Is the good Count planning another war so soon?" As she spoke I watched her carefully, despite her conversational skills her eyes lingered on Dorian much longer than they did anywhere else.

"Stop that Rose, and you as well Dorian. I've told you both to call me by my name. This isn't some state function, it's dinner, and this is my home," I said.

Dorian chuckled; they both loved teasing me with my newfound station. "Careful Rose, we mustn't offend our kind host," he said in mock seriousness.

"Very true Dorian! Please forgive us Mordecai," Rose responded, joining him in the game. As she spoke she put her hand lightly across his forearm. It was a small gesture, one intended to emphasize her words, but I would have bet a pound of gold he'd never move that arm so long as her hand rested there. She probably knew it too. Women are devious.

I sighed, pretending to be annoyed so they could continue their game. "Could I get some wine?" I spoke loudly enough for the man passing behind to hear, for I assumed he was one of the serving staff. Yes, I do have serving staff now… not to mention hiring a full time messenger. Whoever it was ignored my request and continued on, passing through the doorway that led to the kitchen. "That's odd," I said to Penny, "Did I speak too softly?" I hadn't bothered to turn my head so I wasn't entirely sure who had ignored me.

She smiled at me, "It might help if there had been a servant near enough to hear you."

"There was!" I protested, "A tall fellow, almost my own height."

"I'm afraid you're mistaken this time Mort. No one has gone by for a minute or more, but I think I see one of the maids coming now…" She lifted her hand and waved one of our servers over, Lisette was her name I thought. She quickly hurried off to fetch a cup and some wine for me.

I frowned and closed my mouth. In point of fact I hadn't actually looked around but I was so accustomed to using my 'extra' senses that I hadn't needed to do so. I was quite certain a man had passed by, even if Penny hadn't noticed him. There was little point in arguing though; in any case the wine was coming so I had nothing to complain about.

"Mordecai, you never did answer my question," Rose reminded me.

I was startled from my thoughts, "About?" It took me a moment before I remembered. "Oh, the armor!" I exclaimed. "I'd rather not talk about it here. I'd like to keep the details quiet until I'm ready to announce the plans. Perhaps we can discuss it later?"

"Ooh a mystery!" Rose replied with a twinkle in her eyes.

"It isn't anything that exciting, trust me," Penny assured her. "Of much more interest would be the topic of your visit with Cyhan today. You still have not told me how it went."

Apparently Penny was not alone in her curiosity, for everyone leaned closer. I took a deep breath, hoping to finish the tale in one go rather than have to repeat myself. "It went about as well as can be expected. He and I agreed to disagree."

Rose broke in, "That sounds remarkably civilized when the disagreement was over whether you have the right to continue breathing." The humor in her voice was gone now. Rose had been quite angry about Cyhan's decision to end our working relationship so violently. I wasn't quite sure if it was because he had hurt Penny in the process or the fact that he might have killed Dorian in his attempt to get to me.

Dorian laid a hand on her shoulder, as if to calm her down. The gesture made the two of them seem very familiar; although I'm sure he didn't realize it. "Rose, he may be our enemy now but to give the man credit he was only acting according to his oath and his principles." I couldn't help but wonder that just an hour or two prior he had been chiding me for letting my enemy walk free yet now Dorian was defending the man.

Rose gave him a sharp glance, "Honor be damned! He turned his sword against his student and his friend," she said, looking at Penny and me each in turn, "and against you." She punctuated the end of her sentence by jabbing Dorian firmly in the chest. "Any oath that requires such a thing needs to be re-examined. Blind obedience is the refuge of a fool too scared to think for himself!"

Penny's face was a study in conflicting emotions but she put her feelings away and tried to steer the conversation back to practical matters. "All those things aside, what did you do Mort?"

"I sent him back to the king with a message," I replied simply.

"A damn foolish thing to do," Dorian supplied.

Rose snorted, "We agree on that at least."

"You're probably right, but I wouldn't have the man executed for doing his duty," I answered.

Dorian grimaced, "His duty will see you dead and he should not be taken lightly. I can respect his decision but when you have a sworn foe in your grasp you don't hand him a dagger and turn him loose."

"What message did you send him with?" Rose asked quietly.

"The king has asked me to meet with him, privately. I changed the time and place and sent the information along with Cyhan," I said.

Penny looked at me sharply, "You said you weren't going." She kept her voice level but there was a certain amount of worry in it.

"I changed my mind. I'm still not going to meet him at the time and place of his choosing; rather I'll meet him on my own terms."

"That's wise, since it's even odds your meeting would be an ambush. Getting rid of you would solve a lot of the King's problems at one go. Where do you intend to meet him?" Rose asked intently.

I smiled, "In his bedroom."

"Somehow I doubt his majesty will agree to that," Dorian observed.

"He won't be given the option to decline," Penny snapped at him impatiently. The tension in her shoulders was unmistakable. "Are you sure this is wise? This isn't what we discussed earlier." She and I had gone over the topic the night before and now I had changed the plan.

To give her credit, my wife is no shrinking violet. I had come to respect her as a woman of courage and determination, but she was sometimes a bit timid when it came to risking my health. I suppose that made some sense, considering she was expecting our first child. I glanced down at her already swelling waist. Looking up again I met her eyes, "I'm sorry love. I know you're worried, but I have to clear things between myself and the king or we'll never have peace. I think this is the only chance we'll have."

She saw the look in my eye and knew there was little sense in arguing. "You'd best be right, or I'll make sure you spend whatever's left of your life regretting it." It was no idle threat coming from her.

"Our child will have a father," I assured her. Penny's determination was possibly one of her most beautiful qualities.

"A surprise meeting will introduce a certain amount of tension into your discussion. Are you sure that's what you want?" Rose asked, breaking into the conversation again.

"Absolutely," I stated. "Edward needs to understand that I'm negotiating from a position of strength or he'll never respect any bargain we make."

The discussion went on for a solid hour after that, but I had already made up my mind. When all was said and done, no one liked my decision but there weren't any better suggestions made. Only the future would tell whether it was a good idea or not.

CHAPTER 3

The next morning I decided to take a break from my usual routine. Rather than head to the forge and resume work on my next bit of armor crafting I went looking for my other childhood friend. Thanks to Dorian I had paid better attention at dinner the night before and managed to notice a notable absence at the table.

I wondered how many other meals Marc had missed without me bothering to ask about him. Times like this made me realize that I wasn't exactly the best friend a fellow could have. Sure, I had plenty of excuses… a new wife, a county to run, but I still couldn't allow myself that luxury. Excuses would always be plentiful, true friends were not.

I didn't see Marc at breakfast so I headed for the room he had been staying in. Pausing at the door I listened for a moment. I heard nothing and my other senses told me that my friend was inside, alone but awake. I had almost hoped he would have a 'companion' with him… that would have done much to allay my worries. It really wasn't natural for him to spend so much time alone; Marc had always been a highly social animal. I knocked on the door and waited.

There was no response though with my ability I could sense him pouring another drink from a bottle. I could only assume it was wine. I knocked again and spoke loudly, "Marc it's me, open up!" He chose not to answer and instead slumped over as if he were sleeping. He knew I could sense him through the door. "That's not going to work," I yelled at the wooden door, "I already know you're awake."

"Go away!" came a muffled response from within.

I'd had enough, so with a word I unlocked the door and opened it. Marc was sitting on the divan across the room, staring bleakly at me as I entered. He was holding the wine bottle in a curious fashion in one hand. "What are you planning to do with that?" I asked.

"I was giving serious consideration to the thought of tossing it at you," he said dryly, "but then I decided it would be a waste of good wine." He changed his grip on the bottle and turned it up, taking a long swallow directly from the bottle.

"You look like shit," I volunteered.

"Thanks," he replied. "That means a lot to me… coming from you." His tone was surly and I could tell he was ready for a fight.

"If that's your idea of witty repartee you really are drunk."

"Not yet, I just woke up. Give me an hour," he said.

"Why don't you give the wine a rest today and help me with some planning?" I suggested. It was actually a half-truth. While I wouldn't have minded having my friend's advice on my near future plans I obviously wanted even more to snap him out of his dark mood.

"I've got a better idea Mort!" He sat up suddenly, as if filled with energy and enthusiasm. "Why don't you go make your plans, and leave me alone? That way you'll get better plans and I won't have to listen to your bullshit!" He lifted his bottle again and started to take another long draught of wine.

"If you're going to be a sarcastic ass you might as well do it sober," I replied and before he could react I deftly slipped the bottle from his hand. Ordinarily his reflexes were so quick I'd never have managed to do it… but a lot of hard drinking had made him slow.

"You ass!" He was too slow to catch the bottle but planting his hands in my chest he gave me a hard shove. I fell backward over a small table and landed on the floor. Marc leaned forward and started to take the bottle back but I planted a foot in his chest and sent him flying across the room. He bounced off the corner post of the bed and crashed into the dressing table. "Bastard! You'll regret that!" he shouted at me and snatched up a clay water pitcher as it started to fall.

Even hung over and strung out as he was I had to admire his dexterity at the catch… 'til he chose to fling said pitcher at my head. The motion caught me off guard and I failed to duck. Thankfully the shield I still habitually kept around myself prevented me from getting a cracked skull. "Hey! You could have seriously hurt someone like that!" Having fought a few times as children we both knew there was an unspoken rule against throwing heavy objects… or doing anything else potentially permanent.

"As if I could hurt you! You and your stupid shield… why don't you take that thing off and fight like a real man?" he challenged.

"Fine!" I yelled back. "You could use a good thrashing. Did it ever occur to you that your family might be worried about you?" As I spoke I dropped my shield, though there was no visible sign of it.

"My family is none of your damned business!"

"Your sister is worried about you, so is Dorian."

"What about my father eh? I guess he didn't bother to ask after me did he!?" Marc was standing now and approaching cautiously.

"At least you have a father!" I shouted back.

"How long are you going to play the pity card over that one?" he sneered.

"Till I've knocked you on your ass and beaten some sense into your head," I replied a bit more calmly. My anger was only half real, in the back of my mind I was still trying to calculate what the best way to bring my friend to his senses would be.

"Still got your shield up?" he asked. From an outside viewpoint it was almost odd how calm he seemed as he asked that question, but it seemed normal enough at the time.

"No I took it down a moment ago...," before I could finish my words he caught me in the mouth with a quick jab. I stepped back quickly before he could follow up with another but he didn't press his advantage. I wiped the blood from my lip... I could already feel it starting to swell. "Not bad," I commented.

"Might improve your looks," he snapped back.

I stepped forward and took a short swing at him but I found only air. I threw a few more but I still failed to connect 'til finally he blocked one and planted a sharp punch in my stomach. As he delivered the blow I got my left arm around his shoulder, his second strike drove the air from my lungs but I held on and managed to start a grapple.

Things improved for me after that. As with our childhood scuffles I was still no match for him in a straight up punching match, but once we had closed I was the better wrestler. My longer legs and arms gave me better leverage and he lost the advantage his quick reflexes normally gave him. We stumbled about the room for several moments before he tried to drive me into the bed post. With a twist I took his momentum and he wound up getting the hard wooden corner in his back.

With a strangled cry he quit trying to break the grapple. That seemed like a good idea, so I let go and rolled off of him, panting to catch my breath. "Are you alright?" I asked.

"Hell no! It hurts like hell!" He had his hand against his lower back. "That was a shitty move."

"You're the one that tried to run me into it! You're too damn strong for me to hold you down, so it was either you or me," I bit back.

He scowled at me for a long minute while he rubbed at his aching backside. I glared back at him 'til finally neither of us could take the tension any longer and we broke into grins. A moment after that we started laughing and our anger drained away.

"Some things never change," he said once our chuckling slowed down.

"I thought we had outgrown these little chats."

"Me too," he agreed ruefully.

"Desperate times require desperate measures," I announced.

We were lying on our backs side by side now. The hard wooden floor wasn't exactly comfortable but neither of us complained. Then Marc spoke again, "Desperate indeed my friend. I appreciate what you're trying to do, but it isn't going to be enough."

With a sideways glance I could see him staring at the ceiling. "Why not?" I asked.

"Because it hurts Mort, it hurts far more than you can possibly realize." He rolled his head over and caught my gaze. We had been friends for most of our lives and looking into his brown eyes I could see the pain behind them. I watched him for a long moment before he looked away. Tears had begun to well.

"I don't understand," I confessed.

"Nobody does. Even now, even knowing the truth, I want her so badly it feels as though someone is driving a stake through my heart. It's painful Mort… excruciatingly painful." He was referring, of course, to his goddess. Perhaps I should call her his 'ex-goddess', Millicenth, the Lady of the Evening Star.

"We all lose things, it's a part of life," I said softly.

"This isn't like that Mort. Imagine living happily with Penny for years and years, having children, loving them and receiving their love. Imagine everything you ever wanted, love, respect, trust… all of it. Now imagine you wake up tomorrow and discover that it's all gone. Not only is it gone, but it never existed. The woman you loved wasn't real; she was a dream, created for the sole purpose of manipulating you. The children, your life, your happiness, all of it was a lie, fabricated by a being so foreign that it didn't even hate you… you were merely a tool." Marc paused for a moment.

"She made you think you had children?" I asked, puzzled.

"No… idiot! I was using that as an example, it was the closest thing I could think of to convey the sort of happiness she created within me. It wasn't just happiness, it was… everything. While she was with me I had no doubts or fears. Death might threaten but she was holding my hand, and I believed she would be waiting for me beyond death's doors. Every action had meaning, and every moment was full of importance, all part of her plan to better humankind. No… it wasn't just that…" He stopped for a moment, a note of shame in his voice.

"What?" I asked. I wasn't certain I wanted to know, but he wouldn't have begun if he hadn't needed to get it off his chest.

"It was like sex, only better. The entire time I was in her service I abstained from women… I had no desire for them. Whenever I healed someone…" I saw a shudder run through him as he remembered.

"You had an orgasm when you healed people?"

"No! But my shame is just the same, worse, the sensation was far better than an orgasm. It was like a drug, an exaltation of the mind and spirit, as well as an ecstatic sensation of physical pleasure. Why do you think I went looking for people in need?" The look in his eyes was one of abject despair and humiliation. "I 'wanted' to find sick people. I needed it… and when my craving became so bad that I had dreams of hurting people, just so I could heal them… she forgave me. She told me it was normal, a weakness of flesh forced to contain the divine."

I couldn't help the feeling of revulsion his words evoked, "That's…," I stopped myself before I finished with what I was thinking, 'disgusting'.

"I knew it was wrong, but I had to believe her. I needed to believe her. I was like an addict… I am an addict. Even now I have dreams… I want to go back to her so badly." He cradled his head in his hands.

"Yet you rejected her," I said, hoping to remind him of his own inner strength.

"Even in that decision I cannot claim pure motives. Truly I was angry that she refused to aid Penny… that was the moment when I could no longer pretend she had our best interests at heart. I already knew… deep down… but in that moment I was sure. Even so, I would not have had the strength to reject her if I hadn't been so angry."

"Angry that she wouldn't help Penny," I added for him.

"No," he answered in a voice devoid of hope, his face was red and his eyes were swollen with tears now. "I was angry that she wouldn't give me what I wanted… what I needed. It was the anger of an addict who's been told he can't have more."

I stared at my friend for long minutes. He had run out of words and I had none to give him. My only thought was that a man of noble spirit had been broken, and turned into this. The friend I had known so long was ruined, thoroughly, inside and out, more completely than anyone could be. Looking back I think that was the day that I realized anyone could be corrupted, that none of us were immune to evil. No matter how lofty our ideals, we are all susceptible to weakness and depravity. It was a final passage from innocence to adulthood.

Yet we still have choices. Perhaps not good ones, and sometimes they seem insignificant, but they are still choices. At the very least every morning holds the choice, sink into despair or get up and try to do something, no matter how meaningless.

Eventually my thoughts came together and I spoke, "So what are you going to do now?"

He laughed, "There's nothing to do. Let me have that bottle and I'll do the only thing I can to dull the pain." There was no apology in his voice, merely numb acceptance.

"That's just a slow death," I replied.

"Suits me fine," he said. "It isn't as if I want to live anyway. What I have become… isn't something that deserves to live."

"Do you really want to die?" I asked without a hint of mockery.

"Yeah."

"Then let's do it."

"What?" he asked with a note of surprise.

"Not me of course, I still have things to live for… but if you really are in that much pain you should let me help you," I told him earnestly.

"That isn't funny. I'm being serious here Mort."

"I know. I love you Marc. You've been one of my best friends for as long as I can remember. If you're hurting this badly I want to help you." At that moment I was deadly serious, and he could see it on my face.

"Why?"

"Let's look at the alternatives," I explained. "You can drink yourself to death… over a period of months or years, hurting everyone that cares about you, forcing them to watch your slow decline. You could also end yourself in some spectacular manner, shocking everyone and hurting them even more. Or…," I paused and held a finger up, "You could let me help you."

"Help me how? You've lost me," Marc said, but as he spoke I could tell curiosity had replaced his anger and despair at last.

"Help you die. Normally when someone commits suicide they do it alone, and the result usually winds up being someone gets a very nasty and messy surprise when they discover what has happened. If I help you your options are vastly better. You can choose how, when and where and I'll make sure that no one finds your body… unless you want them too. You can just disappear and no one has to know… or I could get 'news' months or years later to give your family closure."

"You would do that for me?"

"I don't think I could call myself your friend if I abandoned you at a time like this, but…," I paused meaningfully.

"But what?" Marc asked.

"You have to swear to let me help you."

"What does that mean?"

"It means you can't do it alone. If you seriously decide you want to do this you have to let me help you.

You can do it however you want… I'll help with any plan you come up with, but you have to tell me first and it can't be something stupid like drinking yourself to death."

Marc stared at me carefully for a long moment; his face held more hope than I had seen in a month. "Fine, you have a deal," he said.

"Swear it," I insisted.

"I swear to let you know when and how I will die, so long as you swear to help rather than interfere," he answered.

"I swear to help, no matter what."

"What now?" he asked.

"I have things to do this morning, how about you?" I told him.

Marc laughed, "There's nothing on my schedule. I had planned to drink myself into a stupor but that seems rather pointless now. I guess I'll start planning."

"I suggest you take a bath and shave first, no sense smelling like a dead rat. Don't forget though… you have to tell me first, no matter what you decide," I stressed the last part.

"I will. I'm not sure about the shave though, I was thinking of growing a beard." He passed his hand over the patchy growth that had sprouted across his cheeks. Marc had never been blessed with a good beard; the hair grew willy-nilly across his cheeks, leaving some spots almost completely bare.

"That's probably a bad idea for you my friend," I said, patting him on the shoulder.

"I think you're just afraid my beard might look better than that paltry goatee you have there," he replied mockingly.

"Believe what you will… but some of us have the gift and some of us have… well whatever that thing sprouting on your face is," I teased him. We kept the banter going for several minutes after that before I finally made my way out.

As I headed to my workshop I wondered what he would decide. My instincts told me whatever it was would be better than what he had been doing. Finally I put the thought aside and decided to trust him. I had a feeling things would work out, but I've always been optimistic.

CHAPTER 4

That evening Marcus made it to the dining hall, freshly shaved and looking much better. He was still pale but he was definitely sober. Dorian gave me a quizzical look… I could almost hear his unspoken question: *What did you do?* Later when I had a chance I told him I had spoken to Marc, but I never did give him the details of our agreement. For that matter I didn't tell Penny either.

Two days later Marc caught up to me in the smithy. I had been spending so much time there lately that almost everyone knew to look for me there when they needed me now. My work was still proceeding at a good pace but it looked as if it would take me months to accomplish my goals.

"That must be the armor Dorian was telling me about," Marc said as he walked up. He hadn't announced himself when he entered but that was hardly necessary anyway.

I didn't bother replying, gracing him with an unintelligible grunt instead. I had my hands full of red hot metal and although I wore heavy leathers to protect my body and had spelled my hands and arms for hardness and heat resistance I still didn't dare relax my attention. Careless smiths didn't work for long, and that probably was doubly true for mage-smiths… if that was the proper term for what I had become. Maybe wizard-smith would sound better?

After a few minutes I found a good stopping point and set my work aside to cool, and then I gave my friend my full attention. "What's on your mind?" I was a little worried he might have come up with a 'plan' but I had decided not to mention it to him until he brought it up himself.

He gave me one of his old grins, the sort that meant he might be up to mischief. "I'm bored," he said finally.

"Nothing new there," I replied. "What are we going to do about it?"

"Well I've been thinking, about your offer. Now that I have that ahead of me it seems I don't need to rush things. Instead there might be a few things I'd like to do first."

I kept my face smooth but inwardly I was smiling. "Such as?" I asked.

"I've been thinking about what you told me before… about the things you read in that book on the history of Illeniel. I'd like to know more," he answered.

"You think you can do something about it," I concluded.

"No, but that's the point. I don't know. Until now I've been a victim, and that's part of what makes it so painful. Not only did she manipulate and betray me, she left me with the knowledge that nothing I do will matter. No action I can take now will affect her or the other gods in the slightest. Mankind as a whole and me in particular, we are insignificant… unworthy of regard or consideration." Marc leaned back and gazed at the cooling metal I had set aside.

"You think there might be knowledge that will help?" I suggested.

His eyes snapped back to my face, "Yes. The story you told me about the sundering, if true, is proof of that. If the gods were once less than they are now—then they aren't immortal, eternal, or unchanging." He clenched his fist as he spoke and I could see the anger simmering beneath his cool exterior.

"And if they aren't?"

Marc gave me a grin that sent a shiver down my spine, "Then they aren't gods, and if they aren't gods then they can be brought to task for the things they have done."

"Even if they aren't omnipotent it's very likely you still won't be able to hurt them," I reminded him.

"I have a friend who might be able to…," he said, looking squarely at me.

I suffered a moment of self-doubt, "That's a big leap. There's little indication anyone might have that sort of power."

"Moira Centyr did...," he said bluntly.

"She was an archmage."

"So are you," he replied.

"Maybe," I admitted. "In any case, she only defeated one god—and that was with a lot of help."

"It doesn't matter Mort. I'll seek what knowledge I can find. If any of it proves useful then I'll have made some sort of difference. If not—well I feel much better knowing you're there to help me… if it comes to that," he stopped there.

"Where do you plan to start?" I asked.

"Your house—there may be more histories in your father's library. After that I'll scour the libraries of the nobility, and if I can get to them, the records of the churches."

That gave me pause, there might be information there that none of us could guess at. "You're an ex-saint, which makes you about as popular with the followers of the evening star as a skunk at a tea party. You think they would let you near their coveted records now?"

"No, but I need a challenge," he declared. There was a light in Marc's eyes again. He wasn't the same man he had been, but he was better than the broken creature I'd found in his room a few days before. Revenge might be a poor motive, but it was better than despair.

"I'm assuming you want me to take you to the capital."

"Of course," he said with a smile.

"I'll take you after dinner this evening. I was planning to make a trip that way in a few days anyway. Now I can use that as an excuse to check on your progress," I informed him.

"Why are you going to Albamarl?" he asked.

I gave him my own evil grin, "I promised the king I would stop by and visit him."

A frown passed over his face before being replaced by a smirk, "You know… since you came and spent that week with me over a year and a half ago you've done nothing but make enemies. The list just keeps getting longer."

"When you have friends as good as mine you have to find a way to balance things out," I replied jokingly. Then I took a chance and asked a more direct question, "Are you feeling better?"

"If you were someone else I would say yes," he answered with a smile that didn't quite reach his eyes. "I'm not going to get 'better' Mort. I'm just going to get even, if possible."

"So your good humor has just been a façade?"

"Mostly. Even so, my façade is better looking than you do, even on a good day," he snapped back.

"Ha!"

"Anyway, Mort, I do need to thank you. I still don't really want to live, but you made me realize I had the choice and if I'm going to stick around a while longer I might as well do something to pay the bitch back for what she did to me. No sense in wallowing in self-pity meanwhile. When I've had enough I'll let you know." He stepped closer and embraced me in a bear hug.

Marc left after that and I collected my thoughts and returned to my work on the armor. As I worked my thoughts kept returning to what he had said, particularly the part about Moira Centyr. I still had a lot of questions about her. I hadn't spent much time exploring my new abilities since the day Penny and I had broken the bond. I wasn't even sure if I should call them 'abilities'. For the most part it just seemed like a broader form of communication.

Things like what I was doing now... working with the metal before me, those were clearly normal wizardry. I was using my own power to shape the material in my hands. So far I hadn't seen anything impressive about this ability that supposedly meant I was an archmage. Sure I could hear the earth, the wind, and a myriad of smaller things, but thus far it seemed to be mainly an informational ability. There were a few things that puzzled me though, such as when the earth had shaken back in Albamarl, when I threatened the banker. Or the way the wind had tossed Ariadne's hair a few days back, just after I had thought about it. In each case something had happened, but I hadn't felt directly responsible. Unlike wizardry, I hadn't exerted my own power, but nevertheless something had happened which coincided with my own thoughts and feelings.

Moira Centyr in particular was a startling example of something far beyond the ken of normal wizardry. Whatever she had done a thousand years before had changed her into a creature of the earth itself, an elemental being. How such a thing could happen was beyond my ability to guess, but as I pondered it I realized that I didn't have to guess.

My last contact with her had been while I was desperately trying to heal Penny. Naturally I hadn't had a chance to ask any non-essential questions at the time, but there was no reason I couldn't ask them now. I had actually been considering trying to contact her since that day, but until now I had had too many things distracting me to make a serious attempt.

The metal in my hands had gone cold. Startled, I realized I had been standing idle for several moments. I set the piece down and decided the time had come to do something. Walking outside I washed my hands and face in the water trough near the door. *I should find someplace a bit more private,* I thought to myself.

I took a walk, through the village and out the gate. As I went I studied the repairs to the outer wall. During Gododdin's siege of my home they had breached the outer wall that encircled the town of Washbrook. After our victory it had been the first thing on our list of important things to rebuild. The work had gone well and now the section of wall that had been torn down was only remarkable by the difference in color between the new stone and the older stone of the undamaged parts of the wall.

The masons were now laying the foundation for a much larger wall that would encircle the area where our palisade had been… and more. The most uncomfortable thing about the siege had been the crowding created by the fact that some of the town was outside of the defensive walls. If it ever came to that again I intended to make sure that we had room and then some for any future sieges. Once the new outer wall was built I would have several large barracks constructed, along with storehouses for food and supplies.

I didn't actually anticipate needing to fill those barracks with soldiers, but if I had to shelter the people of the county again there would be plenty of space for the farmers and their families to stay. *I should probably consider having a second well dug to provide easier access to fresh water,* I thought.

My steps took me beyond the walls and down the road toward the valley. I followed it for several hundred yards before I turned aside and headed into the trees that flanked the road on either side. I kept going 'til I found a comfortable looking spot to sit beside a large oak and there I settled myself, leaning my back against the massive trunk.

Closing my eyes I began slowly clearing my mind. My magesight had already made sure the surrounding area was clear of people so I felt secure in my privacy. A more careful scrutiny reassured me that there were no 'empty-places' that might indicate shiggreth nearby. I had not forgotten them despite the fact that they had remained in hiding since their attack on the village before the war.

Listening I focused my attention on the deep and steady thrumming of what I thought of as the heart of the earth. My awareness of my own body slipped away and was replaced by a more acute awareness of the ground beneath me, the feeling of the stone and dirt that stretched away for miles in every direction. As my connection to the earth grew firm I cast my 'voice' outward, calling her name, *Moira.*

I had never tried to contact her before so I wasn't entirely sure it would work. At first I felt nothing in response to my call but after an unknown period of time I felt… something, a more focused intelligence, approaching. Power moved in the earth around me and I felt the ground rise up slowly in front of where I sat, flowing and forming the shape of a woman.

"You called me," she said quietly. The sound of a purely physical voice surprised me and I opened my eyes to see her standing next to me. As before, she had taken the form of a human woman, perfect in every detail, except for the small fact of being made of earth and stone. Even her voice sounded almost normal, though it had a certain dry quality to it.

"You can speak," I said. I was mildly surprised, in the past she had spoken to me only in my mind.

"Why would you think otherwise?" she asked, though her face betrayed no visible emotion or curiosity.

"I assumed you could only speak to me directly, mind to mind. If you could talk like this you should have been able to talk to me even after I formed the bond with Penny," I told her.

"You are laboring under several misconceptions. I can only speak, move, or indeed act at all because you are *not* bound," she replied.

That made no sense to me. "The bond only interfered with my ability to communicate directly with my mind, how would that affect your ability to speak?"

"Who do you think you are talking to?" she asked.

I sincerely hoped she wasn't going to make a habit of answering my questions with questions, but with a sigh I answered anyway, "Moira Centyr—or have you changed names?"

"That is probably the best name to use, but it is not strictly correct," she said with an infuriatingly calm demeanor.

"Listen, I'm not really in the mood for this, if you aren't Moira Centyr then tell me who I *am* talking to. I'd rather not spend all day playing word games," I said impatiently.

"If I were still alive I'd have you punished for such impertinence," she answered with a faint hint of a smile. "In one sense I am the earth, in another I am a remnant of Moira Centyr, and in the most important sense I am you."

"Well that really clears things up," I said sarcastically. I should have expected an answer like that; magical beings never seem to have straight forward answers. I got my frustration under control and decided to tackle the subject systematically. "Let's start with the first thing you said, 'if I were still alive', I thought you *were* still alive. Did you die after you joined with the earth and defeated Balinthor?"

"The problem is really created by trying to force reality to fit into the form of language. Moira Centyr did not die, she changed, became something else... a part of the earth itself. From a human perspective, and in most ways that matter to humans, she died. I am what she left behind, an impression of her knowledge, an imprint of who she was, preserved within the earth... an echo of her mind."

I had a sinking feeling this was going to be a long introduction. I tried again, "So you're sort of a ghost?"

"No, I am her knowledge, preserved within the earth," she replied.

Same difference, I thought, but I didn't voice my opinion. "It sounds as if the distinction is mostly academic. Rather than split hairs over the details how about we just call you 'Moira' for simplicity's sake," I suggested. "Let's return to the original question, why couldn't you speak to me like this while I was bound to Penny?"

"Because I am *not* Moira Centyr, I am a memory. I have no volition, no will or motivating *self* beyond that which you provide. That is why I said that I am *you* in one sense."

Understanding was beginning to dawn, but I still wasn't clear on everything yet, "then why did you answer when I called you by that name… *Moira.*"

"I answered because you called. Your will, your desire, your motivation compel me to act, to respond. You provide the *volition* that creates this semblance of who Moira Centyr was, without your living will I am no more alive than the ground beneath your feet. I am a memory, given life and substance by your connection to the earth and your desire for answers."

I understood now but I was feeling argumentative, "The ground beneath my feet *is* alive. I've learned that much already."

She smiled then, flashing teeth like white pebbles, "That is true also, but the ground beneath your feet has no desire to speak or debate topics of human knowledge. It was given this knowledge by Moira Centyr and it acquires the desire to speak from your own living will."

"So I really am speaking to the earth."

"I am the earth, but I am not its voice… I am an echo of a woman who has passed beyond the knowledge of how to be human," she said. It might have been my imagination, but I almost heard a hint of wistfulness in her voice as she said it. I felt intuitively that her words were true, but I doubted they were the final truth.

A question popped into my mind suddenly. "Are there others?"

"Others?"

"Other impressions, memories left behind by previous archmages, like you...," I clarified.

"Not that I am aware of," she answered simply.

The answer disappointed me and left me more curious, "Why not? Are you the only archmage to have, er—been lost, or joined with the earth?"

"No, when I was alive I was taught that several had been lost in this way before."

"So why do you exist?" As the question left my mouth it occurred to me that it was a deep question that could just as easily be applied to myself.

"I was created to guard and preserve certain things, the Centyr family has always had a peculiar talent not found in the other great lineages." she said. Her voice had an almost hesitant tone to it, as if she answered reluctantly.

Of course that begged the question, "Such as?"

Her blue eyes bore into mine, "What you see before you... I am a 'splinter' of the original Moira Centyr, a weakened copy if you will."

The idea intrigued me, "This was something unique to your family? Were all of the Centyr mages able to do this?"

"The ability to create a living body is something only an archmage could manage and there have been few of those among my ancestors. However Centyr wizards were frequently able to create semi-sentient enchantments of objects to contain knowledge... I am merely the extreme extension of that ability. As far as I know I am the only example of... whatever it is you would label me," she gestured to her body as she finished.

"And what was your creator's intention when she made you?"

"The preservation of knowledge, to help you... Although I have no will or power to act remaining to me I can teach you what I knew, if you desire my wisdom. And...," she began to say something else but stopped.

"What?" I prodded.

"Nothing."

"It didn't sound like nothing, what else is there?"

"I am not ready to share everything yet, not until I know your purposes better… not until I am sure you can survive," she stated bluntly.

"I thought you acted according to my will," I inquired, "How can a simulacrum be stubborn… or cautious?"

"Some things we are driven to protect so strongly that the desire can survive even this…," she gestured at her earthen form, sweeping her arms delicately downward.

I had the feeling I wasn't going to get anywhere trying to pry an answer from her at this point so I mentally shelved the question for later. A larger question loomed before me, "You said others had been 'lost' like you were… how did you wind up like this? More importantly could this happen to me?"

She smiled again, "A good question… and part of the reason I was created. It involves the fundamental difference between wizardry and what an archmage does. A mage uses his own power to effect change in the world around him, just as a normal man might use the strength of his arm and an axe to fell a tree. A mage wields his power and causes things to happen, in contrast, an archmage listens to the world."

"That doesn't sound very useful, or powerful. The histories say you defeated a dark god, surely you didn't do that by 'listening'," I insisted.

"Correct, I didn't crush Balinthor by just listening, and that is why I became as I am now. I sought power beyond human comprehension, the power of the earth entire, and I gained it," she stopped there.

"I'm confused," I admitted.

She stared intently at me and I found myself fascinated with the light glinting from the deep sapphires that served as her 'eyes'. Finally she opened her mouth to speak again, "An archmage does not wield power, Mordecai. An archmage *becomes* that which they seek to wield."

CHAPTER 5

Moira Centyr, or rather the creature I called Moira, watched me for a long moment, waiting for her words to sink in. I blinked several times as my own experiences over the past year shifted within my mind, reorganizing in light of what she had just told me. Several things clicked into place as I looked back, and my memory of the voice of the wind and the sensation I had had… of losing my 'self'… stood out clearly in my mind.

Just a few days ago I had nearly taken to the skies… just to track a man a few miles further than my regular senses would follow. What if I hadn't come back? What if Ariadne hadn't gotten my attention? Would I have become a zephyr? A part of the wind… lost forever between the clouds, with no memory of my prior life? The implications were startling.

"Could that happen with the wind?" I asked her suddenly.

"An archmage can become anything," she replied, "It is both a blessing and a curse… a strength and a weakness."

"I think it nearly happened to me the other day," I added.

"I am not surprised," she said.

"Why?"

"You are particularly sensitive, in my time you would have been guarded carefully by a *meillte*," she said. The word meillte was familiar to me already, it being the Lycian word for 'watcher'.

"What did these 'meillte' do?" I asked.

"Their job was to make sure an archmage did not go too far. Most of them were mages of limited ability. If the one they were watching became lost they could speak to them directly, mind to mind, to try and draw them back to the world of men," she explained.

"Did you have watchers? And if so… why didn't they bring you back?" Even before I said it I wondered if the question might be too sensitive, but I had to ask anyway.

"I did, but some things cannot be undone. I knew the price and I made my choice, which is why I tried to preserve my knowledge for the future, before I lost myself." She answered plainly, and if the question bothered her she gave no sign of it.

"You say I am 'sensitive', what does that have to do with it?"

"Everything… sensitivity is the way we used to look for possible talents in this regard. In general, once a young mage first showed his power he would be watched carefully. After a year we would test his sensitivity, primarily by checking the range of his magesight," Moira said.

"Does that range or sensitivity give an indication of a mage's power?"

"Not really. Many powerful wizards were too lacking in sensitivity to become archmages… most of them in fact. Conversely, some archmages were fairly mediocre in terms of pure wizardry. I myself was only considered a 'moderate' when my personal power was tested, but my sensitivity was very high. I was closely watched from the time my power first manifested until the time I chose to surrender my life in the attempt to stop Balinthor." She said this with a certain amount of pride.

Needless to say the conversation had taken a fascinating turn for me. I had read about things such as 'emittance' and 'capacitance' being used to characterize the differences between wizards and channelers, stoics and prophets… but what Moira was discussing was more particular to my own situation. "How did you measure sensitivity?" I asked her directly.

"The most common test was to see how far away a mage could sense a particular object or person. Anything over five hundred yards was considered 'very sensitive'. Individuals that tested in that range would be watched carefully to make sure they did no harm to themselves before they could learn to control their abilities. Those judged to be extremely sensitive would be watched throughout their lives… to ensure their own safety."

"Was that really for their safety, or the safety of others?" I questioned pointedly. I was a bit sore on the topic of not being trusted purely because of one's magical ability.

"For their own safety… most archmages that go too far do not endanger anyone, they merely lose themselves."

"What is that like?"

The elemental being stared into me with penetrating eyes, "I was created before my namesake joined the earth completely, so I don't know, but I have her memories of near 'misses' during her life before that day. Becoming something like the earth, or the wind, is too far beyond human experience for it to make sense anyway. Everything you know, everything you are, would be erased, replaced by a vast uncaring reality. There would be no 'memory' of such a thing; memory itself ceases to have meaning when discussing something such as the 'earth' or 'wind'."

"This ability sounds almost useless," I commented.

"That is because we have only discussed the dangers. There are many advantages you have not discovered yet," she informed me.

"And what are those?"

"Before we get that far… you'll need to share some information with me. How far away can you sense a specific individual?" As she asked I could feel the focus of her beautiful gem-like eyes boring into my own. She seemed particularly intent on this question.

"How far were you able to sense a person?" I retorted.

"Nearly a thousand yards," she replied instantly. "Don't avoid the question. I need to know, to assess what you will be capable of learning."

"Fine," I replied. "I can sense a specific person out to a distance of a little over half a mile, probably over eight or nine hundred yards," I lied. The truth was I could sense someone at twice that distance, now that the bond had been broken. I wasn't sure what that might mean in terms of my abilities, but I wasn't about to give the information away without being sure of the motives of the person that wanted to know.

"I suspected as much. Even in my day that was exceptional, especially for an Illeniel," she remarked.

That smacked of an insult. "What does that mean?" I demanded.

She laughed. "Despite their historical honor as the first 'great' line of wizards the Illeniels did not produce many archmages. The Illeniel lineage was renowned for producing powerful wizards but not many of them were exceptional in terms of sensitivity.

Our conversation had begun to fill me with a frustrated energy. To work some of it off I stood and began to pace, hoping to relax my body. I was relieved to finally be getting some answers, but I wasn't sure I liked what they implied.

Finally I spoke again, "I still don't really understand why 'sensitivity' is important for archmages."

She walked beside me as she answered, "It isn't important Mordecai. It is everything. An archmage listens and by listening he understands. Through understanding he *becomes*. The 'ears' that you use to listen are a byproduct of wizardry. The same sense that allows you to perceive magic allows you to listen to the world itself… to become the world itself. Does that make it clearer?"

"Yes, but this power sounds too dangerous to use."

"That is because I have been telling you of the most dangerous uses. An archmage can listen to many less dangerous things, things more similar to his own, human nature. He can also listen in a more limited manner. Power can be gained without passing the threshold. You have caused the earth to shake several times already haven't you? Yet you retained your humanity." She stopped and reached down, into the earth beneath our feet and when she straightened up again she held a dense glassy stone in her hand. "Here take this," she said, handing it to me.

"What is this for?" I asked in surprise.

"A lesson," she replied. "Do exactly as I say and perhaps you will understand better. Crush the stone with your hand." I gave her an odd look but decided to humor her. With a word I encased the stone in my hand with a shield of invisible force and then I began to contract it as I squeezed with my hand. She put her hand on my arm before I could accomplish her request. "Stop," she told me.

"What?"

"Use your hand, not a shield."

"My hand isn't strong enough," I said.

"Channel the energy into your muscles and bones," she explained.

I gave her a stern look. I had seen the effects of physical power on the human body already, mostly by watching what it did to Penelope when she had been my Anath'Meridum. She had once stopped a mace in full swing with her bare hand. To be charitable she had done it to save my life, but it had resulted in a multitude of broken bones in her hand. "No," I said, clenching my jaw.

Moira looked at me with an expression of surprise. "Why not?"

"I would destroy my hand doing that," I said with a flat stare in her direction.

"Too bad, that lesson had two parts, the first being a crash course in healing yourself. Obviously you've spent a lot of time applying your powers in various situations. In my time a mage of your age was usually a lot less experienced in such matters."

"I've been forced by circumstances," I told her.

She smiled, "That isn't necessarily a bad thing. Very well let's move to the more practical application. Listen to the stone… and pay attention to it carefully."

Despite what I had already undergone with the voices of the wind and the earth it hadn't really occurred to me that something as small and innocuous as a rock might have its own voice. Some of the books I had found in my father's library had discussed the matter of sentience and existence… concluding that the very nature of 'existing' included a certain amount of awareness. Inanimate objects were alive in a sense, which is why the earth had a voice, though its awareness was completely foreign to the human mind.

What I hadn't really considered was the full ramifications of that fact… it meant that even small objects, such as this stone, had their own limited awareness… though it might be very minimal. I stared at the rock for several moments before asking, "Is that possible, to hear something so small?"

Her blue stone eyes reflected the light of the afternoon sun, giving her an eerie look for a moment. "Yes it is possible. You must be careful in how you do it though; listen and make the stone a part of yourself, like an extra hand or arm. Do not let yourself become the stone. You must make it a part of you, not the *whole* of you."

I laughed at the thought. "Surely I couldn't *become* something like this."

There was no humor in her expression. "You could."

"Is it difficult to return from a state like that?" I asked. Her seriousness was sobering.

"What do you think the chances are that the stone in your hand will suddenly decide to become a human being?" she replied.

"Oh."

"Stop thinking about it and listen. Clear your mind and focus on the stone. Don't be dismayed if it takes a while, just listen," she repeated.

I did as I was told. Hopefully no one would tell Penny that, she might take it as a hopeful sign. The most difficult part was 'clearing' my mind. In the past when I had listened to the earth, or even the wind, it wasn't very hard. Both of those things were large and in their own way very loud… finding the voice of one small stone, amidst the background noise of everything around me… that was a different matter entirely. I never did succeed in clearing my mind, not completely anyway, but I didn't need to. Soon after I began to focus and clear my mind of its usual clutter I started to hear the voice of the stone in my hand. It wasn't particularly well defined, but once I started paying attention it was fairly easy to find. "I can hear it," I announced.

"Are you sure?" my strange companion asked.

"Yes, I wouldn't have told you if I wasn't," I replied in annoyance.

"Listen carefully and include its voice within your own. Make it a part of your own self. Once you can identify with it I want you to change it," she said.

"Change it in what way?"

"Any way you wish," she clarified.

Typical, I thought. "Thanks for your guidance," I said dryly, and then I got serious. Focusing I listened until the stone did indeed feel as if it were an extension of my own being. It was a curious sensation, but it felt completely natural. It was only afterward, when I had withdrawn myself that it seemed strange to me.

Once I had made the stone a part of myself I tried to think of something interesting to do with it. The most obvious thing would be to cause it to relax... which would result in it falling apart like sand. I think that is what my new 'teacher' expected. Given my contrary nature I decided to try and surprise her. Drawing on past experiences I thought of the first time I had experienced my gifts as a mage, the day I had saved Star from the river. On a whim I coaxed the stone into reshaping itself, molding it to resemble my memory of the beautiful horse. It was a shape far more delicate than you might expect to see in stone, especially at that scale.

I had done similar things frequently with metal, using my power to help shape the metal in my hands but this was different. It still required the use of my imagination, but there was no sensation of effort. I did not force the change myself, I asked... no I *showed* the stone my vision and it obliged me by taking that form for itself. When I had finished I looked up to see Moira's reaction. "How is that?"

Her face was impassive, "Very good, better than most when they first attempt it." Though she gave little outward sign I could sense a feeling of shock in her. She hadn't expected what I had done. More importantly, she was trying to avoid letting me know I had surprised her.

"How good?" I asked pointedly.

"Too good," she admitted. "You're a danger to yourself."

"I've heard that before," I chuckled wryly. "I didn't like it then and I still don't."

"This is no laughing matter. You need a meillte, several in fact, so they can rest. In my day someone like you would have at least three," she declared.

"Why three? I don't see the advantage of having more than one."

"There isn't for *you*. It gives them the opportunity to rest. Three would be enough that one could keep an eye on your mental state at all times, even while you slept," she explained.

"That seems excessive, what would I do while sleeping?"

"Probably nothing, but possibly anything."

"How many of these 'miellte' did you have?" I asked.

"Two… I wasn't judged sensitive enough to warrant a watcher while I slept. The last archmage to require three was my friend, Gareth Gaelyn," she said promptly.

That seemed odd. Gareth Gaelyn had supposedly been defeated in battle with Balinthor, while Moira later went on to defeat the dark god, yet he had required more watchers? *That doesn't make sense,* I thought. "If he was more powerful why did he fail… where you succeeded?" As I said it I immediately realized it was rude, but sometimes my mouth gets the best of me.

"Power… you have to stop thinking like that! An archmage does not possess power! He *becomes* power. Because of this no archmage is intrinsically more powerful than another; the difference lies in the ease with which they can adapt themselves. Gareth's talent made him a brilliant shape-shifter, something most archmages avoid. It also made it easy for him to attempt something that would have daunted a mage with more caution, someone more aware of their own limits!" she spat out angrily.

"I did not meant to offend," I hastily apologized. At the same time I was mentally reviewing what she had said. Shape-shifting wasn't something I had read of in the few books I had had a chance to study so far. The term was intriguing, while also being frightening in its implications. I stayed silent for a while before speaking again, "If you don't mind telling me… what did he do?"

She watched me for a moment, as if considering her words. "We were being driven from the Kingdom of Garulon. It was the first time we had met the shiggreth and they were something of a surprise for us. Balinthor had kept them hidden from us until that day and they overwhelmed our defense of the capital. Because we had not faced such creatures before we had no idea what they could do… or how to fight them. We lost the city and the army routed. Thousands died in the span of a few hours and those of us still able to keep order withdrew, seeking to escape the chaos. The fear and despair drove Gareth to attempt something radical. He was desperate or he would never have done it." She stopped then and turned her back on me, as if to hide her face. Despite her alien body her demeanor was entirely human, as were the emotions I felt running through her.

I waited.

"He became a dragon," she said at last.

Apparently I had used up my supply of 'wisdom' because in my surprise I interrupted, "I thought dragons were only fairy tales."

"They are, or rather, they were... until that day. Gareth had always been fascinated with the stories. In a moment of desperation he sought to create the beasts he had dreamed of from the stories of childhood. I am not sure if his fear and anger twisted his imagination, or if it was purely a foolish thing to begin with, but the dragon he became was a creature of fury and destruction. It tore into the enemy, tossing them about as if they were dolls, incinerating those it could not reach with its claws. Very few of the shiggreth that had come against us survived, and even the avatar of Balinthor left the field, rather than face the dragon directly."

"The history book I found did not mention any of this," I said.

"I doubt any of the scholars would have written of it. The shame of it stained his memory. Before that day Gareth had been well respected and loved by all that knew him," she replied.

"But it sounds as if he succeeded. What went wrong?" I already had a fair inkling of what she might tell me, but I wanted to hear it in her own words.

"After he had killed as many of the enemy as he could find he turned on what was left of the defenders of Garulon. He slaughtered friend and foe alike. Few survived, apart from those I was able to hide."

I had expected something tragic. If anything it helped put my own experiences in perspective, especially the end of the recent war with Gododdin. *At least I didn't kill my own people,* I thought. "What happened after that?" I asked finally.

"We hid for days, waiting for the dragon to leave, but the creature was cunning. Like a cat it waited, catching those who revealed themselves. Eventually, when I felt him leave I emerged from my hiding place in the earth and gathered up those few others who had managed to escape. The dragon that had been Gareth was gone. Whether it still lives or died long ago I have no idea."

We talked for a short while after that, but our conversation had taken on a dark tone and I had lost my enthusiasm for it. Eventually I decided to return to the castle. I had had enough of dark tales and tragic endings. My own life had nearly become one after all.

"I need to return, do you mind if we continue talking at another time?" I asked.

"No need to be polite Mordecai. I am only an echo, turn your attention aside and I practically cease to exist. Call me when you would speak again," she answered. With a wry smile she sank into the earth and as quickly as she had come, she was gone again.

Dusting the leaves from my trousers I headed back toward the keep, people would be looking for me by now.

CHAPTER 6

That evening Marc explained his plan to visit the capital to everyone over dinner. Dorian and Penny had been relieved simply to see him attending the evening meals again, so the news that he would be traveling was rather disappointing for them. Still we were all glad to know he was beginning to find a new purpose for his life.

Dorian had many a question for him regarding his reason for exploring my father's library but Rose was strangely quiet throughout the meal, quietly picking at her venison. Considering her usual chattiness I couldn't help but wonder at her reticence.

"So how long do you think you'll be gone?" asked Dorian. As he spoke he skillfully cut a large joint of meat from a serving platter before passing it along.

Marc smiled, lighting his features with a warmth that made it seem as if his recent depression couldn't possibly have been real. "A while my friend, after I finish there I plan to travel a bit… see if I can get access to some of the records kept by the various churches."

Dorian still wasn't comfortable with the fact that Marc had rejected his goddess. The Thornbear family had been followers of the Lady of the Evening Star for many generations and despite what both of us had told him he still seemed to feel that the goddess must have some good reason for her refusal to help. Deep down I'm sure he secretly hoped that Marcus would reconcile with

Millicenth. "Are you trying to figure out why she did what she did?" he said.

"Partly," answered Marc. He knew better than to voice his desire for vengeance against the gods. It would only upset Dorian and ruin the meal.

Dorian snorted, "'Partly' isn't much of an answer… why don't you just spit out what you're thinking?" Sometimes Dorian could be more perceptive than people expected from such a massive man.

Rose interrupted before I could, "Dorian don't badger him! He's been through a lot, let him enjoy his food."

"I wasn't badgering him," Dorian groused. "I'm just tired of not hearing what's on people's minds."

Marcus spoke up earnestly, "Look Dorian I'm not trying to shut you out. I just need to get away. This gives me something to do and a reason to travel." I marveled at how sincere the half-truth sounded coming from my friend.

"When do you plan on going?" Rose asked suddenly.

"Tonight if Mort doesn't mind teleporting me," Marc answered immediately.

We had already discussed this earlier so I simply nodded my head in agreement. "Would you mind taking a note to my father for me?" asked Rose. "I haven't seen him in months and I'm sure he must be worried."

"Certainly Rose," Marc agreed quickly.

She thanked him and the rest of our meal went quietly after that. I caught Rose looking at me once or twice but she looked away whenever I caught her staring. Even with my advantage in sensing emotions I had no idea what was on her mind. Rose Hightower was a complex puzzle that I had long ago despaired of understanding. It was clear though that she was curious about something.

After we had finished eating I walked with Marc back to his room to gather his things, and then I accompanied him to the teleportation circle I had set to match the one in my house back in Albamarl. He glanced at me in surprise as I stepped onto it with him. "You don't have to come with me."

"Yes I do. I have to tell the house to tolerate your presence. Didn't I ever tell you what happened to Rose that time she went exploring the library without me?" I said. It turned out that somehow I had neglected to relate that tale to him. Consequently we both got a chuckle as I relived the story with him. The part where the golem had Rose upside down left him in stitches.

"I can't believe you didn't tell me about that before," he remarked as we stepped off the circle in my house in Albamarl.

"I guess I was busy. A lot did happen after all," I replied. In point of fact the events we were discussing had been only a few months prior, but now looking back it seemed as if years had passed. I went through the house and made sure it would let him enter and exit through the front door in my absence. I also made particular effort to ensure that the golem in the library would allow him to look through the books without interference. "Are you sure you'll be alright here by yourself?" I asked again for probably the tenth time.

Marc laughed, "I'll be fine Mort… and if I'm not, you'll be the first to know." He emphasized the last part.

"I'll be back in a few days for my meeting with the king," I repeated again. "When you go deliver Rose's note to Lord Hightower don't let them see your face. Just leave it with the doorman. I'd rather no one knows how easy it is for us to enter and leave the city until after I visit the king."

"I doubt he's forgotten your visit to his warehouses already," said Marc sardonically.

"That's certain, but he may not realize I still have a means of entering and leaving other than the circle that was in James Lancaster's storehouse," I said.

"True enough," Marc replied. "I'll keep that in mind. Never fear, no one will know I've returned to the city for at least a few weeks."

After that I said my farewells and returned to Cameron Castle. Penelope was waiting for me when I got back to our rooms. As soon as I entered she looked up, she had been combing out her hair in preparation for bed.

"Already back?" she asked.

I would have thought that was obvious but I decided not to be a smart ass. "Nothing could keep me from your side my dear!" I said chivalrously.

"You say that now. Wait 'til I get fat... I'm already starting to show," she announced with a mixture of pride and trepidation.

"Really?" I asked with a healthy interest.

"Look," she said standing up and smoothing her nightdress. She stood sideways in front of a full length mirror that had been a gift from Genevieve Lancaster. Sure enough there was a distinct protrusion of her belly. There were also more interesting changes.

I stepped up behind her and put one arm around her waist, feeling the modest swelling of her midriff. "That's not all that's grown," I announced as I brought my other hand up to cup her breast in a familiar manner.

"I despair of you ever growing up," she said with a smile, and then she leaned her head back to engage me in a rather distracting kiss.

Sometime later she nudged me; I had almost fallen asleep in the bed. "Do you think our baby will be happy?" she asked with a note of uncertainty.

I tried to focus my thoughts. I have never been sure why she always wanted to talk 'afterward' but I had learned to accept it. Personally I had begun to suspect it was because she knew I was less likely to dissemble and more likely to answer honestly. "I hope so," I replied, "but the future is never certain. And you should say, 'our son'," I added.

"Are you really sure about that? I couldn't have been more than a month along when you healed me," she said.

"Is it so hard to believe? I never question your visions," I told her.

She snorted, "That's because they're always right, and you don't have that gift… how can you be sure?"

"I'm sure," I answered. "You're just feeling nervous because you haven't had any visions to confirm what I said."

"That's not true!" she answered self-righteously, "I'm just nervous. If I decorate the nursery for a boy and we have a girl you're going to be in trouble." She poked me in the ribs as she said it.

I chuckled a bit, "That is a risk I'm willing to take."

—◦——◦—

The next day was quiet and I spent the majority of my morning working on the armor. Over the past month I had gained a lot of confidence in manipulating metal and working with my hands had always given me a sense of peace. These days it also gave me a feeling of connection to my father. I felt a bit like a cheat though, if he could have seen me now, what would he have thought? Using spells I could work metal in ways that he could never have imagined. Much of the skill he gained in a lifetime of crafting involved finding ways to get around the limitations and difficulties of working iron. I was able to completely circumvent many of those limitations with nothing more than my will and some carefully chosen words.

He would have teased me about it, I thought to myself. Deep down I knew it was true… he'd have poked fun and then told me to use whatever tool came to hand. The vision of the final product was what was most important and if that was poorly conceived it wouldn't matter how many advantages I had… the final result would still be junk.

If anything my background in a traditional smithy had taught me to understand iron in a way that no amount of magic could have ever done. That understanding was even more valuable now that I had the ability and the resources to exploit that knowledge effectively.

I can make a suit like this, tailored to an individual, in roughly two weeks, I calculated. *Another two days to finish the enchantments and I'm looking at about sixteen days to equip each of my 'knights'.* Even with my advantages it would still take a considerable amount of time to prepare for what I had in mind. *And I haven't added in the time required for their weapons,* I added mentally.

Dorian's advice had been invaluable concerning the weapons, though. Based on his own experience wearing the armor I had already enchanted for him before the recent war, he seemed to feel that a great sword would be a better weapon. Dorian had told me two days before, "The sword you enchanted cut through everything I put it against, and the armor was enough to stop any normal sword, but I found my shield to be an impediment. If I'd had a longer blade and two good hands free to use it, I could have felled the enemy like wheat before the scythe."

He had also suggested I leave the weapons to a normal smith to produce. I could purchase them far more easily and enchant them afterward, saving myself a lot of time. The main reason I was doing the actual crafting of the armor was because it was simply impossible to get this sort of armor made anywhere outside of the capital itself, and even there it was a year's wait to get a set made.

That didn't suit my needs at all. I wanted enough to arm twenty men within a year. I had seen the effect a few men could make in the last war. Dorian in particular had made all the difference. I had been unconscious for nearly an hour while I was healing Penny, and he had held the breach in the wall almost singlehandedly. Not that I would have said that aloud, many men had died next to him that day. Yet he had been the one that they couldn't put down.

With a lion's heart and armor that no arrow or sword could pierce he had refused to surrender to exhaustion. The sword he had carried cut through men and armor with equal ease. After the dust had settled I couldn't help but wonder what might have been possible if we had had more men similarly equipped.

Of course the man inside the armor had been a primary factor, I wasn't blind to that fact, and there were few to equal Dorian in combat. Still it had been much on my mind since that day, particularly given the continuing threat from the shiggreth. I knew they were out there, but I didn't know when or where they would strike again and I was only one man. Someone encased in enchanted armor would be virtually immune to their touch, and given the right weapons he would be able to give them cause for fear.

That was really the heart of it. Since I had become the Count Cameron I had assumed responsibility for a large number of people, and I couldn't be everywhere. As far as I knew I was the only living wizard left, and the shiggreth could multiply almost without limit. I needed help… powerful help. If no other wizards were available then I would have to create the next best thing.

Dorian had shown me, in his actions against the shiggreth and again during the war with Gododdin, what a well-trained man with superior weaponry could do. Naturally I would have to be selective, and those chosen would have to be carefully trained, but I had a friend I could trust for that task.

Still, Dorian had had one particular weakness, as his fight against the shiggreth had shown… the limitation of mortal strength. If he had possessed the sort of resources that an Anath'Meridum was able to draw upon he would not have been overwhelmed by the press of numbers. My time with Penny as my pact-bearer had shown me just how terrible a warrior could become if they had strength that went far beyond the norm.

I had no intention of renewing my bond with anyone though, much less twenty some ones. I would find another solution. I just wasn't sure how… yet. Shaking my head I focused my attention once more. It wouldn't do to be distracted in the middle of my work.

CHAPTER 7

The next several days flew by and I could no longer put off my trip to Albamarl. I didn't want to give King Edward too much time to brew over my message, and he'd surely received it by now. It was time to pay him a visit.

I had told Penny of my plans several days before and I let her know that today was the day after we finished our breakfast. She was still rather nervous about it, but she had conceded the necessity. "I wish you'd let me come with you," she said again.

"Absolutely not, you're not an Anath'Meridum anymore and more importantly you're with child, we have too much to lose now," I reminded her.

"No need to be mean about it," she complained. "Consider my point of view, if we lost you now what would that mean for me and your child?"

I winced, it always came back to that, and in truth she was right. Still we had discussed it already; I didn't see a better alternative for securing the future for our family… and our people. "I'm sorry love. You know I'd choose a safer path if I thought there was one," I replied.

"So you admit there might be a better way," she said. She was quick to catch on.

"I'd be lying if I pretended to have all the answers. What is true, is that I don't know of a better way," I said honestly.

She ran her hand across my chest, feeling the fabric of my tunic. "I'd feel better if you at least wore mail. Any fool with a dagger could put a hole in your back."

"That would make my task more difficult. I'm actually trying to be sneaky, besides I don't need armor to keep me safe," as I spoke I made my shield flash with light for just a moment. My skill with mundane uses of magic had gotten much greater.

"That didn't do you much good when the shiggreth grabbed you," she noted. It was not only a reminder of my vulnerability but also a reminder of the fact that she had been the one to save my bacon that night.

I grimaced. "There shouldn't be any shiggreth to worry about during this little adventure and if there are… I've prepared a new strategy."

She was cynical, "such as?"

"I can't show you here. It might damage the room," I said evading the question as best I could.

The look on her face was wistful and a bit sad at the same time. "One of these days you're going to find out you're not as smart as you thought and I'm going to have to pay the price."

I laughed, "Did you have another vision?"

Penny frowned, "No, and that's why I'm not objecting too much. I feel certain that something as important as your impending doom would trigger my foresight. Since my 'intuition' has remained silent thus far I'm willing to let you take more risk than is probably wise."

I decided not to argue that point, her 'intuition' and I had already butted heads once before in the past. The result had been her near death. Still I doubted I would back down if I were forced into a corner like that again. I can be notoriously stubborn when I choose to be. Rather than remind her of my penchant for mule-headedness I agreed with her, "I'm glad of that. If things go well I should be back late tonight, or tomorrow at the latest. I may stay and have dinner at the house with Marc. I haven't had many opportunities to explore the library lately."

I finished my good-byes and an hour later I was standing in the hallway of my house in Albamarl. Teleportation was one of the nicer things about being a wizard, although I had very few places I could use it to reach. It required a pre-made circle at both the point of origination and the destination, and the two had to match.

Currently the only places I had available were my home in Cameron Castle, Castle Lancaster, and my house in Albamarl. I intended to expand on that number a bit during my stay in the capital, though. Once I had reminded the king of my traveling abilities he might decide to try and cut down on my options by having my house watched.

I glanced down the hallway and let my senses expand until I had located Marc. True to his word he was sitting at one of the reading tables in the library. My first impulse was to walk in and say hello but after a moment's thought I decided to test out my plan for infiltrating the palace. I had several spells in mind but I hadn't actually tried them out in a practical situation. I spoke a few words and ran my hand over my boots, which should silence any sound my footsteps might make, while leaving me free to speak as need be.

I walked silently until I stood near the door to the library. Marc had thoughtfully closed it after he entered, which made entering the room unseen and unheard more difficult. Perfect. Watching him mentally, I made sure he wasn't facing the door, and then I quietly whispered a few words. They were similar to the ones I had used to silence my boots, and their effect on the door was the same. Putting my hand on the handle I opened the door and stepped inside.

So far I remained unnoticed, Marc was still reading intently but I knew he might look in my direction at any moment and I was far from invisible. I needed to cast another spell but realized that standing in the same room there was a strong chance he would hear me, even if I spoke very softly. I needed a distraction. Glancing toward the opposite end of the room I chanced a whispered word and focused my will. The sound of a book falling to the floor and claws skittering across wooden boards came from that end of the room immediately; drawing Marc's startled attention in that direction. I spoke quietly again and settled what I thought would be the perfect disguise across myself. This last spell was something new entirely, a way of creating a false appearance. I had chosen the likeness of his sister Ariadne in advance.

I had discovered the art of illusion in one of my father's books only a few weeks before and I had been experimenting with them in odd moments ever since. This was my first time attempting to fool another person with a complete disguise however, so I had no idea how well it might work. Walking forward I stood by the table and waited for Marc to turn back around. At the moment he was still tensely watching the corner, wondering at the noise I had created. When at last he turned back around his expression was priceless.

"What?!" he exclaimed, scrambling backward. Or at least he tried to scramble backward, still being seated in the chair he wound up half standing before falling on his ass. It took all my self-control to stifle a laugh, instead I feigned concern.

"Marcus are you alright? I didn't mean to startle you!" I said quickly. If my spell was working properly he should be seeing his sister leaning over him wearing a lovely blue dress that I had once seen her in. Call me a pervert if you will but I always remembered her wearing that dress when I thought of his sister.

"Ariadne?" he said tentatively, a suspicious stare on his features. "Is that you? How did you get here?" He rose from the floor and dusted himself off; although the floor was spotless.

I hadn't considered the conversation beyond surprising him. Now that it was clear my disguise was working I thought I might keep it up a bit longer. My mind raced as I considered my words. "Mordecai sent me. I went to Cameron looking for you and he said you had come to study here. How have you been? Rose told me you have been acting odd lately." *That should keep his suspicions at bay,* I thought to myself with a self-indulgent chuckle. I refrained from hugging him, my illusion lacked any substance and my distinctly masculine frame would be a dead giveaway.

Marc looked around, "Is Mort with you?" he asked suddenly.

"No he said he would return to take me home in an hour or so," I temporized.

"Clever girl," he said with a sly grin. "We haven't had any time to ourselves in ages have we?"

The look he gave me was faintly unsettling. I really had no idea what his conversations with his siblings were like when they were alone but something about his tone was odd. "No, we haven't," I agreed. "I've been worried about you."

He took a step closer and I instinctively stepped back to avoid contact. "Do you still love your brother?" he asked in a wistful tone, "Even after my disgrace?"

I was becoming increasingly uncomfortable with the turn of the conversation, but I didn't want to spoil my joke just yet. "Of course Marcus, you've always been my favorite."

His eyes had a dangerous glint in them, "Your favorite?" he asked. "Don't you mean your *only*? Or have you found someone else?" His voice had developed a distinctly husky sound.

Things had gotten out of hand. "What?!" I shouted in surprise, but before I could say more he leapt forward and kissed me. Shock and outrage were my sudden companions as I tried to throw him off. He clung to me instead and we wound up wrestling on the floor while I attempted to disentangle myself from the sister-loving monster my friend had become.

"Ariadne, I don't remember you being so hairy but I like it!" he growled. I had finally gotten control of our struggle and I was working to get him into an arm lock. He was laughing now and puckering his lips at me as I twisted his arm. At last I realized I had been had. In disgust, I let go of him and with a shove stepped back.

Marc was laughing so hard now he could hardly stand and he collapsed onto the floor again. "Mort you should have seen your face!" he guffawed at me.

His humor was infectious and I found myself chuckling a bit in spite of my indignation. "You're a sick bastard, I hope you realize that! How did you figure it out?" I asked.

Marc's laughter slowed and finally he was able to answer more soberly, "Do you really think my sister's voice sounds like that? That was the worst falsetto I've ever heard!"

Of course, I should have known. I did have a better solution for the voice problem but I couldn't use it without having direct contact with the person I was imitating first. That was academic though, I had thought my generic 'female' voice would be enough. Clearly I was wrong. I frowned.

"And that dress, what was that about? She's only worn that dress to formal balls. Why would she wear that here?" he snickered, but then his eyes went wide. "Oh damn! You have a thing for my sister! Why else would you remember her at her loveliest? Oh that's low Mort! Wait 'til I tell Penny!"

"I do not! You sick sister-lover! Wait 'til I tell your sister you tried to kiss her!" I shot back.

"I knew it was you all along! Who else could get into this place?" he retorted.

I grinned, "She doesn't know that."

"Fine," he said standing up again. "Truce?" he asked, but he was still chuckling as he held out his hand.

I gave his hand a mock-suspicious glare, "I'm not sure that thing is safe to touch," I said, but then I broke into a grin. I hugged him instead and then we sat down to talk. "How have you been doing?" I asked.

"Good," he replied, "When there isn't anyone sneaking up on me and pretending to be my sister."

"I just wanted to test out the new spell," I told him.

He snorted, "It's impressive I'll admit, though the voice needs a lot of work. I've never seen you do anything like that before, though."

"I started experimenting with illusions a few weeks ago. So far they seem fairly simple, as long as it is something I can imagine easily," I said.

"And my sister is someone you imagine regularly I take it?" he said with a wry smile.

"No damnitt! Anyone I've known for a long time is fairly easy. I picked your sister because she seemed the most reasonable person to visit you, besides myself of course. If I try to do a stranger I'd almost have to be looking at them when I cast the spell in order to create a decent resemblance."

Marc sat up straight for a moment. "Mordecai!" he exclaimed, "Have you shown anyone else your illusions yet?"

"No why?"

"Think about it, the possibilities are endless. You could imitate anyone, the king, the head of the bank… or someone you wanted to frame for a crime!" he announced. As he spoke I could see the gears in his head turning. Marc was extremely intelligent, almost as smart as myself in our academic studies as children and infinitely more devious. If anyone could think of useful ways to use deception, it would be him.

"I'm just planning to sneak into the palace, I don't need to commit crimes or blame innocents at this point in my career," I told him.

"Just don't tell anyone you can do this. So long as you are the only one that knows, you have a tool with few limits. Once people know what you can do it will be the opposite… any crime could be laid at your feet," he explained.

I hadn't thought of it in quite those terms but I could see he was right. What at first had seemed like a simple spell was fraught with all sorts of major social implications. If I could impersonate someone, I could do anything… and if people knew I could impersonate anyone, I could be implicated for anything that happened out of the ordinary. Rumor and scandal could easily become the rule of my life. It almost wasn't worth using the spell at all. I shook my head, "Let's just finish this experiment. I need to test another spell, one that should provide a better imitation of someone's voice."

"Anything would be better than that awful falsetto you used," he jibed again. "Do you need me to do anything?"

"Not much, just hold still," I said and then I reached out and touched his throat while vocalizing my new spell. Then I opened my mouth and repeated what he had just said, "Anything would be better than that awful falsetto you used." The words emerged in an exact replica of Marc's voice… at least as far as I could tell.

"Is that what I sound like?" Marc said, rather surprised.

I started to reply, thinking it was an honest question but he didn't wait for an answer.

"Damn, no wonder the ladies find me irresistible!" he stated matter of factly.

I repeated my disguise spell and a moment later he was staring at his own face as well, then I spoke up, "Damn, no wonder people think I'm a conceited ass!"

"That's not what I said," he replied adroitly. "If you're going to copy me you need to stick to the proper dialogue." He stared at me for a moment longer before continuing, "That really is unnerving… like staring into a mirror that has a mind of its own. Hey! I don't suppose you can use that spell on someone else could you?"

I thought about it for a moment, "I think I can, why?"

He grinned, "Make me look and sound like you. I have some things to tell you."

I could only imagine the mayhem that might ensue if we started an insult contest while disguised as each other. In fact, the vision kept me spellbound for a solid minute before I replied, "No, absolutely not."

Marc glared at me, "Why not?"

"This power is too great to be put in the hands of the feeble minded," I told him solemnly.

"Spoilsport," he replied glumly.

"Did you deliver Rose's missive to her father?" I asked suddenly, changing the topic.

He switched gears and leaned back in his chair and putting his feet up on the table, "Indeed I did. I left it with the doorman. None of them saw my face."

"That's a relief then. Any luck with the research yet?" I asked.

His face fell, "Not so far. Do you see how many books are in this place? It could be a year before I've checked them all."

"Well, keep your eyes open for interesting information, even if it isn't directly related to the gods," I reminded him.

He gave me a look that told me I was restating the obvious again. It was a frequent flaw of mine. We talked for a bit more before I took my leave and headed into the city. I had a lot to accomplish and it wouldn't do to waste any more daylight.

I kept my senses alert as I left the house and stepped onto the common road outside. It would be a reasonable guess for the king to figure out I was using my father's house as a means of ingress and egress to the city, but I didn't need to confirm the fact for him. I didn't sense anyone nearby so I relaxed and began walking slowly up the road.

Before I had stepped out I had copied the features of Cecil Draper. I hoped he wouldn't mind and in any case I hadn't known him long enough to do a perfect job of it. I doubted anyone in the capital would recognize him anyway, so I should be effectively anonymous.

I spent the next couple of hours circling the royal palace slowly; paying particular attention to points where I thought the wall might be relatively unobserved. If I could find a good enough spot I might try to enter during the daytime. If not, I would have to wait for cover of darkness.

The palace had an outer wall that encircled the entire building and its gardens, providing privacy and security for both the king and those who enjoyed his hospitality. That outer wall was nearly as impressive as the wall that surrounded the city itself and likewise it was guarded by towers every fifty yards or so. The towers themselves were only fully garrisoned during an active defense. During normal, peaceful times there were only guards stationed in the corner towers, with regular patrols walking the walls between them.

For a normal thief or assassin that would be just as formidable a barrier, but it made things much easier for me. With my senses I could easily find the locations of the guards patrolling and assure myself that there were not others waiting within the wall towers. That made it fairly easy for me to guess at whether I was actually being observed at any given moment.

After my second full circuit of the perimeter I chose my point of entry, a shadowed portion of the eastern wall, near the middle of that side. I left the road and moved up near the wall where one of the towers bulged outward, using it to shield me from view in one direction at least. The afternoon shade made it more difficult to see me but it was by no means impossible. Any passerby would be able to spot me quite easily, as could the guard in the tower on the southern end of the wall I stood against… should he bother to look out and downward.

I had made two plans to handle this situation. The first, which I had chosen before I ever sent Cyhan home to his king, was to use a spell to assist me in climbing the wall. With a bit of cleverness I could imitate the ability of a lizard to cling to walls. The main drawback would be that I would be very visible and exposed as I reached the top of the wall, which made my second option more attractive.

I had only recently been inspired by this idea, mostly by my conversation with Moira Centyr… or her echo. I was having a hard time keeping the two separate in my mind. In any case, her lesson with the stone had given me a new idea, the main drawback being that I wasn't entirely sure I could actually make it work. I would need time, I couldn't rush something new.

I created a new illusion over myself as I stood facing the wall; this one was smoother and less detailed. Once I had finished I looked like a part of the wall, or rather it appeared that the wall possessed an irregular rounded protrusion. It wasn't perfect but unless someone looked closely I should be able to remain where I was for a considerable amount of time without drawing any attention.

I focused on the wall beneath my hands. My mage-sense told me that it was nearly ten feet thick at the base, solid stone for two feet on the outer and inner surfaces, with gravel and mortar sandwiched between. It might be difficult but it was entirely possible for me to make an opening using my power. The problem lay in the fact that I doubted I could do it quietly, and that I couldn't remove the opening without leaving a lot of rather messy evidence afterward. Perhaps if I had a few hours and no one bothering me I could do such a thing, but I didn't think I could do it unobserved.

Closing my eyes I narrowed my attention until the wall in front of me was my entire world. I cleared my mind and listened… listened for the voice of this one small part of a much larger world. Unlike the stone I had held in my hand this wall was composed of many separate stones, and the material between the inner and outer surface was a complex amalgam of material. I didn't let that distract me though; as I listened I began to hear it within my mind, a chorus of many voices. They were all part of the wall, separate and yet joined. Together they wove a harmony of existences joined together for a single purpose and the sudden beauty of it almost drew me in. For a moment I wanted to be a part of that melody, to join the stones in their quiet vigil.

I caught myself in time, and refocused my mind, remembering my purpose. Instead I drew the stones into my own 'self', making them part of my own will. My body was no longer the boundary of my existence, now I also contained a significant portion of the massive stone wall before me. Then I moved, opening to allow another part of myself to pass through. Description fails me at this point, so I'll resort to what would likely have been seen by an outside observer. As my body leaned forward the stones parted before me, flowing like water to let me pass. A moment later I exited the other side.

I found myself blinded by the bright afternoon sun falling on the western side of the wall. My abrupt departure from the stone wall left me disoriented as I became less than what I had been, my sense of self changed and a moment later I was just Mordecai. I stood there blinking the sun from my eyes when a voice found my ears, "Pardon me my lord. I thought the garden was unoccupied this time of day."

My senses came into sharp focus as I realized a woman was staring at me. Mentally I cursed my stupidity but there was no hope for correcting my mistake. The area had been clear when I started but my travel through the wall had distorted my senses, I had been caught completely by surprise. Worse yet, I hadn't renewed my disguise, I was standing before the lady in question with my own face showing. My mind raced to make sense of her words and formulate a response. "Think nothing of it lady. I was caught in reverie of the afternoon sun. I hope I didn't startle you overmuch?" I said calmly.

Her reaction and attire had already told me much. She was garbed as a lady of quality, but not to a degree that made me think she was nobility herself, something about her features belied that assessment. Her deference made me think she might be a lady-in-waiting to one of the more notable peers. Luckily I was dressed in all my glory as one of the ranking peers of the realm. My garb was practical in design but expensive in cut and material, a black velvet cloak trimmed in ermine all but hid the expensive butter soft grey leather doublet I wore. My boots and accoutrements were equally opulent... I was here to meet a king after all.

"No, you didn't startle me. I just didn't expect to find anyone here. Please forgive my ignorance for I don't recognize your lordship and I have no idea if I may have given offence in my familiarity," she said meekly, lowering her gaze, but not before I had caught a glimpse of deep brown. Her eyes had shown little of the humility that her voice conveyed.

Having finally regained some of my balance I swiftly surveyed my surroundings with my magesight. The immediate area was still clear of any other people so I turned my attention to a more thorough examination of the woman before me. Her simple yet expensive dress could easily have let her pass as nobility but her attitude and musculature hinted at servitude. More surprising still she possessed several weapons cleverly hidden on her person. For a moment her armament reminded me of Lady Rose. "Fear not, you have done nothing to offend me," I answered, making clear in my tone that my social standing was such that she was right to be worried. "If you will excuse me I should be getting back to my room," I added with a touch of brusqueness.

She stepped back lithely to let me pass and I was struck by her nimbleness. Unlike Rose Hightower, this woman had more than a casual athleticism, as she moved I could sense the taut muscles under her dress, like steel whipcords, tightly controlling her every movement. I didn't let my observation slow me down, I needed to be away from her quickly but before I got more than a few steps, she addressed me again, "Begging your pardon your lordship, if I might know your name?"

I paused without turning, by now I was fairly certain she was no maid-in-waiting, more likely she was a bodyguard, hired to watch some wealthy noblewoman. Summoning every ounce of imperiousness I had I spoke coldly, "Tell me yours first and I may forgive your impertinence." Benchley would have been proud of me if he could have heard me then.

She answered promptly, "Ruth my lord, one of King Edward's servants." The lack of any honorific confirmed her common status, but her position as one of the king's servitors was a surprise, especially given her weaponry. I revised my opinion swiftly. Whatever she did for the king involved staying in peak physical condition, and women were not highly regarded as bodyguards, so she must be something special indeed.

"*Shibal,*" I said as I turned to catch her. My spell rendered her unconscious before she had a chance to question me further. Gently I eased her to the ground and pulled her back toward the wall where I had emerged moments before. A nearby bush helped to conceal her presence from any casual passersby that might chance along. Since I had been forced to put her to sleep I took the opportunity to examine the heavy blade she had strapped to her thigh. The weapon itself was over a foot in length and wickedly sharp, while the metal had been tempered with a bluish black finish. It was highly unusual in terms of hidden weapons.

I carefully slipped it back into its sheath and then I spoke again, disguising myself as the woman sleeping on the ground before me. Then I touched her throat and used a second spell to imitate her voice. "Thank you for telling me your name, it would have been very inconvenient if someone had asked," I told her. My ears confirmed that my vocal mimicry seemed to be functioning properly and I rose to continue onward.

I smiled quietly to myself as I walked, careful not to move too quickly. I was supposed to be a woman after all. *This should make things much simpler,* I thought. Moments later I was passing into one of the archways that led into the guest quarters of the royal palace.

CHAPTER 8

Iwalked confidently down the corridors, heading directly toward the king's chambers. My senses were on high-alert and I made every attempt to avoid encountering other people in the hallways. The one or two times it was unavoidable I simply nodded at them in passing and moved purposefully onward. Whoever Ruth might be I had a feeling she was moderately important and it was probably normal for her to be moving as if she had someplace to be. I only hoped I wouldn't encounter anyone that knew her well.

As I got closer to the king's personal rooms I noticed a much larger number of guards. Men had been tucked into every available corner and at every doorway along the hall. It hadn't been like this the last time I had come here. Of course on that occasion I had been slightly intoxicated, answering a summons from the king and walking with James Lancaster. It was entirely possible I had missed noticing them, but I doubted it. *Cyhan must have delivered my message*, I thought with a smirk.

As I went I also noticed the guards stood straighter when they saw me coming and whatever small talk they had been engaged in ceased entirely. That gave me all the information I needed regarding Ruth's possible role here. I put a bit more confidence in my stride and boldly met the eyes of any guard who dared to look at me. In every case they met my gaze calmly and without question. I had no more doubts, Ruth was their superior, or at the very least much higher up the food chain.

I stopped before the door leading into the private audience chamber, the same one that King Edward had met me in over a half a year past. Two men guarded it and they seemed worried when I stopped. Protocol for a guest would have been to have them call for the king's chamberlain and request an audience, or at the very least announce my presence. Ruth was not a guest however and I got the distinct feeling they had expected me to enter without pausing for permission or waiting for the chamberlain.

"You!" I snapped at the man standing to the right, "Has anyone entered or left in the past hour?" I was hoping to cover my hesitation with questions.

"No milady!" he answered loudly.

I brought my hand up to rest a finger against my lips and the man visibly flinched. *He thought I might strike him!* Whoever Ruth was, she clearly led an interesting life. "Very well," I told him, "Open the door for me." I wanted him to do it in case there might be a secret signal; one never knew when it came to guarding royalty. If I attempted to open it myself without following whatever the proper protocol was it would be a dead giveaway.

He leaned over and opened the door. If there had been a secret knock or other signal I saw no sign of it, and I wound up feeling a bit foolish. I didn't bother looking at him as I entered. I already knew there was only one person inside, the chamberlain unless I was mistaken. Let me correct that, there was only one person 'within' the room. Two hidden side doors had several guards waiting behind them, watching the area.

The chamberlain started as I entered and rose quickly from the chair he had been resting on. "I hadn't expected…," he began.

"Don't bother," I told him. "Is he in his rooms? I need to talk to the king right away." I was already walking toward the doorway that led toward what I presumed was his Majesty's private living area. That was my first mistake. Apparently Ruth didn't outrank the chamberlain... I should have known.

"Ruth! Stop! What do you think you are doing?" he exclaimed indignantly. I could sense the men behind the hidden doors tensing.

The time for subterfuge was over. I had sincerely hoped I could reach King Edward without kicking up a fuss, but it seemed my wish was not to be. *"Shibal!"* I said loudly, putting a good deal of force into it. The chamberlain went down immediately, as did three of the men behind the hidden doors. The fourth was either a stoic or had something shielding his mind, for he never even faltered, the door he stood behind slid aside and an arrow was already in flight toward my head before I had finished putting his comrades to sleep.

I hadn't been in any sort of serious conflict since the end of the war with Gododdin two months past, yet it that time had left its mark upon me somehow... for I found myself enjoying the adrenaline. I smiled as the arrow shattered against my shield, savoring the look on the bowman's face as he realized he was in more trouble than he was ready for. Since the man was immune to mind affecting spells I spoke again, sealing the door he had just passed through with another shield and as an afterthought I repeated the process to seal the doorway I had entered through as well.

I walked toward the guard... still smiling. He tried another arrow and seeing that fail drew his sword. With a flick of my wrist and a whispered word my magic ripped the blade from his grasp and sent it spinning through the air, only to have it return, pointing at him, scant inches from his face. "Turn around please," I told him calmly. "Put your hands behind your back, I'd really rather not have to hurt you."

The poor fellow was so unnerved he obeyed immediately. Drawing my dagger I cut the belt from his waist and used it to bind his hands. "Lie down on the floor," I added and he readily complied. "Look, I understand you're in an awkward situation here," I told him conversationally. "You're the only one conscious and now you've been tied up, uninjured and unbruised. It might look bad when they free you later. Would you like me to rough you up a bit? I'd rather not get you into trouble if I can avoid it." I honestly meant every word as I said it, but apparently it was a bit too much for the guard. He moaned in an entirely unmanly manner and a moment later I smelled a distinct odor of urine.

"Aww… what the hell?" I said in dismay as I saw the stain spreading on the rich carpeting of the floor. Ignoring his loss of bladder control I took a moment to shatter his sword and rip up his clothes… perhaps that would be enough to keep him from being flogged later. I felt distinctly bad about it though as it only served to frighten him even further.

I left him then and headed through the doorway leading into the king's private demesne. It led into a long corridor, richly decorated and with multiple doorways leading off in every direction. More guards were already heading my way, but none of them were stoics and I put them to sleep before they got anywhere near me. Since my disguise was no longer effective I dropped it.

Taking a second to focus I used my arcane senses to examine the rooms around me. The king's quarters were a veritable warren of chambers, gardens, baths and bedrooms, but it took me only a moment to locate King Edward. He was waiting in his bedroom, sitting calmly at a side table. I have to give the man credit, he might be on the verge of assassination but he faced it with remarkable aplomb.

I followed a circuitous route to reach his bedroom door. I was tempted to knock down some walls and cut a direct path but I figured I should be more diplomatic. There were four men standing in the ante-chamber outside of his room but I didn't let that worry me, they weren't armed and seemed to be wearing nothing more than plain robes. I calmly opened the door to the sitting room and stepped inside. That was when all hell broke loose.

My eyes immediately confirmed what my magesight had already told me; these men were not armed or armored, but as soon as I entered light flared around them. Each one gained an aura, though they varied in color… silver, lavender, greenish gold and blue, these were devotees of the four shining gods. *Channelers, great.*

I was temporarily blinded as their power slammed into me, encasing my shield in coruscating light and nearly crushing me with its force. *I should have expected something like this,* I thought suddenly. Why hadn't I brought my staff? I was trapped… it took nearly all my strength to keep my shield intact. As my senses adjusted I realized only three of them held me, while the third was concentrating on something. The look in his eyes told me it would be something unpleasant and I immediately remembered the spell I had once used to cut through my opponents shields. If he used something like that I would be cut in two. *Shit.*

Individually none of the channelers were powerful enough to be a real threat, but together they were perhaps more than I could handle. I had one advantage though, while they were used to handling power only on rare occasions, I dealt with it on a daily basis. As the free one focused on his spell I changed my shield from a spherical to a tear drop shape, using the force of my opponents grip to send me hurtling sideways.

I wasn't a moment too soon, a flickering beam of green light sliced into the space where I had just been a moment before and cut through the stone walls behind me. As I went flying sideways the three who had held me were disoriented and lost their grip. That was all I needed.

The moment the forces against my shield let up I diverted my strength into a new spell, *"Pyrren ni'Tragen."* Flames exploded outward to engulf the entire room. Two of the men had been using all of their power to pin me, leaving them unable to maintain a shield to protect themselves. Their fate wasn't pretty. The other two had been better able to balance their use of power and were instead merely flung backward by the force of the explosion.

One of them lost his focus and his shield disappeared after he struck a wall. Meanwhile I was already rising from the other side of the room where my shield tactic had tossed me. I didn't bother to waste my power, I already had a stone in my hand and as I stood back up I breathed upon it sharply, *"Tielen striltos,"* I said and it streaked across the room. The unshielded man's head flew back and bits of blood and bone stained the walls.

I walked carefully across the room to the last man who was struggling to focus his power into an effective shield. Something about the clumsy way he wielded his magic made me laugh and a sickening laugh escaped my lips as I approached him. I focused my attention and encased him in a crushing bubble of pure force, much like the one they had used to pin me a moment before. His face went white with strain as he struggled to keep it from killing him. "You're not having a very good day," I told him with a smile.

He grimaced, "You cannot win. The gods are united against you."

I increased the pressure on him a bit. He obviously had too much energy left for talking. "So they have decided to support the king against me?" I glanced around the room, noting the symbols on their robes... Doron, Karenth, Millicenth... all of the shining gods were represented here. Looking back to the man before me I saw the golden flame of Celior on his chest. "Why?" I asked.

The light of madness was shining in his eyes. "You are an abomination," he said between clenched teeth. For a second I wondered what my own face had looked like as I had killed his three companions... at a guess I'd bet it hadn't been much prettier. *I am little better than them. Threaten me for a moment and I turn effortlessly into a merciless killer,* I thought. A feeling of disgust passed over me but I didn't lessen the pressure against his shield.

"If Celior has any messages for me now is the time to pass them along, you won't get many more chances after this," I responded emotionlessly.

His eyes shifted then and I could see them un-focusing as his god came to the fore. Simultaneously the strength of his shield increased three-fold, Celior wasn't pulling his punches. "You bear Illeniel's Doom mortal. You should die now and save yourself from suffering," he replied. His voice now held the dulcet tones of his god.

"You'll ruin your puppet if you push too hard Celior," I rebuked him. Sweat was standing out on my brow now as I redoubled my effort to keep him pinned down.

"His life is mine to use as I wish," the voice of the shining god responded. Blood was running freely from the man's nose and ears now, as he was pressed far beyond his limit.

"You're just like that bitch Millicenth aren't you? No concern for the people who support you. Why are you really doing this? You should be helping us against the shiggreth, aiding us against the dark gods, against Mal'goroth!" I ground the words out from between clenched teeth.

Celior's pawn was now wrapped in golden flames as the force of his god's power overwhelmed his body's limits. "You broke the accord, child of Illeniel; you will get no aid from us now. You must die before Illeniel's Doom destroys us all."

The power being forced through the man's poor body was simply incredible but he was dying already. I felt myself trembling with effort as I kept him trapped and just as I thought I would surely collapse from the strain the god's power fell off sharply and disappeared. I managed to stop myself before I crushed the channeler but it was a useless gesture, the man was already dead. His deity's power had burned him up like a candle, thrown into a furnace; he had been spent in an instant. The sight of his body filled me with anger that we should be so carelessly used and tossed aside. It could have been Marcus just as easily as this man, lying here dead.

The anger was good though, it kept me strong. My struggle with Celior had left me exhausted in a way I hadn't felt since the end of the war with Gododdin, yet I couldn't afford to collapse here; I still had a meeting to attend after all. *What the hell is the 'Doom of Illeniel'?* I wondered. It had sounded like doom with a capital 'D' when he had said it. *I never get any good news from deities. It's always absolutes and ultimatums, no wonder no one invites them to fancy dress balls,* I thought to myself.

Breathing heavily I got myself back on task and made sure the king was still waiting a few rooms away. He was. He must have realized that no amount of running would allow him to escape once his four aces were broken. I strode across the room and opened the door that led to his bedroom. A short hallway faced me and I continued onward 'til I reached the final door that separated us. I still had a shield around myself but it was becoming increasingly difficult to maintain it.

That was a bad sign; normally the strain of my shield was not something I'd even notice, even after a long day. It meant I was surely close to the end of my reserves, not a good thing when you're surrounded by enemies. I decided to try something I had only done once before, when I had needed strength to chase the remaining soldiers of Gododdin back to the river. Focusing on the deep heartbeat of the earth below me I opened myself and drew upon it. *Please share your strength with me,* was my conscious thought, but it was not communicated in words. Instead my mind connected with something far greater than myself, something so much larger as to be entirely alien to my experience as a human being... for a moment I was part of it. I felt stronger and weaker simultaneously... energy was coursing through me now, yet my mortal flesh was weak, nothing like my normal stone and iron. Then I broke the contact and my mind came tumbling back to the present.

I reeled for a second as I became re-accustomed to my humanity again. *That didn't happen the last time I did that,* I noted. Apparently even small uses of my new gift could be dangerous. I had accomplished my goal though; my body was filled with new energy. I felt light and fresh, as if I had slept a full night. *There must be some limit to this.*

Now wasn't the time for inner debates and soul-searching so I drew myself up and opened the door in front of me. A long step took me into the personal bedroom of King Edward Carenval. I have to say I wasn't disappointed by the furnishings. It was every bit as well appointed as one would expect of the room of a king. Silken tapestries adorned the walls and beautifully upholstered furniture graced the room. His bed was a work of art, each of the four posts being lovingly carved to represent one of the shining gods.

I took a moment to stare at the opulence... even the floor was a masterful artwork of wooden parquetry. Finally I settled my eyes upon the man waiting quietly in a comfortably designed chair. He was sitting beside a small table and had a glass of wine in hand already. His outward appearance was remarkably calm, considering how I had arrived but when he sipped at his wine I could see the liquid trembling. "Come, have a seat," he invited me.

Remembering our last meeting I couldn't help but smile at being invited to sit. "Some of your servants were a bit rude out there... I hope you train them better in future," I replied and took a seat on the other side of the table.

"It is difficult to get good help these days," he agreed. "Care for some wine?"

The last thing I needed was to be poisoned after all my effort to get there. "No thanks, I'm not thirsty at the moment."

"We can understand that," said King Edward. "Fortunately that is one worry we don't have at the moment." He raised his glass to me and took a long drink, finishing over half of it at one go. I couldn't blame him; if I were in his shoes I'd have been incredibly nervous as well.

"I trust Cyhan reached you with my message?" I asked.

He looked sharply at me, blue eyes locking onto mine for a moment, "Yes he did. We are surprised you released him."

I smiled in a rather unfriendly way, "You yourself just mentioned how hard it is to find good help. I thought it would be a gesture of good will to return him to you unharmed."

A saw a flicker of hope cross his features but it was quickly hidden. He was perhaps realizing that I hadn't come to assassinate him. "Can we take that to mean you are still concerned with things such as good will?"

I laughed, "Your majesty, you do me a disservice, surely you do not doubt my loyalty?"

"We would be lying if we said we weren't wondering. Your action in defeating the incursion from Gododdin has left us in an awkward position. Our relations were already strained and now we must either acknowledge you as a hero of the realm or see you vilified and replaced quickly. We could not help but notice you made no move to bow or recognize us as your liege when you entered the room," he responded.

I was shocked at how quickly he had gone on the offensive once he realized I didn't mean to kill him. I suppose being a sovereign all these years had made him a tough negotiator. I decided to put him in his place quickly, "We are alone here, with none watching. I saw no need for formal gestures." It was both a statement and a challenge. After a long pause I added, "...sire."

Edward's eyebrows went up, "You play a dangerous game Mordecai. Are you sure this is what you want to do? It might be easier for you if you 'simplified' your situation now."

Did he just suggest I'd be better off if I killed him? I wondered. *That certainly took guts.* After a moment I answered him, "Every choice leads to its own consequences. I would rather look to the safety of the realm. Civil war would only lead to our downfall at this juncture; it is in everyone's best interests if we cooperate."

I could almost see the gears in his head turning. "Do you and James still keep close counsel?" he asked. For King Edward it was a very direct question, and its meaning was clear. He wanted to know if I had an older, 'wiser', head advising me.

I nodded, "Of course, James and I have never been closer. The man has been like a father to me, especially since my own loss." It was a statement loaded with double meanings.

The king's eyes flickered for a moment as he remembered, then they assumed an expression of deep sympathy. "Ah yes, we had heard about your father's death. You have our condolences. It was an unfortunate accident, or so we are told."

My father had been wounded by arrows from a royal guardsman while we were 'liberating' supplies for the defense of Lothion from the king's warehouses. Edward had to be wondering if I held a grudge, even though I bore as much responsibility for that event as he did. Swallowing I kept my tone even, "Yes your majesty, it was a terrible accident. I'm certain that everyone involved regrets what happened."

Edward drank another long swallow of wine. His hand no longer shook, so I could only assume he had at last relaxed. "You have presented us with an interesting conundrum young Illeniel. The clergymen of all four churches have been after me to have you executed. They claim you committed some sort of heresy during the battle. Meanwhile I have received report after report detailing your astonishing victory against the army of Gododdin. Cyhan tells me that you have broken your bond and have likely gone mad."

I nodded in agreement. "I have broken the bond and it is no secret that the gods have turned against me.

Apparently they do not like their chattel to show signs of independence."

"You do not seem like a madman, despite your dramatic entrance today," he observed.

"I like to think that I am not," I said, then glancing at the door I added, "Your men are about to charge the door… there are quite a few of them out there." In fact, there were twenty men preparing to rush the room and more were taking up positions throughout the royal suite. "It might be best if you let them know you are alright before some of them hurt themselves."

"One moment," said the king. Striding to the door he threw it open and began bellowing. I was impressed. I hadn't realized such a volume of sound could come from such an unimposing frame. "Anything that was going to happen has already happened, no thanks to you lot! Get back to your posts… and someone clean up this mess out here!" I could only assume he was gesturing at the bodies of the four channelers. He returned to his chair and refilled his own cup. "Did you have to make such a mess? Between the blood and the fire the room is ruined out there."

I could only wonder at a man who could be so droll in commenting on the deaths of four of his retainers, well… allies at least in the case of the channelers, but I wasn't there to reform the man. "They forced my hand. I would rather not have killed anyone," I told him.

Edward looked at me oddly for a moment, "We do believe you, but sometimes one must break a few eggs to make an omelet."

"They were your eggs, or doesn't that bother you?" I asked.

"No, they were borrowed at best and since you're being so sociable we are beginning to think perhaps we are better off without them. They were beginning to get a bit unreasonable," he replied.

"The church would attempt to force concessions from the king?"

"They have been over-bold since your father's death. Without a wizard we have been forced to rely upon them whenever magical assistance was required. Especially when we thought we might need protection," he gave me a pointed stare as he said that last part.

Something about his statement rang false however. I could not put my finger upon what exactly, but I could tell he was not telling the truth… or at least not the complete truth. "If you had a source of magical support you would not be quite so beholden to them… at the very least you could seek balance by focusing their energies upon a different opponent." I wanted to make it clear that I was aware of my value in other regards… assuming we did agree to get along.

"That fact had not escaped our consideration, though we must confess that we have been very curious regarding your motivations. We understand you care more for the people than your own power, but although avoiding a civil war is a good reason, we still wonder that you think it alone is sufficient reason to follow this course… given your advantage at the moment." It was a very direct question; the king had just openly stated his own vulnerability, something I would have thought unthinkable.

"It is enough for me," I responded. "My wife is expecting our first child and I would rather seek a peaceful solution than bring him into a world torn by strife. The real question is whether you wish to settle our differences or not."

"We did not think it a possibility before now, but you have been persuasive Mordecai. The proclamation branding you an outlaw was certainly a misunderstanding, we shall move to remedy it immediately. Similarly we must think of a suitable reward for the hero that saved our realm. Would two weeks' time be enough for you to prepare for a bit of pomp and circumstance? The crowd does love to celebrate a true hero," he gave me a smile that sent chills down my spine. I might be forced to hard decisions now and then, but this man made them without compunction or regret. I could see him smiling just as easily after sending an army to its death. The callousness of his regard for his people lit my anger again.

"That sounds lovely your majesty. I would be pleased to take this news to James Lancaster as well. I would remind you though... I will not respond well to a betrayal. What happened here today was no mistake. Do not forget it," I gave him a feral grin to answer his cold smile.

Edward stood straight up at that point, his eyes flashing with true anger. "We do not take kindly to threats young Illeniel. Remember that well. Nor will we rule as a puppet to some other master. If you would prefer that, you should make a more direct resolution of this matter... now!" He slapped his chest lightly to punctuate his remark. "Can we count on your oath of fealty... or not?"

I might not like the man, but I had to respect his courage. I waited a moment before replying, "Yes your majesty, you can." I stood up and prepared to leave. I still did not bow to him.

His eyes narrowed, "Did anyone see you enter here today?"

"No, unless you count the four channelers," I told him.

He grinned, "Excellent... that makes things easier for me then. We'll keep this meeting a secret. Do you think you can leave without being recognized?"

"Of course," I replied drawing my hood up over my head. I didn't plan on relying on such a simple disguise, but I still wanted to keep my methods to myself. No one had seen my remove my disguise, although I was certain that a recount of Ruth's use of magic against the guard would lead to a lot of interesting speculation.

"Perfect," he told me. "We shall look forward to seeing you in the capital again in two weeks' time." I left after that, but as I walked I could hear him bellowing orders. "Someone get the Baron of Arundel… I would have words with him!" I could only wonder how he was going to explain the reversal of fortunes to Sheldon. The last time I had seen the Baron I had robbed him of the entirety of his wealth—putting aside the fact that Penny had made a fool of him in front of his men, there was no way he could possibly forgive me, without even considering the fact that I had 'stolen' all of his retainers as well.

I could only wonder how interesting that conversation would be. I made my way carefully through the palace using the stolen visage of a guard. Leaving was much simpler than entering had been.

CHAPTER 9

Ireturned home that evening. I felt a bit bad about not staying to eat dinner with Marc but I wanted to tell Penny the news. If things worked out as expected we would all be visiting Marc very soon anyway.

She received the news with less enthusiasm than I had expected, "He wants you to appear in the capital in two weeks?"

There was nothing wrong with Penny's memory, but for some reason she loved repetition. "Yes, two weeks," I said again.

"And you think he's really planning to welcome you back into the fold?" she asked skeptically.

I sighed. "I made sure he knew the consequences if his offer wasn't genuine."

"You mean you threatened his life," she said flatly.

"Essentially, yes," I replied.

She shifted topics, "How many people did you kill reaching him?" The question annoyed me, and I really didn't want to answer it.

"Four," I told her flatly.

She raised one eyebrow. "Was it worth it?"

"They were channelers, working for the gods... I had no other options," I said.

"They were men, and you said you could get to the king without being caught," she reminded me.

Anger and guilt simmered close to the surface now. "Would you rather we went to war again? I had to meet

107

the king, and I had to do it on my terms if we were to bring him around."

She knew I was close to snapping and her eyes softened. "I'm not blaming you Mordecai, but I can't ignore this. As your wife, your partner, I have to be sure you're keeping your focus on what is important. Stop being defensive and think clearly… was it worth it? Did we gain something worth four lives or should we have tried something different? I don't expect you to be perfect… I just want to make sure you're not forgetting the people that suffer for our choices."

Somewhere in the background of my mind I noted that she used the pronouns 'our' and 'we' frequently. She was trying very hard to keep me involved in the discussion rather than simply creating a fight. I took a deep breath, "I do think that it was still worth it, though I regret the necessity. Perhaps if I had used a better method I could have avoided killing them, but I'm not sure…"

She stepped forward to put her arms around me, "Don't do that. Neither of us is perfect. I just want to know that you're keeping the costs in sight."

"I haven't forgotten the watchman, that night in Albamarl, when we raided the royal warehouses," I told her. "More than any, his death still haunts me…," I began.

"I'm sorry Mort," she interrupted. "I didn't mean to make you think I don't trust you. Let's eat, this conversation has turned entirely too morbid. What will Dorian and Rose think when they see us downstairs?" She took me by the arm and pulled me toward the door.

"Well damnitt woman, make up your mind!" I exclaimed. "One minute you're making me doubt myself… the next you're trying to cheer me up." I gave her an expression that was equal parts pout and smirk.

We went downstairs, and by the time we arrived both of us had replaced our glum expressions with the more positive demeanor expected of the Count and Countess di'Cameron.

⸺•⸺

I spent the next week as productively as possible. I actually managed to finish the first set of armor and brought Dorian in to try it on. He tried to hide it, but the look on his face reminded me of a kid who has gotten too much candy and is hoping no one will notice. It took us a good quarter of an hour to get him buckled into it.

"How does it feel?" I asked.

Dorian didn't answer immediately. Instead he backed up a bit, moving his arms in circular motions, and then he made a sharp lunge forward. He had a very positive expression. I couldn't help but laugh as he began doing warm up exercises.

"Are you going to talk to me or start practicing your ball dances?" I teased him.

He gave me a boyish grin. "I might just try dancing! How did you do this? It's even lighter than the chainmail you magicked for me!"

Though the armor didn't fit me I had already tried it myself… and I had designed the enchantments that produced the effect he was describing. These enchantments were different however, and I was curious about Dorian's reaction. "This armor isn't actually any lighter than normal," I informed him. "You complained that the lightness of the chainmail made you feel like you were being tossed about so I didn't alter the mass of this armor."

"Mass?" he asked without a hint of guile.

I sighed… he never had really paid attention to his tutors in the sciences. If it wasn't military history he just hadn't been interested. "It's what gives your armor weight, what makes it heavy."

"It doesn't feel heavy, I might as well be wearing nothing but my gambeson and a bit of leather for all the weight I have on me," he replied.

"It's all still there, I've just enchanted the armor to move *with* you… at least partly," I explained. It was actually an exceedingly complex enchantment. I had been working on it far longer than I had the actual armor crafting. As usual it was the sort of accomplishment that no one would ever really understand.

"How?" Dorian asked, though he regretted the question almost immediately.

Excited to finally have someone to tell I launched into a detailed explanation, "The armor stores energy from your downward movements, rather like a spring… then the energy is released whenever you move in a direction that works against gravity. The end result is that while you still retain the inertia of eighty pounds of metal you don't have to exhaust yourself moving it around with just your muscles…"

"Mort!" he interrupted me with a pained expression.

The look in his eyes told me I had gone overboard again. I started over, "The armor uses magic to help you move. It's still as heavy as normal, but you don't have to bear all the weight yourself."

Dorian's eyebrows went up, "That's perfect. I'm assuming it's still as hard to pierce as the chainmail you did?"

I chuckled, "I don't know what it would take to cut through that. My guess is that if something powerful enough to pierce the armor hit you, you wouldn't care, the shock would kill you before the armor failed."

"What about one of your enchanted blades?" he asked seriously.

I squinted involuntarily, "It would be unlikely. The edge would have to strike perfectly and the blade would have to be wielded with a strength beyond what a normal man could muster."

"What if he was wearing magical armor that moved with him?" Dorian said pointedly, flexing his arm.

I shook my head, "No the armor doesn't augment your strength. It merely assists you in moving it. It wouldn't be enough."

He looked disappointed. You'd almost think he was trying to figure out a way to kill himself. Finally he opened up, "Well I think it's wonderful, though I wonder if it's really worth your time to be making armor down here."

"There's only one of me Dorian, but I need help. I need men that can fight the shiggreth on equal terms. Scratch that… I need men that can cut the shiggreth into small pieces and send them packing. I can only be in one place at a time… while the enemy is numerous. The valley is large and there are several villages, it just isn't possible for…"

Dorian held a hand up to silence me. "I understand Mort… I'm the one that told you originally remember? You have to trust the people to be your strength."

"Right!" I agreed. "But they need the proper tools if they're to be effective against the sort of enemies we're facing now."

Dorian nodded, "You're right, but you can only make so many suits of armor like this. Even for you it takes too long. How many do you plan to make and what will it accomplish?"

"Twenty or so… for a hand-picked group of leaders and fighters… a new order of knights," I told him. I was a bit hesitant, until now I had kept my idea a secret, and the thought of saying it aloud made it sound a bit like one of the stories I used to read. I feared laughter.

I needn't have worried, though. Dorian's imagination was greater than mine and for all his wisdom he had a simplicity that made such things very believable. His eyes lit with enthusiasm almost before I could finish my sentence. "That's brilliant!" Two words... that's all it took and I could see my dream written in his face.

"Well don't get the wrong idea, they won't be a traditional military order. I'll commission them as protectors, wardens of the people...," I said calmly. I was hoping to calm Dorian's exuberance, although I had to admit it was contagious. He had a habit of saying what perhaps my inner child had been thinking all along.

"So you'll send them out... patrolling the land, guarding the citizens from undead monsters and bandits alike," he exclaimed.

"Well yes..."

"And they'll pledge absolute loyalty to you Mort... the defender of Lothion!" Dorian was pacing now and nothing I could say would get through to him, his head was filled with visions of knights errant and deeds of chivalry. I smiled to myself as I watched him. If I could find nineteen other men like him, perhaps it wasn't such a foolish dream after all.

"Ideally they'd pledge fealty to the...," I started to say 'king' but I knew already that it was a bad idea. "Perhaps they should swear to James of Lancaster," I amended.

He stopped and glared at me, "Say something like that again and I'll wallop you!"

"You object to James?" I started.

"No, fool! I know you're trying to be modest and all, but it's time to own up to what you've done. You defeated an army of over thirty thousand men, saved the realm, and won the hearts of thousands of people. Do you honestly think you could create some new order of knights and just hand it over to someone else? Do you think people would be inspired by that?" he said angrily.

"Alright, you're right," I said trying to placate him. I knew there was no use in arguing once he got riled up like that.

"Don't agree with me and think I'll shut up! You always do that. I may not be a genius but I'm smart enough to spot your patronizing ways. Listen up… the people need inspiration, just as much as they need protection. We just fought off a massive attack; many of the people lost loved ones. The first harvest was nearly a complete loss and you and I aren't the only ones who know that there's a lot of damned undead wandering around unaccounted for. This idea is brilliant and it's just what they need, something to hope for. Nothing inspires hope like a hero, and you're planning to give them twenty… but they need to be led by a hero, someone the people know. Someone the people believe can do anything… in case you haven't been paying attention, that's you Mort." He poked me forcefully with his index finger.

Sometimes Dorian could embarrass the hell out of me, even when we were alone. I tried to change the subject, "Actually Dorian you brought up something important. This new order will need a captain… aside from whoever they answer to… and you made a lot of good points. Naturally I want you to be that person."

He blinked for a second, "Well I knew that already, the real question is who else you want, you need nineteen other men if you're to have a force of twenty."

I had done some thinking on that already but it was a difficult subject. I had to be selective. I wanted men who had already been tested in battle, veterans who were also trustworthy. There were a number of capable warriors in my livery now but I had no way of judging the integrity of many of them. Quite a few were ex-mercenaries with questionable backgrounds. Finding killers was easy; finding men like Dorian was a daunting task. So far I had only come up with two names. "Joe McDaniels and Harold Simmons," I said at last.

"Joe won't do," Dorian commented. "He's too old and he has a business to run. Much as I love the man I wouldn't saddle him with something like this in his later years. Harold might be a good choice though, what made you choose him?"

"He's young and bright eyed. You've mentioned him several times in the past, regarding his skill with weapons. He's also a native son of Washbrook. He knows the people here and they'll trust him. More importantly he'll care about them far better than one of our transplants from the capital," I explained.

Dorian nodded. "I like your thinking. I may know one or two more that meet those criteria among our new guards. I'll work with them and let you know if I think they'll work."

"Perfect, I want you training them anyway," I added.

"I figured that, but you've omitted one key piece of information here," he told me.

I stared blankly at him, "What?"

"What are you going to name this new order?"

"Oh…," I said eloquently. I didn't have a single idea, and it didn't take long for my vacuous gaze to communicate that fact to him.

"Ha! Don't worry! I've been dreaming about something like this since we were kids," he reassured me. Long experience prevented me from being reassured. Dorian drew a dramatic breath. "The Mystic Guardians of Lothion!" he pronounced, as if he stood upon a stage.

I groaned, "Mystic?"

"Well you are outfitting them each with magical weapons and armor," Dorian explained. "Alright how about: The Defenders of the Flame!"

"What flame?"

"The flame of life that burns in all of us, we're supposed to be protecting people from the undead right?"

"I don't know… I was thinking it should be something shorter," I mused. "Let's think about it a while, there's no need to rush into a name yet. Besides, I have a question for you."

"What about?" Dorian asked.

"I built this armor with you in mind. Now that you have it, I still feel it isn't enough. You've fought them before, hand to hand and wearing enchanted armor… what would have helped you most?" I said, trying to elaborate so that he would understand my question.

My friend pursed his lips for a moment, concentrating. "What helped most was your father tossing oil on them and setting them on fire when they had me helpless."

I smiled ruefully at the thought, "If I could bring him back to follow us around and haul our asses out of trouble every time things went badly… I would, and I'd bring your dad back as well. I'm sure that with the two of them around we could just take it easy from then on."

Dorian grinned, but I could see a hint of sadness in his eyes at the thought. "Well I suppose the next best thing would be something that would prevent me being borne to the ground and overwhelmed by sheer numbers. I was always rather jealous of Penny's strength when she was your Anath'Meridum. If I had been strong like that, they never could have forced me down."

I winced, "There's no way I'm renewing the bond, with you or anyone else."

"I understand," Dorian replied hastily, "but isn't there some other way?"

I frowned as I thought… "I don't know, maybe. I'll see what I can figure out."

CHAPTER 10

The next day I took a break and went out looking for some privacy. I wanted to talk to Moira again. Finding a quiet place in the forest I sat down and called her silently. I probably could have chosen a quiet room in the castle just as easily, but the weather was nice and it seemed more appropriate to call her in a more natural setting. She appeared within moments, rising silently from the earth.

"You need me again?" she asked. Today her eyes were composed of some translucent blue stone, making it look as though they had clouded over. I wondered if she actually saw through them or if they were just for show. Each time I called her it seemed her body was created on the spot from whatever materials were at hand.

"I just wanted to continue our conversation. I have more questions. You don't mind do you?" I replied.

"Mind?" Her lips curled into a smirk. "Remember Mordecai, I am not a living person. I am a memory of a person, I only exist because your will breathes life into that memory."

"Well you must have some feelings. You just smiled at me… and as you've shown before you definitely have your own opinions," I said in return.

"Do not confuse 'seeming' with 'being'," she said. "You might paint a picture of a person, but it still is only oil on canvas. I am not much more than that."

"So I am supposed to believe you aren't much better than a clockwork mechanism? Do you honestly propose to tell me that you have no emotions either?" I said bluntly.

She stared at me intently, "No... I do have emotions... I think. I am as much a victim of the illusion as you are. While we talk, while you invest your focus on me, I feel... much as I did once, long ago. But I still remember this is an illusion, as soon as you turn your will aside I will return to dust."

"What if I kept my focus on you? It doesn't seem to cost me anything. You could live again perhaps..." I suggested.

"No!" she interrupted loudly. "I could not bear it. The longer I am here, the more I remember, the more it hurts."

"But you succeeded... I would think perhaps you would have at least a few good things to remember," I continued.

"I won," she agreed, "but that is not necessarily the same as success. I lost everything I was fighting for, but I won. Almost everyone I knew or cared about was dead by the time I made my final choice and the one good reason I had left for fighting was rendered..." She stopped then and her face told me she had gone further than she intended.

"Forgive me for prying," I apologized, but inwardly I wondered what she had been about to say.

"It isn't your fault. I am not ready to share the more painful parts of my story yet, but perhaps someday I will." She closed her eyes and lowered her head, as if communing with the long dead spirits of her friends and family.

I waited for a long minute before continuing, "Actually, I had a more practical reason for disturbing your rest."

The memory of Moira Centyr opened her eyes, "Good, my reason for existing is entirely practical. It might be best to stick to such things." Staring into those alien stone eyes I could not help but be touched by the emotion I felt lay behind them, but I kept my tongue firmly in check this time.

"When Penny and I were bound together, she gained great physical strength and speed. Cyhan told me it was a side effect of the bond. Because of it she gained extra strength in proportion to my power," I said explaining. "Do you understand how it worked?"

"No. I can guess, but in my time such bonds were not made. Such a thing would be dangerous for both people involved, exposing them to pointless risk of life and, as you discovered, limiting the sensitivity of the mage," she said. "Why do you ask?"

"I just thought it might be useful for other warriors to possess such physical advantages, if there were some way to do it without putting my own life at risk," even as I spoke it seemed frivolous. "It's probably a foolish question isn't it?"

She laughed showing white pebble teeth as her mouth opened, "Not at all. You just want to create a *targoth cherek.*" My knowledge of Lycian now was good enough that I already understood the words, 'earth guard', though the context was foreign still.

"I'm not sure what that is," I admitted.

"That is no surprise," she said, "There haven't been any since the last archmage passed into the earth."

"You mean yourself?" I asked.

"Yes, Gareth Gaelyn and I were the last to create such bonds," she replied.

"So they were men?"

"And women, occasionally. They were given power to protect their charge."

"So they were similar to the Anath'Meridum?" I questioned.

She frowned, the expression seeming almost completely human despite the exotic composition of her cheeks and lips. "No, the Anath'Meridum, from what I understand, were created by wizards… after the sundering. They were an effort to appease the church and the people of the time I do not doubt. Very likely they were inspired by the memory of the targoth cherek."

She paused for a moment before elaborating. "Despite the superficial similarities they were entirely different than your pact-bearers. Each targoth cherek was given his or her power to protect an archmage. They served as bodyguards, rather than executioners."

I couldn't help but interrupt, "Were their lives connected to the archmage they served?"

Moira snorted, which seemed odd given her form. "Absolutely not, they were connected to the *earth,* not another human being. We weren't stupid enough to link two people's lives in such a foolish manner."

"Why weren't there any more created after the war with Balinthor?"

"There weren't any archmages," she said matter-of-factly. "The creation of the Anath'Meridum made sure of that."

"So only…," I began.

"Yes, only an archmage could facilitate the bond between a mortal being and the earth," she said answering my unfinished question.

"Hmmm," I said sagely as I considered her words.

"You don't understand why, do you?" she asked pointedly.

"No," I admitted.

"Any such bond, such as the bond you took with your wife, is a bond between two mutually consenting beings.

It cannot be forced. A wizard is unable to communicate with the earth… and for that matter so is everyone else. An archmage must facilitate, must communicate with the earth or no such bond can be formed," she explained.

I was beginning to get the general idea, but I still had many questions. "Were the 'miellte' you mentioned before, the watchers, were they also 'targoth cherek'?" I was referring to the watchers that observed archmages to keep them from overusing their powers.

Moira laughed, "No… that would be pointless. The 'miellte' were wizards themselves and such a bond would have limited their ability to listen, to communicate, just as your pact kept you from hearing the earth. A bond with the earth, or anything else, would keep the miellte from hearing the mind of the archmage they were tasked with watching."

Now that she said it aloud it made more sense to me. "So the targoth cherek were created as guardians?"

"Of a sort," she replied. "They were almost exclusively bodyguards for the one or two archmages alive at any given time."

It was time to get down to brass tacks. It sounded as if the earth-bond she was describing might be perfect for my purpose but I needed to know what its effects were, as well as how to create it. "So to be more specific, is there a limit to how many of these earth-bonds an archmage can create, and what are the drawbacks?" Experience had taught me that there had to be problems.

Her eyebrows, or what passed for eyebrows anyway… shot up in surprise. "You would attempt something like that? You have barely begun to learn to control your ability."

"My life, since learning of my magical gifts, has been rough. The only thing I am sure of is that I rarely have as much time as I should. If I don't move forward I will be caught by my enemies before I have learned how to deal with them," I told her.

"You just slew an army of over thirty thousand men, how many enemies could you have left?" she asked, but there was more than a question in her eyes, there was a challenge there as well.

"More than when I started. Those men were never my enemies; my true enemy was always the dark god behind them, Mal'goroth. Since I stopped them he is only stronger and the shiggreth he created are loose upon the land. Even now they are multiplying somewhere that I cannot see them," I replied.

"Are those your only enemies?"

Her question gave voice to my fear and suddenly I knew for a fact that my paranoia must be correct. "No, there are others. The other dark gods certainly, and I suspect the shining gods are worse than neutral; they may actually be malign as well. Beyond that I have no idea, but I must assume I have a growing crowd of 'admirers' among my own kind as well."

She nodded her head in agreement, "You are right to fear the shining gods. They may be your greatest foes. Whether they are malign to humanity I do not know, but they certainly bear you no good will."

Her statement reminded me of my recent run-in at the royal palace. "I spoke with Celior not long ago. He said something I didn't understand."

"It is rare that they say anything worth hearing," she commented.

"He said that I bore 'Illeniel's Doom' and that I should die before destroying us all," I told her. "Have you heard of it before?"

She sat for a long time and I almost gave up on her answering. "I have heard of it. My Mordecai, the one that died long ago, mentioned it once," she said. Her expression had grown distant, as if she was remembering times and places far removed from the present. I suppose she must have been thinking of her lover, the Illeniel she had known in her time that had born my name. At last she stared at me again, "I do not know what he meant. It was related to some sort of secret your family kept. All he would tell me was that it was an old family shame, something that went back to the founder, the first Illeniel."

That's just what I need, more secrets, I thought quietly to myself. "How will I find out?" I said aloud, more to myself than to her.

"That's for you to figure out. Perhaps you will never know, though if it were that important I would think your family might have kept some sort of record," she said.

"Perhaps in my father's house," I said, thinking aloud. There was still a lot that needed exploring there. I had barely begun to scratch the surface of the books there. In fact, I had only read four of the books from my father's library so far… one of history, one regarding teleportation circles and a couple relating to the use of illusions. Those last two I was still coming to grips with. I shook my head and spoke again, "You've let me get sidetracked. I wanted to know about the limitations and drawbacks involved with the targoth cherek."

She smiled, "It isn't my job to keep you on track. Besides, only one of us is completely 'real', so I can't be blamed." Her face took on a more serious expression then. "To answer your question, yes, there are limitations and drawbacks, very serious ones. You remember the stone I had you work with the last time we spoke I am sure. Let us use it as an example. That stone, small as it was, had a small amount of latent power of its own, as well as a minimal level of consciousness. When you listened to it your task was to make the stone a part of yourself, a part of your consciousness, a part of your 'body'. The risk, which I described to you then, was that you might accidentally make yourself a part of 'it' instead of the other way around. You remember all of this, don't you?"

"Yes of course," I said immediately.

"You also should remember the loss of self you experienced when you tried to 'listen' to the wind and went past your limit. An occasion like that is why having a miellte present can be very important, that girl… Ariadne, she saved your life when she got your attention and brought you back to yourself. The same principle applies when you work with the earth. A small stone is a small risk; it is easy to maintain your 'self'. A large stone is more risk, and more difficult to make a part of yourself, without you instead becoming a part of it. Does all of this make sense so far?"

It seemed logical, so I nodded my head in agreement.

"There are two factors that are important to the creation of the bond. One is the person being bonded… particularly how resilient their mind is to being in close contact with something as alien and different as the earth itself. The second factor relates to the archmage and how great a portion of the earth he or she attempts to bond to the subject. The greater the portion is, the more powerful the targoth cherek will be and the faster they will devolve. An archmage can only bind as much of the earth as they can actively work with themselves, without being overwhelmed so that…"

I interrupted, "Wait, what do you mean 'devolve'?"

Moira gave me an irritated look, "I hadn't gotten to that part yet, but it is a pertinent question. A human being is not meant to be in constant contact with the earth, along with the power they receive they also find themselves becoming more like the earth itself. The effect is similar to what happens to an archmage when they go too far, except that a targoth cherek has little control over the process. They cannot break the bond on their own, or reduce the amount of earthpower they are bonded to. Eventually they become creatures of stone and earth themselves, or very nearly so. They become golems, intelligent, sentient creatures of stone, with minimal will or self-awareness. At that point there is little anyone can do to restore them."

"Like Magnus," I said remembering the golem at my father's house in Albamarl.

"What?!" she said, startled. "Where did you get that name?"

I carefully related the story of the golem I had met guarding my father's library. I didn't get into too much detail regarding how it had 'inverted' Rose, though the memory still brought a smile to my face. When I finished I noticed that Moira had gone rather still and her face was somber.

"I never expected to hear that name again, though it makes sense… poor Magnus," she said after a while.

"Did you know him?"

"He was the only targoth cherek I ever made, as well as being a close friend. He was a noble man. I had hoped to free him before it got so far but events got away from me. I sent him away, to protect 'my' Mordecai when things got desperate. I can only assume he succeeded… since you are here." Her voice was thick and crystal tears had formed at the edges of her eyes.

Her obvious pain should have made me more sensitive, but my curiosity overrode my better sense. "What do you mean 'free him'? Is there a way to prevent what happens to them?"

"Yes," she answered. "The archmage that created the bond must unmake it, before they go beyond the point of no return. In my time, though it was risky, most of those who became targoth cherek were freed before they suffered irreversible effects, usually after a matter of years or sometimes decades. It was rare for one to be left to his fate as Magnus was. It could only happen as an act of deliberate cruelty or perhaps if the archmage died without warning, before the bond could be broken." Shame and sorrow were written in her gaze.

"I'm sorry," I said, realizing I had asked too much.

"It isn't your fault. I hadn't thought of it since that time. Not 'til I heard his name again. I was cruel, and my love for your namesake was so great that I ignored the consequences. I sent Magnus to protect him, and I did it knowing that I would probably be unable to return later to remove the bond. It was a selfish request on my part, yet he swore to do it anyway. My guilt is not your fault." She had sunk to her knees now, and her stone dress had spread out around her like water upon the ground, her posture was one of dejection.

"Moira…" I started but she interrupted me.

"Would you mind letting me go, for now? Let me return to nothing and forget. These memories are too much. Please?" She looked up at me then and I could not refuse her.

"Rest Moira, I will call you another time," I told her and before the words had finished leaving my lips she was gone. This time she had vanished so quickly she didn't even bother to return the body she had fashioned from the earth to the ground. Instead she left it there, like some exquisitely perfect statue of a woman kneeling upon the soft earth. I might have thought she was still there but for my arcane senses, I knew she was no longer present.

I sat staring at the form she had left behind for some while, wondering at the woman she had been. Clearly she had her own demons, things she would rather forget. Her story was already finished, yet because of me she was repeatedly forced to return and relive it, neither alive nor properly dead. For a moment I considered not calling her again, but my need was too great and her knowledge too valuable. No matter how much I might wish to leave her in peace the things she could teach me were too important to ignore. *I suppose someday I will be able to add this to my own list of regrets, torturing a woman from the past with her memories that she might teach me,* I thought to myself.

I rose and began trudging home, there was nothing more to be gained in the forest today.

CHAPTER 11

Several days had passed and I still had not called on Moira again. I had dozens of questions for her, but something told me to wait. I felt she deserved that at least. Instead I focused on the task I had in front of me. I began working in earnest on a second set of armor, using measurements for Harold Simmons. Dorian had been kind enough to get them for me, though we hadn't told poor Harold the reason they were needed. By mutual consent we decided to keep the plans for my new order of knighthood a secret until they were more fully developed.

That didn't stop Dorian from taking Harold aside for more direct and personal training however. I might have felt sorry for the man, except that he seemed to take delight in the personal attention. He seemed to positively enjoy sweating himself half to death in the practice yard. *Some people are just masochists,* I thought. It never occurred to me that I probably sweat just as much working in the smithy each day. That was different after all.

Today I was hard at work shaping the metal that would hopefully someday be worn by Harold. While my hands were busy, my mind had drifted away, thinking of the upcoming trip to Albamarl. I had decided to seek a blacksmith to employ while we were in the city. It might be hard to convince one to relocate, especially if he had a successful practice in the capital already. It might be better to find a young journeyman, someone who had recently finished his apprenticeship and might be looking for an opportunity abroad.

Perhaps I could find a master and a journeyman. Washbrook had many needs beyond my personal projects and with my father gone I was the closest thing to an actual metal worker in the area. With my skills and a bit of cheating I could do anything that needed to be done, and very quickly as well, but it was distracting. Plus I needed help. Hopefully I could find someone with experience in weaponsmithing. That way I could hand over the job of forging the great-swords I planned to enchant later.

The metal in front of me had gone cold again, but rather than reheat it I set it down and stepped outside to wash my hands and face. *I should probably find someplace a little more private before I attempt this*, I thought to myself. Using a towel I had brought with me I was drying my hands and face when I felt an intent stare on my back. My magesight could easily locate the man watching me; he was standing at one of the windows looking down from the main keep.

Being a member of the nobility now, as well as the only living wizard known, I was quite used to gathering curious stares but something about this man caught my attention. I studied him carefully without looking up to let him know I was aware of his gaze. Without using my eyes, I could tell he was a fairly nondescript man, medium build and middling age, not old yet but far from young. He was already starting to go bald, though I couldn't tell what color his hair might be without using my eyes.

Then I realized what had gotten my attention, there was a fine aura of power rippling in the air around his body, something similar to my own shield but far subtler. My shield was bright and shimmering when viewed with my magesight but this was a dim shadowy aura, almost undetectable. He kept his power close to his skin and it was woven so delicately it was hard to understand what purpose it might serve, though it was clearly not meant to be used as a protective shield.

At last my curiosity got the better of me and I turned to look upward at him. My eyes immediately found the window he was standing at, but there was no one there. That was in direct opposition to the fact that my magesight could still see him standing there quite clearly, looking down at me. I squinted as my eyes tried harder to see the person I knew had to be there. As I did, I sensed (but didn't see) the stranger's eyebrows lifting in surprise, as he realized I knew he was there.

I started heading for the door that would lead me inside. "Wait there! I need to talk to you!" I shouted upward as I moved. I wasn't entirely sure why I thought the man might listen to me but it couldn't hurt. I didn't really fancy having to chase him around. Visible or not I was certain he couldn't escape me now that I had taken notice of him.

That proved to be hubris on my part. As I ran across the yard he began to fade. My last impression was of him closing his eyes before he simply wasn't there anymore. I stopped dead still. *That's not possible… is it?* I wondered. I opened my mind to its fullest and scanned the area carefully. I made doubly sure there were no 'empty' spaces that might indicate the presence of a shiggreth either. I found nothing.

As far as I could tell, the stranger had simply faded out of existence. He had gone from merely invisible to 'maybe I just imagined it' in the span of just a few seconds. Still, I had enough confidence these days in my senses not to doubt them. He had been there, which left me with some uncomfortable possibilities. "He was there, but he was not visible… not to the naked eye," I mused aloud.

"And when he realized I was aware of him he either transported himself away or managed to hide himself from my magesight as well as my normal sight."

I didn't think he had transported himself. I would have felt something and I doubted he had a circle prepared there in the middle of the hallway in my own castle. I resolved to check that immediately and I continued my journey inside so that I could examine the place where I had seen him.

A minute later I was standing where he had been. There was no circle. Searching the corridor and nearby rooms I didn't find any nearby either. Yet he had vanished. My recent study of illusions had made me quite aware of some of the possibilities magic held with regards to fooling the eyes but I knew of no way to make a someone completely undetectable to normal vision. Setting that aside I couldn't imagine how he could hide from my magesight, even the shiggreth left an empty place that could be sensed if I paid enough attention.

So is he still here, or not? The thought set the space between my shoulder blades to itching. I double checked my shield and began walking briskly toward the training yard. As soon as I spotted my burly friend I shouted, "Dorian!" Surprised he looked up and after he spotted me he gave the men a few more instructions before walking to meet me.

"You look worried," he said. My friend had a gift for understatement.

"There's an intruder inside the castle," I told him without preamble.

"What?!"

I began explaining what had happened, which took longer than I had expected. Dorian was full of questions and my story was less than clear to him since he didn't really understand magic in the slightest. Finally he summed up the story for me, "So you don't know if there's someone here now, or if they've gone… and it's possible you were just imagining things, since you never actually saw them with your eyes."

"That sums it up, except for the imagining part. There was someone there and he was using magic of some sort," I replied. "What do you think we should do?"

Dorian gave me a look that spoke volumes… his mouth gaped and his eyes were wide. "A rogue wizard is loose in the castle and you're asking me? If you can't find him I don't have a clue what to…" His eyes got wider for a moment. "Go find Penny! Stay with her 'til I find you."

"Wait," I said in confusion. "Why Penny?"

"Just make sure she's safe! I'll take care of the rest!" Dorian shouted back. He was already heading toward the training field and before I got to the stairs I could hear him yelling instructions to the men at arms there. I ran in the opposite direction and cursed myself for not thinking of Penny. It was a sign of my own growing vanity. I had assumed that whatever risk the intruder posed must be directed at me. As I ran I found her with my mind… she was never too far from my thoughts so I located her easily.

Inside the keep I took the stairs two at a time and as I reached the floor we lived on I started yelling her name. She was in the nursery, probably decorating again, or 'nesting' as she called it. She was alone as far as I could tell, and in fact the only other person was a maid cleaning rooms at the opposite end of the hall. She looked curiously out of the room as I ran past but I paid no heed to her questioning.

I burst through the door to our rooms without slowing down and nearly knocked Penny to the floor, she had been running the other way. "What the hell?" she exclaimed, in her hand she held a sheathed sword.

"Damn, you almost skewered me with that thing!" I said, ignoring the fact that my shield would probably have protected me. *Then again, I did enchant her blade... it might well cut through my shield,* I thought, remembering my fight with Devon Tremont.

She arched an eyebrow at me. "That's why I don't take it out of the scabbard until I see someone worth cutting, genius," she replied tartly, waving it in front of me.

I couldn't help but smile inwardly. *My girl definitely has a mouth on her. Can't help but love her,* I thought to myself. I took her hand and with a word and a thought I built a shield around both of us. My breath was still coming heavily after my sprint up the stairs.

"Are you planning to share the details with me?" she asked.

Drawing another deep breath I replied, "I found someone in the castle, watching me. Dorian suggested I find you first." I was still panting and even I will admit it wasn't the most complete answer I have ever given.

"So you need me to protect you from your secret admirer?" she asked.

Laughing made it harder to catch my breath but I was almost fully recovered by then anyway. "Maybe," I said with a grin. "The intruder was using magic of some sort, and he was able to hide himself from me. I think Dorian thought you might be a target so he suggested I find you first."

Penny patted her softly rounded stomach, "I'm definitely a good target and getting easier to hit by the day."

I should have known she'd bring that up. Women never seemed to miss an opportunity to bring attention to their growing waistlines, even though they complained about it. "You aren't that big yet," I said, another half-truth on my part, but all part of a husband's duty. "You do bring up a good point though, should you really be picking up steel and fighting unknown foes in your condition?"

"Would you rather I lay down and wait to die if someone attacked me?"

Alright, I had to admit... looking at it from that perspective she made a lot of sense. "Point taken," I said.

"No... no point taken... that's the point," she replied.

I groaned, "How long are you planning to keep this up? It really isn't that funny."

"Fine, but if you keep acting like a wet blanket this princess isn't going on any more adventures with you," she answered with mock seriousness.

Obviously Penny was in an interesting mood, something that had become rather common since her pregnancy started. I stared at her, wondering at her sanity. "You aren't a princess, and even if I *went* on adventures I wouldn't take you, you're pregnant!"

She stared at me intently for a moment before I noticed how still she had become. Her eyes had gotten wider and were beginning to well with tears. A chill went up my spine as I realized her mood had just flipped. "Have I gotten that fat already?" she asked. There was a tremor in her lip.

Oh bloody hell! I thought. "No, no, that's not what I meant!" Thankfully one of the guards arrived and knocked on the door. I opened it quickly, hoping for a distraction.

"My lord," he said quickly, "Where would you like me to take up my post?"

My mind was blank for a moment 'til I realized Dorian must have sent him to guard our rooms. I concentrated for a second until I recalled his name. "Barnabas, right?" I said, snapping my fingers.

"Yes your lordship," he answered hesitantly.

"Come inside. You may take your post there by the door," I told him. Ordinarily I'd have set him outside the door, but if the intruder was using magic it would just make the guard an easy target. Plus if he were inside it might help stabilize Penny's mood.

After that we moved into the antechamber adjoining our bedroom and sat down. We held hands while we sat and I cast my senses outward, trying to follow the movements of our guards through the castle. Dorian seemed to be conducting a room to room search of the entire place.

"Do you think it was another wizard?" Penny asked, breaking the silence.

"There aren't supposed to be any others," I said, except that there had been. The late Devon Tremont came immediately to mind. "But we've already seen that that may not be true I guess. It's more likely to be a channeler, though."

"And if it is a channeler?"

"Then he isn't friendly. The dark gods are definitely our enemies and the shining gods seem to want me dead now too," I said. Another knock at the door interrupted our conversation. "You can let them in," I told the guard. "It's just my mother and more guardsmen."

Barnabas opened the door and five more guardsmen entered, escorting my mother. She seemed none too pleased about having been suddenly uprooted from her house and forced to quick march into the castle. "What's going on Mordecai?" she asked me.

"I found an intruder in the castle, but he escaped. Dorian sent the guards to make sure you were safe, and he must have felt you'd be safest if you were with us as well." I agreed with him on that point. I also appreciated the fact that he had sent no less than five guards to make sure Miriam was safely escorted. "Are you still wearing the necklace I gave you?" I added.

My mother huffed, "I've never taken it off." It might be worth mentioning that as an only son, and an adopted one at that, my mother had always been quite attached to me.

I ignored her irritability and began explaining the situation. Dorian and Rose joined us as I finished. It was worth noting that he had escorted her personally. "We didn't find anyone," he announced.

I hadn't really expected him to, but it bothered me. *Whoever it was, is far better at sneaking around than I am,* I thought. That wasn't very comforting. I was used to thinking of channelers as inept, except when it came to healing. In general their gods didn't spend a lot of time letting them practice 'borrowing' their power to learn practical skills. "I didn't think you would, but I'm glad you searched," I replied. "Did you really think Penny or my mother might be in danger?"

"I couldn't afford to think anything else," he replied.

That didn't really add up in my mind and I wasn't used to Dorian reaching conclusions before I did. I made my doubt plain, "I still don't understand your reasoning."

Dorian gave me a look that indicated I might have been born naturally slow. Then he explained, "You have to remember Mort, the Thornbears have been protecting the Lancaster family for several generations now, not just Lancaster Castle. I learned quite a bit from my father. What do you think the easiest way to hurt you would be?"

I could see the direction his thoughts had taken but I still wasn't sure I agreed. "That might be true, but anyone that hurt my family would only earn themselves painful retribution."

Dorian snorted, "I doubt the dark gods are that frightened of you, but that is beside the point. Anyone that wants to control you has to be giving serious thought to kidnapping your family."

His words struck me like a thunderbolt as I realized how clueless I had been. Rose patted me on the shoulder and added, "That's what I love about Dorian, he's often a lot smarter than his simple exterior would lead one to believe."

I almost felt bad for him. Dorian's moment in the spotlight went from calm and in control to red and embarrassed almost instantly. His mouth formed a perfect 'o' as he stared at Rose. Eventually he looked back at me, shaking his head before he spoke again, "Anyway, I think your mother should move into one of the rooms adjacent to yours and we need to post extra guards on both doors and the stairs leading to this floor."

"Will it matter if our intruder can move about without fear of detection?" I asked. I didn't really think guards would be very useful if magic was involved.

"He may be able to sneak about in safety but I doubt he can take someone out of here by force without a struggle. With you nearby that would be the most foolish thing anyone could attempt," Dorian replied, his face was gradually returning to its normal color.

I was flattered by Dorian's confidence in me and I had to admit he had a good point, "Alright, I agree with you. What else do you think we should do?"

My mother had other ideas however. "Now wait a minute!" she interrupted. "Are you telling me that I have to move into the castle?" I knew already she wouldn't be happy about leaving the small house she had shared with my father. Dorian and I exchanged helpless glances, neither of us wanted to be the one to force this on her.

Luckily Rose intervened, "Miriam, I'm sorry but Dorian may be right. Would you want someone to use you as a tool to coerce your son?" I started to say something to support her but Penny gave me a look cautioning me to silence.

"Well of course not," replied my mother after a brief pause. "I just don't think it is right to have me barging in on them. They've only been married a few months and now Penelope has to put up with her mother-in-law living right on top of her?"

Penny spoke up then, "No Miriam, that's not a problem! I'd love to have you closer to us."

I watched the two of them carefully. I had never suspected that might be the reason my mother had refused to leave her house before. Now that the veil had been drawn I found myself watching Penny as well. Perhaps it would bother her, even though she denied it now. The more I learned of the world of women, the less I understood.

In the end my mother agreed to move into the adjoining rooms, though she swore up and down we'd never know she was there. The entire process involved quite a bit of hugging and even a few tears as the ladies (all three of them) shared their love for one another. Meanwhile Dorian and I quietly worked out the other arrangements which primarily involved having guards following my wife and mother everywhere.

There really wasn't a practical way to stop the movements of a channeler that could hide his presence from anyone, so we decided the best thing we could do was make sure it would be nearly impossible to kidnap either of them.

Later that evening, as I lay in bed listening to Penny snoring, I couldn't help but wonder at the turns my life had taken. A year or two ago I would never have imagined that power could make me so vulnerable. I resolved to look in my father's library and see if I could find ideas on how to protect my family better. Some sort of ward to alert me to intrusions while sleeping would be good. As it was I could hardly sleep. Paranoia seemed destined to become my new bed companion.

CHAPTER 12

The cool linens were soothing against Cyhan's skin. The large man slept with little more than a sheet despite the crisp night air. His body had always seemed to produce far more heat than he needed.

Glancing upward he couldn't help but be glad to be home again, if his room in the palace could truly be called home. Residence would probably be a better word. Even so, two months in a dungeon had given him a new appreciation for a proper bed and fresh sheets. Not that he would have ever admitted such a thing where anyone could hear it.

"I must be getting old," he mused aloud. Truthfully the cell he had occupied in Lancaster hadn't been bad… as far as prison cells went anyway. The good duke had made sure he was properly fed and given fresh water daily, but it had not been a comfortable existence.

Despite the fact that he was back in his accustomed place he still found little peace. Mordecai's words bothered him. Cyhan had always been proud of his service, training the next generation of Anath'Meridum (when there had still been the possibility someone would need one), and serving his king when that was no longer necessary. He had also prided himself on not second guessing himself once he had given his oath. His life had been built around the principle of fidelity.

Intelligence and wit were meant to serve a purpose. Little was to be gained by debating a choice over and over after it had been made. Yet the older he got the harder it was to maintain his rigid principles. Life seemed determined to color him in shades of gray.

Though his eyes were closed his room was softly lit by moonlight coming from the balcony facing the royal gardens. A flicker made him open his eyes slowly. Had something just blocked the light momentarily? He kept his body relaxed and still while his ears became more sensitive. If there was an intruder his hand already knew where his blade was... he felt no need to reach for it yet.

A hint of sandalwood came to his nose and he smiled in the semi-darkness. The sharp cold edge of a blade pressed against the skin of his neck and he could see a shadow leaning over him. "Has your time away made you soft *zaihar?*" The voice that spoke was soft and sultry.

"If you had come to kill me I doubt you would have worn perfume," he answered without moving.

"When I kill you it will be while the jasmine is blooming and your nose is already filled with its scent," she said, leaning in close enough to see his face in the dim light.

Her hair fell around him as she leaned down and the smell of sandalwood grew stronger. Moving slowly Cyhan slid his hand up the outside of her thigh, tracing her curves. The knife pressed harder against his throat, its sharp edge warning him. "Careful zaihar, your life is in my hands," she told him, her face mere inches from his own.

"I'll take my chances," he replied as his hand roamed into more sensitive zones in the darkness. A moment later the woman gasped and the pressure on the blade let up for a moment. With a twist he took the blade from her hand and tossed it across the room. A brief struggle ensued, earning him a few bruises and a scratch. His opponent was naked but for a sheer nightgown.

The woman was much stronger than she appeared and a capable wrestler, but she still proved no match for him. He was nearly twice her weight after all. Forcing her into an armlock he held her captive against the mattress. His other hand continued to roam even as she growled at him. "Has my time away made you soft Ruth?" he asked.

She bit him then, but softly. "Release me and I will show you soft," she teased.

He did and despite his reflexes she caught him across the cheek with a stinging slap. He had forgotten how fast she was. He ignored the blow and drew her in fiercely for a kiss. Several minutes passed before she spoke again. "I thought you weren't coming back," she said.

"I almost didn't," he admitted. "What would you have done?"

She had her legs around him by then, and pushing him back down she leaned closer to whisper into his ear, "I would have left a trail of blood and dead men from one end of this kingdom to the other, until I found your killer."

"And if I wasn't dead?" he asked, holding her waist. The nightgown had already been ripped to shreds during their struggle.

"Then I'd have killed you myself," she said nipping at his ear.

He smiled at that but didn't reply. No sense spoiling the moment. A long time went by before either of them resumed the conversation. They had more pressing issues to resolve.

Eventually things calmed down and they lay tangled in the ruins of Cyhan's bed. "I was starting to think you were mad at me," he said referring to the fact that he had been back in the capital for more than two weeks before Ruth had chosen to 'visit' him.

She snorted, "I was, but you seemed too thick-headed to understand the message."

He grunted but stayed silent.

"Besides," she continued, "I'm leaving soon. I didn't want to go without saying goodbye."

He levered himself up on his elbow to see her more clearly, "Does this have anything to do with you being found unconscious in the garden the other day?"

She grimaced. That had been one of her most embarrassing failures since she had begun working for the king over ten years ago. "I suspect I would have been given this mission anyway but that didn't help matters any."

Cyhan didn't ask what her assignment was; he knew she wouldn't tell him.

She spoke instead, "I need information."

He took a deep breath; he had guessed it might come to this. He could feel something inside his chest clench uncomfortably. He ignored the sensation. "When are you leaving?" he asked, but he already knew the answer. If she left tomorrow she would reach Castle Cameron a day before the public ceremony with Mordecai in the capital. The timing would make sure she was there while the new Lord Cameron was absent.

"I can't answer that," she replied. "I need to know what she's like."

"You mean my recent student of course," he said bluntly.

She nodded, "I already met her husband."

"Don't judge him by that. He's two different people in some senses. Hard under pressure but still naïve when he can afford to be," he said.

"He seemed quite capable, but I need to know about his wife," she pressed.

Since he won't be there, Cyhan thought to himself. "She's no pushover. I trained her well, but she is still young and inexperienced. She has spirit, but without the bond she is no match for you."

"The reports say she is pregnant," Ruth added.

"Probably," he answered. "I never saw her after the battle and they didn't see fit to keep me updated while I was locked up."

"That might complicate things," she commented, staring at him.

"How so?" Cyhan asked.

"Women fight harder when their offspring are endangered," she replied. "I'm surprised you would forget that. Why do you think Elena broke her bond?"

"Have you ever given any thought to having your own children?" Cyhan asked suddenly. Even he wasn't sure where the question had come from.

Ruth's eyes widened in the darkness, "Is that your way of proposing to me?"

He tightened his jaw, "If it were… what would your answer be?"

She relaxed. "I don't know. Perhaps if you were younger it would be easier to answer that question," she said teasingly.

His hand tensed painfully on her arm for a moment before he relaxed his grip and looked away. "You need a new job," he said finally.

Ruth laughed and wrapped her arms around his shoulders, draping herself almost casually over him. It was a gesture both sensual and warm in equal measure. "Are you worried about me or the countess?"

He gritted his teeth. "Both," he said at last. "They're good people."

"All they have to do is keep his majesty happy and no one will need to shed any tears," she replied. "Are you having doubts about your oath?"

"I'm tired of blood. Maybe we should retire," he replied, avoiding the question.

Her face was behind his line of sight so he never saw the expression of pain that crossed her face. When she spoke her voice was playful, "People like us don't retire zaihar, and we die the same way we have lived."

"Stop calling me that, I'm not your teacher anymore."

"My! Aren't you testy this evening? I'm starting to think you're worried about me," she said.

"If by some chance you encounter Mordecai during your mission… don't fight him," he answered, ignoring her remarks.

"You have so little faith in me now?" she said.

Cyhan frowned. "He's too dangerous, especially if he thinks his family is in danger, and if anyone is going to slip a blade between his ribs it should be me. I owe him at least that much."

Ruth kissed him along his jaw and ear. "I don't think I've ever seen you so melancholy, or so poetic. They really got to you didn't they?"

He shook his head slightly, "No, I've just been re-thinking some things lately."

"Don't think so hard," she answered, running her hands lightly down his stomach. "I take that back…," she said throatily in his ear. "Think as hard as you like."

"Shouldn't you be resting before tomorrow," Cyhan replied.

Ruth laughed, "I can rest when I'm dead." Holding him she traced her hand across his chest 'til it found the iron pendant resting there. The enchanted pendant Mordecai had made for him to protect his mind. "What's this?" she asked.

"Something you need," he replied, reaching up to untie the thong around his neck. "It prevents magic or other influences from affecting your mind. If you had been wearing it the other day you wouldn't have taken your sudden nap." Turning he put it on her.

"Where did you get such a thing?"

"Mordecai made it for me," he said with a chuckle. "I think you'll be far more likely to need it in the coming days than I will."

She stared at him in disbelief. "He gave this to the man who tried to kill him?"

Cyhan shook his head. "He made one for everyone in his town, to protect them from the shiggreth. He gave it to me before breaking his bond, before I tried to kill him."

"And he let you keep it?"

"You would have to know him for a while to understand," he replied, his eyes were staring into the distance now.

"He must be a fool," she said.

Cyhan's attention returned from the recesses of his mind and he began kissing her once more, easing her gently back onto the pillows. "Maybe," he murmured softly to himself. "I'm not so sure anymore."

CHAPTER 13

The days passed quickly, probably because I worked myself harder than ever. I wanted to make sure the second set of armor was finished before I left for the capital. The recent scare and the ensuing paranoia had made me more aware than ever that I needed help. I couldn't be everywhere, nor could I protect everyone.

A knock at the door to the smithy drew my attention away. "Come in Lisette," I called. I had already recognized the castle maid though she hadn't spoken or opened the door yet.

She poked her head through the door, "Pardon me your lordship, but Sir Dorian asked me to tell you that it's time for your planning session." For some reason my eye lit upon a bright ribbon she had tied her hair up with. On rare occasions I can be highly perceptive. Penny might say those occasions usually involve pretty women, but that was only true some of the time… like today.

"Is that a new ribbon Lisette?" I observed as I followed her out of the smithy.

She blushed, "Yes your lordship, though I thought such things would be beneath your notice."

"You must have an admirer," I guessed. "One of the lads in the village?" as I said 'lads' I couldn't help but laugh at myself. I sounded like an old man, though I had yet to pass my twentieth birthday.

Her color deepened, "No your lordship, one of the armsmen." Her embarrassment had caused her to lower her head even more deeply. I could no longer see her eyes.

"No need to be embarrassed, it's only natural. Do you fancy him?" I felt bad as soon as I asked. I had pressed her beyond the ability to speak, she nodded mutely instead.

I tried to put her at ease. "I'm sorry Lisette. I shouldn't have pried into your affairs. If he mistreats you though, let me know. I'll have no discourtesy among my men."

For some reason that remark roused her from her flustered embarrassment. "Oh no your lordship! Harold would never mistreat me. He's a true gentleman, by nature at least… if not by birth." Finishing her sentence she realized she had said more than she intended and lapsed again into silence.

The name surprised me. "Harold Simmons?"

She nodded a 'yes'.

"From what I've heard he's a good fellow," I said. We had reached the stairs by then and our paths were separating. I couldn't help but feel I had bungled the conversation somehow as she curtseyed and escaped down the hall. I still wasn't used to people being afraid of me.

A minute later I stepped into the planning room. Unlike a few months prior, it now held its own table and chairs, so we were no longer forced to use the high table in the great hall. Many of the chairs were in use already, occupied by Dorian, Rose, Penny, and Harold Simmons. Dorian had suggested we include Harold today since he would be important to our plans in the near future. Better to start his education early than late.

"Sorry I'm late, I lost track of time," I told them.

Penny rolled her eyes at me and I caught a hint of a smirk on Rose's face, but Dorian spoke first. "Well now that you're here we can get started."

I took a seat. "I'm sure you all know why we're here. The recent incident with the intruder has raised certain issues. Issues that we need to prepare for while I am in the capital."

"Security," Penny clarified for me.

"Right," I agreed. "Dorian you said you had a plan worked out, why don't you explain?"

Dorian stood up. I don't think he could have addressed the room and remained seated. It just wasn't in him. "The first thing we need to discuss is who will be going to the capital and who will remain here…"

"Wouldn't it be simpler if everyone just came with me?" I asked.

Dorian glared at me for interrupting him so quickly. "Perhaps," he answered, "but you will be busy and distracted in the capital. There is also the possibility of intrigue while you are there. I think it would be easier for you to focus on the matters at hand if you bring only the bare minimum of people with you."

"So primarily just Mort and myself?" Penny asked.

Dorian shook his head in negation. "I'm sorry Penny but no. I would like for Mort to go alone, except for his honor guard."

"Won't I be more exposed here without Mort close by?" she countered.

"You won't," he replied. "It would be much more difficult for an enemy in the capital to coordinate any scheme at such a distance."

My wife wasn't to be so easily defeated however, "What about our mysterious channeler?"

"I have a solution for that as well. The day Mort leaves you will be moved to Lancaster, along with Miriam and your guards," he said smugly. "No one outside of this room will know about your trip until you are already gone.

Without knowing what our enemy intends I can only presume that a sudden relocation will seriously disrupt any plans they might have, especially if they don't know where you have been taken."

I broke in, "Lancaster is a rather obvious location, though."

"It is, but without certainty they will have difficulty deciding on their response, if they are even able to cover the distance quickly enough. If they do manage to follow they still will be on unfamiliar ground. They won't know what rooms your family is staying in, the locations of the guards or how long you plan on being there."

Harold spoke up suddenly, "Who will be guarding the countess?" He spoke evenly, despite his obvious nervousness at being in a room full of his superiors.

Dorian answered, "I will. You will be assigned to the count while he is in the capital."

"No disrespect Sir Dorian, but you would be far more qualified to protect the count," said young Harold.

I chuckled, "I think you've misunderstood his priorities Harold. Dorian is sending you with me because he's guessing I'm much less likely to face a threat."

"Oh," said the young fighter. He hid his embarrassment quickly.

"Don't take it too hard Harold," Dorian said, trying to cheer him up. "After all you will still be leading the contingent guarding our illustrious count. That's no small feat for a man your age."

Rose spoke up then, "From what you said before, I gather you intend for me to remain with Penny and Miriam?"

For the first time since he had begun, Dorian looked directly at Rose. I hadn't realized 'til then that he had been avoiding direct eye contact with her, probably because it frequently left him unable to speak clearly. "Errr… yes! That was exactly what I intended and astute it was of you to… I mean it was very astute of you… I…," Dorian ended on an uncomfortable pause. At last he looked away and spoke again, "Yes. Sorry, I lost my train of thought."

I could see Penny smiling at me from across the table. Naturally she found all of this vastly amusing, while I couldn't help but be a bit embarrassed for my friend. Rose broke the silence, "Ordinarily I wouldn't mind, but in this case I think I need to go with Mordecai," she said.

Dorian was still recovering, so I spoke in his stead, "Why?"

"I'm not on the list of primary targets, so I should be in little danger and I have several matters of business to attend to in the city. Not the least of which is helping you to acquire a new blacksmith," she said.

I had forgotten that. I had asked her advice on the matter the day before. "What other business do you have in the city?" I asked.

She smiled, "Since you seem to be redeemed in the eyes of the king it appears that my Dorian may not be an outlaw forever. I thought I might talk to my father regarding some personal matters." The way she said 'my Dorian' left little doubt in anyone's mind how she felt about him. It was the first time I had ever heard her speak so openly about her feelings for him.

Dorian seemed on the verge of apoplexy. "Well that sounds fine," he said in a remarkably clear voice. "Does anyone else have objections or clarifications to bring up?" Though he spoke without a stammer his face was a deep red.

I couldn't help myself. I put up my hand like a school boy and asked, "Yes, I was just wondering when you intend on meeting with Lord Hight…oww!" Penny had just kicked me under the table, and not delicately. I exclaimed more from surprise than pain though; as usual I had a shield closely woven around myself.

"Anything else, Your Excellency?" Penny asked with one eyebrow raised.

I gave her a hard look before answering, "Actually yes, I do have something else… Harold!"

Poor Harold looked up as if I had slapped him, "Yes, your lordship?"

"Do you understand the position you are in now?" I asked.

He gave me a blank stare. He reminded me a lot of Dorian in some ways, though he was quite different in others. "I'm sorry, Your Excellency, I'm not sure what you mean," he said at last.

"There is a reason you've been invited to this meeting. I have a real lack of men I can personally trust in my employ. Dorian has said a number of good things about you of late and I have done some checking around on my own. You seem to be a man of integrity as well as skilled at arms," I said.

I hadn't asked any questions so Harold was left wondering what to say. "Thank you, Your Excellency," he ventured at last.

"To make a long story short I need your service, and not just in your present capacity as a man at arms," I told him. I went on to describe the new order of knighthood I intended to create.

Harold stood up from his chair near the end of my explanation. "Begging your pardon sir, you can't be serious!"

I was nonplussed. Not understanding his perspective I assumed he was criticizing the idea of a new order of knights. Dorian put his hand on my arm before I could respond, "We are serious. Before you discount yourself think about how you acquitted yourself during the recent war against Gododdin. Lord Cameron did not make this decision lightly and you might consider that before you question his reasons." As Dorian spoke I realized Harold had been objecting to his own selection, not the plan itself.

"Do you intend to decline this burden?" I asked young Harold somberly, giving him my most gravid look.

Harold dropped to one knee as if he had been poleaxed. "No my liege, I will accept whatever you place upon me, insofar as I am able."

I raised an eyebrow and glanced at Dorian. I had not expected Harold to be so well spoken. "Very well, rise for now. We will hold the accolade tomorrow so you will need to prepare your vigil tonight."

He rose and left with Dorian and Rose while I exchanged a meaningful glance with Penny. Once everyone had left the room I spoke, "Are you sure you're alright with this plan?"

She stepped closer and I wrapped my arms around her. Tipping her head back to look at me she gave me an appraising look. "I'd rather be with you but I understand the need. Just don't make me spend too many nights alone or you'll have a very cranky pregnant woman on your hands when you return."

She laid her head against my chest and I leaned mine forward, resting my cheek against her soft brown hair. We stood that way for a long minute before finally making our way to the door. Looking back Penny studied the room for a moment and frowned. "This room is entirely too dusty. I'll have to remind Lisette to give it a thorough cleaning."

I almost felt sorry for the castle staff… having been a maid once herself, Penny held high standards for them. "Don't be too hard on her dear, it doesn't look so bad to me," I told her.

"You're too nice," she said. "Look in those corners… the dust is so heavy there you can see footprints."

I had to admit she was right. "Just try to go easy on Lisette; she's a young woman in love you know. She might have a few things distracting her." I led Penny from the room and with our backs to the room I didn't see the dust stirring behind us or the extra footprints that appeared once our attention had moved away.

CHAPTER 14

That evening I returned to work in the smithy. I was close to finishing the armor I had been crafting for Harold. If he was going to be my body guard in Albamarl I wanted him to look good, as well as being properly equipped. Besides, I had a feeling Lisette would like seeing her young man in his new finery, at least until it began to smell. I chuckled to myself at the thought; even magical armor had a tendency to rankle the nose after a while.

My best estimate saw me not finishing until after Harold's knighting. Hopefully I would complete it before we left for the capital. He would simply have to be understanding. It was a surprise anyway, he had no idea I planned to armor all of my knights in such gear.

While I worked I found myself in an awkward position, needing an extra set of hands and having only my own two. I considered calling in the guards that Dorian had positioned outside but I really didn't want to give away my secrets to anyone else yet. Then an idea came to me. "Moira," I called softly, wondering if asking for her help with such a minor task would annoy her.

She rose up from the packed earth floor with fluid grace. "No, it doesn't annoy me," she replied to my unspoken words, "Though I never expected when I created this repository of knowledge that it would someday be used as a smith's apprentice."

She held the hot metal with hands that felt no heat and watched me as I worked. Her eyes today were made from two pieces of glossy slag metal, giving them a strange grey cast, similar to polished hematite. Neither of us spoke for a while as I was fully focused upon my task, smoothing and stroking the burning steel into shape. Eventually I paused to let the metal cool while I used a rule to measure it. This piece was to be part of the greaves that protected the lower leg and it needed to match the already finished piece for the other leg.

While I did that Moira examined the already finished breastplate and pauldrons, running her hands over the metal and studying the lines of the enchantments I had already laid upon them. I could sense her astonishment as she examined them. "I suppose they must seem rather crude compared to the enchantments created during your time," I observed.

She looked up at me, "Not at all. What you have done here is novel, unlike anything created while I was alive, and the sophistication of the enchantments is nothing to laugh at. Your talents would have earned you praise as a mage-smith in my day. Where did you learn this?"

I wasn't sure how to react to her compliments. "I just worked with what I already knew, about wards and such. I nearly blew myself up a few times," I told her, thinking back to my first attempts to create enchantments by storing heat energy.

"You have no idea how few men possessed the talents to create things like this, even in my day. This alone would set you apart, without even considering your strength as a wizard or your potential as an archmage. Your ancestors would have been proud of you," she said.

"So far I've only managed to kill a lot of innocent people, I'm not sure how that fits with your assessment," I said bitterly. For some reason her praise had irritated me.

"I won't debate the merits of your actions with you. Your forebears were hardly innocent on that score," she replied. "The Illeniels were well known for the many mage-smiths and skilled enchanters they produced throughout history. It is interesting to see that the trait has bred true in you despite your lack of guidance or formal training."

"That's not entirely true," I said defensively.

"How so?"

"My father taught me from the time I was old enough to work the bellows. I watched him working with iron for most of my life and when I was old enough he showed me everything he could of his knowledge of it."

"And you think that explains this?" she laughed, waving her hands at the armor lying on the table behind her. "Are you even aware of the fact that you are using more than mere wizardry as you shape the metal?"

"I'm just spelling my hands to make them stronger and heat tolerant. There's nothing more to it than that," I said brusquely.

"There is much more to it than that," she insisted picking up the piece I had just been working on. "Do you think metal can be shaped so simply, so gracefully, just because you have given yourself stronger hands? You are talking to it, even as you work. Nothing as profound as what you did with the stone that day, but quietly, subtly, your mind is coaxing it to shape itself under your fingers."

I stared at her, stunned, for as she spoke I knew she was telling the truth.

She set the metal down and pointed at my staff, which I had left leaning by the doorway. "And what of this? Look at the runes… do you realize that the geometry needed to align them like that has to be perfect? Where is the master that taught you that?"

I did have an answer for that at least, "The duke's tutors taught me mathematics. It was one of my favorite subjects."

"And from that you discern how to create a rune channel to focus power? Doesn't any of this give you pause to think? At a time in history when wizardry had almost completely died out... you appear, an untaught prodigy. You are a mage as strong as any I have ever heard of and possessing amazing potential as an archmage as well. And after you appear you manage to defeat the only other remaining wizard, one who was about to summon a dark god to finish the job Balinthor started in my time. Then you rediscover the lost art of enchanting and use it to turn back an army of over thirty thousand men. All in the span of less than two years, does none of this cause you to question the nature of your existence?"

I hadn't really considered it, though to be fair I hadn't had her perspective. As a young man without any external guidance I had no way to judge the merits of what I had done. Moira had the benefit of a viewpoint based on the height of mankind's civilization, over a thousand years gone. "I am what I am," I replied. "Now that you have pointed it out it does seem odd, but how should I have questioned the gifts I was born with? They all seemed natural to me. What are you suggesting?"

She was silent for some time before she replied, "I don't know, but I think you should be aware that you are far beyond the pale, even for my time. I cannot help but see the hand of some agency at work in this and that should make you cautious."

I snorted, "I already have half the world and all of the heavens for my enemies. How can I be any more cautious?"

Moira bowed her head, looking at the floor, and then she returned her gaze to mine. "Just keep this thought in your mind and be watchful. Whatever has set this course for you has been moving along this path for over a thousand years. Until you have discovered whether its intentions are malign or not you should be watchful lest you are maneuvered into doing something you might not wish."

"Illeniel's doom," I muttered.

"That may well have something to do with it," she agreed.

"And you know nothing of it?" I asked again.

She shook her head regretfully. "Unfortunately I do not. You will have to discover that on your own."

I was sick of mysteries and conspiracies and I decided to change the subject to something more practical. "I have another question for you then," I began.

She didn't respond except to give me her full attention.

"Will you teach me to create the bond between a mortal and the earth? Will you show me how to make my own targoth cherek?"

"I will," she answered, "on one condition."

"And that is?"

"You must promise never to deliberately leave one to his fate as I did with Magnus," she said.

I could understand her reasons but experience had taught me some hard lessons already. "I cannot agree to that," I told her.

Her stony eyes widened, "Why not?"

"Life has shown me its dark side already. I will not gainsay my ability to make choices in the future, even bad ones. Just as you had to choose between your lover and your guardian's welfare, so I may have to make hard choices. If you will teach me this, do so freely and I will promise to exercise my best conscience in how I choose to use that knowledge." I stared evenly into her eyes.

"You have grown in wisdom at least," she said at last. "Very well, I will teach you and the consequences of your actions will be on your own head."

"I appreciate your trust."

"The first thing you must understand is that you can only bind a certain amount of the earth's power to one person. The greater the amount the faster they will inevitably turn into a part of the earth themselves," she said, starting upon the topic already.

I nodded, "You implied that during our last discussion."

"You also are restricted as to how much of the earth's power you may bind to others. The limit is set by how much you can control yourself without losing your own humanity. Though you can create more than one targoth cherek the sum of the power you bind to them cannot exceed your own limit. Is that clear?" she asked.

It seemed straightforward. "So I can only bind a certain amount and I can choose to divide that among more than one person, so long as the total is no more than my own limit?"

"Yes, a little among many or a great deal to a few, ideally you should bind as little as possible to achieve your goal. This will extend the time your targoth cherek can retain his humanity. If you are sensible they can survive for decades before they begin to suffer. You must also caution them to exercise prudence in how they use the power. If they continually draw upon it they will turn more quickly."

It was late that evening before I finally retired, but I felt more hope for the future than I had in a while when I did. I might not understand all the forces moving around me yet, but the more I learned the better armed I would be in the future.

Penny growled at me as I tried to reclaim some of the bed sheets to cover myself. "Blankets are reserved for husbands that come to bed at a reasonable hour."

"Husbands?" I chuckled. "How many are there?" I eased up against her backside for warmth.

"There's going to be one fewer if you keep skipping dinner and leaving me to go to bed alone like some spinster," she replied grumpily.

CHAPTER 15

My dreams were filled with the sound of drums. Men marched and fire fell from the sky while through it all the drummers kept up their hellish rhythm, and then I woke up. The deep booming drums were replaced by the sound of someone beating on the door, which alarmed me in and of itself. Then I remembered the guards and my extra senses confirmed that they were still there.

Penny was nowhere to be found and the windows were still dark, dawn had yet to arrive. *How does she wake up so early?* I wondered as I stomped toward my door. *Probably her unhealthy bedtimes.* I threw the door open to glare at Dorian standing outside. "I hope you have a damn good reason for this," I growled.

He had his characteristically cheerful morning face on. "Good morning sunshine!" he proclaimed.

That was enough for me; I slammed the door shut and stalked back toward the bed. "There's no sunshine yet you sadistic bastard!" I yelled at the door behind me.

"Tell that to Harold," he replied through the heavy wood.

I stopped halfway across the room while my muddled brain worked through that statement. I had told Harold Simmons to prepare his vigil, which meant he had spent the night awake, meditating before his dubbing this morning. I grinned evilly to myself. *Well at least one person will have had less sleep than me, I* thought. Then I remembered the ceremony was to be held at dawn, with the rising of the sun. For an instant my selfish side warred with my better half, telling me to postpone the dubbing until noon at least, but I knew that would be disrespectful.

Despite the perception many people have of nobility, it isn't all parades and roses. Perhaps some lords wouldn't have been concerned, but I didn't intend to show so little care for the people that served me. *Unlike the Baron of Arundel*, I thought. I went back to the door and opened it. "I hate you sometimes," I said to my dear friend. He was still smiling… the bastard.

"Just be glad it was me," he said.

"What do you mean?"

"Penny wanted to have a bucket of water thrown on you for coming to bed so late," he said chuckling.

"And you decided you'd rather have the pleasure of waking me up?" I asked.

"No I was worried you might hurt the servant if you were startled awake so suddenly," he replied.

"Ahh Dorian, you always have my best interests at heart don't you. I'm still going to kill you slowly after breakfast, but it can wait 'til Harold's dubbing is over. I wouldn't want to spoil the occasion," I said in mock seriousness.

"The accolade is first then breakfast," Dorian corrected. "Harold can't eat 'til after it is done."

A barbaric damn custom if you asked me, but then no one had. "Help me dress, the sooner I get down there the sooner we can all feed ourselves," I said callously. Dorian did the honors since I still didn't have a proper manservant and Penny had gone on strike. I woke up more thoroughly as I got ready and by the time I was presentable I felt a slight bit of guilt over my poor temper. Not that I told

Dorian. He deserved to learn prudence, but I did want to do right by Harold.

We went downstairs and headed for the small chapel that had been repaired when the castle was renovated. Although I no longer revered the goddess the ceremony was traditionally held there. I had been tempted to forbid her worship entirely but I had contented myself with threatening every priest that had applied to minister at the chapel. As a result there was no priest in residence in Castle Cameron any longer, or Washbrook either for that matter. I hadn't officially made my position known to the people yet, but I was pretty sure that rumors were already starting to circulate.

"How do you plan to handle the vows?" Dorian asked. He was referring of course to the references to the goddess that were traditionally a part of them.

"Millicenth can go to hell for all I care!" I said vehemently.

Dorian winced visibly. His eyes darted upward for a moment and I was sure he was wondering when the lightning bolts would strike. "You can't say things like that Mort!"

"I'll be damned if I don't!" I responded. "She isn't the goddess they taught us about when we were growing up. She all but ruined Marcus and Penny would be dead if she had gotten her way. If she or any of the other gods want my respect they can start acting like gods instead of spoilt children."

Dorian's face was white as ash now, so I saved him the trouble of answering and walked into the chapel. Harold was kneeling inside, with nothing more than a single candle to provide light. The young man's shoulders straightened as he heard us enter. I was pretty sure he had been struggling against the urge to sleep.

Seeing him there I found myself reflecting on my goal. Harold was young, younger even than Dorian and I. He was filled with enthusiasm and an irrational belief that the things would work out for the best. Or perhaps I was just projecting my own past naivety onto him, I couldn't really be sure. Still I wondered what effect our choices today would have upon his future.

I walked to the front of the chapel, stopping in front of him. He had remained on his knees and his head was still bowed. "Lift your head Harold Simmons," I told him. As he looked up I exerted my will and spoke a word, "*Lyet,*" lighting the candles around the room. Soft golden light surrounded us, accenting the bronze candlesticks and golden oak pews.

"Today we gather to form a new order of knighthood. One pledged to the protection of the innocent and the defense of the helpless. This order will draw strength from the earth, and its knights shall be known as 'earth wardens'. As a member your first duty will be the protection of mankind from any and all that would see it harmed. That duty will precede any and all allegiances to mortal men, even myself. Should you accept this honor Harold, you will be the first knight created by this order and the second to join it. Do you still wish to join?"

"Yes my lord," he replied. The earnestness in his face almost caused me to lose my train of thought. I had spent some time adapting the ceremony to include what Moira had taught me the night before. I had also re-written the lines I would say. Hopefully I could remember them properly.

"Sir Dorian, please come stand beside me," I said, gesturing to my friend where he stood behind Harold. He came closer, 'til he stood next to me on the dais.

"Dorian you shall henceforth serve as the grandmaster of the Order of Stone. Do you accept this duty?" I asked.

"I do, my lord," he answered.

"The young man in front of me has come to my attention as being worthy to join our new order. Do you feel that he is acceptable in mind and body?"

"He is, my lord," Dorian replied.

"Give me the sword, Sir Dorian," I commanded. This part of the accolade was fairly standard so he was already holding a scabbarded long sword. He held it toward me with the hilt free for my hand and I drew it smoothly from its sheath. I lifted the naked steel to point upward with the hilt even with my eyes. "Throughout history the knight's sword has been a symbol of his faith and trust, to both his liege and to the gods. The Knights of the Stone are granted their power by the earth itself, rather than any heavenly agency. You will give fealty to me and pledge to protect humanity itself, even against the gods if necessary. Will you swear to this Sir Dorian?"

Dorian's face was a study of warring emotions. I thought for a moment he might faint at the words I had chosen, but then I saw his jaw clench and color returned to his cheeks. At last he answered, "I so swear, I will uphold these vows, and even though the gods themselves may curse me I will not fail in my duty."

I looked down on Harold and his blond hair almost seemed to glow in the candlelight. "Will you swear to this Harold?"

He never hesitated. "I swear it."

"Then by the power I hold in trust as Lord of Cameron and the power granted me by the earth itself I dub thee knight," I intoned, bringing the sword down to lightly touch each of his shoulders once. "Rise Sir Harold and take up your sword." The young warrior in front of me stood and as I handed him the naked blade I saw there were tears in his eyes.

Dorian stepped behind him and knelt down. I wasn't sure what he was doing for a moment, 'til I saw him buckling the spurs onto Harold's boots. *I always forget that part,* I chided myself. Then Dorian stood and buckled the scabbard and belt around Harold's waist so our new knight could sheath his sword. When he had finished he struck Harold hard between the shoulder blades, almost sending him to his knees. Even the blow was traditional, a welcoming 'buffet' given by a senior knight to a new peer. "Welcome brother knight," he said and then he embraced him.

"There is yet one thing left undone," I told them. Both of them looked at me with questioning eyes, traditionally the ceremony was already done. "The Order of the Stone is more than just a name. Now that you have sworn your oaths I may invest you with a small part of the earth's strength. This does not come without some risk however, and someday you will be forced to relinquish this power lest you become part of the earth itself. Are you both willing?"

After a short pause they both nodded and responded with 'ayes'.

"I must speak with the earth. When I am ready I will hold out my hands silently, each of you take one and respond with these words: 'I accept this gift freely and freely will I return it when my time is done.' Do you understand?" I asked. Again they both nodded.

I sat as Moira had shown me, so as to avoid falling when my mind was too far gone to steady my balance, and then I opened my mind. *Moira watch over me,* I called mentally. For this she would serve as my miellte. She flowed upward from the stone floor beside us, this time she was composed utterly of grey granite. I sensed more than saw the two men in front of me flinch in surprise, but they held their ground.

"You may proceed," she said aloud.

The deep thrumming of the earth grew louder as I focused upon it, until it seemed to drown out every other sound. As I listened it seemed as if I could almost understand it, though it was unlike any human voice. My mind expanded and I struggled to maintain my balance, to do as she had taught me. "Keep your center," she had told me last night. "Include as much of it within yourself as you can, but do not let yourself be included within it."

And so I did, until it seemed I was composed of nothing more than a giant stone heart, beating in time to some ancient cosmic rhythm. When my thoughts began to disintegrate, to fade into its vastness I stopped... somehow... and I held back. *Now to prepare the gift*, I thought. Mentally I divided my earthly vastness into three portions, two very small ones and a vast remainder. *Their portions must be small or they will not last.* Once I was ready I extended those two smaller parts, upward and outward, into a world I could see but barely understand. Lifting my 'arms,' I held them out toward the two beings that would become my companions... at least for a time.

They reached out and grasped me with soft appendages, while making sounds I could not comprehend, yet I could feel their acceptance. With an inward 'click' I felt the bonds form as a small portion of me was given into their care. It was finished. Using what seemed like alien eyes I studied the strange space I was in, wondering at its purpose. Now that my goal was accomplished I struggled to remember what I should do. Then another mind touched mine, *Mordecai, it is over, you must return to yourself. Leave the earth behind and return to the world of men.*

The sound of my name resonated with something within me and everything began to make sense again. With a dizzying sensation the world seemed to 'snap' back into place. I studied my hands for a moment, for everything seemed smaller. Finally I tugged on them a bit, to remind Dorian and Harold they could let go. They both seemed to be dazed and it took them a moment to release me.

I glanced at Moira. *I'm fine now, thank you,* I told her mentally. With a nod she sank downward into the stone floor. I looked back to my two companions. Now that I had released my connection with the earth I was no longer connected to them but I could see that they were both connected to something. I could feel an almost subliminal power radiating from them.

"Mort...," said Dorian, staring at me. He couldn't seem to find the words he was looking for. Harold didn't even try.

"Take it easy. Your bodies will feel different and it will take a while for you to get used to it," I told them. I assumed that much from what Penny had gone through when she had formed her bond with me.

"I feel different," said Harold.

"You are. You are stronger than before, possibly faster as well. You also possess extra reserves of energy, so you will not tire quickly. In times of need you can draw upon the earth itself to increase your strength even more but it is unwise to do so. The more you use, beyond what you have now, the faster you will change," I replied.

"Change?" he asked.

"Into stone," I answered. "The strength you have now you can use safely, for decades at least. Eventually you will start to notice changes, when that happens it will be time to retire and give up your extra power. I will help you release the bond then."

Dorian grinned, "So we're like Penny was?" He was clenching and unclenching his fist slowly as he spoke. I could almost see him trying to decide what to test his newfound strength upon first.

"Not exactly," I said. "You are not bound directly to me for one thing, which means that if one of us dies it isn't a death sentence for the other. You are bound to the earth. The power you gain from it will probably be similar to what Penny gained from me, but I think there will be differences. Not the least of which is the risk that if you draw upon extra strength too often you may begin to turn into stone yourself."

"That doesn't sound so bad," Dorian replied. "A warrior made of stone would be nigh invulnerable."

"A man of stone has no care for the things you love. Nor could he have children," I said bluntly.

Dorian's face went still as he considered it. I could almost see the exact moment Rose entered into his thoughts, for a blush appeared on his cheeks.

Harold could see it too, "Perhaps it would be best to take care of the 'having children' part of it sooner rather than later Sir Dorian, just to be safe."

That was the first sign I had encountered of Harold having a sense of humor. I definitely approved. "Mind your manners… 'brother'," Dorian snapped angrily at the younger man.

Together the three of us walked from the chapel. "Rose did say something about meeting with her father. I wonder what that's about," I pondered aloud. Dorian shot me a look that warned me not to speculate further so I stopped there. He'd had enough stress for one day I figured. As we stepped through the doors we met Penny and Joe McDaniel waiting outside for us.

"Is your 'secret' ceremony finished?" she asked.

Dorian was already looking for a distraction so he clapped Harold heartily upon the back. "Meet our newest knight!" he exclaimed. Unfortunately he hadn't anticipated his strength and Harold was sent hurtling face first into the opposite wall of the corridor. If Penny had been a foot or two to her right he would have knocked her down.

"I think you two should be careful for a while, until you adjust," Penny said. I saw her eyes dart toward me for a second with a sad look in them. She never complained but I knew she still missed the bond we had shared when she was my Anath'Meridum. "Let's go and have breakfast," she continued in a cheerful tone.

As we entered the dining hall a cheer rose up, echoing from the walls. Penny stepped back and raised her hands with the crowd and I knew she must have organized it then. "Three cheers for Sir Harold!" she yelled and the people responded. Three times they cheered and each time poor Harold's face got redder with embarrassment.

Dorian smiled enough for both of them. My friend wasn't shy at all… so long as the attention was focused on someone else. He soon had our newest knight moving through the crowd so that everyone could clap him upon the back as he made his way to the high table. As they went I watched Penny with new eyes. She never failed to surprise me. I hadn't suspected she was organizing a celebration such as this at all.

Now that she had it was obvious to me that someone needed to do it, but it had never occurred to me. I was grateful again that she had seen fit to marry me. Seeing how the people responded to her enthusiasm gave me even more joy. If something ever happened to me I didn't worry that they would follow her in my stead, she had already captured their hearts.

She turned to look back as we walked, meeting my eyes with a smile. Her body was swelling at the waist, and in more interesting places, yet her expression still held the sparkle of the girl I had always loved. Something in my face must have told her my thoughts then, for she leaned back and kissed me sweetly. "You look happy," she said, whispering directly into my ear, the room was too noisy to be heard otherwise.

And that was when I finally realized it. Despite the recent war, despite my father's death and all the terrible things that had happened, I was happy. My people were cheering, not for me, but for someone else, and I was happy. I had a place, friends, love, and the beginnings of a new family. Certainly there were problems to be overcome still, but at that moment they seemed small. Negotiate peace with the king and then all I would have to do would be to protect the people from a few unnatural enemies. It seemed almost simple.

"That's because I am happy!" I yelled back at her over the ruckus. She laughed and we sat down to the best breakfast I could recall eating in years.

Sometimes mornings aren't as bad as they seem at first.

CHAPTER 16

I made sure to get to bed early that night. I had finished Harold's armor early and he and Dorian had left me to make sure all the fittings were adjusted perfectly. Consequently I made it to dinner on time and spent a quiet evening with Penelope. In short, my day had been almost as good as the morning was.

Penny and I rose early the next day. The preparations had already been made but we wanted to get a good breakfast in before we had to part ways. Today was the day I would be traveling to Albamarl. Rose and Dorian arrived almost as soon as we did, and even more suspiciously, they arrived together. I gave my friend a hard stare as he escorted her to the table and he rewarded me by blushing bright red.

Penny elbowed me and I lost my fierce glare, lapsing into a smile instead. "Don't tease him Mort!" she hissed in my ear. "He's terribly embarrassed and it's taken her months to get him to this point."

I looked at Penny in astonishment. *They've been plotting this for months!* I thought to myself. I wondered idly whether Dorian had just escorted Rose from her room or if he had been inside… I shook my head. No, that simply wasn't possible. It couldn't be. "So does that mean…?" I asked curiously.

She gave me a hopeless look. "No! And wipe that stupid smirk off your face!" she told me. I finally complied and we both tried to put on normal expressions before Rose and Dorian sat down with us. I could tell Penny wasn't really angry though, she had been struggling to keep her composure too.

Dorian held Rose's chair for her with an expression of absolute concentration. He had the look of a man who knew if he lost his focus for even a second something terrible would happen. I did my best not to stare at him but apparently no one had given my mother the message. She was sitting across from them and she watched him with approval.

"About time you starting courting her properly Dorian," Miriam observed. Dorian turned red and I had to stare at my plate to avoid laughing at his discomfort.

My friend stepped back from her chair and backed into one of the kitchen servers. The poor girl lost her tray and stumbled forward trying to catch it as fresh baked bread went flying in all directions. In spite of his social awkwardness Dorian had never been clumsy and with surprising dexterity he reached out to keep her from falling forward.

Naturally his hand landed firmly on her bosom and the lass in question jerked backward reflexively. I had given up cataloguing the many shades of pink and red Dorian was displaying but he wasn't done yet. As the girl fell backward he lunged and turned, swept her up and caught her deftly, while his face shifted to a lovely shade of beet red. All the noise in the dining hall stopped expectantly while Dorian stood behind the high table holding the maid in his arms.

Every head in the room focused firmly on him and it was then that something in Dorian's head finally snapped. He had been pushed beyond some limit of absolute embarrassment and his sanity shattered like a glass dropped on a stone floor. He stared at the room for a long second before breaking into a country jig. After a few steps he twirled and set the girl on her feet but kept one of her hands in his as he spun her out and away as if she was his dance partner.

At the end he released her hand and made an elaborate bow to her. The girl was quick on her feet and returned the gesture with a remarkably well done curtsey. The room exploded with applause and cheers. Penny and Rose were standing now as they clapped and I had nearly fallen from my chair. There were tears in my eyes and I felt sure I would die from laughing too hard.

Dorian picked up one of the fallen loaves and sat down triumphantly. "This really is good bread you know," he announced calmly. "Would you like a piece Rose?" he said offering it to her.

She had already lost her composure with all the laughter, but her wits were second to none. "I think I'd like some privacy first," she said with a wink.

Dorian's mind must have returned to normal already, for the remark cost him his ability to speak. He stared at her with his mouth open.

And then Rose did something quite remarkable. She reached up calmly and closed Dorian's mouth gently before leaning in to kiss him softly on the lips. It was brief but left little doubt about her feelings.

My friend's eyes refocused as she pulled back. "Would you like to go riding tomorrow?" he asked without blinking.

"That won't be possible," she replied with a smile. "I am leaving for the capital in an hour, remember?"

Dorian's courage was still holding. "Then when we both return?" The hall had gone dead silent again as every ear strained to hear their conversation.

Rose's playful side was in full control however. "Perhaps...," she answered coyly.

That was more than Penny could take, though. "Rose!" she snapped.

"It was a joke!" protested Rose. "Of course I will Dorian," she assured him before turning her attention back to Penny. "I'm pretty sure he would have realized I was teasing."

"Don't be so sure," Penny advised her. "I've known him most of my life and he can be terribly thick sometimes."

Dorian looked to me for help while they talked as if he wasn't there. I shrugged and stuffed a piece of bread in my mouth. Who am I to give advice regarding women? I finished chewing and pointed at the food. "You should eat while they're ignoring you. Otherwise you'll be hungry later," I told him pragmatically.

It was closer to two hours before we actually got underway, but eventually we were all gathered near the circle that would take us to Lancaster. Since I was the only one that could activate the teleportation circles I would have to take Penny and her escort to Lancaster first before returning to take myself, and those coming with me, to Albamarl.

We still had told no one of Penny and Miriam's unexpected visit to Lancaster. According to our plan I would tell Joe McDaniel and some of the household staff right before I took my final jump to Albamarl. If anyone had plans for Penny or my mother that should effectively disrupt them.

During the war with Gododdin I had constructed an outbuilding in the castle courtyard to house the circles leading to Lancaster and Arundel, as well as one or two other places. Since then I had had the barn like structure replaced with a heavy stone building with double doors to allow for wagons. The larger circles were individually housed within the building, in stone partitioned rooms. Each room was also closed with a heavy wooden door and kept locked.

I had learned the hard way what could happen when an enemy capable of using a circle gained access to my home through one of the matching circles. It had left enough of an impression on me that I still kept a guard on watch inside the building at all times, in case doors and locks weren't enough.

I stood in the circle for Lancaster now, with Penny and Miriam beside me. Dorian stood before us, resplendent in his new plate armor, and behind us were four more men he had chosen to accompany them. I focused my will and spoke a word and then we were in Lancaster. At my urging James had had it locked up as well, but I was able to unlock the door from within, letting us out into the yard.

The guard there wasn't expecting us, so he seemed a bit startled when we emerged. Ordinarily if someone unexpected showed up it was just me, or me and one or two other people. Today we came through the doors with five armed men, and one of them looked ready to take on an army.

"It's me, Willem! No need for the horn!" I said quickly. The poor fellow had his instrument almost to his lips before I got his attention.

He paused, horn in hand, while his eyes finally came unstuck from Dorian and focused on me. Once he recognized me he relaxed. "Oh it's you Lord Cameron!" he said promptly. "Why do you have an army with you? You scared me half to death."

Dorian laughed inside his armor, with the visor down Willem hadn't recognized him at all. He lifted it to grin at the guard. "What? No greeting for an old friend?"

"Dorian!" shouted the man, recognizing him at last. "Where did you get that armor?"

I was a bit proud that my handiwork would elicit such an excited response but I had other things to do. While they caught up with one another I gave my mother a hug before turning to Penelope. "I'll miss you," I said.

"It's just a week or so," she answered. "It will be nice catching up with Genevieve and Ariadne. I haven't seen either of them in almost two months. I'm more worried about you. Try not to start a civil war while you're in Albamarl."

She was smiling as she said it, but there was a definite undertone of seriousness. My mother leaned forward to interject, "Think about Lady Rose. If you start a war she'll never be able to marry Dorian." I could only guess that she was referring to the fact that Rose's father served the king rather closely. I doubted that her father's disapproval would stop Rose from marrying anyone she chose, but I did have to admit it could make things awkward.

"I'll try to wait 'til after they're married before I start a war then. Will that be alright?" I asked jokingly.

Dorian naturally picked that moment to tune back into our conversation. He turned around and asked, "Who's getting married?"

"No one currently my friend," I replied. "Would you mind giving the duke and duchess my regards? I'm afraid I need to get on my way," I said hoping to distract him.

"Certainly," he said.

I leaned forward and gave Penny a quick kiss before stepping back into the room housing the circle. With a wave I was gone before Dorian could ask any more questions. The ladies could tell him whatever they liked; I wanted no part of it.

Back in Castle Cameron I gathered up Harold, Rose, and my own set of four guards. The circle that led to my house in Albamarl was smaller, so I would be able to take no more than two people with me at a time. I turned to Joe McDaniel before making the first trip. "I'll be gone for at least a week. Try not to tell anyone that Penny and Miriam have gone to Lancaster until this evening. If someone is planning something I'd like to give them as little time to recover as possible."

"Don't worry your lordship! Dorian will take good care of them and I'll be sure to keep my lips sealed 'til dinnertime at the very least," he said in return.

With that I began taking my companions to Albamarl. I transported Harold and the guards in two trips before making the final one with just Rose. "Are you ready my lady?" I asked her while offering my arm.

She raised an eyebrow. "This is far different than the manners you displayed the last time I went through a portal with you."

I had forgotten that incident and it embarrassed me when I remembered. I had been in a rush and had brought her back to Cameron by force. Worse I had slapped her rear to get her moving, much like a drover might slap a mule. At least that had been how I explained it to Penny. I blushed, "I'm sorry Rose. I should have apologized sooner."

She took my arm and we stepped into the circle. "No need to apologize. You were under a lot of pressure at the time. I just wanted to make sure you knew that *I* had not forgotten."

I started to ask her what that meant but then I decided I probably didn't want to know. With a word I took us to Albamarl.

CHAPTER 17

Penelope watched Mordecai step into the circle and vanish, feeling a sudden pang that they had not had time for a longer goodbye. She felt a gentle hand on her shoulder. "It never gets easier," Miriam told her. "Royce used to take trips into the city to buy materials and I had to do without him for two weeks at a time."

For a moment Penny wondered if her mother-in-law were trying to make a point of the fact that her husband's trips had lasted twice as long, but then she pushed the thought aside as petty. "Did he make many trips?" she asked instead.

"At least two a year," replied Miriam. "But sometimes he returned with really wonderful presents… like Mordecai."

Penny smiled wistfully, "Your son really is something special isn't he?"

Miriam loved nothing more than to hear her son complimented. She linked arms with Penny before answering, "Yes, but don't tell him too often or it will go to his head."

Dorian turned to face them. "If you ladies are ready we should probably go inside and give our greetings," he said.

"Well certainly…," Penny said, but before she could finish her statement the world exploded. Chaos enfolded her and everything became a blur as her consciousness left her body behind and the future blossomed before her eyes.

What seemed like an eternity passed, as scenes of violence played out in front of her, while she watched helplessly. Before the end she saw reality split along two possible paths, one dark and featureless while the other held some hope. At the juxtaposition of possibilities stood Mordecai, holding a balding man by the front of his tunic.

There was death in Mort's eyes, and anger beyond anything she had seen in him before. "You killed her Prathion!" he said bitterly. "You slew them both."

The eyes of the man he held were bulging in terror. "Please, I have a family…" he begged.

At the utterance of the word 'family' Mordecai began to laugh. It was an evil sound, and one Penny hoped never to hear again. Flames began sprouting from Mordecai's hands as he laughed and while they didn't burn him the man he held was not so fortunate. "Family is the last thing *you* should offer in your defense!" he yelled and soon both men were screaming, one with rage and the other in pain and terror. Mercifully the vision ended before it was over.

Penny found herself on her knees being held steady by Miriam's strong arms. "Are you alright girl?" Miriam asked, but it was then that Penny's stomach decided it had had enough and she emptied its contents onto the ground.

It took a few minutes but eventually the retching stopped and she let Miriam help her to her feet again. "I'm sorry, I don't know what came over me," she said.

"Think nothing of it. I was just worried for you. Your eyes rolled back and for a moment I thought you might be having a seizure. I almost didn't catch you before you collapsed," said the older woman. "Let's get you inside and find some water. I'm sure you want to rinse your mouth after that."

Penny kept Miriam's hand in her own as they began walking, "Yes I think that would be a good idea," she answered. Dorian stayed close by her on the other side, in case she showed signs of collapsing again, while the four guards spread out around them as they walked.

A few minutes later she was seated at a table in the great hall of Lancaster Castle, drinking water from a metal goblet. The crisp taste helped her clear her mind but her thoughts wouldn't stop racing. *What do I do?* she thought. *I have so little time.* In the background she could hear Dorian explaining to James what had happened and why they were there so unexpectedly.

A particularly vivid memory came to mind and tears started fresh from her eyes. Using her sleeve she dabbed at them quickly, hoping no one noticed. *If they start to suspect I know what's about to happen it will be even worse,* she thought. She turned to Miriam, "Do you think you could get someone to find Ariadne for me?"

"She's here already Penny," said Miriam, nodding in a direction past Penny's left shoulder.

"Oh, of course, thank you Miriam," she said and rising she walked quickly to Ariadne.

"Are you alright Penelope? I heard that…" Ariadne started.

Penny gave her a look that would brook no interference. "Ariadne, do you trust me?" she said quietly.

"Yes of course," the other woman answered.

"Do you have writing materials in your room?" Penny asked.

"Not much, but I have pen and paper," Ariadne replied.

"No I don't mind at all! Let's go take a look," Penny said loudly, taking Ariadne's arm in her own. "I'll be back in just a minute," she said addressing the room. Genevieve had arrived by then and though she looked concerned she nodded her agreement. Miriam seemed positively mystified.

Once Penny reached Ariadne's room she wasted no time before preparing to write a letter. "Who will that be for?" asked the younger woman.

"It's for Mordecai, but I need you to keep it a secret," she told Ariadne.

"You seem awful serious Penny, are you sure there isn't something else I can do?"

"No, you've done enough, but I need you to promise me a few things," said Penny.

Ariadne gave Penny a long look. "You have the same sort of intensity about you right now that you did the night you tried to murder Devon Tremont on the dance floor."

Penny was surprised by Ariadne's acute perception but she couldn't afford to lose her support now. She decided to try honesty. "There is a bit of similarity between the two occasions Ariadne, but I need you to trust me."

"Why?" asked the younger woman.

Penny took a deep breath. "I trust everyone here, but I've *seen* something and if they realize that, it will change the outcome of things. Does that make sense?" she replied anxiously.

Ariadne nodded, "You've had a vision?"

"Yes, that's why I collapsed in the yard. It came on me right after Mordecai left, which makes everything more difficult," Penny said.

"Because you need to tell him something?"

"Yes," said Penny emphatically. "I need to send a message to him. A message to him in the future, when he returns, and I have to do it without arousing anyone's suspicion in the present."

"Shouldn't that include me then?" Ariadne asked.

"I only need you to keep my secret for a few hours," Penny told the younger woman. "After that it won't matter very much, the worst will have happened already."

"Why do I want to let the worst happen?"

Penny shrugged, "It isn't the worst for everyone, just for a few, but if it doesn't happen everyone will die."

Ariadne squinted suspiciously at her. "Define everyone?"

"Everyone."

"Everyone in Lothion?" asked Ariadne.

"Everyone," said Penny.

"Everyone in Gododdin?"

"All humanity," replied Penny. "I'm talking about the possible extinction of our race."

Ariadne Lancaster drew herself up carefully before answering. "That sounds fairly dramatic, but knowing you I will suspend my normal disbelief. Tell me something else… assuming I help you, who are the people that something terrible will happen to in the short term?"

Penny shook her head negatively, not trusting herself to speak.

"Is it that bad?" Ariadne asked.

Penny's courage could only carry her so far, and it finally gave out under her, leaving her to dissolve into tears. Ariadne wound up consoling her for long minutes before her composure returned. When she had regained control she asked, "Will you help?"

"I don't see that I have much choice, assuming I believe you, and I do. What do you want me to do?" answered Ariadne with some resignation.

"Let me finish this note. Then I will seal it and hand it over to you. Tomorrow or the next day I need you to find someone to take it to Joe McDaniels, in Washbrook. Tell no one about our talk," Penny said.

"That doesn't sound too hard," Ariadne observed.

Penny gave a bitter laugh. "It will be. Things will happen between now and then. Please don't be tempted to tell anyone what I've said," she told her.

Ariadne hugged her. "I don't know what sort of burden you are carrying Penny, but I won't let you down. Trust me."

Her pronouncement almost brought Penny to tears again, but she fought down the urge. With a nod she returned to writing her note. She struggled, trying to decide exactly what to say, too much and Mort would figure out what was going to happen, too little and he would balk at doing what was necessary. In the end she settled on keeping the note short and simple, trusting that Mordecai would heed her advice. *I won't know the outcome either way,* she thought ruefully.

A short time later they returned to the main hall and Penny had to make a few graceful excuses for her absence. It seemed everyone was worried about her now. Eventually she side stepped the issue of her possible illness by claiming fatigue. "If you wouldn't mind, I'd like to rest," she told Genevieve.

"Why naturally you do!" said the duchess sympathetically. She wasted no time calling one of the servants over to lead her to one of the guest bedrooms.

"I'll go with her," announced Miriam. "I wouldn't dream of leaving my daughter without a watchful eye," she said with a protective tone.

Although Penny appreciated the gesture, she wished she could convince her otherwise, but there was little hope of that. Dorian and the guards formed up to escort them through the halls. "That won't be necessary,"

Penny protested. "Dorian you're enough by yourself, why don't you let the men take their leisure?"

Dorian hesitated before answering, "I'm sorry Penny. I'll have to insist, I promised Mort that we wouldn't leave you unguarded." He removed his helmet as he spoke, since its presence seemed rude within the castle.

She sighed regretfully. She had known it wouldn't work but she had felt compelled to try. Taking Miriam's arm she allowed herself to be led down the corridor.

"You're shaking something dreadful Penny! Are you sure you're alright?" asked Miriam worriedly.

"Don't worry Miriam, I think I just need to eat something after what happened in the courtyard. My stomach feels dreadfully empty," she lied. Her stomach was full of butterflies. As they walked Penny thought of something and glancing over she realized Dorian still had his helmet off. "Dorian would you mind putting your helmet back on?" she asked.

The large man looked askance at her. "We're inside the castle Penny," he said, stating the obvious.

She put on her best stubborn look, "If you're going to insist on following me around playing bodyguard all day then I'll have to insist you wear the armor my husband made for you."

He stared at her for a long moment before settling the helmet back down on his head. "There, is that better?" he asked with a slight tone of condescension.

"Yes," she replied, "but I want you to put the visor down as well."

"You can't be serious," he said disbelievingly.

She stopped walking, forcing Miriam to stop with her. "I am absolutely serious Dorian. If you don't put the visor down I won't take one step further." Everyone was staring at her now, including Mort's mother. Unable to think of a rationale for her behavior Penny resorted to letting a bit more of her frustration show in the form of a wild expression and some tears.

Miriam waved her hands at Dorian, "Just put your damn visor down Dorian, we need to get her to a room." Miriam's face gave him an expression showing she understood his confusion.

Dorian complied with the request, though his body language showed how silly he thought it was. Penny didn't care though, she was just glad to see his armor fully in place. A few minutes later they reached the guest room.

Once inside Penny was taken to the bedroom while three of the guardsmen were arranged in the antechamber. The fourth was set to stand guard outside in the hallway. Miriam was still paying her considerable attention, "Why don't you lie down for a bit?" the older woman asked.

Penny found herself feeling bad for worrying the other woman. She embraced Miriam while speaking softly, "I'm sorry for causing such a fuss, but I'm not actually sick."

Mort's mother looked at her suspiciously, "What does that mean?"

Penny crossed the room to close the door. Before she did she looked out and saw Dorian lifting his visor again. "I said keep your damn visor shut!" she barked. Dorian glared at her for a second before his hand drew his helm's faceguard back down. Penny shut the door and turned back to Miriam. "I'm sure Mort has told you about the visions I've had," she began.

Miriam's eyes grew wide. "In the courtyard?" she said suddenly.

Penny nodded.

"How bad is it?" asked the other woman.

"Bad, and I can't tell you how or why, but I need you to trust me," she said.

"What does that mean?" asked Miriam.

"It means I want you to follow my lead. Something bad is about to happen and I may say some things that don't make sense but I want you to ignore that and go along with me," Penny replied.

"Like Dorian's visor?"

"Yes."

"Something violent is about to happen isn't it?" said Miriam.

A knock at the outer door interrupted their conversation and both women held their breath to hear what was happening in the outer room. One of the guards exchanged words with whoever was in the hall but they couldn't make out what was said. A moment later Dorian knocked on the bedroom door. "Excuse me ladies," he said politely.

Penny opened the door quickly. She was full of more nervous energy now than she could stand. "Yes?" she asked.

Dorian still had his visor down this time, which made his voice sound odd. "James has sent one of his men to request I attend him in his rooms," he said plainly.

Penny swallowed before answering, her mouth had gone dry. "Then you should go," she told him.

Dorian raised his hand to his helm, "What about this?"

Penny started to laugh but she stopped herself quickly as she felt hysteria creeping into her voice. "Keep it down until you reach James. Obviously I don't expect you to wear it while you're speaking with him," she replied.

Dorian sighed again. Though she seemed normal Penny was obviously suffering from some sort of stress induced eccentricity. "The guard who brought the message will remain here in my place 'til I return," he told her.

"That will be fine," she answered.

Dorian turned and strode from the room, feeling ridiculous walking out with his visor down. As he went he stared for a moment at the guard James had sent to summon him. Something about the man's face bothered him, but he couldn't figure out what it was. In any case, he didn't recognize the fellow anyway.

After he had gone Penny returned to the outer room. She had too much energy to stay pent up in the bedroom. Her presence served to stifle the idle banter her guards had been engaging in and an awkward silence fell across the room. They didn't have long to wait however, less than two minutes after Dorian left another knock sounded at the door.

The guard outside opened the door without waiting for a response, revealing a highly unusual woman framed by the opening. She was garbed in soft leathers, like a huntsman, though she bore more steel than would be necessary for such an occupation. Her hair was black and curled into delicate ringlets, it might have draped past her shoulders but she had it tied back into a businesslike pony tail. She strode forward into the room as though she owned it.

Penny locked eyes with the strange woman and a chill ran down her spine. *This woman is death,* she thought and her knowledge of what would soon happen did nothing to change her opinion. "Wait," she said suddenly, before the woman could speak. "I'd like you men to leave so we can talk in private."

The man closest to her, Samuel was his name, answered first, "I don't think that's what Sir Dorian had in mind when he left." He might have said more but a dagger appeared, lodged in his left eye. It happened so suddenly almost no one reacted for the first few seconds, aside from Penelope.

Penny no longer had the superior speed and strength she had possessed while she had been Mordecai's Anath'Meridum, but she had been trained by one of the most skilled warriors in all of Lothion, and she had already known a good deal of what would happen. As the first dagger flew toward Samuel's head she was already drawing a long bladed knife from her skirt and though she was too far to save him she managed to bat a second blade from the air before it reached one of her other guards.

The room grew still for a moment as Samuel slowly collapsed to the floor, twitching as he died. The other guard, Cole, had just begun to register the fact that a similar blade had almost reached him as well. The strange woman looked at Penny appraisingly, "Not bad, I see Cyhan did a good job with you."

The other woman's patronizing tone got under Penny's skin immediately and she wanted nothing more than to teach her a lesson, but she kept her wits about her. "This is a mistake. No one else needs to die if you'll just let me explain," she said.

The dark haired woman drew two long knives, each with a blade almost eighteen inches in length and advanced. "I'm afraid the time for talking is over sweetheart," she replied.

To their credit the two guards that remained never wavered in their resolve. Cole drew his sword as the woman stepped forward, as did the man beside him, but they never stood a chance. Their opponent feinted toward Penny and Cole took the bait, lunging sideways to protect his ward and the woman cut his throat wide as she swept back in the other direction. Ducking a swing from the second guard she moved in closely and slashed at his midsection.

That move was purely a distraction however, his breastplate made it impossible for her blade to hurt him there, but he flinched and drew back reflexively... or at least he attempted to do so, but she had pinned his left foot under her own. With a small push she sent him falling backward and followed him downward, using his weight to start a tumbling roll. Penny had stepped over Cole and her own blade narrowly missed the woman's back as she rolled away.

The stranger came up and into a crouch several feet away, but the man she had tripped didn't rise. One of the two long knives was lodged under his chin and a pool of blood was already spreading underneath him. Penny stared at him in shock, she hadn't seen the attack that killed him, or even expected it. All three of her guards were now dead and she assumed that the one outside the room was gone as well. The fight was effectively over, unless she intended to take the intruder on singlehandedly.

Given her condition that seemed foolish. The woman before her was more deadly than anyone she had ever seen, except perhaps Cyhan. Without the extra speed and strength she had had as Mort's Anath'Meridum there was no way she could hope to overcome her. That didn't mean she was ready to surrender however. *What is it that Mort's always saying? Stupid never dies. I guess that describes me as well,* she thought to herself. *If there's no way to overpower her directly perhaps I can make her underestimate me.*

Penelope began edging sideways around the room, backing further from the woman as she moved, until she had reached the place she started. Cole's now still form lay on the ground behind her, but before she could begin her opponent spoke. "I'm not here to kill you," the other woman said.

Penny knew this already but she feigned ignorance. "Who are you?" she asked.

The woman laughed, "Ruth is my name. If you put the dagger down I won't hurt you."

"And if I don't?"

"Then I might put my knee right in the middle of that big belly of yours," Ruth replied with an evil sneer. "You wouldn't want to endanger the baby would you?" she said with mock sympathy.

Penny decided to risk some of her information on a bluff, "The king would be very displeased if something happened to me or my child."

Ruth stepped forward without bothering to reply. As she did Penny stepped sideways but her foot came down awkwardly on Cole's body, causing her to trip. Ruth lunged thinking Penny vulnerable but her eyes widened in surprise when Penny sank gracefully to one knee instead, bringing her dagger up and in-line with Ruth's mid-section. Twisting like a cat she narrowly avoided being gutted and the sharp edge slid over the outside of her ribs, ripping a deep cut through her leathers and scoring deeply into the skin beneath. The motion threw her completely off balance and she fell awkwardly beside the pregnant woman.

Penny cursed as her thrust failed to eviscerate Ruth but she followed through, trying to make the most of her opportunity. As Ruth fell Penny leaned to her left and drove her left elbow into her attacker's side. If she had been more limber she could have tried for a better target but her belly was hampering her movements. She felt as much as heard the grunt of pain that escaped her attacker's lips as the blow connected. Bringing her right hand around she wasted no time, trying to catch Ruth with her blade before she could recover.

Ruth was moving already though, she rolled to the side before Penny could connect with the dagger and lashing out with her leg she caught her solidly in the side of the head. Penny was thrown sideways by the blow, crashing into the wooden doorframe between the two rooms. Struggling to clear her vision Penny tried to get up, when a second blow she failed to see knocked her down again.

A moment later she was caught. Ruth's long legs were wrapped around her waist and one arm was around her neck. With crushing pressure Penny felt Ruth's forearm cutting into her neck, choking off her air supply and making her head feel as though it were about to explode. "You're going to pay for that cut bitch," came Ruth's voice next to her ear. "You've got me so worked up I might just choke you to death."

Penny wanted to reply, but she couldn't, the pressure on her throat was too great. She was unable to even croak and she knew her face must be blood red… the world was starting to go dark.

Then the bedroom door flew open and Miriam entered the fray. The older woman had been searching the bedroom for weapons and not finding any had finally settle upon the only workable item in the room, a slender wooden chair that had been used with the writing desk. Swinging the chair wildly at Ruth's back she charged. "Get your hands off my daughter!" Unfortunately her approach was far from stealthy.

The pressure on Penny's throat abruptly vanished as Ruth released her and leapt aside. Miriam struggled to stop her swing before she hit Penny but only partially succeeded and Penny felt fresh pain as the heavy wood struck her legs. Ruth was smiling now, with a new blade in hand as she approached Miriam, like a cat that has found a new mouse to play with. "I don't really have to keep both of you alive."

Penny felt fresh horror sweep over her as Ruth prepared to attack Miriam. *No! This isn't what's supposed to happen!* She thought to herself while her body stubbornly refused to listen to her commands. She couldn't get up, and there was no way she could reach Miriam in time to save her.

CHAPTER 18

Dorian was troubled by a nagging doubt as he walked. Something about the guard that had come to summon him bothered him, but he couldn't put his finger on it. He was halfway to the duke's family suites before it came to him.

He hadn't recognized the guard… at all. Having been raised in Lancaster, as well as trained there amongst its guards, he should have known him. At the very least the man's face should have been familiar. There was always the possibility that he was new to the duke's service, but unlike Washbrook, Lancaster hadn't had a large influx of new settlers, so the chances of that were small.

I'd better go back, he thought, and turning he began to walk back the way he had come. The further he went the more urgent it felt and before he had gone twenty feet he was running. *Keep your visor down,* she had said. *Damnitt Penny! You knew!* A minute later and he was rounding the corner of the hallway their room was on, and as soon as he saw the men in the hallway his fears were confirmed. There was no reason for four strange guards to be standing outside her room.

Despite his conversation with Mordecai previously Dorian still didn't have an enchanted great sword yet, and for once he was glad of it, the hallway would have been an awkward place to use such a large weapon. Roaring he drew his long sword and dagger, charging down the corridor at the men he knew must be there for the women he was sworn to protect.

The guards started at his appearance and drew their weapons. They bore only swords and truncheons, but many of them wished for a shield when they saw Dorian bearing down upon them. Raising their weapons they prepared to face him.

They might as well have laid down their arms, for all the good their weapons did them. Dorian ignored their attacks completely, trusting to his armor to protect him. Instead he focused his attention on his own weapons and within a span of seconds four of his opponents were down, dead or mortally wounded. Two others had entered Penny's room, bolting the door behind them. Apparently they weren't ready to be part of the massacre.

He reached the door in a panic, knowing Penny and Miriam were inside, presumably unguarded now. Naturally the door resisted his first attempt to open it. In frustration he struck the heavy oak with his gauntleted fist, sending splinters and shards of wood flying. The door shook in its frame as if a battering ram had been used upon it. Dorian stepped back and threw himself, shoulder first against the wooden barrier. Impossibly some of the wooden timbers snapped and the door nearly collapsed in on itself. A blade shot forth through one of the gaps, attempting to wound him, but it skittered harmlessly from his breastplate.

Raising his sword he began chopping away the remaining wood, the enchanted steel cutting through the damaged wood as easily as a knife through bread, within seconds he would be inside. He was so focused on getting to Penny and Miriam that he failed to notice the balding man fading into view ten feet down the hallway, nor did he pay any heed when the man began speaking in a foreign tongue.

Through the gaps in the wood Dorian could see dead bodies scattered across the floor. Blood was everywhere and Penny was being carefully bound by a woman with dark hair. He thought he could see a glimpse of Miriam on the floor to one side, lying utterly still. The two men inside were busy piling furniture against the rapidly disintegrating door.

Still unnoticed the man in the hallway gave Dorian a strange stare, for his words had had no noticeable effect upon him. Biting his lip he tried something different and lightning streaked across the distance between him and the armored warrior.

Dorian's body convulsed momentarily as electricity coursed over his armor. Despite being encased in metal armor he still lived, for Mordecai's enchantments somehow absorbed much of the strike. Still twitching he looked over his shoulder, spotting the man who had tried to kill him. Not daring to waste time he threw his dagger at the stranger, hoping to distract the man while he finished cutting his way through the door.

Oddly enough the balding man never wavered or ducked and he seemed strangely surprised when the blade lodged solidly in his shoulder. Letting out a cry of pain and frustration he fell backward, clutching at the wound. Dorian continued tearing a path through the ruined furniture and debris that still blocked his path. The woman had finished binding Penny and stood behind the two male warriors, berating them in their attempts to keep him out of the room.

Not satisfied with how the situation was resolving she searched about for a moment before finding a heavy table leg and… as Dorian finally forced his way in, she struck. Her blow was not the more usual swing, but rather a thrust, as one might use a spear. Normally such a strike would carry enormous force, having the weight of the wielder's body behind a small point of impact. She struck so rapidly and with such force that Dorian was unable to duck, being still entangled in broken furniture, and the end of the table leg slammed into the face of his helm.

The blow would have killed him outright if he had not had his visor down. Even protected as he was it still sent him stumbling to fall backward over the broken wood behind him. The two fighters with the woman wasted no time, and following her directions they each lifted one of their captives and bore them quickly from the room.

Dorian struggled to rise but Ruth gave him no room, she had leapt through the doorway and now circled him, using the table leg as a cudgel. She struck madly, at his legs, arms, and head, making sure he was unable to regain his balance. She was grinning and sweating as she attacked him but even in her frenzy she was looking for vulnerabilities. Her blows seemed to have little effect on the massive warrior, besides keeping him from regaining his feet. His armor showed no signs of denting, or even being scratched.

"Walter!" she yelled. "Isn't there something you can do about this metal beast?" That was when she spotted the wizard, wounded and struggling to rise on the other side of the hall. The sight distracted her and Dorian's mailed fist caught the table leg on its next swing. She struggled to pull it from his grasp for he seemed to be impossibly strong.

With a yank Dorian pulled himself upright and drew Ruth into his reach. Moving with a speed she hadn't suspected he caught her throat in his left hand and drew her face close to his helm as he stood. Rising up like a shining colossus Dorian held her in the air while she kicked desperately at him. She could see his face through the numerous slits in his visor and the look in his eyes sent a shock of adrenaline through her body.

"If you've injured either of those women I will rip that head right off of your shoulders!" he growled through clenched jaws. Turning his head he addressed the two men carrying Penny and Miriam, "Put them down or I kill this bitch." They stared at him helplessly, unsure what to do.

Ruth glared at them while her face grew red and her eyes bulged. Her mouth gaped as she struggled to speak. Thinking she might give the order Dorian loosened his grip enough for her to breathe. "Release me fool or I'll have them killed…," she choked out but Dorian never gave her a chance to finish the sentence. With two long strides he lifted her up and slammed her against the stone wall.

"Then you die first!" he roared. He was beyond madness now and the men holding Penny and Miriam began to lower their captives to the ground. Then Dorian heard strange words and a sledgehammer blow of pure force struck him behind his knees sending him to the ground again. In the course of the fall he lost his grip on Ruth's throat, but his gauntleted hand left deep bloody gouges on her neck as she fell free and went tumbling away.

Rolling over Dorian rose up again. The balding man, the wizard, was facing him again while Ruth choked and gasped ten feet away. Dorian leapt at him but struck an invisible shield that barred his path. Searching with his hands it seemed to block the width of the corridor. Penny and Miriam were on the other side of it… along with their enemies.

The wizard, Walter was what Ruth had named him, smiled and began backing slowly down the hallway. Ruth was rising unsteadily to her feet, still gasping for air, and the two remaining soldiers they had brought lifted Penny and Miriam again. Desperate Dorian slammed his fist against the invisible barrier in front of him. Walter winced visibly at the force of the blow.

Two steps and Dorian recovered his sword. He had spent enough time with Mordecai to know the effect enchanted blades could have, even on a wizard's shield. Turning back one swing cut through whatever held him back and then the resistance was gone. Walter's eyes grew wide in fear.

"Run!" shouted the panicked wizard. "I can't hold him!"

Dorian had almost made it to the spell caster when another bolt of lightning struck and stunned him momentarily. His entire body was tingling and pain robbed him of his senses for a second, and then he began to advance again. "You're going to regret that," he said in an ominous tone.

Walter stumbled back, fear written on his face. Dorian could see the front of the man's shirt was covered in blood where the dagger had struck him earlier. In desperation the wizard uttered a sharp phrase in an unfamiliar language and Dorian braced himself, but nothing happened. With a cry he leapt forward to grab the older man, but his feet suddenly flew out from under him and he fell to strike the floor, a floor that was now as slick as ice.

The wizard moved quickly back, following his companions, and as he went he repeated his incantation… ice now covered the floor for thirty feet between himself and the almost helpless Dorian.

"What the hell?" Dorian shouted as he tried unsuccessfully to lever himself up onto his arms and legs again. He struggled desperately but only managed to flounder more spectacularly, his frenzy making it even more difficult to find purchase on the ice beneath him. Every second that passed Penny and Miriam were being taken further away as their attackers carried them down the hall.

In frustration Dorian slammed the floor with his fist, sending splinters of ice flying every direction. His hand found solid purchase on the stone underneath. Inspiration struck and moments later he was beating the ice with both fists to clear the ground. Within a minute or less he was past the ice and running after them. Rounding a corner he found nothing but an empty hallway, his foes were nowhere to be seen.

He bounded in the direction he assumed they would have gone, the stairs… still he found no sign of them. Looking back he scanned the floor and considered the doors he had passed. He could see blood on the ground, probably the wizard's. It appeared he was losing a fair amount of blood. The blood stopped a good twenty feet from the entrance to the stairs.

Squinting he examined the floor there, hoping to find some clue, and as he stared at the area a second spot of blood appeared, as if by magic. He glanced upward, suspecting they had somehow climbed the walls, yet he saw nothing above. Dorian took another step, getting closer to the mysterious area. He could hear someone breathing heavily… perhaps several some ones.

Suddenly the light changed and standing before him appeared the entire group. Ruth appeared to be helping to keep the wizard on his feet. Said wizard chose then to speak, "Why the hell won't you just give up!?" Another strange word and lightning enveloped Dorian again, sending pain shooting throughout his body. This time the surge of electricity didn't end immediately, it continued for what seemed an eternity as the wizard focused his fear and desperation on him.

"You should be dead already!" cried the man, almost sobbing with emotion.

Yet Dorian did not fall, though smoke rose from his armor and his body had begun to shake uncontrollably. More and more the electricity seemed to be affecting him, though the armor blunted the majority of its deadly effect. Eventually it was too much, and losing his balance he collapsed onto the stone floor. His body grew still, as if after the constant spasms his muscles seemed content to rest at last. Dorian struggled to maintain consciousness.

He could hear the woman drawing the exhausted wizard away, toward the stairs. The man seemed to have lost control of himself and was crying uncontrollably now. "Shut up you damned coward!" Ruth yelled at him. "What's wrong with you?"

"I've never killed anyone before," the wizard answered in a voice that sounded devoid of hope.

"Nothing's changed then imbecile!" she shouted back at him. "He's still breathing."

Their voices grew more distant as they descended the stairs and Dorian struggled to move. Though his body felt like it was made of jelly he was desperate inside. *Move damnitt! Move!!* he yelled inwardly at his stubborn muscles and slowly but surely his limbs began to obey him again. Several minutes passed and finally he began to drag himself forward, working his way to the stairs.

Within five minutes he was walking, trying to navigate the steep staircase leading downward. More than once his legs gave out on him, sending him tumbling down five or ten feet before coming to a halt again, yet he refused to rest. *He wanted to know why I won't give up,* he thought, recalling the wizard's panicked question… *because you have my friends.*

By the time he reached the bottom his legs had become significantly more reliable. He noted that there were still spots of blood scattered along the way, which made his task much easier. "You should get that looked at," he said quietly to himself, thinking grimly of the wizard he had wounded. "Man could bleed to death like that."

He followed the path out into the castle yard; there the blood and heavy footprints of the men carrying Penny and Miriam were even easier to follow. No one along the way seemed to have seen them. "Rouse yourselves! Enemies in the keep! Close the gates!" Dorian shouted. "They've taken the Countess!"

Men began running as he yelled. Guards came alive on the walls, manning the battlements and scanning the surrounding area. Others approached Dorian as he walked steadily across the yard, following the trail of blood. Questions were asked but he had no time for them. "Close the damn gates, they might still be inside!" he shouted.

As he drew closer he could see that the trail had not yet reached the gate. They were moving slowly, invisibly, and trying to avoid detection. Yet his eyes spotted the end of the trail, and more fresh blood as they moved again. They were almost through the gate now. A large collection of guardsmen had gathered beside him now. "They're right there, in front of the gate!" he yelled. "Fan out and search the area 'til you lay hands on them. They're invisible," he ordered and men moved to obey.

Men looked at him oddly, as if he had gone mad. "It's a wizard or some servant of the dark gods, with the power to render himself invisible to sight… and they're right there!" he shouted, pointing at the area they had to be in. As he spoke a boot print appeared on the hard packed earth, the tread of a man carrying a heavy load. Having just pointed in that direction a few of the guards saw it appear and gasps of astonishment could be heard among them.

Dorian didn't pause, sheathing his sword to avoid the possibility of hitting Penny or Miriam he charged toward the place where his enemies had to be standing. That was when all hell broke loose.

A shadow fell across the earth and looking up he saw a beast straight out of myth and legend. The creature that was descending was sixty feet in length if it was an inch. Dark green scales shimmered in the afternoon sun and its wings seemed to block out the light.

Dorian stared at it in shock. "A dragon?" he muttered disbelievingly. Cries of fear and dismay rang out as the men of Lancaster keep took shelter. Such a thing had never been seen before but they ran instinctively nonetheless. Within seconds the courtyard had cleared and Dorian was left to stand alone.

The scaled monstrosity landed with an almost inhuman grace and delicacy, barely stirring the ground as it came to rest. Its forelegs were nearly as thick as Dorian's chest, yet it made hardly a sound, until its mouth opened to issue a challenging roar.

Dorian gritted his teeth as he fought against his instincts. His legs had started to shake, yet he refused to look away and somehow his sword had gotten into his hand. His mind had gone blank, but deep within he could feel the stirrings of anger and despite his fear Dorian began to walk forward. The first step was slow and hesitant, but each one that followed was firmer and surer, and in a moment he was striding boldly toward the massive beast, head up and unbowed. "I will be thrice damned before I let something like you get in my way!"

Then the dragon drew itself up on all fours and took a deep breath, staring squarely at Dorian's approach.

He flinched and then stopped as it opened its mouth and exhaled, sending a wave of searing flames out to engulf him.

Dorian crouched, keeping his head down and shielding his visor with his arms until the blast of fire had passed. He felt no heat from it and realized that once again his armor seemed to shield him from more than just physical blows. In fact, it had worked much better against the flame than it had against the lightning. Standing again he charged forward and threw himself against the great beast, seeking to pierce its breast with his sword.

It was a complete shock to him when he passed through the thing without the faintest resistance, as though the dragon had been conjured from nothing but smoke. Light and shadow swirled around him until he emerged from the other side. A glance backward revealed the dragon still rampaging behind him but if he had any doubts about its solidity they were dispelled as its tail swept through his chest while he watched.

Ignoring the phantom monster behind him Dorian faced the main gate. No longer distracted by the dragon he spotted the now visible abductors passing through the open castle entrance. The portcullis was part way down but had stopped before reaching the ground, held up by some invisible force. The wizard stood next to it, red-faced and sweating. It was obvious that the strain of maintaining both the illusion and keeping the portcullis from closing had pushed him to his limit.

Wasting no more time Dorian ran after them, toward the wizard first, he understood now the man was too dangerous to ignore. The older man watched him come, sweat running down his cheeks, as he tried to do too many things at once. He was almost under the heavy steel portcullis by the time Dorian reached him and he had already given up trying to maintain the illusion of the dragon.

At the end, seeing he could not escape, the stranger released the barrier that was holding the portcullis and threw himself down, trying to roll under before it struck the ground. Unfortunately for him, he didn't quite make it, and one of the massive steel spikes ripped through his right thigh, pinning him under the heavy metal.

It also barred Dorian from pursuing the men carrying Penny and Miriam steadily away. He could see someone riding hard from the tree-line, followed by a string of horses. The abductors had obviously planned carefully, within moments they would have their targets on horseback and any chance of catching them would be much smaller.

In a fit of rage Dorian struck at the metal bars that kept him from following. Although his sword was enchanted and razor sharp the metal was far too thick to cut through, his blade kept sticking a half an inch or so into the heavy two inch iron bar. The wizard on the ground beneath him groaned audibly. "Raise the portcullis!" Dorian screamed, but he knew it was futile. The sight of the dragon had unmanned the guards. It was doubtful anyone was within earshot to obey him anyway.

Sheathing his sword, he eyed the iron portcullis carefully. He knew from experience that it weighed many tons. It was designed that way to enable it to be dropped quickly in time of emergency, and its weight was all that prevented an enemy from lifting it. Since the day he had received the earth bond Dorian had been aware of a noticeable increase in his strength and stamina, but this seemed far beyond possibility.

In the distance he could see them loading Penny and Miriam onto the waiting horses. "To hell with what's possible," he said and crouching down he took a firm grip of the bottom of the portcullis. Drawing a deep breath he began to lift, keeping his back straight and his arms locked while his legs strained to lift him up. At first nothing happened, but while he struggled he began to hear a great thumping beneath him, like a massive heart, beating in time with his own. *Give me the strength*, he thought.

Something answered his call, for he felt energy suffusing his limbs and while his face turned red and his body trembled, the portcullis began to lift. As he came up a long drawn out cry of pain and effort issued from deep within him, while the portcullis gathered upward momentum, rising faster as it approached chest height. Not daring to pause he used that momentum and centering himself under the heavy metal he thrust it upward above him.

Time slowed for a moment as he held the massive structure above him, and by all rights the weight alone should have crushed him. Looking downward he saw the wizard watching him. "If you're going to move, now would be a good time…" he ground out slowly between clenched teeth. Comprehension dawned on the stranger's face and he began dragging himself out of the way… leaving a trail of blood behind him.

Once he was clear, Dorian stepped outward and let gravity take its course and the massive portcullis slammed down behind him. He looked at the wizard lying on the ground on the other side. "Let them help you when they finally get over their fear of your 'dragon' and you might live. I want to talk to you when I get back," he told him. He wasn't sure if the fellow was still conscious but he thought he saw him nod an acknowledgement. The man was in such a bad state he might have imagined it.

Turning away Dorian began to run toward the group of men and horses that were beginning to ride away. They were over fifty yards away and he could clearly see Penny being held in front of one of the riders. Miriam had been slung sideways over the back end of another horse. He took that as a bad sign, since in general only corpses were slung across horses like that. If she were alive the position would do nothing to keep her that way.

Running in armor was an interesting proposition normally, something usually reserved for very short charges. In the chain mail that most men wore it was a difficult affair… the weight of the armor served as a limiting factor. In the plate armor he now wore it should have been even more awkward, not because of weight, plate actually weighed slightly less than chain, but because of the more restricted mobility the armor afforded. Yet again Mort had worked a miracle. The armor was cunningly crafted and moved very freely with his body. It still would have hindered a run, but because it worked to augment his own motions it made it feel almost as though he were running without armor at all.

It still wasn't perfect however, and it did slow him down more than running in normal clothes would have. Fifty yards wouldn't have been too much for a normal charge, but the riders were now spurring their mounts to a canter, creating more distance between him and those he was determined to reach. Hopeless as it was he ran anyway.

Dorian thought of nothing else besides running. He had never been a great sprinter but being tall and athletic he was no slouch either. His breath quickened as his legs drove him forward, pumping rhythmically. A minute passed and still he ran, and the riders seemed no further away than when he had started. The party ahead of him consisted of six horses bearing riders and several without a rider; those had probably been for the men he had slain.

One horse carried double, having an armsman plus Penny aboard, while another carried Miriam alone slung across it like so much dead weight.

Because of the heavy burden on the horse carrying Penny and her captor the others were forced to maintain a slower pace, and incredibly it appeared to be one he could match. He pushed himself harder, hoping to close the gap, though in the back of his mind he couldn't help but wonder when his stamina would run out.

Apparently his quarry had begun to wonder the same thing. Two of the riders, who had brought the horses to meet the fugitives, were looking backward with incredulous faces as they watched him run. On the face of it, it was ridiculous… a man in heavy armor could not hope to keep up with horses, even at a moderate pace such as they were riding at now, yet he was beginning to gain on them.

Finally with a word to his fellows one of the riders turned aside and made to intercept him. Drawing his sword the man urged his mount to a full gallop, charging directly at the maniac following them. With barely forty yards between them when he turned Dorian's opponent wasn't able to get his horse up to full speed; not that he needed to do so.

Dorian crossed the distance rapidly while the fellow turned his horse and prepared to ride him down. They drew together with surprising speed but Dorian never slowed, opting instead to run straight for the horse rather than try to avoid it. Seconds later the animal grew large in his view and he could see its rider leaning out to catch him in the sweep of his sword. Just before they met the horse tried to adjust its course enough to avoid a collision, but Dorian wasn't having that and he headed straight into it.

The poor beast reared as they came together and he came up under its right shoulder as it flailed and tried to keep from losing its balance. With a shock he straightened up as he passed under the horse and drove all of his momentum up and forward; the move cost him most of his forward speed, yet after stumbling drunkenly for several yards he was able to regain his rhythm and begin running again. The horse he had struck was nowhere to be seen but he didn't pause to ponder that mystery, choosing instead to focus on catching up to Penny and her abductors. They had gained several tens of yards in distance after his collision.

Dorian ran on. His breath was coming heavily now, and he was starting to stagger every so often as he ran, but he didn't slow. His mouth tasted of blood and iron while his lungs sounded like a raspy set of bellows, but he ran on. Those he was chasing didn't make the mistake of sending anyone else back to delay him, but he saw Ruth looking over her shoulder frequently. She seemed surprised at his perseverance, and she didn't give the impression that she surprised easily. Dorian grinned at the thought.

Long minutes passed and still his chase continued. They had turned off of the road near the forest, a mile or so from Lancaster, and now they were following a small trail. They had probably planned the route in advance to help avoid any patrols or pursuit, but they hadn't counted on Dorian. The smaller trail with its tendency to wander and the occasional low limb forced the riders to slow even more and now Dorian was gaining rapidly. He was now within ten yards of the last horse, an unused palfrey following the rearmost armsman's mount. The man had wrapped its reins loosely around the front of his saddle, keeping his hands free while he nervously watched Dorian closing on them.

The rider's face was a study in fear as he watched Dorian draw close, 'til he was almost able to touch the free horse the man was leading. Drawing his sword in one economical motion Dorian neatly severed the left rear leg of the horse several feet from the ground. Screaming in pain the animal fell and began tumbling; its cries of pain combined with the jerking of the lead rope connecting it to the horse ahead of it created instant pandemonium. In seconds the trail was littered with the bodies of both horses along with the unfortunate rider.

Dorian ignored the carnage and ran on, though he was forced to leap over one of the horses as it fell. He regretted killing the horses, but at the time he had only one thought on his mind… the two people he was charged with protecting.

Ruth rode in the lead, with Penny in front of her and looking backward she gauged Dorian's distance carefully. The look on her face worried him for a moment for it had changed. It was no longer the face of someone desperate to escape but rather the face of someone planning their next move. Drawing her sword she cut the lead line that tethered Miriam's mount to hers, leaving the unguided horse to drift away. Then she faced forward again and leaned to the left, stretching out her sword arm, as if she meant to cut down an invisible foe.

Her action puzzled Dorian until he saw the rope, which she gracefully cut in two as she rode past, and then he felt the rumble in the ground. It was one of the oldest and simplest traps, a deadfall of cut logs piled and braced up and to the left of the trail. Once the rope was cut the supports keeping the timbers in place fell away and the logs began rolling sideways across the trail, sweeping horses and men away, like some wooden tide. The only one that escaped the trap was Ruth… along with Penny naturally.

The horse bearing Miriam's body went down as its legs were swept sideways by the first of the rolling timbers. Luckily her 'mount' had been slowing down already and Dorian was nearly beside it when the cascade of logs arrived. Leaping forward he caught her as her body tumbled from its back and without knowing what else to do he dropped to the ground and tried to shield her body with his own. Chance as much as good reflexes allowed him to get her onto the ground so he could cover her body with his own before the rest of the wooden avalanche arrived.

The cut logs averaged more than a foot in diameter and they thundered and bounced across the trail, sometimes bouncing over him and occasionally glancing off of his shoulders and back. The impacts came with tremendous force and Dorian was driven hard into the ground, until he feared he might crush Miriam with his own body. Then the logs stopped coming and silence rose up suddenly in the aftermath.

Examining himself he saw that his arms had been driven into the ground past his elbows, and one knee had gouged a deep divot into the earth. Yet somehow both he and Miriam were still whole, though he still was unsure if she was alive or if he had wasted his time protecting a corpse. Everyone else, both the remaining riders and their horses were strewn, broken and mangled across the trail. It was very apparent that they were dead, though one horse was still whinnying pitifully as it died.

Pushing carefully away from the earth Dorian pulled himself free and shook the dirt loose before picking up Miriam's still body. He carried her to the verge of the trail and laid her gently among the ferns, away from the area the logs had torn up. As he did he noticed blood seeping down his armor, staining both of his gauntleted hands where they touched her. Somewhere within the seemingly invincible plate he wore he was bleeding... probably in several places, though he couldn't see any place where the armor had been breached or compromised.

One rider had escaped, Ruth, and with her she carried Penny. The two of them were no longer in sight but Dorian could hear the sound of the horse bearing them away. Standing upright he began walking, following the direction they had gone down the trail. His body had become a throbbing mass of pain and now that he had stopped running Dorian wondered how he had managed to do it for so long. Exhaustion and weariness had taken on entirely new levels of meaning for him.

"Faster… I have to move faster," he told himself, urging his legs to move more quickly. Each step was agony but his legs did seem to be responding, though he couldn't seem to manage to get past a fast walk. This went on for several minutes, while the sound of Ruth's horse got further and further distant. Eventually he could no longer hear it at all, yet he continued to walk.

After an indeterminate time, in which the only sounds to be heard were those of his labored breathing and the noise made by his armor as he walked, he heard something new. It was the cry of a horse in pain followed by a heavy thumping sound, as if something heavy had struck the soft earth. This was followed by the sound of Penny swearing, until her voice was cut short. Silence followed.

Without realizing it Dorian had begun to run again. Energy he knew he did not possess was flowing into him and his battered body responded by running faster. Droplets of blood flew from his hands as his arms and legs churned with increasing speed. He raced forward and his pain receded into the back of his mind.

"Cut me loose!" he heard Penny shout. "I can help. At least let me defend myself!"

He knew he was close now and then he saw the forms of people ahead of him on the trail, a lot of people. They were heading along the path in the same direction he was, so most of their backs were to him. As he approached some of them turned and their emotionless stares brought the truth to his mind. *Shiggreth!*

Memories of that night over a year past, when he had fought a mob of them outside of Washbrook, came flooding into his head. Everything about them seemed familiar, from the strange unnatural movements to the expressionless faces. He drew his sword in a fluid motion and without slowing he drove through them, cutting aside anything that blocked his path.

The throng of shiggreth seemed endless until suddenly he broke through and found himself standing in a small clearing in the forest. Penny and Ruth stood in the center of it, next to a crippled horse. At a glance it appeared the poor beast had stepped into a shallow concealed trench, breaking both of its forelegs. Beyond the two women were more of the undead, and looking to the sides he could see them there as well… they were completely surrounded.

This is bad, really, really bad, he thought to himself. He reached the two women in seconds and wordlessly the three of them formed a triangle, each of them facing outward. Ruth had already cut Penny's bonds and given her a sword to use. Apparently she knew enough about the shiggreth to realize their personal issues were no longer the priority.

Dorian estimated their enemy numbered at least a couple of hundred strong, which wasn't encouraging. "I get the feeling this wasn't part of your plan," he said loudly over his shoulder.

"No," Ruth answered, "it appears to be a deliberate ambush, though."

"They've never shown signs of being able to plan ahead like this before," Penny interjected.

"According to the histories they were just as intelligent as men," Ruth replied. "At least that's what my teacher said," she added.

"Who was your teacher?" Penny asked.

"Cyhan," was Ruth's reply.

"That explains a few things," muttered Dorian, but he had barely finished speaking before the shiggreth closed in on them. None of them had time to talk after that.

The battle, if it could be called such, was short and bitter. In the open, surrounded by foes and with plenty of room, Dorian wished he had the great sword he had talked to Mort about. It would have been the perfect situation for such a weapon. Instead he made do with his long sword, though he had no shield or dagger to complement it.

Of the three of them he was the only one protected from their foes weakening touch. Despite their best efforts Penny and Ruth were overcome almost immediately. He saw them dragging Ruth away while she struggled uselessly, her sword cutting flesh that could not feel its bite. Penny grew faint after being touched several times and collapsed to the ground. She might have been drawn away as well, but for the fact that he stood over her, cutting away arms and legs as they reached for her.

Standing alone he fought for an unknown time. It certainly seemed like an eternity. Despite their numbers they could not drag him down, as they once had, though they mobbed him in droves. Hands gripped his arms and legs yet he moved anyway, dragging them along as he hewed their fellows into pieces. Cutting and cursing he fought under the weight of their numbers until at the last he felt Penny dragged from beneath him as his own legs were lifted up.

He fought on, though he knew he had already failed. She was dead and his best friend's child with her. Tears appeared in his eyes and he wept with sorrow and rage even as the mob bore him up. The sun and sky seemed to mock his tragedy as the countless numbers of his foes tried to strip the armor from his limbs. His struggle went on hopelessly and it was a long time before the trees were cloaked in silence again.

CHAPTER 19

It took me several jumps to get my entire entourage to my house in Albamarl. I took Sir Harold and my honor guard first before bringing Lady Rose on the final trip. Including Harold I had ten men with me, all of them armed and well acquainted with battle. Unlike most of the nobility in Albamarl I had a large number of veteran warriors now, men who had already faced death once and were ready to do so again.

Dorian and Harold had spent an excessive amount of time worrying over which men to send with me and I had no doubts that some of them were being considered for eventual induction into the Knights of Stone.

Marc took a long look at Sir Harold, resplendent in his enchanted plate, and the other armed and armored men that had come with me. "You've decided to invade the capital?" he asked.

I laughed. "Not yet, I think the king can be trusted to hold to his end of the agreement."

"Ten men won't be enough if he doesn't, not even with that one," he replied, pointing to Harold. "Where did you get that armor?"

"I'll explain that later, for now suffice to say that Sir Harold here is much more of a threat than he appears," I said.

"Glad to make your acquaintance my lord," Harold said politely with a small bow in Marcus' direction.

Marc gave him his full attention, "I'm not a lord anymore. I surrendered those rights already. Still I am happy to have met you as well, though we were not properly introduced." He gave me a pointed stare as he said that last part. "If you're going to start knighting people you need to learn better etiquette Mort," he added for my benefit.

"Actually, since you 'surrendered your rights' as you put it, he isn't required to introduce anyone to you," Rose informed him with a wicked smile.

Marc winced visibly, "Ouch Rose! I see you haven't lost your sharp wit." He waved us all down the corridor toward the stairs leading to the first floor. "Would you like some wine? I took the trouble of restocking Mort's cellar while I've been here."

I gave him a sharp glance.

"Don't worry I haven't been over doing it. Our promise still stands," he reassured me quietly.

Several minutes later we were all seated in the front parlor on the ground floor, sipping at our wine. I tried to have the honor guard join us but Harold explained that would only make them more uncomfortable. Instead he set them the task of figuring out their sleeping arrangements in the guest bedrooms.

"We've had a lot of excitement here since you left," Marc began.

"It's only been two weeks, I wouldn't think a shut in would see much in that period of time," I commented with a grin.

He gave me a somber look, "It wasn't necessarily good excitement if you take my meaning."

"How about we stop talking and you fill us in," I answered.

Lady Rose snorted with suppressed laughter at that but she held her tongue and we let Marc give us the news. "The Baron of Arundel has been executed," Marc said bluntly. I gaped but Rose leaned over and put her hand over my mouth before I could speak. I unconsciously noted that she smelled pleasantly of lavender.

Marc continued, "Two weeks ago, immediately after you met with the king, he announced that the Baron had entered the royal palace and attempted to assassinate him during a personal meeting. Apparently this was Baron Arundel's reaction to being notified that he would be stripped of his lands for his cowardly behavior during the recent war with Gododdin."

"That's bullshit!" I exclaimed.

Rose looked at me crossly, "Would you just let him finish?"

I closed my mouth and Marc looked back and forth between us a few times, trying not to smile. Finally he went on, "He was apprehended red handed inside the palace. According to his majesty he slew four priests, one of each of the various churches, before then attempting to take the king's life. Several guards stopped him and by their accounts the blood and violence in and near the king's chambers was something remarkable to behold. I'm sure you wouldn't know anything about that would you Mordecai?"

"You know damn well what happened in there, I told you myself," I said.

Rose broke in, "Don't goad him Marcus. What else happened?"

"Poor Sheldon was taken into custody, clapped in irons and the next day he was marched to the gallows. He was kept bound and gagged and was hanged without preamble, pretext, or even being allowed last words," he said smugly. "Couldn't have happened to a nicer fellow if you ask me."

Sheldon was the baron's first name as I recalled from our brief and unpleasant meetings half a year ago.

"But he was a lord!" I protested. "Isn't there some sort of rule about executing nobility?" I didn't bother bringing up the matter of his actual innocence. I had been in the circles of the powerful long enough to know that guilt or innocence were tools of convenience for those in control.

"The king retains the right of high justice," Rose informed us. High justice, in case you were wondering was what the courts called cases involving the death penalty. She continued, "In a case involving treason or a direct assault upon his person he is well within his right to bypass the Lord High Justicer and pass sentence directly upon the offender without trial."

In a moment of exceptional wisdom I closed my mouth and tried to think things through. Obviously Sheldon had been innocent of the charge, but that was irrelevant. What really mattered was *why* the king had chosen to execute him after our conversation.

Marc spoke first, "You were a real inconvenience to his majesty, but after your meeting with him your circumstances changed. Now, assuming he can capitalize upon your heroic efforts in the war, you could be a great asset to him."

"Which would tend to make Lord Arundel's position a complete reversal of that," Rose added.

Marc nodded, "On top of that, Edward had a rather large mess that needed an explanation…"

"And he decided to kill two birds with one stone," she finished for him. "Though it might be better to say he killed one bird to take care of two problems." The two of them were nodding and smiling smugly at each other, seemingly satisfied with their mutual cleverness.

I put up a hand as though I were in class, trying to get the tutor's attention. Neither of them noticed. "What is truly amazing," said Marc "is how quickly he came to a decision after Mort left."

"Excuse me…" I said.

They both ignored me as Rose spoke again, "He's been the monarch for a long time, but it really is frightening how quickly he came to such an effective choice. Most men would have blundered or hesitated."

"Hey!" I said loudly, waving a hand between the two of them. They paused to grace me with curious looks. "Would either of you political masterminds care to explain this to me in terms an ex-commoner can understand?"

"I've never thought of you as a commoner," Marc objected.

Rose pursed her lips thoughtfully. "Well he is a little common you have to admit Marcus."

Marc chuckled, "True, but I'd never have said it."

"You just did!" I complained. "Besides, the last time I checked being a commoner was nothing to be ashamed of, and after meeting Sheldon, being a noble certainly isn't always something to brag about."

Rose patted my shoulder, "Don't act so wounded, we were just teasing. After all, you still hold the highest station here, and Marcus is the commoner these days."

Marc winced visibly at the reminder. "What her ladyship is trying to tell you is that the king decided to simplify his situation after making peace with you," he said, returning the conversation back to its intended course. "Returning you to the fold and rewarding you for defeating Gododdin makes you a hero and would have put Sheldon in a very awkward position. At the very least it would have created division and in-fighting amongst the nobility. Many of the other lords would have felt a lot of sympathy for Arundel after the way you abused him."

"He abandoned his own people," I reminded him.

"I understand that, but what you have to understand is that for many of the lords that is a small matter beside humiliating the man, abusing him in front of his servants, taking his possessions, and then sending him packing with nothing but the clothes on his back. Especially since the man that did all that was seen as a 'commoner' as you just mentioned," Marc explained.

"And executing him will make them feel better about me?" I asked sarcastically.

Rose spoke up, "Not exactly. What it does is send an immediate message that the king is very serious about rewarding you. It eliminates your most prominent enemies at the outset and also neatly clears up the matter of several violent deaths that occurred within the royal palace. That will give pause to anyone that might think to create trouble, for they will know quite clearly which side of the matter the king is on."

It all sounded very neat and precise but I didn't like it. As usual human lives were being treated with little more concern than a player has for his chess pieces. "That's wonderful for me then isn't it?" I announced with a bitter tone.

"For the most part," Marc replied.

"And what happens when I become 'inconvenient' one fine day?" I asked pointedly.

"That's a possibility that all men of station have to consider. In general there are two practical strategies for dealing with it," he said.

He paused and I gave him a flat stare, I didn't feel like playing twenty questions. Eventually he decided to continue despite my lack of prompting.

"The first," he said sourly, "is making damn sure you don't become 'inconvenient', as you put it." He paused again, but I merely stared at him some more.

Rose winked at me. "What is the second Marcus?" she asked gaily.

"Thank you Rose," he told her. "The second is making sure you always use a taster before you eat, keeping a lot of men like Sir Harold there around, and always wearing a chain shirt."

I raised an eyebrow, "I don't recall you ever doing any of that."

"I was never important enough," he said bluntly. "You, on the other hand, have more attention focused on you than even the king does at the moment. It pays to be ready for the worst."

"You'll be glad to know that you and Dorian are in complete agreement," I said dryly.

"You can add me to that list," said Harold, speaking for the first time.

"How would you like to be my new food taster?" I shot back, but I smiled to let him know I wasn't serious.

CHAPTER 20

I was sitting in the same private reception chamber I had met King Edward in for the first time, back when James and I had been slightly inebriated. On this occasion I was entirely sober and prepared for the worst. Harold and one of my other men at arms were waiting outside, beside the king's own armsmen. Weapons weren't permitted in the presence of his royal majesty, except in the case of high ranking nobility, though I had declined to wear a weapon myself, partly because it was considered respectful and partly because I really didn't need one.

I had sent a messenger to the palace the day before, after my arrival, to notify his majesty of my presence in the capital. He had sent my man back with a summons to meet him this morning, to discuss the plans for my award and recognition ceremony. Consequently I now found myself facing him across a small table, watching him sip carefully at a cup of hot tea.

"You haven't touched your tea," he said mildly, looking at my own cup.

"Pardon me your majesty, my stomach has been very delicate this morning," I replied before raising my cup to my lips. Rose had assured me that it was highly unlikely Edward would try to poison me at this point, especially under these circumstances, but I still couldn't bring myself to drink. I tilted the cup as if I was sipping but I never opened my mouth. In fact, I even kept a thin shield between my lips and the liquid, lest some contact poison were present. Was I paranoid? Perhaps, but I was beyond caring.

King Edward watched me without concern, though something told me he was well aware of my deception. He smiled before speaking again, "We are pleased that you returned so quickly."

"I prefer to waste as little time as possible your majesty, especially when it is your time," I answered carefully.

"Now that you're here, we would like to hold the ceremony in two days. That should be enough time for most of the local nobility to arrange their affairs so they can be present. Ideally we should like as many of them to see it as possible," he said.

I would have preferred to get it over with immediately so I could return home sooner, but I had expected this. "I am not very fond of public honors and accolades, is it really necessary to have such a display your majesty?"

"You possess a keen intellect along with your many other talents Mordecai, but questions such as that one serve to remind me that you were not raised among the nobility," he replied. I started to answer but he held up a hand before continuing, "Public ceremonies and displays are as much a part of ruling as councils and private meetings. In some ways they are more important, for they cement a ruler's place in the forefront of his subject's minds. They also serve to reinforce the nobility's memory of their own standing in relation to the king and to the one being honored. Never doubt the importance of such occasions."

I found Edward's lecture condescending and it re-ignited my anger of the previous day. "Was Arundel's execution also a reminder?" I asked. My tone was even but my eyes held a dangerous light.

His face took on an amused expression, "One would think that you would be more pleased at the news. We were given to understand that there was no love lost between you and the late baron."

I fixed him with a direct stare before I spoke, "I dislike seeing people used as pawns, to be played or discarded for matters of convenience."

Edward's countenance grew red and his brows drew together as he heard my words. "When you have seen as many winters as I have, buried as many friends and allies as I have, been betrayed and manipulated as I have, then you may judge me. When you have grown old and jaded from long years wielding power, then you may debate my relative worth on the scale of good and evil, until then you can keep your damned opinions to yourself!"

I couldn't help but notice the king had dropped the royal 'we' during his tirade and somehow it made me feel as if I had won a small victory. My own anger dissipated somewhat allowing me to think more clearly. "You assume I will live to such an age your Majesty. Considering my position, there isn't much chance of me reaching a ripe old age." Our eyes locked as I spoke and I was certain he could see my resolve, as well as my honesty.

His own anger flickered out as he gazed at me, to be replaced by a sardonic expression. "Don't count on it Mordecai, I once said the same thing, yet I am here still, long past my prime."

I gave him a grim smile. "Should I be so lucky as to live long enough to judge you I doubt you will still be alive to hear my explanation of your faults," I said.

"Arrogant bastard!" he exclaimed. "If you do live that long you will have become just as dark and jaded as I am, and wishing you could find my shade that you might apologize for your impertinence." We glared at each other for a tense moment before we both began to chuckle. It was a dark laughter, born of anger and tension, but it defused the dangerous emotions that lay between us… at least temporarily.

Shortly after that I excused myself. I don't think either of us really wanted to continue making small talk. Neither of us liked the other, but as long as we could manage a working relationship that was all that mattered.

⌖

Later that same day I took the opportunity to do some research in the library. I was hoping to find another book about illusions, or possibly some explanation for how someone could hide from my magesight. The memory of the stranger in Cameron Castle still bothered me. However such a thing was accomplished it should be something the wizards of old would have known about.

I spent a fruitless span of hours looking for the information I wanted before I stumbled across something unexpected. I was replacing books that I had taken down earlier to peruse, when I noticed something odd about the wall behind the bookshelf. The pattern of runes there was different.

Every stone that formed the house was enchanted, which meant that spotting something simply by virtue of the presence of a magical aura was useless. In this case however I could discern a very different pattern to the runes woven into these particular stones. There seemed to be five specific points within the pattern that were unconnected, but I wasn't sure why.

I studied it for a long time before I decided to do something foolish. I knew Penny wouldn't have approved, but since she wasn't there to give advice I figured I'd have to do the best I could. And my best was telling me that the five points were meant to be connected by using the fingertips of my left hand. I really couldn't be sure what would happen then. Surely it wouldn't be anything bad… right?

I started laughing softly to myself. "It takes a special sort of fool sometimes," I said to no one in particular. Then I reached out and carefully placed my fingertips on the appropriate spots. The pattern around the five touch points began to glow visibly, rather than just in my magesight, and I could feel a tingling in my palm. For a second nothing else happened and I discovered I was holding my breath, I let it out with an audible sigh. Then I removed my hand and stepped back.

The glowing faded quickly and I thought I must have done something wrong when I heard a click and the wall began moving silently aside, taking the bookcase with it. Seconds later I found myself staring into a small but brightly lit room, one that had been hidden within the library despite all my previous searches. "Well I'll be damned," I said to myself.

I stepped inside and the wall closed silently behind me. That worried me a little, but I hoped that getting out would be as easy as entering had been, otherwise I was in for some fun later.

The room I was standing in wasn't large, being only around six foot by six on each side. It was brightly lit by enchanted lamps that weren't too dissimilar to the ones I had created for my workshop at home, though I could tell at a glance that the patterns were slightly different from mine.

A long low bench was built against the far wall, and it held an assortment of small tools, hammers and chisels primarily, things that would be useful shaping small pieces of jewelry, or perhaps wood, if one was into carving. None were magical in the slightest, except for one small silver implement. I drew closer to examine it.

It was perhaps the size of a small quill pen, if most of the feather had been removed. At a guess it was about six or seven inches in length and less than a quarter inch in diameter. One end was blunt and the other end tapered gracefully to a fine point. The entire thing looked to be fashioned of pure silver, though it hadn't tarnished in the slightest. It was also completely covered with tiny and intricate runes, from one end to the other.

At first I was completely mystified regarding its function, until I realized the pattern of runes was familiar, though they were much smaller than the ones I had seen before. They were nearly identical to the runes that formed the main shaft of my staff. The tiny silver implement was a rune channel, created to facilitate the focusing and fine control of power. Its size still puzzled me, though.

My staff was large, and rightly so, I could use it to channel a blast of energy over much greater distances, or use it to focus my power into a razor sharp beam, for cutting through an enemy's shields. Creating a rune channel this size made little sense. I picked it up and held it carefully in my hand, as I would a pen or brush. As I considered its function I moved it idly over the surface of the bench and channeled a tiny bit of power through it. It left beautifully graceful lines of energy across the wood, much finer and more delicate than any I had ever managed using my fingers alone; and as simply as that I understood its function.

It was a stylus of sorts. At least that was the only name I could think of to call it. Historically ancient man had used similar metal implements to incise letters on clay or wax tablets, back before paper had come into wide use. This was similar to that, except it was used to create magical runes, quickly, easily and more precisely than could be done using bare hands. Having seen it I could hardly believe I had never thought to make one for myself before now. It was such a plainly useful thing I felt like kicking myself for not having done so already. *Think of the time I could have saved!* I thought to myself.

I tucked it into my belt pouch. I could create one myself if need be, but I didn't see any reason not to take the one I had already found. Then I returned my attention to the room around me. Aside from the stylus, the only remaining objects of possible interest were a small silver bound book and an intricately carved wooden box. The box caught my eye first, for the artistry that went into its carving took my breath away.

I opened it carefully and found myself puzzled by the contents. The interior was lined with soft fabric, now dry and brittle with age. Nestled within that fabric were a number of plain gold rings. Each was identical and scribed with delicate runes set in a very particular pattern. It looked like an enchantment but there was very little residual magic contained within them.

Worked into the pattern were Lycian letters, spelling out one word on the exterior, 'Illeniel'. I turned one of the rings over carefully in my hands and spotted more writing on the inside of the band, again in Lycian. The words were tiny but they appeared to read 'trusted guest'. *That's an odd phrase to put in a gold ring,* I thought.

I counted the rings and found there were twenty one within the box, though it appeared there might have been more originally. I pondered them for a good while before I set them aside for another day. I had a feeling their purpose would become clear to me later... probably while

I was sleeping or bathing. I always did my best thinking when I was relaxed.

Finally I turned my attention to the book. I had been restraining myself thus far, since it was what I desired to look at first. I had saved it for last since I knew it might well take me a long time to make up my mind about its value.

It was a very compact item, no more than six inches in width and only slightly taller. Even though it was bound in silver it wasn't more than half an inch in thickness and would easily fit into a shirt pocket or pouch. The metal exterior was covered in runes, but unlike the others I had no idea what their purpose was. The arrangements were unlike anything I had ever considered which made it hard to guess whether it was safe to open or not.

"I could stare at those patterns for a year and probably not understand what they're supposed to do," I said out loud, as if giving voice to my thoughts would make them more reasonable. "Sooner or later I'll have to take a chance, and one thing I rarely have the luxury of is time." Having said that, I felt sure it was true. *It's still stupid to open something like that without at least having witnesses in case something bad happens*, said a small voice in the back of my head. I quickly hustled that voice down to the basement of my mind and had it locked away where it wouldn't bother me anymore.

"No time like the present," I said, and then I undid the metal clasp that held the book closed and flipped the cover open. As I did the runes around the edge of the metal began to writhe and move, as if they were alive, something I had never seen runes do before. A golden light suffused the metal and it felt as though the book itself jumped in my hand, in fact it startled me so much that I nearly dropped it. Gritting my teeth to steady my nerves I watched as the book expanded to slightly more than twice its original size. Once it had finished growing the runes grew still and the book resumed its more usual dormant state. I let out a long held sigh, grateful there hadn't been some sort of trap.

I looked at the title page and felt my heart jump with excitement when I read the words there. *'Index of Enchanting Schemata'* was the name of the book. As I stared at it I remembered Moira's words, *"The Illeniels were well known for the many mage-smiths and skilled enchanters they produced throughout history."* This was the first sign of that. Nothing else I had found in the library had so much as hinted at the secrets of enchanting, much less providing full-fledged schemata. I had despaired of ever finding any guidance in the lost art I had somehow re-invented.

I began thumbing through the pages idly, wondering what I might find. One page was titled, 'Schemata for trans-spatial storage apparatus'. The designs seemed strange but I recognized some similarities with teleportation circles, though the resemblance didn't go very far. Another page held a diagram for something called a 'self-locking door', and yet another contained the schemata for a 'stasis field effect', whatever that was.

A cursory examination told me that the book held very little in the way of instruction or explanation. Whoever had owned this book previously had obviously made it to be portable and durable, and he or she hadn't needed much in the way of explanation. This was a book for someone already well-practiced in the art of enchanting, for what it contained were formulae and fully functional diagrams of enchantments.

Still I would rather have a book of functional designs rather than a primer with no real world applications. I had already discovered the basics on my own anyway, or most of them I hoped. I felt certain that using these I could work backward to figure out how they worked. Many of the designs I found were similar to ones I had already created. I gave myself a mental pat on the back, *not bad for a beginner,* I thought.

Eventually I decided I should go back outside before anyone started looking for me. Closing the book I watched as it quickly shrank back down to its previous size. It really was an amazing effect, though I still didn't understand how it worked. Looking around I tried to discern the mechanism for re-opening the door.

Thankfully it was just as simple as entering. The wall behind me held a similar pattern to the one I had activated on the other side. I reached up to touch it but a stray thought made me pause. Given that I was in a secret room it seemed obvious I should make sure no one was outside before I opened the door again. Normally I would simply use my arcane senses to check whether anyone was nearby, and I did try, but I failed.

In most cases failure isn't that unusual, but this time was an exception. I was unable to sense anything beyond the small room I stood within. It was as though I had entered a small bubble of reality, encapsulated by an endless void. Now that I was paying attention the sensation was shocking.

It reminded me somewhat of my first experience with the shiggreth, when I discovered I was completely unable to sense their physical presence, except as an absence. This was similar, except now the effect had extended to the entire world; the only thing I could perceive was the tiny room I was inside. My heart rate sped up as an involuntary moment of panic sent adrenaline coursing through my veins. I got my fear under control quickly. I had never been one to let fear trump reason.

Taking a slow steady breath I put my hand out to the pattern, where my fingertips should activate the enchantment that controlled the door. As my fingers touched it I felt the same tingle I had felt before and then I became aware of the world beyond the room I was in again. The door didn't open, for I hadn't withdrawn my hand yet, but the connection between me and the enchantment had restored my ability to sense the world outside.

Interesting, I thought to myself. *The enchantment must make the room itself invisible to magesight, and conversely it makes it impossible to sense the world outside when you're within it.* It was a cunning piece of work and I found myself admiring the cleverness of whoever had originally designed it. Not only was the room undetectable from the outside, but whoever was inside could see to tell if anyone was outside before opening the door, although that would probably make them visible to magesight.

"Can't have everything I guess," I said to myself and then I took my hand away from the enchantment. Seconds later the door opened and I stepped out into the main library. The door closed behind me and once it was shut I could no longer sense anything of the room I had just been inside. *That really is a clever piece of work,* I thought. I hoped the pattern would be among the other schemata I had inside the book I now held. Not that it mattered… I could copy it from the walls themselves if need be. I felt sure it might be useful to me someday.

I turned and made my way to the door. I could sense Marc on his way up the stairs and something about his stride told me he had something important to discuss.

CHAPTER 21

Imet Marc just outside the library, pretending to some surprise at finding him there. I did things like that often, pretending to be surprised when I met people, mostly to put them at ease. I had come to the conclusion early on that it only upset people when they knew I was aware of their every movement when they were near me. No one likes to feel as if they are continually being watched. It wasn't as if I really watched people constantly, usually it was more like the background noise in a busy room. You hear the voices but you don't know what they're saying until you pay attention to one or another of them. My magesight was similar, I could focus upon an individual and see as much as I liked, up to about a mile away, but in practice I couldn't possibly watch everyone. It would have driven me insane.

If they knew how much I could see I doubt anyone would have been comfortable living within Castle Cameron. In reality though, people's lives are… for the most part, incredibly boring. Still I pretended to be as normal as possible, to avoid making everyone uncomfortable.

"Don't act surprised to see me," Marc said, as if he could read my thoughts.

I frowned, "What do you mean?"

"You always overdo your acting. Since it's just me you don't have to bother. I know you can see me from one end of the house to the other, so you don't have to pretend to be surprised when I find you."

I couldn't fault his logic. *Bastard knows me too well,* I thought with a grin. "You're too sharp for your own good. I hope you realize that?" I said.

He struck a pose of intense concentration, putting one hand on his chin and the other on his hip, "The thought had occurred to me," he said smugly. "I try not to flaunt my gifts too much though; it might make others feel inadequate."

I laughed. "Are you going to tell me what you found or spend all day congratulating yourself?" I asked.

He pretended to ponder my words seriously for a moment. "That's a tough one," he said at last, "but the real question is how do you know I found something?"

"Magic," I answered immediately, "that and the fact you have a book tucked under your arm and you were looking for me with a certain air of urgency."

He looked down at the book he held. "I guess you have me on that one." He walked past me, into the library I had just left. "Here let me show you," he said sitting down at the closest reading table. I followed him and sat down in a nearby chair. "I took a stack of promising books to my room last night, to look through before I fell asleep. I found this tucked inside one of them." He pulled out a neatly folded sheet of paper, yellow from age.

"Which book was it in?" I asked.

He held up the book he had been carrying, *'An Illuminated Guide to the Birds of Lothion'*, read the title.

"Why would you have even taken that one to search through?" I said curiously.

Marc smirked sheepishly. "Sometimes I get tired looking through so many serious tomes. This one has a lot of really lovely illustrations, all carefully hand painted. I was looking through it purely for enjoyment." He shrugged helplessly.

I shook my head. Even though we'd been friends for nearly twenty years now I had never known he was interested in birds. Perhaps I wasn't as observant as I thought. I opened the paper carefully, for it was brittle. Once it was unfolded I could see it was a letter, and the handwriting was familiar to me.

My Dear Friend,

I cannot say much here, for I fear this letter may never reach you. I must assume you received my last letter for I have not gotten a reply yet but that is not unusual these days. They watch my correspondences carefully, of that I am sure. Quite possibly they have stolen your replies to keep me from seeing them.

Vendraccus moves more freely now and I suspect he will attempt to unseat me soon. There are none left now that I can trust. I hate to sound morbid, but this may be my last letter. A source close to Vendraccus has given me information that I think may be of importance to you, though I do not understand its meaning. I cannot even be sure if it is the truth; my own spies are untrustworthy and may be feeding me misinformation.

I have been told that Vendraccus has been charged by his god to find something known as 'Illeniel's Doom'. My informant was unsure what 'it' might actually be, but he said that by the conversation he overheard it sounded like something living, such as a person or creature.

Whether this helps you or not, I do not know, but I assumed that the name would have some meaning to you.

Good luck. I cannot tell you how much your friendship has meant to me over the years, especially now that I find myself alone, surrounded by strangers.

Sincerely,

V.

I had seen a letter similar to this one previously; in my father's writing desk the first time I had explored the house. I was also sure it had been signed much the same way, with a simple initial. At the time I had been unsure who had sent the letter to him, but given the content of this one I was starting to believe it really had been Valerius, the last king of Gododdin. I had no idea how he had become friends with the man, but then my father's life was still mostly a mystery to me.

I looked at Marc, "You know what this means?"

He shook his head negatively.

"Me either," I admitted. "Although it really does seem that my father had some sort of on-going friendship with the king of Gododdin."

Marc let out a deep sigh. "I had really hoped you might be able to make something of that."

"It isn't your fault," I said. "So far my only sources of information about this thing have been from the gods themselves, and we know how reliable they are."

My friend looked sharply at me as I spoke. "You're absolutely right."

I grinned, "I'll need you to write that down and sign it for me. I can use it the next time you're being stubborn."

He shook his head again, "No, I really mean it. All the information you have about this 'Doom' comes from the gods, first from Celior, and now indirectly from Mal'goroth. I should be looking through the church archives, not this library."

"I don't think your search here is entirely a waste," I told him. "After all this is the only known library of the Illeniel family, so it seems an obvious choice to search."

"True," he agreed, "and I have learned a lot of interesting tidbits while I was looking here. We'll have to sit down for a week or two sometime. You would be surprised at some of the general information about wizardry, the gods, and even people like Dorian that can be found here."

"Dorian?"

"Yes," he said smugly. "Dorian is, as far as I can tell, what your ancestors called a 'stoic'." He folded his arms in front of him, waiting for me to ask the inevitable questions.

I waved a hand nonchalantly at him, "Oh yes, I knew that. I learned about them in Vestrius' journal, but I would like to see what books you found the information in… I'm sure there's a lot more I need to know." I knew my phrasing would irritate him, but then, that's what friends are for… right?

"Sometimes you really are a wet blanket. You know that?" he said with resignation. "You could at least pretend to be excited, just to make your friend feel better."

I winked at him, "A friend told me recently that I 'overdo' my acting and I should just be honest. It seemed like good advice."

Marc grimaced in mock pain, as if my joke had wounded his delicate sense of humor. Rose appeared in the doorway before he could prepare a good come back, though. "From the look of things I doubt you gentlemen are up to anything good," she said.

Marc held up his hands, "For once I am innocent of all wrongdoing, though I cannot be so sure of our friend the incipient thespian here," he said pointing at me.

An arched eyebrow was all the response he got. Rose ignored our banter and asked a question instead, "I need to visit my father, would either of you gentlemen care to escort me?"

I knew for a fact she wasn't afraid to walk the streets of Albamarl by herself. After all the last time we had been here together she had crossed half the city at night, alone. She was simply being polite, and perhaps offering us a chance to stretch our legs. She could have just taken one of my guards with her if all she wanted was an escort.

I glanced at Marc and found him watching me. We knew each other well enough that it only took a glance for us to communicate volumes. I was planning to volunteer if he didn't feel like going out, but he wanted to go. I waited and Marc answered her, "I'll come with you Rose. I was hoping to stretch my legs in town today and I couldn't think of anyone who would be better company."

"Thank you for the offer Rose, but I'll let you two go without me. I have some things I'd like to take care of," I said, chiming in.

"More research?" she asked.

"Essentially," I replied. "I found some interesting information in the library and I'd like to test some ideas."

"Experiment, that's what he really means," said Marc said with a chuckle, "It's probably safer if we leave anyway Rose."

"I wasn't planning to try anything dangerous," I said without humor.

"Sure, sure… I believe you," he replied, "but I made a promise to Mother after all, and I can't go back on that."

I stared at him quizzically, "You made a promise to Genevieve?"

He gazed at the ceiling innocently, "Yes, she said that she had to shout at you once over tea… when she had come to visit. Apparently you had nearly blown yourself to bits during some experiment and you were half deaf as a result. I had to promise her that I wouldn't go near you if you were doing any future experiments. She was very worried…"

I knew for a fact she would never have forced him to make such a promise. Well, I was pretty sure anyway. The more I thought about it the less sure I became… he was her son after all.

Rose started laughing and then exclaimed, "Oh that's nothing! You should have seen him the day he first tried to get into this house! He nearly fried himself and his hair was standing on end for hours afterward."

The conversation was rapidly devolving into one long joke at my expense. "I'd have thought you two had already told each other these stories," I put in.

Rose smiled at me, "We all have other things to talk about you do realize? We don't just sit around talking about you all the time."

"Well no, I didn't think that," I said caught off guard. My legendary wit had abandoned me, so I settled for escorting them to the doorway.

Rose gracefully took Marc's arm and the two of them left the library. They kept talking as they went, having stumbled upon a juicy subject. As they went down the stairs I could still hear them. Marc was telling another story, "You should have seen the day he tried to tell Penny he was a wizard. He nearly convinced her he was working with the powers of darkness and when I saw her bolt from his room I thought he had tried to assault her…"

It was several minutes before I turned my attention back to the silver-bound book I carried. I had the rest of the day to myself now and I didn't intend to waste it. Drawing out the silver stylus I started thumbing through the book, considering what I should try first.

CHAPTER 22

The sun was shining down like the wrath of a vengeful god, causing me to squint. While some people love sunny days I found them to be intrusive. The bards sing of cloudless skies and bright sun, but I honestly preferred a few clouds and a bit of shade. Not that I minded the sunshine, it was a welcome respite from the past winter… it was just that sometimes it was too much. Especially with hundreds, perhaps even thousands of people staring at me.

That many eyes watching made me understandably nervous, and with the glare from the sun overhead I couldn't see their faces clearly. Of course I could have closed my eyes and simply relied on my magesight, but sometimes there's just no substitute for seeing something with your own eyes, a mob of strangers staring at me being at the top of that list.

"…and while the Baron of Arundel abandoned his people to the unkind mercies of the enemy, *this man*, stayed to defend them!" King Edward's voice rose to a crescendo while his arms waved to highlight me standing beside him. "This man stayed, to protect his people, to protect his neighbor's people… and to protect us! All the while his fellow lord, the craven Baron, was here… spreading lies and dissent. Even so, this man, the Count di'Cameron, stayed to do his duty, both to kingdom and crown, and so doing he saved us all."

I was finding it difficult to keep from fidgeting as I stood there. Being the object of an unrestrained river of praise and compliments was more uncomfortable than I had imagined. Not that I had ever imagined such a barrage of half-truths and exaggerations. Well I had to admit the last part was true, but much of what had come before had been outright fabrication.

Apparently the late Baron was a scoundrel and coward of immense proportions, who had not only run from danger and abandoned his people, but also a tremendous liar who had worked tirelessly to have our hero, yours truly, deposed so that he could receive my lands. This ignored the fact that my lands would have reverted to the Duke of Lancaster if I had had my title stripped from me. According to the tale, the baron was soon confronted by our wise and good king, once he had learned of the plot. Naturally the villainous baron had attempted to kill the good king once he realized that he would not be fooled by the baron's wicked lies.

All of this led of course, to today, when I, the loyal servant would be rewarded for my faithful service in protecting the kingdom from both treacherous cowards and powerful armies. The tale was so sickeningly sweet I could almost hear my mother warning me that I would get a tummy ache if I listened to any more.

While I wasn't particularly heart-broken about Sheldon's sudden execution I didn't think he fully deserved to be hanged for his cowardice. Worse I knew he had been executed simply to smooth the way for my 'reward' today. My thoughts flew apart at that moment, for Harold had just nudged my elbow and I realized I had lost track of what the king had been saying. I looked at the king with a question in my eyes.

"Kneel before the king," Sir Harold whispered to me and I realized I had nearly made a grave mistake.

I hastily genuflected, hoping the pause had not been noticed by the crowd.

Edward drew forth a simple gold circlet, set with a large blue sapphire. He had had it made specifically for today, to symbolize the accolades I was receiving. Gently he placed the circlet on my brow and then rested his hands on top of my head. "Take this as a small token of our gratitude for your service, and with it we name you the Protector of the Northern Reach, in honor of your victory. In addition to this title we also bestow upon you the lands formerly held by your neighbor, the late Baron of Arundel, to keep or use for your own vassals."

When he had finished speaking he put his hands on my shoulders and lifted upward as a signal to rise. As I stood I felt a wave of disgust crash over me, disgust for the entire ceremony, and for myself for participating. It was nothing more than an overblown lie, meant to sooth the people and create more support for the king, a man I could barely stand, much less respect.

Raising my head I saw Cyhan standing beside and slightly behind our monarch and as our eyes met he saw the look in my eyes. An imperceptible shake of his head cautioned me to hold my tongue. Taking a deep breath I knew he was right, the wrong words now could start a civil war, and that was precisely what I was here to prevent.

I wondered at his calm. His last words to me had cautioned me that our next meeting would be an unpleasant one, yet now he stood calmly by the king, acting as his bodyguard. I could only surmise that his oath to our monarch superseded his oath to execute unbound wizards. *I bet it keeps him up at night,* I thought. I gave Cyhan a polite smile when the king took his eyes from me, letting him know I appreciated his tolerance… and his advice.

"Perhaps our hero would like to say a few words to the crowd?" asked the king graciously.

"Certainly, your Majesty," I answered quickly. He stepped back and I turned to face the people. The sun was no longer in my face so I could see them more clearly now. "Our king has honored me today, but I want you to know that the honor is not just my own. The defense of Lothion is not something any one man could accomplish alone; it was done with the aid of hundreds, nay thousands of men and women. People just like those here today. I did no more, and no less, than I would have expected any loyal citizen of our nation would do." I stopped there.

I was tempted to continue, to tell them that they should prepare to do the same, should fate again threaten our nation, but I withheld those words. I knew they would be badly received by Edward. I had already given him a slight insult by insisting that the honor was not my own, by sharing it with those who served me. Despite Cyhan's unspoken warning I could feel my temper flare, but I went cold when I saw a young man staring at me in the crowd.

It was a surreal moment, when the world slows down and everything becomes crystalline. Though there were hundreds of people before me, for those few seconds the only other person I was aware of was the young sandy haired man whose eyes burned into me. It was a look of utter hatred, the look of someone who saw in me the personification of all the ills in the world. In that timeless moment of focus my mind saw him clearly, even to the knife he held clutched at his side, hidden under a ragged cloth. This man, who seemed to be even younger than I was, had come today with no other reason, than the hope that he might get close enough to kill me.

It was a shocking thought, but I knew it was true, with a surety that pure logic can never provide. Whatever his reason, this fellow desired nothing more than to end my life. A woman's voice rang out through the crowd. It was but one voice among many, but he knew it and he turned his head to see the girl who called for him. I followed his gaze, and when his eyes settled upon her I saw her as well.

She was young, and she resembled him, *probably his younger sister,* I thought. She struggled to get through the crowd, to reach him, and her face bore a look of profound fear and worry. *She's come to stop him,* I realized. The crowd went on cheering while the king put his hand on my shoulder. Unnoticed by everyone a tiny drama played out within the crowd, and yet I saw them.

The king began speaking again but I did not hear him, all my attention was upon the young man and his sister. She had reached him now and they argued with one another in the midst of the crowded square. Realizing his chance had vanished with her arrival his shoulders slumped and he turned away, letting her lead him toward home. As he did she cast her eyes toward me and I found myself transfixed by her gaze. I had hoped my expression would convey my thanks to her, but her face was lit with a fury and hatred every bit as intense as his had been.

What could I have done to make these two young strangers despise me so? I wondered. Sir Harold jostled my elbow again, alerting me to the fact that the king had left the platform. We were supposed to follow. I got myself moving but I kept a portion of my mind on the young man and his sister. They were leaving now, dispersing with the crowd, and heading in the opposite direction.

I felt sure I could follow them, mentally, so long as I wasn't too distracted and they didn't travel too far away, but I worried the king would want to discuss matters once we had gotten free of the crowds.

I needn't have worried. As soon as we got within the palace Edward turned to me, "We have more business to tend to this afternoon so we won't keep you. Our steward will send someone around later with the documents you need to sign."

"Documents?" I said questioningly.

"Deeds and letters, relating to the late Baron's estate… now yours," he smiled, though the effect his smile produced was more unnerving than reassuring.

"Of course your Majesty," I said, giving him a deferential bow. My mind was still distracted, trying to follow the young man and his sister, steadily drawing further away. Thankfully the king merely nodded at that and soon enough I was on my own again. I waited a long minute until Edward had gone from my sight.

I started walking briskly in the direction of the man I was still tracking, much to Harold's dismay. "Your Excellency!" he said, trying to get my attention.

"What," I said gruffly.

"Would you mind telling me where we are heading?" he asked.

"I have something to take care of… I'll meet you back at the house in a short while," I informed him.

"I'm coming with you, your lordship," he said firmly.

"No, I'm afraid you are not," I replied.

"Lord Dorian's orders were very clear sir," he explained, almost apologetically, "my duty is to protect you, no matter what the circumstances."

"Who is your liege-lord?" I asked him.

"You my lord," he said promptly.

"I'm ordering you to return to my house and wait for me there," I said sternly.

"I cannot obey that order your Lordship," he replied.

I laughed, "Be glad I am tolerant." I started walking back through the crowd. "Most lords would have you cut into pieces for that sort of impertinence." Before he could reply I reached out and touched a stranger and spoke a phrase in Lycian. My appearance changed instantly to match that of the man I had just touched. Poor Harold was confused immediately.

Before he could sort things out I moved further away and touched someone else, trading appearances as easily as some people might change shirts. Soon enough I had lost my guards, and more specifically Harold, completely. I almost felt bad about it. I knew he would be sick with worry until I returned later. *Sorry Harold,* I thought.

I still had my mind fixed on that young man and his sister. They were heading steadily away, close to the limit of my range now as they made their way toward the city gates. I jogged when possible to close the distance and soon I had caught up enough that I didn't have to worry about the range anymore. I followed at a fast pace then, to avoid attracting attention or running into someone, since the streets were still crowded.

I thought they might perhaps pass through the gates but they turned aside before they reached them, heading into one of the poorest districts of the city… a ramshackle collection of houses built near the walls. I followed them, making note of the street names until at last they entered a small dilapidated cottage. They stopped there, which allowed me to catch up.

I dawdled in the street near their house for a short while before I finally decided to simply knock on the door. I was still wearing a stranger's appearance so I didn't think it could hurt. I gave the door a few sharp raps and waited. After a minute it opened slightly and I saw the young woman peering at me from one side. "Can I help you sir?" she asked.

"Yes miss, I hope you can. Could you tell me what address this is?" I replied politely. I did in fact have no idea what the address was, and I needed the information for the next part of my ruse.

She opened the door slightly wider, probably thanks to my courteous tone. "This is number fourteen, Redbird Lane sir... why do you ask?" she answered cautiously.

I tipped my head deferentially. I almost attempted to tip my hat to her, but I wasn't really sure if my appearance included a hat or not, or what would happen if I tried to remove an illusory cap. "Pardon the intrusion ma'am, my name is Stephen Dryer and I'm trying to find my friend, a mister John Wheeler." Of course none of that was true, but sometimes a false statement is better than a question for getting facts.

She pursed her lips, "I'm afraid there's no one here by that name sir, this is the Tucker residence."

My face fell in an expression of dismay. "Are you sure? This is the address I was given and I don't know where else to look. Could he possibly be one of your neighbors?"

Her look was sympathetic, "I don't recognize the name, perhaps if you describe him to me."

I smiled inwardly. I already had the address and their last name, anything more was icing on the cake. "Certainly ma'am, he's a young fellow, younger than me, perhaps seventeen years old by his features. He's got sandy brown hair and brown eyes and he stands about so tall." I held my hand up near my face to indicate my estimate of her brother's height.

She frowned, "That sounds just like my brother sir, but his name is Peter, not John, so I doubt it could be him."

I let my eyes widen in excitement, "Is your brother in Miss? Perhaps he knows the fellow I'm looking for… if I could just talk to him for a moment."

I could see her hesitate as she considered my words. "Well sir, he's home at the moment but he's not in a mood for visitors," she said finally.

I gave her a look of sincere disappointment, "Please Miss, it would mean a lot to me."

"Alright, just let me fetch him," she said with a sigh. "The house isn't fit for visitors so you'll have to wait out here."

I told her I didn't mind and she shut the door. Inwardly I was congratulating myself. I might not be as good at courting and wooing women as Marc was, but I had a fair hand in dealing with people in general. After a minute or two the door opened again, this time fully, and standing in it was the man I had followed here, Peter Tucker. He didn't look very happy to see me.

He'd be even less happy if he knew who I really was, I thought. I held out my hand but kept my face neutral. A smile might have annoyed him given his current mood. "Sorry for bothering you, my name is Stephen Dryer. I'm looking for a friend named John Wheeler."

He shook my hand carefully, but didn't make the gesture any friendlier than it had to be. "Looks like you wasted your time, there's nobody by that name around here. What did you want to find him for?" he asked.

"Just wanted to let him know about a job. He'd been lookin' for a while he said. I wanted to let him know about this one before he ran off and… well never mind," I said, as if I had reconsidered my words.

Peter's eyes lit with interest at the word 'job'. "What sort of job was it? I might be interested," he said.

I paused, frowning, as if I was giving serious thought to the question. "Well I don't know if I should be sharing, since I don't know how many men they need...," I let my sentence trail off uncertainly.

"I don't want to come between you and your friend, but if they need more than one man I could use some luck right about now," he said carefully, as if he was afraid he might scare me off. Now that I had him it was time to set my hook and see what sort of information I could catch.

I looked him up and down. "You seem like an alright fellow, and truth is I might not run into John for a few days. I don't think the offer will be open that long so I might as well help you out." My mind raced while my tongue wagged, I needed a job that might entice this young man. His reaction would tell me much, but on the off chance he didn't give anything away a job that interested him might allow me to keep the conversation going longer. Unfortunately I knew very little about him, other than the fact he wasn't very muscular.

"What sort of job is it?" he asked, obviously somewhat anxious. As he spoke he lifted his hand to his face, scratching the stubble of his fledgling beard; that was when I spotted the ink stain.

"Well before you go getting excited I should tell you first that the job needs someone that knows his letters," I informed him.

"Ha!" said Peter excitedly. "No problem there."

"Really?" I said with feigned surprise, for less than a third of the common folk could read.

"My dad taught me, and I even had a job as a clerk for a while," he said proudly.

I grinned and slapped my leg. "This might be your lucky day then!" I said excitedly. "One of the nobles is looking for a messenger and junior scribe to come work for him, and the pay is supposedly good."

The younger sister had been listening behind the door, but this news was too good for her to keep her distance. She darted her head around the doorframe, "That would be perfect Peter! Think of what we could…"

"Lily!" he barked. "Go inside and stop eavesdropping!" Her face flinched at his tone and she ducked inside and shut the door. He turned back to me before speaking again, "Which noble is it?"

"The new Protector of the Northern Reach," I answered loudly, "the Count di'Cameron, don't ask me to tell you his proper name though, I can never keep it straight." I told him this with some enthusiasm but I was watching him closely to see his reaction. I needn't have bothered; he didn't hide his disdain at all.

Peter spat on the ground in disgust. "Bah! I'd rather work shoveling manure for the rest of my life as take a job for that blood-thirsty whoreson!" he announced.

I gave him a shocked look, "Well I didn't think you'd be offended…" I was hoping he might feel like elaborating on his reasons.

Peter started to open his mouth but then he shut it again, thinking carefully. Finally he replied, "Sorry, it really isn't your fault. I'll let you get back to looking for your friend." He turned and headed into back inside, but he was visibly upset.

"Let me give you the details in case you change your…," the door closed before I could finish. I stared blankly at it for a moment. I had hoped to find out more than that. *To hell with it,* I thought. I knocked on the door again.

Lily opened it and this time she didn't bother hiding behind it. "I'm sorry. Peter's not interested in that job."

"Here, let me at least tell you the address, in case he changes his mind. They might have a job that would suit you as well," I suggested.

Her face hardened. "There's no way either one of us would ever work for that bastard," she said evenly and there was steel in her voice.

My ruse had run its course, and there wasn't much hope I could get anything else from it so I took a chance on a direct question, "But why not?"

Her expression changed then, it wasn't the burning fury I had seen the first time she looked upon me… this was a look of despair mixed with resentment, a cooler anger, more acceptable for sharing with a stranger. "He killed our grandfather," she said coldly, and then she shut the door. There was no doubt in my mind the conversation was over now.

I stood still for a long moment, before turning away. A chill had washed over me, leaving me numb as I started walking toward home. *He killed our grandfather,* she said over again in my mind. I wasn't sure who her grandfather was, but a deep sense of guilt welled up. I had killed many men, but I only knew the names of a few.

I walked without paying attention to my direction, wandering aimlessly while my mind ran in circles. *He killed our grandfather.* I wondered how many families cursed me in Gododdin as well; I had killed many more of their men. Assuming any of their families survived to hate me, considering Mal'goroth's assertion that he would sacrifice the families of any soldier I killed.

Memories of the past year chased each other through my mind, memories of people that had died. *This is the Tucker residence,* she had said. *Tucker!* I screamed inwardly as I remembered. "Jonathan Tucker!"

When I had come to 'liberate' my goods from the royal warehouse last year, I had used my power to destroy a steel gate and inadvertently killed an old guard. The heavy metal had been blown backward with incredible force, completely severing his head. The tag carefully sewn into his shirt had read, Jonathan Tucker. Had I just met the girl that had embroidered that tag? Unbidden, a vision of a thirteen year old girl diligently working to mend her grandfather's shirt rose in my mind, tormenting me.

Did they have any other family? Had the old man been their only income? Was young Peter now desperate to find work to support his sister? These questions and many more ate at my conscience. Even if I wanted to help them they would not accept my aid. I walked without purpose or direction for an hour more before I finally resolved to find some way to help them.

It didn't ease the black cloud in my heart, but it gave me enough purpose to return home at last. Harold was *very* happy to see me, in the sense that he was fairly put out. Being his lord though he was obliged to keep much of his opinion to himself and when he saw my face he knew better than to try and pester me about abandoning him.

I ignored his questions and sought privacy in my room, locking the door behind me. Then I stared at the ceiling for a long time.

CHAPTER 23

The next day started much as I had anticipated. Rose and Marc were both in good moods and feeling entirely too chatty. I ignored them through most of breakfast. Eventually of course they tired of my reticence and started asking more direct questions. I suspect Marc would have waited, he knew me well enough to recognize my moods, but Rose was having none of it.

"Are you going to tell us what's wrong or spend the entire day brooding?" Rose said finally.

My first impulse was to lash out at her. I badly wanted to hurt someone, to give vent to my emotion, but I didn't. Instead I reminded her of that night, when we raided the warehouse, and the man I had killed. The one she had suggested hiding afterward.

"You're still beating yourself up over something that happened over a year ago?" she interrupted.

"No, if you'll let me finish, I'll tell you," I ground out with some irritation. "I doubt you recall, but the man I killed that night was named Jonathan Tucker."

She started to argue about my use of the term, 'killed', I could see it in her face as she opened her mouth. Luckily Marc stopped her, putting a finger to her lips. As smart as Rose was she still hadn't picked up on the heart of the problem.

"I met his grandchildren yesterday," I said at last, and then I stopped. They both stared at me in astonishment. Rose had put her hand over her mouth in an expression of more shock than I could ever recall her showing before. "Their names are Peter and Lily Tucker and they hate me with a passion. Peter came to look for a chance to stick a knife in me during the ceremony yesterday, but his sister forced him to go home."

"How did you learn their names?" asked Rose.

"I took on another man's appearance and followed them home," I answered her, and then I described the conversation I had had with them.

Marc whistled admiringly, "That was quick thinking my friend."

"It still doesn't help me help them," I replied. "From the looks of things they were desperate for money and I don't think either of them have an income."

Rose stood up and took my hands. "Stand up," she said sternly. I humored her, not sure what she had in mind, but after I had risen she put her arms around me and embraced me. Then she leaned up and kissed me on the cheek. "You are a sweet man Mordecai, I can see why Penny loves you, but you cannot take the weight of the world upon your shoulders."

I returned her hug, and then I replied, "What would you have me do? Ignore them?"

She didn't let go of me. "No, let me take care of it. I know the city and my father has the resources here to help them. I'll make sure their fortunes change for the better and they need never know you were the cause." I felt another pair of arms around me as she finished. Marc had joined the hug.

"I second the lady's idea," he said.

"Fine!" I answered with some exasperation, shaking myself loose from the two of them. It was impossible to fall into despair with friends such as these. "I want to know everything you discover, as well as how you help them," I told Rose.

"Naturally," she said. "You can trust my discretion."

The sound of a knock came from the hallway. The door to the dining room was open but Harold had knocked on the doorframe to let us know he was entering, since we appeared to be in a personal conversation. I had to give him credit, for all his brawn Harold was as considerate as anyone I had ever met. "Sorry," he said as he entered. "Hope I didn't interrupt, but I'm terribly hungry."

Marc answered, "No, come in and eat. You should hear all this as well." Marc pointed at a chair and slid a plate of sausages in that direction. Rose and I sat down as well and after a few minutes she and Marc had brought Harold up to date on our conversation.

"So that's why you ran off and left me yesterday," Harold said after they had finished.

"That about sums it up, yes," I told him. I could see he was still upset. He was probably having trouble figuring out how to express his anger toward his liege-lord. Honesty, integrity, and respect for my station were waging a hard fought battle in his mind.

"I really wish you had told me what you intended to do," he said at last. "My job here is to protect you and if you don't trust me I can't possibly succeed."

His wording impressed me; obviously he had a brain between his ears. "That makes sense Harold. I do trust you by the way, but when you told me that you couldn't obey my order you effectively ended our conversation. Do you understand why?"

He shook his head, "But Lord Dorian told me…"

"Lord Dorian nothing!" I interrupted. "I understand why he told you that but when it comes down to the line you have to know who makes the final decisions, even if they conflict with your assigned task."

"Yes your Lordship," he answered a bit sullenly.

"You may think I'm being heavy handed here but nothing that occurs around me is normal. I frequently learn things long before anyone else is aware of them. Therefore if you are to serve me you must accept that sometimes I will give an order that may not make sense. Can you accept that?"

"Yes sir," he replied.

I let my expression soften. "I'm sorry for putting you in that situation Harold. I will try to avoid doing that in the future. I will also try to give you more information whenever possible."

The tension between Harold and me was much better after that. Eventually Rose got up and headed for the door. Marc spoke up then, "What's your plan for today Rose?"

"I still haven't found a blacksmith that wants to move to Washbrook yet so I thought I would get an early start," she announced.

"I don't plan to return for a couple of days," I said to reassure her.

She frowned, "I didn't think you had anything left to do in Albamarl."

"Well I don't, but I plan to use my time productively. I have a lot of distractions at home, but here things are relatively quiet. I thought I'd use a couple of days to make use of the library and work on some things I've learned recently," I said. More specifically I wanted to try and understand some of the unfamiliar enchanting schemata I had found in the book I had recovered.

"I see," she answered. "Perhaps if I'm lucky I will find your smith for you before you finish."

"If not I'll come back for you in a week," I told her. "It really isn't a bother for me."

She left after that and I retired to the library. Marc had some sort of plan to approach the church of Celior. He was hoping to gain access to their archives somehow. I had already asked him if he wanted my help but he was being very tight-lipped about his plan so I gave him some space. I had faith in him, if he needed my help he would ask.

That left me and Harold on our own. Let me clarify… that left me to my own devices, while poor Harold was stuck trying to figure out how to keep the guards we had brought with us from Washbrook from becoming too bored. I felt a great deal of sympathy for him, and then I put it out of my mind entirely.

———◦———

I had been trying to understand the 'trans-spatial storage device' design for hours. It seemed maddeningly familiar, since many of the runes involved were used in teleportation circles, yet the rationale behind it still eluded me. A large part of the problem was probably the fact that I didn't really know what it was meant to do, so the design confused me.

The enchantment seemed to be broken into two parts, much like teleportation circles were, but both halves were kept perpetually activated. That was the simple part, what really bothered me was that one half seemed to be designed to constantly alter itself according to a mathematical algorithm. Even worse, that algorithm was dependent upon the exact location of the first half of the enchantment.

"This makes no sense," I said running my hands through my hair for the hundredth time. "It's as if they intend for one side of this thing to be permanently affixed while the other moves constantly." There is something to be said for talking to yourself aloud. Sometimes it enables you to see what should have been patently obvious to you all along.

"I can't believe I've been so stupid," I told myself. I had let the mathematics obscure my vision of how it was meant to work. One end would be designed around some sort of collapsible opening, such as a hinged ring for example, but any circular opening would work. Whenever that end was opened and took its full shape, the enchantment would be activated, forming an open link between two spaces. A simple design would be a bag or suitcase, that when opened would create a perpetual portal, between the bag and a permanent storage space somewhere else.

Now that I understood what it was for I could see a lot of immediate uses. I reached down and felt the small leather pouch at my waist. Inside it I carried a collection of small iron spheres, each loaded with energy and ready to explode when activated. I had found them so useful during the recent war that I had made sure to keep a supply of them ready at all times, yet the danger of carrying them still worried me. Using something like this enchantment I could store them in a safely remote location, yet still access them easily when I needed them.

I thought about the implications for a few minutes. A portable storage container that could hold heavy or dangerous items was only one possibility. Another would be connecting the portable 'mouth' to a place other than box or closet. If the immobile end were underwater, say positioned on a river bottom then the other end could be opened to provide a seemingly endless stream of fresh water. I was no expert on agriculture but I could immediately see that it might easily solve many of the difficulties involved in digging canals for irrigating crops.

The enchantment could also be easily modified to create something more like a permanent portal, or gateway between two places. Then my magically disadvantaged friends could travel between locations without needing me to activate a circle for them. My imagination ran rampant as I thought about the possibilities. I dreamed of building a house in which each room was in a different place. I could look out of a window in the kitchen and see the beach, or walk into the bedroom and gaze out upon a sylvan forest scene. My mind was whirling with ideas.

I spent hours studying the design before I finally began working on my own 'portable storage device'. I had Harold send one of the guards out to buy a durable leather pouch and a heavy duty strongbox for me and once I had them I spent the evening connecting them via enchantment. I found the process much easier using the stylus that I had discovered. It made creating precision runes a snap and allowed me to work much more quickly than usual.

Even so it was late that night before I finished my first project. Looking at the plain leather pouch on the table I felt a sense of pride. It didn't look like much, but I knew what skill had gone into it. I immediately wished Penny were around for me to show it to her. "No matter," I said to myself, "I'll see her in another day or two and she'll be just as excited then."

I imagined her in my mind's eye, smiling with her hand resting upon her swollen belly. That thought got me to thinking about our baby and that eventually led me to yet another use for my new favorite toy.

"Waste disposal!" I said out loud. That idea made me laugh and then I realized I was getting a bit silly with sleep deprivation. It was probably past midnight already. I decided to put myself to bed but I was still chuckling as I walked down the hallway to my room.

The guard Harold had stationed outside my room gave me an odd look, for I was still chuckling as I wished him good night and shut the bedroom door.

CHAPTER 24

The next day I tackled the 'self-locking door' schemata, which turned out to be a lot simpler than I had imagined. It was also about as exciting as it sounded. Essentially it was a method for making sure a door or similar closure would close itself and automatically lock after being left unattended for a period of time.

What I did find fascinating was the method for creating a delay before the action of closing the door occurred. It could be adjusted, so while the standard door would close within seconds of being used, I could use the same technique to create a delay of minute, hours, or even longer. Although I might never want a door that waited that long to close itself, I could imagine any number of other enchants that might be useful if I could set them to activate after a delay.

A trap for example, or perhaps a timed event that should happen on a regular basis… my mind was full of possibilities. The more I learned the more ways I could imagine recombining the various elements to achieve different effects.

I spent most of the day working on ideas and jotting down notes. I didn't want to forget anything. Rose and Marc were both gone on their individual tasks for most of that time so I suffered few interruptions.

That evening I made a half-hearted attempt at understanding the schemata that detailed how to create the effect that shielded the secret room from my magesight. I soon realized that a half-hearted effort would not be successful and decided to save it for another day. I had already used up my quota of 'clever' for the day it seemed.

After dinner with Rose, Marc, and Harold, I retired early. I was looking forward to returning home the next morning. I had considered extending my stay another two days, to make it a full week but I missed Penny. I could still work on things back in Castle Cameron anyway; there would just be more distractions.

I went to sleep while thinking about whether I should make our doors 'self-locking'. It made me laugh to think of people's reactions when the doors closed without aid behind them. What can I say? I'm a man of small amusements.

⟞———⟝

The next morning I rose early, anticipating the return home. The night before Rose had told me she was still searching for a suitable smith so I would be going back without her. I told her I'd check back in a week and see if she was ready to return.

Harold had his men ready shortly after breakfast and I could see that I wasn't the only one glad to be returning. Certainly many of them had families they wanted to get back to just as I did. I made my goodbyes with Marc and Rose and soon enough I had Harold and the guards back in Castle Cameron.

A guard was posted, as usual, in the building where the teleport circles were housed. He got my attention as soon as I brought the first group of guardsmen across. "Excuse me your Lordship!" he said nervously.

"Just a minute," I told him. "Let me get the rest of these men home." It took a couple of minutes to finish that and dismiss the men and then I turned back to him. "Alright, you look like you have something to tell me…"

"Yes, Your Excellency, Joe McDaniel wanted me to tell you to see him as soon as you returned, before doing anything else," the man answered, dutifully reciting his message.

"Tell Joe I'll see him as soon as I get back from Lancaster. I have a lady waiting on me there," I gave him one of my disarming smiles.

"Your pardon sir, but Joe said I should tell you he needs to see you first. He said it was very important," he replied. I could tell he felt uncomfortable telling me that.

"Well Joe shouldn't really be expecting me for another day or two, so I doubt a few minutes will make a difference. I'll see him as soon as I return…," and so saying I ducked into the room holding the circle that led to Lancaster. Before the poor fellow could muster the courage to restate his message I had transported myself.

I hastily unlocked the door that protected the circle in Lancaster and stepped outside. Today there were no fewer than three men guarding the building, something I knew to be unusual. As soon as I stepped out two of them snapped to attention while the third drew his horn to his lips and blew a loud note.

"There's no need for that!" I said immediately.

The man with the horn finished and put it down. "Your pardon sir, the duke's orders were that we sound the horn the moment you appeared."

I frowned, "What's going on?" The tension in these men had already set my hackles to rising.

"The duke will explain sir," he replied apologetically.

"Fine," I said and began walking toward the main door of the keep. Before I could reach it the door flew open and Ariadne darted out, running as quickly as a young woman can in full skirts, which was surprisingly fast. Before I could utter a greeting she flung herself into my chest, and buried her face against my shoulder.

"I'm so sorry Mordecai!" she cried into my tunic. My apprehensiveness went up several notches and transformed into true anxiety. I hadn't seen Ariadne cry like this since she was a child, and that had been over a dead puppy. Something told me this had nothing to do with furry animals.

"Where is Penny?" I asked suddenly. A cold feeling was running down my spine now. Ariadne said something but I couldn't hear her clearly, most likely because my shirt was muffling her voice, that and the tears. The door opened again and I saw James approaching with an angry expression.

"Ariadne! I told you to stay inside. You're only making this worse," James spoke loudly, and I could tell by his voice he was close to snapping.

She turned to him, face red with tears. "I had to see him Father. I had to tell him how sorry I am."

His next words were spoken with such a tone of controlled anger they made even me flinch. "Get... to... your... room..."

"But Father!"

"Now!" he barked.

She broke and ran for the keep and I gave James a questioning look. It was unusual for him to be so stern with his family. "Where is Penny?"

His face changed, switching from anger to tired sorrow in a heartbeat. "Come inside Mordecai. Let's talk at the table so everyone can hear. Your mother is anxious to see you as well."

I followed him into the entry hall, my anxiety only becoming greater. "Where is Penny?" I asked again.

"Let's sit down first lad," he said in an informal tone, I could tell he was trying to calm me down but it only served to drive me to anger.

I jerked back from his hand, "Where is Penny damnitt!? I'm not taking another step until you explain yourself!"

His face showed little, but knowing his self-control it told me a lot anyway. "She's missing Mordecai. Now come, sit down so we can explain what we do know."

I started walking rapidly, my strides eating up the ground between me and the great hall. I wanted to know everything, and I wanted to know it immediately. I burst through the doors into the dining hall with James still ten paces behind. The room had been cleared and the only people in the room sat at the high table. I noted the faces of those present instantly, my mother, Lady Thornbear, Genevieve, William Doyle, who was the duke's master huntsman, as well as Sir Andrew, the new seneschal for Lancaster Castle. Most notable to me were the absences, neither Penny nor Dorian was present, nor were any of the guards I had sent with them.

No one looked particularly happy to see me. Most of them were trying not to meet my eyes, and they all seemed torn by painful emotions. Only my mother met my gaze squarely. "What happened? Where is Penny?" I asked as soon as I was less than ten feet from the table.

Genevieve spoke first, "She was abducted Mordecai. Almost immediately after their arrival she and your mother were abducted from the guest room where I had placed them."

I looked at my mother, "Obviously they weren't successful. Where is Penny, and why isn't Dorian here to explain?"

My mother rose and walked over to me. "I was badly wounded son, and Dorian managed to rescue me, but things did not go well after that."

I shrugged her attempt at a hug off and stepped away. I was far too wound up with tension to accept an embrace. "How did they get inside? How did they know you would be here?" A thousand questions were rushing up in my mind.

James spoke then, from behind me, "They had magical assistance, a wizard of some sort. He was able to hide their presence. They walked in without a soul seeing them, and if it had not been for Dorian they might have walked out just as easily."

I could almost see the walls moving around me, as if the keep itself were breathing. My emotions were spiraling out of control, yet still hidden behind the backdrop of my superficially calm mind. Deep down I could hear a voice screaming and I knew I had to keep it from reaching the surface or I would never get answers. I could not afford to panic… not yet. "Why isn't Dorian here explaining this? Where is he?"

My mother took another step toward me but avoided reaching out this time. "We aren't sure Mordecai. Let me explain from the beginning…" And so she did. I held my tongue while she spoke though I wanted to jump up and shout as she told her tale. With each passing moment the story grew worse. Penny had been abducted and my mother stabbed by some madwoman. Their guards were slain and Dorian had fought like a berserker to stop their enemies.

A dragon had appeared, sending the Duke's men into hiding, though it turned out to be illusory once all was said and done. Dorian hadn't faltered though; he had somehow forced his way past a closed portcullis, wounded the enemy wizard and chased down several men on horseback. They had found corpses and a few dead horses along the path he had taken. He had also somehow saved Miriam. She had gone unconscious after being stabbed but had been found in the forest, alive and safely nestled in the bushes beside an ill-traveled path. Her wound had been healed, but no one knew how or when that had happened.

Of Dorian and Penny, no trace had been found. No, that wasn't true; there had been a lot of traces found. There were bodies and parts of bodies hacked and mangled in the forest, all of them still moving. The shiggreth had somehow ambushed the kidnappers. According to William, the duke's huntsman and chief tracker, there had been several hundred shiggreth there. Yet the bodies of only a few dozen were found, those that Dorian had cut into too many pieces to move effectively anymore.

More telling, the bodies of Penny and Dorian had not been found, nor had the body of the woman who had apparently been in charge of the abduction. There was but one probable explanation for that. We all knew what happened to the victims of the shiggreth.

"Mordecai! Look at me!" that was my mother's voice. She was standing in front of me now, and I got the impression she had been trying to get my attention for more than a few seconds. I focused on her and blinked a few times.

"What?" I said and I noted that my voice sounded very dry, as if I hadn't had any water in a long time.

A look of relief crossed her face, "Don't scare us like that. You closed your eyes and everything started shaking. I thought you might bring the castle down on top of our heads."

"Really?" I said in a daze. I sounded calm but my heart was a churning turmoil of emotions. I had no memory of making anything shake.

I tried to draw my thoughts together. Addressing James I finally verbalized a question, "You said the wizard was wounded. Do you still have him? Alive?"

"Yes, he's in the dungeon, same place we kept Cyhan," he replied.

"How are you keeping him?" I was curious since I couldn't imagine how they would prevent such a person from escaping.

"We tended to his wounds and then we drugged him. We've kept him bound and gagged. Whenever he regains enough consciousness to wake we feed him, give him water and drug him again. He's barely been conscious for more than a few hours since he was captured," he told me.

I was surprised. Drugging someone into unconsciousness was a tricky business. You might just as easily kill them as render them insensible. "Who had the skill and art to manage that?" I asked.

Lady Thornbear spoke up, "That would be me." I stared at her in astonishment. I had never known her to have such skills.

The Duchess spoke then, "Elise learned much of the healing arts from her mother, and she practiced them often on our behalf. Gram himself benefited from her skills on more than one occasion when he was wounded." Gram was the first name of the late-Lord Thornbear, Dorian's father, and Elise was Lady Thornbear's given name, though I had never heard anyone use it before.

I pushed my surprise aside. "I want to talk to this wizard." I could see concern on James' face when I mentioned it.

Lady Thornbear broke in, "He's unconscious at the moment. He probably won't wake up for a few more hours. That should give you a little time to get your bearings as well."

Her face plainly told me that she feared I might commit murder if I met him now. I doubted a few hours would change that risk, though. I turned to William Doyle, "Did you search the area where they disappeared?"

"Of course my Lord," he said promptly.

"You could not follow their trail?" I said questioningly.

"After their battle the shiggreth dispersed, taking many paths through the forest. I had no way of knowing which way they took Dorian and the Countess," he answered.

"Did you find any personal items?" I asked hopefully.

"Not personal items your Lordship, I found a few torn bits of cloth from her dress, and a dagger, nothing else," he replied.

"No jewelry? The Countess wore a necklace I made for her," I told him.

"No your Lordship," he said.

I felt a tiny spark of hope. One thing we had learned in our few encounters with the shiggreth since I had made the enchanted necklaces to protect our people was that the undead did not like the enchantment. A few of our men had been taken since Dorian's famous battle with them and in every case we found each man's necklace not far from where he had been 'turned'. Apparently once they had gone over to the other side they found the necklace to be unbearable and removed it. If Penny still had hers it meant she had not been 'turned', it meant she might still be alive.

Dorian of course did not wear one, his natural ability as a stoic had made the enchantment unnecessary for him. I wondered what that would mean if he was taken by the shiggreth. Would he go mad? He had no necklace that could be removed. I was still uncertain why the mind protecting enchantment bothered them so much after they had become undead.

I looked at the people around me. "I will go and see where they were ambushed. I'd rather do something while I wait for this wizard to wake up. I don't think I can sit still." I glanced at William Doyle and without waiting I indicated the door that led out. "Let's go." I started walking toward the door before he had even risen from his chair.

With my magesight I could see him look toward the Duke, who merely nodded, and then he ran after me.

CHAPTER 25

Iwalked through the courtyard from the keep to the main gate, scanning the ground as I went. William walked beside me silently. He obviously had a good sense of my mood. We passed the stables on the way to the gate, but I never even spared them a glance. I didn't intend to ride. I wanted to examine the ground carefully from here until the trail went cold, and possibly beyond.

"Tell me what you know of what happened here," I said. William was a smart fellow and he did as I asked, giving me only the information pertinent to where we stood. Once we got beyond the gate he showed me the area where they had mounted horses and ridden away.

"And Dorian was on foot here?" I asked.

He nodded affirmatively. I walked on without commenting. William led me to the trail where they had turned off the main road to follow a small forest trail. I watched the ground along the path with both my eyes and my other senses. I wasn't sure what I was looking for but I didn't want to miss anything. Unfortunately I didn't find anything that William hadn't already noticed.

"What was this? The ground is all churned up here," I pointed at a place where the earth had been disturbed.

"I didn't see with my own eyes but some of the men on the walls were watching. According to their reports the enemy sent one of their riders back to stop Dorian's pursuit. The rider charged him with weapon drawn and if the witnesses are to be believed Lord Dorian threw him over his shoulder." William hesitated as he spoke, unsure if I would believe such fantastic details.

"What the man dismounted first?"

"No your Lordship, according to the people watching Dorian picked the horse and rider up and threw them both over his shoulder," he clarified.

I stopped and put my hand on the ground. I couldn't imagine what my friend had been going through at that moment, but I knew he had done his best. I might have laughed at the image of him throwing a horse, but the fact that he was probably dead now stole the humor from the thought. I straightened up and resumed walking. Despite the emotions within I still had not had the urge to cry. I was somewhat numb, though I felt a cold fire burning inside my stomach.

William led me along the path, showing me where they had found Miriam before leading me on to the place where their last stand had occurred. I surveyed the area carefully. "What happened to the body parts that were found?" I asked.

"The Duke had them collected and burned," William replied.

I nodded approvingly. "Give me a moment alone William," I told him.

Without a word the huntsman retreated back down the path and waited at a distance. For being a man of few words William was remarkably adept at discerning my intentions from a few words. I imagined his perceptiveness must come in handy when tracking and understanding game.

I closed my eyes so that I could better focus on my magesight, then I took a deep breath and began to search the area carefully with my mind. I hoped to find some indication of which way they might have gone but I knew that it was a long shot. After a quarter of an hour I had nearly given up when I detected a faint gleam of magic, something that had fallen to the ground.

It was a few hundred yards to the north of where we were now and I had a sickening feeling I knew what it was. I pulled my mind back rather than examine it more closely. I didn't want to know, not yet, not 'til I could see it with my own eyes.

I waved at William and pointed north so that he would understand my intention, then I started trudging through the brush. It took me almost twenty minutes to reach the spot where it lay and the closer I got the more I shuttered my mind, to keep from seeing it before I could pick it up. Now I stood over it and I could not avoid looking at it any longer. Lying at my feet was a silver necklace with an enchanted pendant, the first of its kind I had ever made. The necklace I had given to Penny for her protection.

Kneeling, I gently picked it from the leaves and draped it across my left hand. The chain had snapped, as if its wearer couldn't be bothered with the clasp. In my mind I could see her eyes glazing over as the life was drawn from her, 'til at last her dead hand had reached up to pull the last remaining annoyance from her prior life away. The creature she had become had ripped the pendant from her neck and tossed it as far away as possible.

There were tears on my face now, but I paid them no heed. Standing I tried to think of a course of action, but all my paths seemed dark and meaningless without her. *I will have to hunt them down, all of them,* I thought to myself. The shiggreth were a scourge meant to destroy humanity. Too long I had waited to act, and now my wife and unborn child had paid the price. Eventually I would find her too. *And I'll have to burn her as well,* came the unbidden thought to my mind. With it came a torrent of rage as the floodgates of my soul opened up.

The air turned red as my anger boiled up, like blood from the earth, filling my mind and erasing my doubt. My heart beat like thunder and my body swelled as adrenaline filled my muscles with energy. A small voice in my mind warned me, I was losing control, but I didn't care, not any longer. Power filled me with exhilarating potential to match the rage that had consumed my mind. I could see the world below me for miles; I could feel the earth's blood deep below, crying out in anger and pain to match my own.

Around me the world grew smaller with each passing heartbeat and soon I could see all the way to Albamarl and further, beyond even that. Below it all the earth boiled and seethed in anger. The world of men was built upon a thin skin of crusted rock that barely covered the hot reality underneath it. It would take very little to unleash the fury below and wipe the surface clean with fire and magma. The thought had just occurred to me when I knew I must do it. Too long I had lain dormant, too long I had slumbered while the world grew cold and strange around me. I would wipe it clean.

I felt a hand resting atop mine now, a woman's hand, long and slender. I looked down to see whose it was and I was surprised to see that my arm was red and swollen. It appeared to be made of molten rock. Resting atop it was a dark brown arm and following it I found its owner, Moira Centyr. "Stop Mordecai, this is not the way," she rebuked me softly.

I gazed at her with tears in my eyes, tears that fell to the earth and set the dry leaves there aflame. Moira was tiny now; she had never looked so small to me before. "Who is Mordecai?" I asked her. The name felt familiar but it held little meaning for me.

"Mordecai is the man you were, the man you must remain," she answered sadly. "Do not let your anger destroy everything you have worked to build."

Her words brought my memories back and I suddenly understood my anger. "They must be punished," I told her.

"No," she said. "Not all of them, if you do this everyone will die. Does your mother deserve to suffer?"

A face appeared in my mind when she said those words and I remembered Miriam. I didn't want to hurt her, yet my anger was beyond restraint. "I cannot stop now," I told her.

"You must Mordecai, let go of your anger. You must not give up your humanity, not yet. Let the fires cool. Remember how your father banked the hearth at night? Relax… the fire will not die, just let it slumber, it does not need to burn so hotly." As she spoke I grew calmer and I began to breathe again, though it seemed an unfamiliar practice.

After an unknowable period I finally regained myself. Moira talked to me through it all, soothing me and reminding me of things from my mortal life, helping me to regain my perspective. When I had finally recovered my sanity I was astonished at the change in my physical body.

I seemed to be made of molten rock; I was so hot I glowed like an iron pulled from a furnace. Now that I had calmed down though I was cooling off and my color had changed to a dull orange. I was also a lot bigger than normal. I stood at least fifteen feet in height and everything else had increased proportionally. Now that my mind was back to normal I felt close to panic at the changes in my body. I had no idea how to return to being flesh and blood again.

I looked down at Moira, desperate, "What do I do now?"

"I'm just relieved you've finally recovered your senses," she replied.

"What about this?!" I said in a panicked tone, holding up my enormous stony hand.

"Now that you are yourself again I would think that part should be simple for you," she said. "In case you don't remember you just nearly wiped the face of the earth clean of all life. I think the rest of us deserve a minute to collect our wits."

"Perhaps if you could just explain how I got this way," I offered.

"I'm not sure how you did any of what you just did," she said in an odd tone. "Normally when someone melds with the earth the way you did their mind is completely absorbed and they lose all conception of their prior emotions, yet somehow you projected your emotions onto everything else in the process. I even felt angry. You didn't just become part of the earth, you made the earth become part of you."

"What is that supposed to mean?" I asked.

"I don't know," she said. Her voice held an almost petulant tone. "Except that you shouldn't still be yourself. You went too far, and that's an understatement. You should be like me now."

I glanced at my body, "I think we do share certain features."

"That's not what I mean," she snapped. "I'm not real; I'm a shadow of a person that once existed. You are still yourself."

"I can't go back to Lancaster like this," I informed her.

She sighed, if elemental beings can be said to sigh that is. "You have shifted your physical body. In this case it was a side effect of your joining the earth but if you had gone any further your body would have completely lost humanoid form and become indistinguishable from the earth itself, does that make sense?"

I nodded. "So how do I undo this?"

"Idiot," she said suddenly. "To think you would do so much yet be unable to manage the most fundamental part of shape shifting."

"I haven't had the most communicative teachers," I replied sarcastically.

"Close your eyes and envisage yourself as you were before," she replied, not deigning to respond to my remark. "Block everything out but your personal self, cut your ties to everything else. You must not think of anything but your body, and it must be the body you remember. Listen to the substance of your current self and coax it into becoming the self you remember."

I thought about what she said for a moment before speaking. "Can I change anything?"

"What do you mean?" she said with a frown.

"I had a chipped tooth," I said by way of example, "could I reimagine myself with a whole tooth?"

"You occupy the body of a giant, composed of rock and magma, and you want to know if you can rebuild yourself without a chip in your tooth?" Her expression was less than sympathetic.

"Yes."

She stared at me for a long moment, pondering before she spoke, "Yes you could rebuild your body with a perfect tooth; however such a thing would be risky. You must remember your body, not just mentally, but viscerally. If you make a mistake you could die. Trying to alter your remembrance during the process could produce a tragic failure."

I clenched my granite jaw, "I just discovered my wife is dead and my best friend along with her, I don't really give a damn if I fail." With those words I closed my eyes and tried to do as she had said, imagining myself as I had been. At first nothing happened, until I listened to my body.

Once I had its voice in my mind I began to change it. It was a shocking realization, I was a rocky giant because my body's song said I was, and by simply changing its reality, I became the flesh and blood human I remembered.

When I opened my eyes again I was human, though my tooth was no longer chipped. I smiled at that thought. I also now knew how fine the line between reality and illusion was. My body was in some fundamental way a product of my 'vision'. If I changed the way I thought of it, it would change in response.

It occurred to me that I should test my theory. I closed my eyes again, but Moira's voice broke my concentration, "Don't," she said.

"Don't what?" I asked.

"Don't try that... you haven't learned enough yet. Shape shifting is in some ways the simplest of the arts but it is also fraught with the most dangers. The only thing you should attempt until you've had at least some basic advice is what you just did, returning to your proper form," she answered.

"How did you know what I was thinking?"

"I have been acting as your miellte, since you badly need one. I am 'listening' to you, as best I can," she responded.

"You can see my thoughts?" I asked curiously, and perhaps secretly a bit alarmed.

She smiled, "Not exactly. I can anticipate your actions and feel some of your emotions, but I don't know exactly what you are thinking."

For some reason that was the point when my normal human emotions kicked in again, while I had been in the form of an earthen giant I had felt only anger, the emotion I had been feeling when I changed. Now that I was flesh and blood again my normal 'range' seemed to be restored and my grief came back to me, washing over me like a river of sadness. "So you can feel my emotions now then?" I said in a voice devoid of the emotion I was feeling.

Though she was made of earth Moira's features were as finely done as any mortal's, her eyes revealed a deep sympathy within them. "Yes, I can feel your sorrow. I have known times such as these myself."

"But you do not hear the question in my heart?"

"No," she answered.

"Today I have seen the power I possess. A power so great it could destroy everything, yet I was unable to protect those most dear to me. I want to know why. Why?" As I asked the question I felt my anger returning, but I didn't allow it to overwhelm me this time.

Moira's expression changed as I spoke, becoming more stern. "Listen to me son of Illeniel, and I will tell you what I learned at great cost, once, long ago, ages before you were born. The ability to destroy is the least form of power, though it is the first form that any power will take. Even an infant is able to destroy things, weak though it may be. Using your talent to build, to create, or to restore, those are the greater forms of power; and those forms require time and cultivation to mature."

I listened carefully, despite my anger and sorrow, even then my mind was working, looking ahead. "What of the power to protect?" I asked.

She closed her eyes. "That is an illusion. There is no power to protect, only to destroy and create anew. Protection is a result of the mind and clever use of power to manipulate the actions of those that would harm you, but it is not a result of power itself."

"That makes no sense. If you try to destroy something, or someone, and I prevent you I have exercised my power to protect."

"How would you prevent me?" she replied. "You would either destroy me, or use the threat of destruction to alter my actions. The protection of whomever or whatever is a secondary result, not a primary result of power. Power only creates or destroys."

I didn't want to agree with her, but I couldn't see the flaw in her reasoning. Tired, I decided to put the discussion aside for another day. "I don't like your answer, but I'm too worn to debate it."

She continued, "All that belies another point you must be aware of…"

"What's that?"

"As I told you before, an archmage does not possess power, he 'becomes' it. The power you use is not your own, you merely borrow it, and if you use too much it will own you. Remember that."

I gritted my teeth but said nothing. I knew very well what she meant but I was convinced there was more to it than that. At every turn I was being told that all power had a price, that the power I used would cost me my very life if I tried to use the amount I needed to stop a being such as Mal'goroth, or the shining gods. Yet I could see that there were many unknowns in this game, even Moira didn't understand the full limitations, or possibilities of an archmage's ability. If she did she would already understand what had just happened to me, and she had already admitted to some uncertainty there. *And I am not just an archmage,* I thought to myself. I possessed power in my own right, as a wizard, though it might pale before some of the foes arrayed against me.

Beyond that I knew that the power of the mind might provide answers that no amount of brute force could. Moira underestimated the importance of intelligence that I was sure of, because all of her training taught her that the greater uses of an archmage's power would obliterate his (or her) mind or ability to think. The natural progression of that train of thought was that all power, beyond a certain point, would render meaningless an individual's power of thought or personal will.

I refused to accept that notion. I knew from my time in the smithy that sometimes small applications of force could have great effects. *Skillful use of power magnifies what is possible.* I turned my back on Moira and began walking back toward Lancaster. "You may go for now Moira," I said curtly. For once my patience and courtesy were gone, and I didn't really care.

◆━━◆

Somewhere deep, in one of the dark places of the world something woke. It stirred restlessly, stretching a body that had been still for almost a millennium. The world itself had shaken, as if it would throw off the shackles of dormancy and drown the world in fire. Things were still now, but it could feel a lingering expectancy, as if the world had merely gone quiet, hushed in waiting for some larger event.

Slowly it shook the dust from its ancient form and began making its way toward daylight and fresh air. It was hungry, for it hadn't eaten in nigh on a thousand years.

CHAPTER 26

I returned to the Duke's castle with William. I wasn't sure what he had seen or felt, and for that matter I wasn't sure what I had seen or felt either. My mind had been different in that other form and my memories were strange to me. William didn't say anything when I found him and I didn't volunteer any information. I did notice that he kept his distance and he gripped his bow with a certain anxiety I hadn't seen in him before.

Walking through the main gate I noticed the guards looked shaken. I had an uneasy feeling that I might be the cause, but I said nothing, merely kept walking. When I reached the main door of the keep James met me. "Did you feel the earth shake?" he asked.

I could only assume he meant my theatrics an hour past. "Yes."

"We've never had earthquakes here before, any idea what might have caused it?" His face was drawn in worry and concern.

"Not really," I lied. I had a feeling he would learn the truth soon enough, if he didn't suspect already, but I didn't much care. I only had one goal now and it was hard to see past it.

Something in my demeanor must have tipped him off. "What is that look? You don't seem very concerned about what happened."

I shrugged, "I'm not particularly." I stepped around him and started walking again.

"Where are you going?"

"To talk to that wizard you captured," I said calmly.

Despite James' age, experience, and smooth face, I felt a flicker of anxiety when he spoke again. It was very plain to see in the aura my magesight showed around him. "He isn't awake yet."

I stopped but didn't turn to look at him. "Don't lie to me James. I understand what you are trying to do, but please don't try to lie to me." After a brief pause I resumed walking, not waiting for a response.

He didn't move to follow me but before I left the hall he shouted after me, "What are you planning to do?"

I didn't reply, at least no loudly enough for him to hear. I muttered my response quietly to myself instead, "I'm just going to ask some questions." *And find out who is behind the murder of my wife and unborn child,* I added mentally. A cold stillness had swallowed my heart, leaving only an icy anger mixed with determination. "Then I'll start burning parts off of him… but not too quickly. I wouldn't want to rush things after all." I smiled.

As I passed through the corridors heading for the stairs that would lead me down to the dungeon my mother and Genevieve found me. They were the last people I wanted to see so I ignored them and with a word I blocked the hall with a shield of invisible force. My sanity was mostly gone but I still didn't want them to see what would happen below. *Better they should stay up here,* I thought to myself.

I was almost to the stairs now and as I walked a quiet part of myself watched in detachment. If Marc or Rose were here they might have been able to calm me down, but they were much too far away to help. *Penny would have been even better*, and that thought made my stomach tighten. Inside all I could feel was an icy knot of pain, but my mind held nothing but images of flames.

I turned a corner and found Ariadne standing before the door leading to the dungeon stairs. "Mordecai I need to talk to you."

"Please move," I said flatly.

"I have to talk to you," she said with a look of determination, gone was the girl frightened of her father I had seen earlier. Idly I wondered when she had become a woman; it seemed just a day ago she had been Marc's annoying little sister. The part of me that was doing the wondering wasn't in charge though; I didn't have any room for indulging my nostalgia... not anymore.

I already knew she was wearing one of the necklaces I had made so I didn't bother trying to put her to sleep. I didn't want to hurt her but my patience was extremely short on supply. *"Borok Ingak,"* I said, blowing the door behind her apart with a precision I had lacked a year ago. The sudden loss of support behind her caused her to stumble backward and she might have fallen down the stairs but I had already stepped forward to catch her by the hand. "Careful, Marc would never forgive me if I accidentally hurt you," I said softly as I pulled her away from the doorframe.

The frightened look in her eyes told me everything I needed to know. Something in my tone had already given away my secret. I had gone feral; worse, I was consumed by the desire to commit murder. "Mort you have to listen to me!" she cried as I pushed her back and used a shield to seal the doorway between us.

I turned my back on her and began descending the stairs. The quiet part of me observed that the darkened stairwell might well be a metaphor for my own spiritual descent into darkness. "You don't want to see this Ariadne," I said as I went. I didn't particularly worry about whether she heard me or not.

"Penny left you a note! Did you see it?!" she yelled at my back. Her words were muffled slightly by the screen of force blocking her way, but I heard them nonetheless. My feet stopped of their own accord.

"What?" I turned back in annoyance. The poor girl, beautiful as she was, was in tears.

"She left a note for you. Joe McDaniel was supposed to give it to you."

My anger made room for a bit of ordinary irritation. "I can read it later, nothing is going to change my mind at this point."

I started to turn away again but she screamed at me, "She had a vision! She wanted you to read it before you did anything else… she knew Mordecai! She knew!"

My cold rage was becoming a rather more normal hot anger, "Just tell me what it said damnitt!" I removed the shield from the doorway and walked back up to her. I wanted nothing more than to finish our conversation so I could go down and take care of my unfinished business. My hands were itching with impatience.

"I don't know!" she said desperately. "I don't know. She wouldn't tell me, but she wanted you to read it. She knew what was about to happen and she said only you should see the note.

For the first time since I had resolved to slowly torture the man held below to death, I truly paused to think. *If she knew then she must have had a plan*, I thought. *That might mean she isn't dead, but for some reason didn't want anyone to realize that fact.* That meant her note might have been left to prevent me from making a mistake, based on that assumption. There really wasn't any way to second guess her without reading it first.

I looked at Marc's sister. She was a wreck. Tears stained her cheeks and her eyes were swollen. I had given her quite a fright. Still my heart was not capable of much compassion, not yet anyway. Mechanically I embraced her, "I'm sorry for scaring you." Then I pushed her away and headed for the teleportation circles. I needed to see Joe. "Tell your father I'll pay the bill for the door," I said absently as I went.

At first she didn't answer but as I passed from her view I heard her mutter behind me, "Nobody cares about the damn door, least of all Father. We just want you to stay sane Mordecai." She probably thought I hadn't heard her, not that it mattered.

⸙

I found Joe pacing outside the building housing the teleportation circles in Castle Cameron. His eyes lit on me emerging from the double doors with obvious relief. "Thank the gods you came back!"

I gave him a grim stare. "You know better than to praise the gods in front of me Joe."

His face registered shock at my tone, "It's just an expression of habit…"

"Well change it. Where's the note she sent you?" I said bluntly.

"Ya know I've spent most of every day waiting out here for you to return and sure enough you show up when I'm in the privies…" he said nervously. His slightly foreign accent became more pronounced when he was anxious. Reaching into his jacket he withdrew a sealed envelope.

I took it from him and began walking. He fell in beside me. "I'll take lunch in my rooms," I told him.

"Pardon ser?"

"I'll be in my rooms for a while, thinking." I held up the envelope and waved it at him. "I'm sure I'll have a lot to think about. Make sure I'm not disturbed, except for some food and wine."

"Of course your Lordship," he said and when we entered the keep proper he headed in the direction of the kitchens to relay my instructions to the cook. As he walked away I felt a twinge of guilt for my abrupt behavior. Joe was a friend, and I had rarely treated him roughly. Hopefully he would understand later.

Pushing that thought aside I mounted the stairs leading up to the apartments I had until recently shared with my wife. That thought made me clench my teeth anew.

Once I had closed the door behind me I carefully opened the envelope Joe had given me. It was still sealed with the bit of wax she had carefully pressed onto it. The impression in the wax showed the delicate seal of a woman's ring, small and bearing the Cameron arms. I held my breath as I pulled it loose and looked at the contents.

My Love,

I know how frustrated and angry you are, for I have seen the events that have led you to this moment. What I do not know is how you will react to these words. My hope is that you will take my advice and do what is best for everyone. The vision I saw was one in which you did not receive this, and I did not like what I saw. You must not let your anger blind you, if you do so, you will damn us all, starting with yourself.

The man I know, the man I love, is given to compassion. Do not let this break your spirit. I have seen what will happen if you pay heed to your darker impulses. It is a bleak and empty path, and you will no longer be the man I have loved. There is still hope if you do not despair. I cannot say more than that.

I must apologize for the deplorable lack of information here. I cannot tell you most of what I have seen, lest it change things even further beyond what I have seen. You will have to trust me yet again. I will say that I had no intimation of any of this until you left us in Lancaster. That was probably for the best, for I doubt I could have kept it a secret if I had known. You would have seen through my acting and drawn the secret from me, possibly dooming everyone.

Here is the important part, the part that might change the future for the better. Do not let your anger rule you. The wizard in Lancaster's dungeon is not your enemy. His surname is Prathion, and if you will open your heart he may be your greatest ally. Ask him who healed Miriam; his answer should help you understand.

Do not seek vengeance with the king. That may come later. Your answers lie with the shiggreth for now.

That is it. I can say no more, nor can I offer you any consolation. Do not let grief warp your heart and soul. You are not the first, nor the last to suffer a tragedy, but your actions from this day onward could do much to reduce the number of people that lose their loved ones. Do not lose hope. Show the world the kind heart that I have always loved.

Love,
Penelope
P.S. If you ignore my advice I will make you regret it for the rest of this life and into the next one, if there is such a thing, and I'm not joking.

The last line made me smile through my tears. "Your handwriting is still simply awful my dear," I said to myself with a chuckle that turned into a choked sob. Taking hold of myself I drew a deep breath and carefully refolded the sheet of paper and set it aside on my writing table. I didn't want it marred or damaged by a thoughtless accident or poor judgment on my part. Once I had it safely tucked away I slowly collapsed on the floor. I lay there for a long time and my sorrow threatened to drown my reason, but I didn't let it. *That's not what she wanted,* I thought to myself.

What she would want me to do is think, and think carefully, I mentally reminded myself. "I cannot promise you I will retain my kindness and compassion," I said, speaking as if to her directly. "But I won't let anger control me, I will be cold and clever, like a viper, until I have gotten my vengeance. Justice can be damned, I will make those responsible pay." I clenched my jaw as I said the words.

I lay there on the floor for some time, until a servant knocked, delivering the meal I had asked for earlier. I opened the door calm and composed, with little trace of the turmoil inside remaining on my features. After I had eaten I spent the rest of the day thinking. My next steps would be made carefully lest I give away my intentions to my enemies.

That evening I took out the silver stylus I had found and began working on an item I thought might prove useful. It took several attempts before I got the rune structure properly balanced, but luckily I was able to test my device upon myself to ensure it worked properly. The final adjustments were trickier, since I had to be careful not to accidentally trigger it and possibly injure myself. I did that part while using the strongest shield I could create, but I still wasn't certain it would protect me at such a close range if I made a mistake.

By the time midnight had arrived I had finished and I felt my plans were as complete as I could make them. I decided to put myself to bed.

I had taken to approaching each step with methodical carefulness, as if it was a ritual. I did the same with retiring. I washed up and removed my dirty outerwear, taking care to neglect nothing. It almost felt as if I had a duty to Penny to properly manage the mundane tasks of life. She would have wanted me to take care of myself. Still, it took me a half-bottle of wine before sleep would claim me, and my dreams were far from restful.

CHAPTER 27

I returned to Lancaster bright and early the next morning. I had taken particular care with my grooming and when I appeared every hair was in place. My beard and mustache were carefully trimmed and my clothing was immaculate. Again, I felt it was something Penny would have wanted, though upon further consideration it might have been a symptom of the effort I was taking to control the emotions within myself.

James met me soon after I had entered. He appraised my appearance with one look and I saw a look of approval in his eyes. "You look better today Mordecai."

"Indeed, Your Grace, I am much improved. I hope you can forgive my behavior yesterday, I was distraught," I told him in overly formal tones.

"No need to be so serious, we're family after all," he told me. In point of fact his wife was my aunt, a fact I had learned only two years previously.

"The formality is perhaps part of my way of coping, sir. I hope you'll understand, but I cannot afford to be too loose with my emotions right now," I replied.

"Are you referring to the 'earthquake' we had yesterday?"

William must have seen more than I had thought and of course he had spoken with his master. Of course I couldn't have reasonably expected them not to connect the dots even without William's account. "I got a bit carried away. The worst is over now, please don't worry. I won't let something like that happen again," I reassured him.

James' eyes crinkled into an expression of sympathy. "There's more to come lad, you know that from your father's passing. It never really goes away."

"How has Lady Thornbear taken it?" I asked suddenly. I felt a bit selfish for not having thought of her before; she had lost her only son after all. I was not the only one suffering.

I could see the duke's jaw clench, "She has dealt with it admirably, like all those of her lineage. Still it has been hard on her, having just lost Gram two years ago, and now her son as well. She has kept to her quarters for the most part, though Genevieve and your mother have visited her frequently."

I nodded, for I didn't know what to say. We walked on toward the hall and James asked if I had eaten. I hadn't and so we took breakfast together that morning in his sunroom. Somehow he kept everyone else away, though I'm sure they all wanted to see me. My mother in particular certainly, but I wasn't really ready to deal with her emotions. My own were almost more than I could stand.

We didn't talk too much as we ate, but eventually I brought up my main reason for showing up so early that morning. "I'm ready to talk to the wizard now," I said without preamble.

James set his plate aside. "You nearly frightened poor Ariadne to death yesterday."

"I need to apologize for that, and to thank her. If it hadn't been for her I might have made a serious mistake," I replied. "I'd also like to pay for the damage to your door."

He waved his hands in a dismissive motion, "Don't worry about it, we've been through too much to squabble over doors. I'm curious as to what Ariadne might have said to you though, you've calmed down considerably since yesterday."

I looked down in embarrassment, "She simply reminded me of things Penny had said before, and what she would think of what I was planning to do." I told him the truth, but it was in a roundabout manner, neglecting entirely the fact that the information had come from one of Penny's visions.

We talked for perhaps another quarter of an hour before I excused myself and went to find my mother. There wasn't much use delaying the inevitable. I found her sitting alone in the room Genevieve had given her. I didn't fail to notice it was located directly next to the duke's own suite, or that there were two guards posted outside it.

The guards stepped aside without a word as I approached, both of them knew me. I knocked on the door. I already knew Miriam was inside, and awake, but I didn't want to startle her. "Yes?" came her voice a moment later.

"It's me Mother, may I come in?" I asked.

"Of course," she said drawing the bolt and pulling the door back. "I wondered if you would show up today."

I gave her a solemn look, "I am sorry about yesterday. I was not myself."

She nodded, "I think everyone knows that already. As far as grief stricken reactions go I don't think yours was too far beyond what anyone might have done." She stepped forward and slid her arms around me after I had shut the door.

I held her silently for a moment. No matter how old I might get I didn't think that simple gesture would ever fail to comfort me, though I couldn't help but notice how small she was. Had she always been so small? "In my stupidity yesterday I didn't even stop to ask how your recovery was coming. How badly were you wounded?"

She let go of me and returned to the table where she had been working on some embroidery. She rarely let her hands stay idle for long. "I don't really know," she answered. "I'll show you the scar if you're not too embarrassed to look at your old mother's bosom."

A moment later she bared her chest and midriff and what I saw there made me gasp. A long silver line traced its way up from her belly, from just above her naval to her short ribs on the right side. It had been an ugly wound, yet even more surprisingly; it appeared to be fully healed. "Does it still hurt?" I asked immediately. She was already pulling her under tunic down to cover herself again.

Miriam grimaced, "Yes it does. Some of the tissues underneath are not fully healed as far as I can tell."

"But how?"

"The last thing I remembered was that woman's nasty blade gutting me like a sow in a slaughterhouse. I was trying to hold my insides in when I blacked out. When I woke up again I was back here, in bed, and my wound was sealed," she explained.

I questioned her for a bit longer, and she described in more detail exactly what had happened: Penny's words to Dorian about his visor, the way the assassins had entered… the resulting fight. From her description I could see that Penny had clearly been expecting what had happened. *But why didn't she avoid it?* I wondered. She had seen her death approaching, she could have hidden instead of following the expected routine, but she didn't. What could have been so terrible that she had accepted her own death to prevent it?

I looked up and realized I had missed my mother's last few words. "Pardon?" I said.

"I asked what you were thinking."

"I was thinking I should examine your wound more properly," I said to cover my distraction.

"Will it hurt?" she asked, a bit nervously.

I drew my chair close beside hers. "It shouldn't, unless I need to fix something."

"Maybe I should lie down then," she suggested. I almost smacked myself, I should have thought of that.

"That's a good idea," I replied. Once she had gotten comfortable on the bed I sat beside her and put my hand on her midsection. Closing my eyes I turned my attention entirely to my magesight, focusing on the woman beside me. I hoped that whatever I found would be simple, if it were too much I might have to leave my own body, as I had with Penny once before. Something like that was risky as I had already learned.

After several minutes I had satisfied myself. The cut had severed the skin, fat, and muscle of her abdomen. It also appeared that her liver and one of her lungs had been damaged, but those had already been repaired. The abdominal muscles hadn't been completely rejoined however, which was probably what was causing her pain. I damped the nerve impulses in that region and carefully knitted them back together.

Opening my eyes again I looked at her, she had been watching me carefully the entire time. "I think I found the problem. It wasn't anything serious, but it would have hurt for a long time."

"Do you know how I was healed?" she asked.

"Magic," I said simply, "but I don't understand why."

She put her hand over mine, "You will find out."

I smiled at her, "I will."

"Just don't do anything stupid along the way," she cautioned.

"I'm in much better control of myself today."

She shook her head. "I don't mean that you shouldn't punish those behind it. Just make sure you know for certain who the blame falls on before you do anything permanent."

"I understand," I said to reassure her.

She continued anyway, "Then when you're certain, you make damn sure they never have a chance to hurt anyone else we love ever again."

We agreed on that at least.

Lady Thornbear and one of the duke's guards preceded me into the cell. The man imprisoned there was bound and his eyes were covered with a blindfold. He moaned quietly as we entered. A soft bed had been placed in the cell and I looked at Dorian's mother questioningly.

"I didn't want him dying before you returned," she said. "If we had left him on the floor he might have developed sores and died of infection."

I nodded, "Is he awake?"

"He should be close to conscious but it hardly matters. After a week of this his mind is muddled, it will be hours after he wakes before he regains his senses completely," she replied.

I was learning to see Lady Elise in a new light. As a child she had simply been Dorian's mother, strict, but kind and loving as well. Now I was forced to face the fact that she was also a skilled herbalist and poisoner. Somehow the two pictures refused to come together for me.

"You've done this before haven't you?" I said without thinking.

There was a gleam in her eye as she answered, "Never a wizard... that made it much more difficult. When you find out who sent him let me know, I'll make something special for you to give them."

A shiver went down my spine as she said it and I remembered, this was a woman that had just lost her son. *She probably wants revenge just as badly as I do.*

"I'm going to move him to Castle Cameron," I told her, and then I nodded toward the guard. "I'll need your help moving him since he's not quite sensible yet."

She looked at me questioningly, "Are you sure that's wise? You have no dungeon in your keep."

"The dungeon isn't what kept him here milady, you were, or rather it was the use of your arts that held him. I will keep a close watch upon him using other means," as I finished the statement I leaned over and carefully clasped a delicate silver necklace around the prisoner's neck. I kept my movements casual but I was very careful as I did so.

"What is that?" Elise Thornbear asked.

"Something I devised," I said smugly. "It will keep him contained until I can decide his fate."

"Is it dangerous?"

"Very," I answered.

She smiled, "You were always a good boy Mordecai. My son thought the world of you."

"I was never as good as Dorian, but I hold him as an inspiration for what people could be," I replied with complete sincerity.

Lady Thornbear leaned over then and surprised me with a kiss on the cheek. It was sudden and gentle, but I imagined I felt a trace of her tears there as well. "Thank you for that Mordecai. Here take this." She thrust a small glass phial into my hands.

I didn't question her but my look said the words for me, with one eyebrow slightly raised.

"It tastes sweet, like honey liquor. Flavor a drink with it, or use it as a sweet garnish for a dessert and the recipient will fall into a deep slumber, never to awaken again," she said quietly.

"Why me?"

"If anyone is going to find those responsible for this it will be you. I doubt you'll need it when you find them, but sometimes subtlety is the only way, even for a wizard," she answered.

"How long does it take to work?"

Her eyes twinkled in the dim light, "Good question... a day at least, sometimes two if they don't get a large dose."

"A day before they fall asleep or a day before they stop breathing?" I said to be sure.

"A day before they sleep, death follows hours after that."

I frowned, "That seems terribly slow."

"You have much to learn. Speed is not usually the poisoner's friend. Slow and certain is better, and it gives you more time and distance to allay suspicion. People tend to blame the last meal eaten rather than the one from the day before."

The more I learned of Lady Thornbear's secret profession the more she frightened me. How could a creature so well versed in subtlety and lethal deception have been the same woman who raised my friend Dorian?

My confusion must have shown on my face for she patted my cheek reassuringly, "Don't fret about it Mordecai, we all must take on various roles in our lives. Some people confuse their identity with what they do. Don't mistake a 'role' for your 'self'. I have done many things, but I am none of them, I am Lady Elise Thornbear. I have been a healer, a wife, a mother, and sometimes when necessary, a poisoner."

Her words struck a chord within me, resonating with some inner truth. I knew I would remember them for a long time to come. "Thank you Elise," I said, using her given name for the first time in my life. "You were always kind to us as children, except when strictness was called for. I never doubted you, no matter what hidden talents you possess."

I turned to the guard, "Help me get him up. I want him back in Castle Cameron and in a soft bed before he comes to his senses."

CHAPTER 28

The man I had brought back was still lying in the bed where I had had him placed, but he hadn't shown many signs of consciousness yet. Occasionally he would open his eyes and stare about the room, but his pupils were dilated and his gaze seemed unfocused. After a week in a drug induced slumber I imagined he was very confused. Instinctively I worried that the treatment he had endured might have permanently damaged his mental faculties. Then I caught myself, *Why the hell would I care if he's damaged?*

A knock came at the door, but I already knew that it was Lisette. "Come in," I yelled in the direction of the door. She came in followed by several other maids bearing a large copper tub and towels. "Just set the tub over there," I directed, pointing to one side of the room.

Harold entered a moment later, his eyes following Lisette as she bustled about the room. I didn't say anything, not wanting to embarrass either of them, especially since he didn't realize I knew about their relationship already. After a moment he pulled his gaze from her and addressed me, "I still don't understand why you have him in this room, your Lordship."

I sighed, "I don't have a dungeon and even if I did he'd probably sicken if I kept him there. From what I can see he lost a lot of blood before he stopped his leg from bleeding. James says he was pinned under the portcullis for a short time."

"You only need him conscious and awake for as much time as it takes to find out what he knows," he replied implying that I would have the wizard executed shortly after that.

"I don't intend to execute him," I said simply. Harold looked shocked and given my behavior the day previous I couldn't blame him. I had been close to doing much worse than mere execution. The memory made me shudder for a second, and I had to struggle to suppress the visions of fire and torment that still seemed somewhat attractive to me.

Harold stood, agitated, and after a moment he spoke. I was quite certain he had thrown out the first several sentences that came to mind. I had to admire his self-control. "I assume you have some particular reason for putting him up in a soft bed and nursing him back to health."

"I do. I intend to put him to work on my behalf. I believe he may be more valuable to me alive than dead, though only time will tell."

Harold's eye twitched. "What about Lord Dorian? What about your wife?"

My temper snapped and I stood up to face the young man Dorian had left behind to serve me. With two strides I came face to face with him, our noses nearly touching. Harold was a tall man, for his eyes were nearly level with my own, and his shoulders were much broader. "Don't test me Harold and be damned sure you don't suggest that my feelings for my wife or my friend are insincere or lacking in some fashion."

He held my gaze for a second before looking down and away. "Pardon me my Lord. It was not my place to address you so."

I regained my balance quickly. "Someday it will be Harold, someday it will. I respect your honesty, but you do not know me well enough yet." I put a hand to his shoulder, "Help me get him out of his clothes, they'll be bringing in the hot water in a moment."

His eyes widened, "Shouldn't we let the maids do that?"

I almost laughed but I kept a serious face, "Hmm you may be right. I'll ask Lisette to undress him. Perhaps she could help bathe him as well."

He shook his head, "No that wouldn't be right either." After a few minutes we had him stripped down and ready for the tub. Our prisoner's eyes were open now and he seemed more awake though whenever he tried to speak nothing but gibberish came out. Harold was looking at the man's right leg, which was bent and swollen. A long silver scar marked where it had been pierced by the portcullis. "That looks bad," he observed.

"You're right about that," I agreed. "I'll see what I can do about it. Don't let anyone disturb me until I'm finished."

"How will I know when you're done?"

"I'll be looking around and talking to you," I said, giving him a wink and a smile. Harold shook his head and I knew he wanted to comment on my being a smart ass but he held his tongue. I sat down by the bed and closed my eyes, turning my vision inward and then shifting my focus to the man lying on the bed beside me.

His heart was beating strongly but his body was hot with fever. His wound was obviously infected but I wasn't entirely sure what to do about that. Instead I examined his leg and the tissues around his wound carefully to see if there were any obvious problems. His femur was broken and had begun to heal at a bad angle, next to it an abscess had formed around something foreign.

I shifted my focus, examining the area more closely. A small piece of stone had lodged there and the infection had spread from there, creating a large pocket of pus and fluid around the bit of rock. It might take a while, but eventually the infection would kill him, if the abscess weren't drained and the stone removed. If he survived that he would most certainly be lamed by the badly healed bone. Luckily both problems were things I could easily deal with.

I decided to fix the bone first. Draining the wound would be a messy process; it could wait until after the bath. Briefly I considered letting him feel the pain when I straightened his bone. The man was conscious enough that the pain would be intense. After a brief moral struggle I damped the nerve impulses from his leg and carefully straightened the bone. An audible 'click' could be heard when the part that had already begun healing came apart again and I sensed more than heard Harold's gasp beside me as he watched. I aligned the ends and then carefully knitted them together. It wasn't quite as good as it would be after a month or two healing naturally, but the join was strong enough he would be able to walk on it without fear. The swelling and pain from the infection would probably make that a moot point however.

I opened my eyes and looked at Harold, "All done… for now," I said.

"That made my skin crawl," said the big warrior.

I chuckled at that. "Help me get him into the tub." Harold got behind the wizard and put his arms around the man's chest and then lifted him up by main force, leaving me to lift his legs and guide them into the copper bathing tub. "Mind his head, I'm not sure if he can keep it above the water," I cautioned.

Surprisingly the fellow sat up on his own, so we didn't have to work too hard to keep him from drowning. His mouth worked and strange sounds came out but I still couldn't make sense of anything he said.

Half an hour later we had him back in the bed and he smelled much better. "How strong a stomach do you have?" I asked Harold.

He grimaced, "I considered myself strong stomached before, but I have a feeling I'm not up to whatever it is you have in mind."

"I need to drain the pus from his wound and clean it out."

"I'll get Joe to help you. He's done a lot of minor doctoring for the soldiers and his belly is as strong as any man's I know," he said.

"That'll be fine," I said and twenty minutes later I had Joe McDaniel beside me instead.

"I'll just wait out here in case you need me," said Harold as he stepped out of the room.

"Find Lisette for me," I called after him. "I'll need more hot water and some towels. After she brings those she can wait with you… in case we need anything else." I smiled to myself, *might as well give them some time to chat.* That pleasant thought was followed by a sharp pang as I realized I'd not be having any more chances for small talk with Penny. Gritting my teeth I pushed that thought aside and concentrated on the task at hand.

I looked into the wounded man's eyes, "I know you're probably still confused, but I need to clean out the wound on your leg. Do you understand?"

The man nodded and grunted something. He was half bald and the hair remaining showed some grey already coming in, if I had to guess I would have judged his age at around forty. I glanced at Joe, "I need you to keep the towels and water handy to clean up the fluids when I drain his wound."

"Don't you need to heat up a knife first?" he asked.

"Not my way, just watch. You'll see an opening in a minute," I told him. Closing my eyes I relaxed and then drew my mind sharply into focus. Working within his leg I created a channel from the abscess to the surface and then opened a hole in the skin there. Then I began drawing the small piece of stone outward, following the channel I had created. As it moved pus began flowing out of the hole and a putrid smell threatened to break my concentration.

Ignoring the stench I gently eased the stone out and then helped the rest of the pus and sanguineous fluids to exit the abscess. When I had finished I left a small opening in the skin so that the fluids that would collect in the wound afterward could drain as well. His body would have to heal the infection on its own; I had done as much as I knew to do at that point.

Opening my eyes I looked at Joe, "I think that's it."

"For such a young man Mordecai you've become far too familiar with wounds like this," the older man noted.

I nodded in agreement, "I got more experience than I wanted after the war with Gododdin." Which was true, even though we had won we had had plenty of casualties and a lot of those had led to septic wounds. Unfortunately many had died before I found any books detailing the best methods for dealing with such injuries.

My prisoner was watching me carefully and his face held an expression of curiosity. His mouth opened and closed but only a hoarse croaking sound came out. He kept trying though, and eventually I made out a single word, "Thanks."

For some reason his gratitude enraged me. "Don't thank me. I may yet kill you for what you've done." Agitated I stood and left the room. Lisette was waiting outside, still talking with Harold. "Feed him," I told her.

Turning to Harold I addressed him directly. "Keep an eye on him. I'm going to rest for a while. If he attempts to remove the necklace get everyone out of the room."

He looked at me strangely, "Do you mind if I ask why?"

"Because I like you with all your limbs still attached," I said brusquely. "I'll be back in a few hours." With that pronouncement I left, I needed some air to clear my head. Hopefully the prisoner would be better able to talk by the time I returned.

CHAPTER 29

In spite of myself I didn't return until much later. After a quick lunch I wound up falling asleep for several hours. I hadn't realized how tired I was, but stress and the events of the past day had prevented me from sleeping much the night before. When I appeared that evening the sky was already turning dark.

I found Harold still keeping watch in the room. He seemed glad to see me. "He's been talking," he informed me.

"Why didn't you send for me?"

"I did, but they told me you were sleeping so I decided it could wait," he replied.

My nap had improved my mood, so I didn't argue the point, "What has he said?"

"I just told him my name," said the man lying on the bed.

I ignored him, keeping my eyes on Harold. After a moment he realized I was waiting on his response. "That's it, he volunteered his first name and I told him to keep his mouth shut 'til you had time to talk to him."

I nodded, "You did well. Wait out in the hall for now. I want to speak to him alone for a while."

After the burly knight had left I turned my attention to the man watching me quietly from the bed. "What's your name?"

"Walter," he stated simply. I could see by his face that he had been tempted to mention that he had already told Harold this, but his better sense had won out.

"And your family name?"

"Thatcher," he replied. I could see the aura around him flicker as he lied.

I briefly considered letting him continue to see what sort of tales he would spin but I didn't think it would be very constructive. "Don't lie to me Walter. It's a bad way to start our conversation."

He gave me a nervous smile, "Sorry, I had to try."

"My wife is dead Walter. It's a miracle you're still alive at this point and my sense of humor is non-existent at the moment," I said bluntly.

"Why did you heal me?" he asked.

It took every bit of self-control I still retained to keep from killing him then. "If you don't tell me your name things are going to get ugly, and I'll regret healing you even more than I already do."

"Walter Prathion," he answered.

"That's a better start," I told him. "I'm sure by now you've noticed a few things about your situation."

Walter nodded, "I can't sense anything. Is this?" He held up the pendant I had clasped around his neck the day before.

"Yes, that's the reason you can't sense much. It will also restrict your magical ability."

He frowned, "Where did you get something like this?"

"I made it last night," I replied. *Using my dead wife's necklace,* I added mentally. I had changed the enchantment to completely lock the mind it protected away from the world, blocking his magical senses as well as his power. It was a side effect I had noticed when I first made this necklace to protect Penny and it was the main reason I had never worn one of the pendants I created. Now I was exploiting and strengthening that effect to effectively shackle Walter's power. I had also replaced the clasp with one of my explosive iron balls. To avoid causing it to explode with my tampering I had spoken to the metal in the necklace and the metal in the iron sphere to convince them to fuse together seamlessly. The end result of my efforts was a necklace that contained two intertwined enchantments, break either, or break the circle, and it would explode. Only an archmage would be able to remove the necklace without breaking it.

"I thought the craft to make things like this was lost," he rambled.

I cut his line of reasoning off there. "I'm not inclined to explain my history or abilities to you at the moment. Today you will be doing the explaining. The necklace will restrict your ability to sense or manipulate energy. Given enough time you might be able to break the barrier it creates around your mind, but if you do so it will be the last thing you do."

Walter stared at me with silent eyes. For a moment I had an odd sensation, *this isn't the first time he has been given a deadly ultimatum.* I ignored the thought and continued, "If you break the enchantment by force, magical or physical, it will kill you. If you escape, I will break the enchantment, and it will kill you. If you attempt to unclasp the necklace, it will kill you. If you catch the chain on something by accident and it is broken, it will kill you."

Walter closed his eyes in resignation. "I probably shouldn't ask, but is there any way to remove the necklace without triggering this explosion?"

I smiled, "Yes, actually there are two methods that I know. The best is for me to remove it without disturbing the enchantment. The other is for someone to sever your head at the neck, allowing the necklace to fall free without being damaged."

He brought his hand up to grasp the silver chain. "You should have killed me," he said solemnly. There was a look of ineffable sadness in his eyes. "I'm half tempted to finish myself now."

I had to work hard to keep my face smooth. "That's your choice," I said, concealing my worry. "Until you decide to do that… who paid you to kidnap my wife and mother?"

"No one," he replied. "I wasn't paid. It was by order of King Edward… or so his agents told me."

I had expected as much, though I had thought it would take longer to get the answer. "Even the King pays his servants. Surely you didn't spend weeks skulking about my castle watching me and preparing for nothing but the glory of serving your monarch," there was a bitter tone to my words.

"He has my wife and children."

I went still and our eyes locked for a long moment. I had sensed no deception in his reply, but his answer made me suspicious nonetheless. The only explanation he could give that might deflect some of the blame was that he was acting under duress, and I couldn't be certain he didn't know some method for hiding his falsehoods. He had already shown that he knew certain types of magic I was otherwise ignorant of. Finally I spoke, "That's an easy answer for you to make."

He didn't waver, "I have no other."

I decided to leave that issue aside for later. "How long were you observing us here?"

"Almost two months," he answered promptly.

"What were your orders, in specific?" I asked.

Walter hesitated, "If the King discovers I've been taken prisoner, and talked to you… he'll kill one of my children, or something worse."

I leaned in to stare into his eyes, "My wife and unborn child have joined the ranks of the living dead thanks to your efforts. Eventually I'll have to find her and render her corpse to ash to give her peace. I'm having some difficulty feeling much sympathy for you."

His eyes widened, "The shiggreth?"

It hadn't occurred to me that he wouldn't have known what happened to his party after he was captured. "They were ambushed by them in the forest, just a few miles from Lancaster. None of them escaped alive."

Walter's face registered genuine shock, "I had no idea."

For some reason his chagrin reminded me of the night that I had slain the night watchman guarding the royal warehouses. Of course I hadn't been kidnapping anyone, but a number of people had died that night, starting with Jonathan Tucker and eventually culminating with my father. "That's what happens when you roll the dice and take risks with other people's lives Walter, some of them get hurt," I said bitterly.

"You didn't mention your mother," he said suddenly. "What happened to Miriam?"

Hearing a complete stranger use her name like that was a bit of a surprise, until I remembered that he had been observing us closely for two months. *Ask him who healed Miriam; his answer should help you understand,* Penny's words ran through my head. "You healed her didn't you?"

He looked down for a moment, "Yes I did. Ruth… that's the mercenary who was in charge of our group, Ruth stabbed her."

"Why did you bother?"

"I never wanted to do any of this. Miriam was a gentle soul, I didn't want to see her hurt, or anyone else in your family for that matter," he said softly.

That was when I felt my first pang of empathy for the man. "What are your children's names?" I asked on a sudden whim.

"Elaine, my daughter, is the oldest. She will be sixteen this year. My boy, George, just turned eleven last month."

The name George rang a bell in my mind and I remembered my father's letters. "George… is he named after your father?"

Walter looked up, "No, George was my older brother."

That surprised me; I had assumed that the George Prathion my father had known was this man's father. I made a mental note of the fact before continuing, "How long has it been since you saw your children Walter?"

"Four years."

I stood up. "I still don't know if I believe you Walter. But if you're telling the truth I'll do my damnedest to make sure they're safe again."

The older wizard's eyes stared at me intently, and I could see both hope and fear written on his face. I turned away and opened the door. "I'll check on you again in a few days. Rest up and heal, we can talk more then. If you try to escape, or if you aren't here when I return… I'll assume you were lying and kill you." I snapped my fingers to illustrate my point. I could feel his eyes still watching me as I shut the door.

CHAPTER 30

Istepped away from the teleportation circle and looked around, within seconds my senses told me the house was empty, both Rose and Marc had gone elsewhere. *That's rather inconvenient,* I thought to myself. I had hoped to find both of them at the house. That would have simplified my task. They needed to know what had happened to Dorian and Penny. Deep down I was slightly relieved though, I was dreading the conversation. Still, they had to be told and I couldn't leave the task to someone else.

A piece of paper caught my eye; it had been tacked to the doorframe leading into the hallway. It was ideally positioned so that I wouldn't fail to notice it after arriving. I took it down and recognized Rose's elegant handwriting immediately.

Dear Mordecai,

I'm sorry there's no one here to meet you, but I decided to return to my own home. I have been away from it for quite a while now and there were a number of matters that needed my attention. If you need to see me quickly please seek me there. My house is located at 17 Hightower Street, not far from the traditional Hightower residence. I'm sure you remember it, since you broke in there once.

Marc hasn't been back in several days either and he may not return for a week or more. He has contrived a plan to gain access to certain religious archives. I won't say more regarding it here, but I will be glad to give you more information when I see you next. Assuming he hasn't already returned by then. I'm rather worried for his sake, as usual his idea is bold and daring, not to mention risky.

I found a suitable blacksmith for you. His name is Gavin Traylor and he's a rather accomplished journeyman. He trained under Brian Turbrook, the chief weaponsmith and armorer for King Edward himself. His skills are excellent and he should probably have been promoted to master already in his own right, which I believe is the reason he seeks to leave the capital. My guess is that his teacher has kept him back for fear of creating undue competition for himself.

In any case, his difficult circumstances have created a wonderful opportunity for you. He readily agreed to your terms and should be arriving in Washbrook within a week or two. He said he would make the trip as soon as he had finished arranging his affairs and packing his own tools and such.

If that were not good news enough, I have another surprise for you as well. Peter and Lily Tucker showed up on your doorstep just a few days after you left. They seem to have had a change of heart and were interested in seeking employment in, Your Excellency's service. I wasn't sure what you would have wanted but I felt fairly safe in offering them terms on your behalf. Even now they are making the journey to Washbrook. I told Peter that you had need of another messenger and I told Lily that you needed more help among the castle staff.

As for their motivations… you can be sure there is more to that story than I know.

Last, and certainly not least, you should be aware that I spoke with my father, regarding a certain friend of yours. He responded very positively and hopefully you can arrange for Dorian to make a trip to the capital soon. Given your talents I don't think it would be too much of a hardship. When you see Penny be sure to tell her. I think she will be almost as excited as I am. She and I have much to plan for. Say nothing to Dorian however… I don't want you to spoil my news.

Sincerely,
Lady Rose Hightower

The innocent hope in Rose's letter tore at my heart and I found my eyes watering as I stood there in the dim hallway. I had to deliver the news to her, though it would destroy her dreams for the future. I wondered as well how Marc would handle the news. Two of our best and oldest friends were now gone. Would this wreck his recovery from what the goddess had done to him?

It was too much to figure out alone. We would have to help each other. I couldn't shoulder my own burden and theirs as well. I took the stairs down to the main floor of the house and made my way to the door. Since I had no way of knowing where Marc was I would definitely be looking for Rose first.

I was on high alert as I left the house, with my mind stretched out to its fullest. I was curious as to whether anyone had been watching the house, but although I found several people in the buildings nearby none of them gave any indication that they were interested, or even aware of my appearance. I kept my pace casual as I walked through the city, but I didn't bother to disguise my features. As far as the king knew I might not have even returned home yet.

I found Rose's house less than a block from the tower where her father lived. I knew she possessed several estates in her own right even though her parents were still alive. The Hightower family was so well placed they could afford to pass certain titles on to her while Lord Hightower himself still lived. The house was modestly sized for someone of her relative social standing but it was obviously well cared for.

While most houses in town had large iron knockers on the doors, this one bore a cleverly wrought brass bell. I pulled on a small rope that hung below it and an almost melodic chiming issued forth. It seemed perfectly suited to Rose.

Within a span of breaths the door opened and a woman with neatly coiffed hair answered, "Good day sir. How can I help you?"

"I am here to call on Lady Rose Hightower," I said in cultured tones, doing my best to imitate Benchley's voice. *I haven't thought about that pompous bastard in a while, I wonder how he's doing?*

The woman's eyes made a rapid examination of my clothes as she replied, "May I ask who is calling sir?" Her own clothing was trim and sharp, a dark blue dress with light blue accents. I might have taken her for noblewoman herself but for the practical apron she wore over her front.

"Please tell her that the Count di'Cameron is here, if she is available," I answered.

The door opened wider at that pronouncement, "You may wait inside your Lordship. I'll inform the Lady immediately." She ushered me into a small waiting room near the front hall.

After she left I spent my time examining the furnishings. As expected the room was well appointed. In fact, although the style and decorations weren't as lavish as those at the royal palace, they were better chosen and more tastefully arranged, at least in my opinion. I sat down in a comfortable chair to wait. The cushions on it were covered with a patterned green fabric that matched the rest of the room perfectly.

I didn't wait long however. Almost immediately after sitting the woman who had let me in reappeared. "Lady Rose would like you to join her in her bedroom sir," she told me, though something in her voice gave me the impression she would rather have chewed dung than to say those words. Her expression was definitely disapproving even as she tried to hide her opinion on the matter from me. "If you will follow me," she added and then turned away leading me further into the house.

The house really wasn't that large, and it only took a few seconds to reach the bedroom. The door was still open and Rose called out as soon as she heard us, "I'm so glad you've returned Mordecai! Please come in."

I gave the maid a winning smile and did as I was bid. She entered with me. I knew she simply couldn't bear the thought of me being in the bedroom alone with Rose. *She probably thinks all men are beasts just waiting to get into a lady's boudoir.* Then I got my first look at Rose and my breath caught in my throat.

She was standing in front of a large window with the afternoon sun streaming in around her. Another woman was kneeling behind her with a mouthful of pins and performing some arcane ritual of feminine mystery upon the dress that Rose wore. The dress itself was breathtaking. It was constructed of yellow material and embroidered with pink roses. The hem was far too long for it to be a ball gown, without even considering the train. *Train?* My brain had frozen up, but my eyes continued to explore. The neckline was daring, but not scandalous, showing a graceful neck and hints of her shoulders. Topping it all were Rose's dark curls, except that for once her hair wasn't carefully arranged, or even brushed and loose, instead it had been gathered into an ungainly mop and tied or pinned to the top of her head.

Her eyes caught mine. "Well? What do you think?" she said with an almost girlish smile on her face.

I was frozen in place. The dress could be only one thing, a wedding dress. Knowing her family it had probably been worn by her mother or great grandmother and she was having it fitted. She was pleased by my shocked face. "I'll take that look as a compliment," she said at last.

My mouth worked as my mind tried to come up with some way to rescue what was already one of the most tragic moments I could imagine. "But he hasn't even asked you yet...," came the words from my mouth. Apparently that was the best I could manage.

Rose's eyes darted to her maid and then to the woman pinning her dress, "Mistress Kenwick, now should be a good time for a break. Angela, would you mind taking Mistress Kenwick to the parlor for some refreshments? I'd like some privacy."

Angela, the woman who had escorted me in, dipped her head and ushered the seamstress out. "I'll just leave the door open milady," she replied.

"Shut it please."

Angela pursed her lips unhappily but did as she was told and then I was alone with Rose. I glanced at her again and started to say something but she was quicker and spoke first, "Father said he would be looking forward to meeting Dorian again, which is as close to giving his outright approval as I could expect. I don't think it will be very long after that."

"Still, this seems a bit sudden," I said, floundering for better words.

Rose left the window and came over to greet me more warmly, putting her arms around my shoulders. "Relax Mordecai, I know it could be a year or longer even. I've been waiting years already; this is just a bit of fun. No sense in being caught unprepared after all."

"Years?"

She stepped back and gave me a serious look. "Since his parents sent him to foster under my father's tutelage."

That had been years ago, when Dorian was a growing boy of just thirteen years I recalled. "He told me that he rarely spoke to you then."

Rose laughed, "*He* rarely spoke. I followed him about and teased him frequently. I had never met such a serious young man, nor one so easily embarrassed." The memory put a sparkle in her eyes as she spoke.

I could tell by her mood she was ready to continue the story but I stopped her, "Rose."

She grew still and her eyes searched my face carefully. Her euphoria had blinded her usual perceptiveness, but now her attention had focused fully upon me. In the span of a few seconds she read the sad tale written on my visage and I saw her own features darken. It was like watching rainclouds cover a previously sunny sky. "What happened?"

I had kept myself under control pretty well for the past two days but her simple question undid me. My eyes were watering as I looked away, "I don't know how to say this Rose."

Her voice hardened, "How bad is it?"

"They're both dead Rose… Penny and Dorian both," somehow I got the words out, though my heart felt like lead as I said them.

I had taken my gaze away from her but my magesight showed her clearly as she registered the dire news. An almost imperceptible shiver went through her frame, and then she became utterly still as if she were made of stone. For a long moment she didn't move at all, not even to breathe, the only motion in her was that of her rapidly beating heart. When at last she did move it was a smooth graceful motion, as if she were focusing utterly on her walk.

She sat down on a small couch some fifteen feet away, facing the window. Her face was hidden from me, but I could sense that her eyes were closed when she spoke, "I'd like you to tell me what happened please, while I still have my composure."

I couldn't help but admire her reserve and I wished I had done half as well when I first found out. Slowly, carefully, I began the tale, leaving nothing out. If she was impatient for the important details I couldn't tell, for she never interrupted me or uttered a single word.

Not until I was done and my story ground into an awkward silence did she finally speak again, "Thank you, Mordecai. That was well done." She stood slowly and nodded in my direction. "This is still fresh news for me, if you don't mind I think I'd like to be alone for a while." She had hidden her hands in the folds of her dress but my magesight could still see them trembling.

I took a step in her direction, "Rose…"

"No Mordecai, please," she interrupted. "You may call upon me tomorrow. I need some time to collect myself." The trembling in her hands had moved on to become a more generalized tremor throughout her body.

Her conviction gave me pause and I considered leaving. It seemed a lot easier than facing the storm she held tightly shuttered behind her eyes. Then I remembered my own night, alone in my room, after I had nearly committed murder to quench my thirst for revenge, rather than face my own sorrow. I took several more steps toward her. *You won't face this alone.*

"Please go, Mordecai. You don't understand, that's not how my family deals with things like this," she spoke in a tone of command, but it was undermined by a sudden gut wrenching sob as her voice broke in mid-sentence. Her balance wavered and I caught her before she could fall.

"No Mordecai!" she screamed into my shirt. "That's not how we do things!" She was crying as she yelled at me. "I'm a Hightower, we don't mourn in front of others…," she was sobbing and beating my chest at the same time.

I held onto her firmly, until her violence had lapsed into a more subdued weeping. "Then your family needs to find a better way," I told her softly. She cried for an unknown span of time, and the afternoon shadows grew long and vanished into dusk before she had finished. Eventually she lapsed into silence and I simply held her and stroked her hair. Outside the sun had dropped below the roofline and the city seemed to be holding its breath in expectation of the night.

"I'd better return home," I told her.

She nodded and I noticed her eyes were swollen and puffy. With her hair askew and her red face I couldn't help but think it was the first time I had ever seen her so disheveled. Another day I might have laughed. She walked me to the door herself, while Angela watched disapprovingly. I couldn't imagine what her maid-servant might be thinking.

As I stepped out she grabbed my hand, "Don't go too far. I'll be looking for you tomorrow. Make sure I can find you."

"I need to find Marc still. He hasn't heard the news."

She released my hand. "I can help with that."

I smiled weakly, "Tomorrow then." I turned away and began walking back toward my own city home. The door closed behind me briefly before opening again.

"Mordecai," she called.

I looked over my shoulder at the unkempt Lady Rose, peering from her door, "Yes?"

"Thank you," she said, and then she shut the door again.

I walked on, into the deepening dusk.

CHAPTER 31

The next morning found me still abed when Rose showed up at my door. Actually that statement isn't quite true. The more accurate statement would be that Rose found me still abed when morning showed up at my door. At least morning had the decency to knock first, for she had not.

I stared blearily at the red-clad woman who stood at the foot of my bed, "Damnitt will you stop shaking the bed!"

"Fine I'll be back in a moment," she replied unconcernedly.

That woke me up further as my suspicious instincts kicked in, "Where are you going?"

She smiled wickedly, "To get some water."

I sat up, "Fine, I'm up. Get out so I can put some damned clothes on!" She left promptly and I did indeed rise, though I wasn't about to 'shine' so early in the day. I had stayed up late the night before trying to understand the 'stasis field' enchanting schemata. It was either that or go burn down the royal palace, but Penny's note had been very explicit that I should save the king for later. That was alright, I knew where his majesty lived and it wasn't as if he'd be moving soon.

The enchantment still frustrated me, which was a large part of the reason I hadn't gone to bed early. I had trouble letting go of a problem once I had started on it. In this case I had figured out how to construct the rune structure without problem, it was intricate but the pattern was repetitive enough that I had no trouble memorizing it. I just didn't understand what it actually 'did'.

In the end I had constructed a working model using the stylus and small wooden box. The field was supposed to permeate the interior of the box when it was activated, that much was clear. Still, nothing seemed to happen to anything I put into the box... either before, after, or during the time it was activated. I had gone to bed puzzled and frustrated.

I found Lady Rose downstairs in the kitchen. She had brought a basket with her and was laying items out on the small breakfast table. "You look awfully domestic," I mumbled.

She looked at me sharply, "You look thin. How many meals have you eaten since you found out?"

"None of your damned business," I told her self-righteously as I sat down and began eating the scones she had brought. I couldn't remember when I had eaten last.

"Those taste better if you put some of the jam on them," she suggested.

I was in no mood, "I prefer them plain," I said around a mouthful of scone. I doubt any of the words were intelligible. Then I picked up the tea and promptly burned my tongue.

"Take your time, the food won't escape," Rose said with a slight smile.

I swallowed and took another sip of the tea, this time without burning myself. "I didn't expect you to bring breakfast."

"Penny wouldn't like it if you starved to death and... well you can think of it as a thank you," she answered.

I snorted, "A thank you? For what?"

"Yesterday," she said simply.

"That's what family does."

"Family?" she said, raising an eyebrow.

I raised my own eyebrow, just to show her she wasn't the only one with witty brows. "I've never had a large family, so I've been adding my friends to it since I was very young. Congratulations, you've been adopted. Would you like to be my little sister, cousin, or aunt?"

"Aunt? I think sister would suit better," she said crinkling her nose.

"Little sister it is then," I said in a final tone.

"I am a bit older than you though," she reminded me.

"Don't worry I won't tell anyone."

She laughed a little at that. It was clear neither of us would recover our brighter spirits anytime soon, but I was determined not to give in to despair. "Do you know what else family does?" I asked.

She had just filled her mouth with tea so she merely shook her head in negation.

I narrowed my eyes, "Family gets even."

She raised that lone eyebrow again, "Why do you think I wore red today?"

Half an hour later we were walking through the city, heading toward the temple of Doron the Iron God, if Rose was to be believed.

"Can you explain to me exactly why he thought he should be staying with the Iron Brothers?" I asked her again.

"He thought they would be easier to fool," she replied.

That didn't go far toward explaining the entire scheme to me, "But you said he was planning to examine the archives of Karenth the Just. Why is he here?" By here I was referring to the large brooding structure looming over the street on the right hand side. While most of Albamarl was constructed of local rose granite that hadn't been good enough for the Iron Brothers, they had felt the need to import a lot of drab grey granite to face the walls with. It probably hadn't been cheap to achieve the depressing look they had wanted. I was also willing to bet that underneath the surface most of the bulk of the building was built with rose granite.

"He's taken on the identity of a visiting priest of Doron, who is interested in viewing the Karenthian archives," she explained.

"And he thought disguising himself as a priest of Karenth would be more difficult? Doesn't actually staying here among the Doronites increase his chances of detection?" I had a lot more questions where those came from, but I was pacing myself.

Rose sighed, "Talk to him about it when you see him."

I grunted and then replied, "Let me see if I can find him first." Closing my eyes I focused on my other 'sight' and extended my mind to a much greater extent, so that I could search the temple in front of us. It was larger than it appeared; the building actually had been built on top of an extensive underground complex. Some of it even extended underneath our feet. There were cells and storerooms, and a variety of living quarters. There were also quite a few people. At a rough count I would have guessed at least three hundred people were within the building at the moment, and they weren't holding services currently.

"There's a lot more Doronic clergy in there than I expected," I said at last.

"Doronic?"

"I know they prefer 'Iron Brotherhood', or 'Doronite', but I like 'Doronic'. It sounds a lot more like moronic."

Rose groaned, "Did you find him?"

"Not yet, it's more difficult when there are more people. I have to examine each one," I closed my eyes again. Several minutes later I had found him, though his situation confused me. He was in what appeared to be one of their cells for visiting clergy, but he wasn't alone. I had initially passed over him because I had assumed he would be by himself if he was in the living quarters. *That was my mistake.* "I found him."

"What is he doing?" asked Rose.

I was torn between my desire to keep my friend's private business, well… private, and the desire to snicker. Trust Marc to find a priestess with an 'itch'. I looked at Rose and scratched my head, "He's discussing matters with one of the other clergy members."

She watched my face carefully, "He's only been in there a few days and he's already bedding the women?"

I was embarrassed by proxy, "That's a long time for him, and how did you know it was that?"

She held up a finger, "One, I can tell he likes women. Two, your eyes darted off to the side right before you spoke."

I was curious, "How can you tell he likes women?" As far as I knew he hadn't had any lady friends that she knew about.

"You watch the eyes," she replied. "That and posture tell me all I need to know."

"Posture?"

"People lean toward you when they're interested."

I filed that information away without looking at it too closely. I didn't want to know what Rose might have read in my eyes over the past few years. "Well you guessed correctly," I told her, and then added, "about Marc's activities in there."

"So do we wait for him to emerge?"

"I'd rather not. Let's go in and find him," I replied.

Lady Rose shook her head, "If you weren't a wizard I'd think you were mad. How do you plan to accomplish that, without exposing him?"

"Do you trust me?"

She looked up into my eyes, "More than anyone else still living." Then she looked away. Even with her self-control some things were just too painful to say, and neither of us could afford to start crying in the street.

"There's an empty storeroom under the street over there," I said pointing to an alley running alongside the temple. "We can enter there without anyone noticing us and it should be a short walk from there to the cells the priests sleep in."

A minute later we were standing beside the building, in the alley I had indicated. "I don't see an entry," commented Rose.

"There isn't one. It's directly underneath us," I informed her.

Her eyes widened as she looked at me, "How far beneath us?"

"Fifty feet or so, would you like to come with me or wait up here?"

"I'm coming with you. What do I have to do?" she asked.

I was surprised at her easy acceptance. "Shouldn't you be warning me not to do anything stupid?"

Her face softened, "I'm not Penny dear. I expect you to make your own judgments regarding magic, but if you damage this dress I'll take it out of you in blood."

Her remark made me want to laugh and cry at the same time, so I ignored it and moved on. "I'll need you to get close to me for this to work."

"How close?" she said.

"I'm not sure, in physical contact at least," I told her.

She stepped into me and wrapped her arms around my waist, "Is this sufficient?"

I had been thinking that holding hands would suffice, but I wasn't going to tell her otherwise now. I put my own arms around her and tried to concentrate. It took longer than I had expected. Rose smelled very nice.

Pushing those thoughts aside I listened carefully to the stone beneath us. It was a complicated mixture of cobblestones laid over gravel and sand. Beneath that was layer of clay and then more stone, this time natural stone. I struggled to integrate it all into my 'self', while at the same time maintaining Rose as a separate physical entity. I didn't want to think about what might occur if I accidentally blurred the boundaries between us.

After a moment I began to sink into myself, or rather into what I would previously have called the ground. Rose wasn't moving however and I had to make a conscious effort to allow her to pass through me. If it sounds confusing that's because it was. It was hard enough to visualize and language isn't really made for describing the mixing of perspectives between animate and inanimate.

Eventually we both emerged from the ceiling of the store room deep below. The ceilings down there were low so we managed to reach the floor without much of a drop. I took a moment to disconnect myself from the stone and earth above us and return my consciousness to normal. Once I had regained my proper perspective again I realized I was still holding Rose.

Holding her close like that felt good, and for a second I didn't want to release her. I hated myself for that thought immediately. I took my arms away, "It's safe to let go now."

"I wasn't sure," she said. "That was the strangest experience of my life. It felt as though the stone and earth itself were *flowing* around us." She was staring upward at the ceiling in wonder. "I can't imagine what the world must be like for you."

"What do you mean?"

"You have the power to change the world around you, to suit your whims. If I had such power I'm not certain I would use it wisely."

I'm not sure I will either, I thought to myself. "I never had a choice in the matter. I'm just doing the best I can to use it for the greater good." That was a presumptuous line, but I didn't know how else to phrase it.

"You will succeed Mordecai. You're a good man," she patted me on the cheek as she said it.

"Not as good a man as Dorian was," I said thinking of my lost friend.

"True," she agreed with a sad note in her voice. "He was the truest, most honest, and chivalrous man I ever met. Not just in his word and deed, but right down to his very bones. You are not as 'good' as he was."

Her explanation was a bit excessive, but it was accurate in every particular.

"But still, I think you are the best one to bear the burden of that power," she added. "The choices and responsibilities that your power will thrust upon you would undo someone as pure as he was. Your power and goals will require compassion, adaptability, and cunning."

I didn't really want to engage in excessive philosophic discourse in a moldy storeroom, though her words did strike a chord in me. "Let's go find Marc before we talk the day away."

"What if we're seen? We don't exactly blend in," Rose pointed out, gesturing to her red dress. It was of a practical cut, but the color and the woman wearing it would draw attention no matter where you put them.

"There's no one in the halls. Those that are moving around are up above. I think I can get us to his room without encountering anyone from where we are now," I explained. It was very useful being able to explore the layout without venturing there, and even more useful knowing where all the inhabitants were.

I opened the door and led her into the corridor. It was a short walk and a few turns before I led her into the hallway that served the cells where Marc was currently 'engaged'. We reached his doorway without being seen. The noises coming faintly through the door made it plain that we had reached the right room.

"Now what?" said Rose.

"Shibal," I said sternly in the direction of the door. The sounds inside changed, as one of the partners abruptly stopped vocalizing. Marc of course was wearing the necklace I had given him. The door had no lock, but was barred from within; another word and I removed the bar. Rose and I stepped inside quickly and closed the door behind us.

"Son of a bitch!" Marc exclaimed coarsely. "You bastard, you scared me half to death."

"I can see that," I said smugly, glancing down at the woman who had collapsed beside him.

"Boys... behave," Rose admonished us. She leaned over to pull the blanket up over the woman's naked form. I was oddly disappointed, but no one else needed to know that. Rose looked at Marc, "And you... cover that thing up, no one wants to see that."

I stuck my tongue out at him from behind her, while he responded with wounded dignity, "I'll have you know that a number of ladies have expressed quite the opposite opinion." He drew the other side of the blanket up to cover himself as well. "I'm assuming you have a good reason for barging into a young priest's room without so much as knocking."

As usual I found myself smiling at his banter, until I remembered the news I had to give him. "I do. I can't spend too much time in the city and I didn't know how long it would be before you returned to the house."

"You must have important news then. Is it safe to talk here? How long will she be out?" he patted the woman next to him gently on the rump.

"An hour or more, but my news can wait. It will take longer than that to discuss," I replied.

Marc answered quickly, "If you like I can come and meet you at the house, say around noon?"

It was closing in on somewhere past nine already at my best guess. "You can leave without ruining your disguise?"

"Certainly, I do so all the time. This cell is just a courtesy for a visiting brother," he said gesturing with his hand to include the room, as if he were in grand surroundings.

"Why exactly did you need to stay here?" I said suspiciously.

He grinned, "It helps further the disguise. I've learned innumerable things while sharing meals and accommodations with the Iron Brothers."

"And?"

He smirked, "and your house is rather unfriendly to strangers that you haven't personally vouched for, like sweet Marissa here."

Rose spoke up, "Can we save the chatter for later gentlemen?" I got the impression the setting made her uneasy.

"Noon then," I said looking at Marc. He nodded in acknowledgment and drew Marissa closer as if to snuggle as we started through the door.

Rose stopped in shock, "Have you no shame? The girl's still unconscious!"

Marc was unabashed, "That's disgusting. You should wash your head out for having such dirty thoughts; I was planning to wake her up first." Then he tilted his head as if thinking, "Though your idea does have some merit, sick as it is."

I ushered Rose out the door before she could kill him, trying not to laugh as I did. "That man is unbelievable!" she said as we moved quickly down the corridor.

"Shhh," I told her, "Let's wait 'til we get somewhere else to talk about it."

To her credit she did hold her tongue 'til we got back to the old storeroom. "Your friend is a cad," she said simply.

"As you so recently told me, I'm not exactly a saint myself," I replied.

She looked at me with a worried frown, "Do you think he really woke her up?"

That did start me to laughing. *She really is worried he might ravish the poor girl in her sleep,* I thought to myself. "Do you want me to check?" I answered. "Really?" I had been deliberately keeping my mind from observing Marc's room up until that point.

Rose was torn, "No." She chewed her lip for a moment before speaking again, "Yes, but don't be a voyeur about it."

"Alright, let me focus for a moment," I said more dramatically than necessary. Stepping back I closed my eyes, though at such close range it really wasn't necessary. After a few seconds I made an expression of interest. "Oh, now that's original," I said aloud.

"Stop looking!" Rose admonished me. "Did he wake her up or not?"

"I don't think she's fully awake yet, but she will be before long I'm quite certain," I said with authority. "Now let's head back…"

Rose glared at me suspiciously, "*How* is he waking her up?"

I looked upward, not wanting to meet her eyes. "Well he's kissing her… sort of."

Rose blushed until her skin tone matched her name, "That's enough, let's go."

I laughed so hard it was several minutes before I was able to concentrate. Somewhere in the middle of it Rose joined me.

CHAPTER 32

Marc arrived a half an hour before noon, just before we had finished preparing for lunch. We had bought some food on the way back, and Rose had tested her cooking skills warming it up while we waited.

Unfortunately her skills had not extended much beyond setting the table. Although we had bought nothing more complicated than fresh sausages and bread she had managed to burn the sausages while heating them in a pan. Thankfully she hadn't tried to warm up the bread.

The experience had her more flustered and upset than I had ever seen her, since she was normally the epitome of grace and reserve. It had never occurred to me that her sheltered upbringing might have left her short on a few skills that most people from my own social background took for granted.

Although cooking was generally considered a woman's art, most of the men in Washbrook knew the basics, and quite a few went well beyond that. Joe McDaniel was an excellent cook I happened to know from experience. My father had also been a fair hand with a skillet. I made sure to mention none of this to Rose as I helped to fix the mess.

Marc wandered into the kitchen as I was helping to cut the burned part off the sausages so I could reheat them. While they had burned in places most of them were still partly raw as well. As a result Marc had no idea that it was

Rose that had burned the food. Obviously he never would have expected Rose to have tried her hand at cooking.

"What is that smell?" he observed upon entering.

I glanced at Rose before answering, "I got distracted and left the sausages on too long. They burned before I caught my mistake."

He grinned, "And here you always bragged at being such a fine cook. You should have brought Penny with you. Now there's a girl that knows what she's doing behind a stove."

Rose made her way past him, visibly agitated, "I'll be outside. I need some air. I'll be back in a few minutes."

"What's wrong with her?" Marc asked after she had left.

"Aside from the fact that she was the one that burned the sausages, not much, idiot," I told him.

He winced, "Ouch, I'll have to apologize when she returns."

"You know better than that, I already said it was me that burned them," I replied.

He looked me over carefully, "Both of you seem awfully high strung today. What news do you have?"

I turned the sausage over in the pan to avoid repeating Rose's mistake. I was grateful for something to do to disguise my reaction to his question. "Let's save my news for after yours. I'm curious as to what you found out," I said over my shoulder.

He paused at that and I could almost hear him thinking. He had known me for long enough to know when I was stalling for time. Finally he decided to ignore it and play along. "I've learned all sorts of interesting things this past week," he began.

"Are you sure? It seemed to me that you were more focused on learning the ins and outs of a certain Doronic priestess," I observed.

He put a finger to his lips as if in thought, "Doronic, I like that. It definitely has a certain ring to it. However you are still wrong, Marissa isn't a member of the Doronite clergy."

"She certainly seemed to have the proper calling," I said. I was pretty proud of that one.

Marc laughed, "Actually I agree with you on that. She's definitely grown on me. However the key point is that the Iron God doesn't accept women among his exalted clergymen. There is also the small matter of her being a devotee of Celior instead."

I turned and stared at him, "Wait, let me get this straight. You are impersonating one of the Iron Brothers in order to seek access to the Karenthian archives, while at the same time you are bedding a priestess of Celior. Do I have all that in order or should I be confused about a few more things as well?"

"More specifically, I'm a visiting priest from Verningham," he corrected me.

"My pardon, a visiting priest... what name did you give them by the way?"

"Marc."

"And you don't think anyone is going to make the connection between your features and that name? You made quite a splash last year as the new channeler for Millicenth," I reminded him.

"That's why I chose Doron's temple as opposed to that of Millicenth's. Besides, I prefer using my own name, it simplifies all the lying."

"How so?"

He made a serious face as if he were beginning a lecture. "First, it means I don't have to worry about not responding when someone calls me from a distance using my assumed name and second, it makes the cut by satisfying my third rule of lying."

We had had a few conversations like this one before, but I struggled to remember which rule was the third one. After a minute he took pity on me and explained without waiting for me to ask. "The third rule is that if a lie cannot follow rules one or two, it should be so preposterous or unbelievable that no one will doubt it. Using my own name is so silly that anyone hearing it will discount the possibility right away, since I would never use my own name to impersonate a priest, especially given my rather famous past." He crossed his arms smugly as he finished.

"Remind me what the first two rules were," I said blandly. I wasn't going to give him the satisfaction of laughing.

"Rule one was do not lie, or if you do, do so by omission. Rule two states if you must lie, always do so by including as much of the truth as possible," he rattled off immediately.

"It worries me that you have these rules memorized."

"You yourself are reaping the benefits even now. Since I disinherited myself you might consider hiring me as your spymaster general. I think I have a talent for it," he said modestly.

"I won't disagree with that," said Rose from the doorway behind him. She appeared much more herself now that she had returned.

Marc bowed in her direction, "Thank you milady."

"Back to what you discovered," I prodded.

"Oh yes, that! Well after I showed my credentials from the chapter in Verningham the brothers were kind enough to put me up at the temple here in Albamarl and from there it…"

"Credentials?" I interrupted.

"A letter of introduction from Abbot Simon in Verningham," he clarified.

"How did you get that?" I questioned.

He sighed audibly, "I forged it Mort. Are you going to keep interrupting every time I get going? It really drags the story out."

"Sorry," I apologized. I also made a note that Marc still had talents I had yet to discover after all our years as friends.

He glared at me for a second, then opened his mouth as if he were about to speak. When I said nothing he finally went on, "So from there I went to the temple of Karenth and presented myself as an itinerant scholar and gained permission to search the archives."

I marveled at his brazen accomplishments, but I had come to expect surprises from Marc over the years. Before I could ask another question he went on, "So I began my search and I quickly discovered that the damned place is a maze of books and moldy scrolls. It would take most of my lifetime to search that place and I still might miss the information we're looking for, so I sought out expert advice."

Rose swallowed the piece of burnt sausage she had been idly nibbling at and broke in, "You mean you began sleeping with people."

Marc gave her an indignant look, "Marissa is not people. She is a promising 'light' in the church of Celior, not to mention an accomplished scholar of history."

Rose rolled her eyes but said nothing.

"Anyway, I met Marissa in the stacks, and it turns out that not many men share her interest in ancient church history. She was very pleased to share her knowledge and to help answer my questions as they arose," he said somberly.

"If you were in the Karenthian archives, what was a priestess of Celior doing there?" I asked.

He pointed at me, "See! Now you show your ignorance. The archives are a resource shared by all four temples. The Karenthians are simply the ones in charge of managing it."

"So what did you find out?" I asked impatiently.

Marc frowned. Obviously I was ruining his hard won tale. "Well if you want me to shorten things up, Marissa helped me do some research on the city's early days, before and immediately after the events of the Sundering. Unfortunately there was very little of practical use recorded about Moira's battle against Balinthor, other than the usual, she summoned a colossal giant of earth and stone that battled and eventually overcame Balinthor. Although she won there is no mention of her afterward, so I'm assuming she died during or shortly after the battle."

I nodded, "That's essentially true."

He looked at me oddly. I hadn't gotten around to telling anyone about my ongoing conversation with Moira Centyr, not even him. As it was I didn't want to spoil his efforts, it had been hard enough for him to find a purpose after his depression. "Do you know something about that?" he asked me.

"Not much, but what you found agrees with what I've read," I told him. *Now there's a perfect example of the subtle use of rule number two in lying,* I thought to myself.

After a moment he continued, "What I did discover of importance, was that during the chaos of Balinthor's war against humanity the Illeniel family moved something here of great importance. Something they didn't want falling into the hands of strangers, or malevolent gods."

I leaned forward. I was all ears now, "Go on…"

Marc smiled, "Apparently the early churches were all watching the remaining wizards carefully, particularly after the war was over. There are several missives detailing their activities, especially those regarding the Illeniel family. From what they could piece together it was suspected that something called 'Illeniel's Doom' was moved to Albamarl."

"If that were true then the most likely location for it today… would be here, in this house," I noted.

"Assuming they didn't have a secret storehouse somewhere," Rose pointed out.

"True," I agreed, though I personally doubted they would let something that important be kept away from this house. Usually the best protection a wizard can provide is his own presence. "What else did you discover?"

"The early clergy believed that Balinthor was primarily after Illeniel's Doom, and that his attempt to wipe out humanity was merely a secondary goal of revenge."

That was news to me. Moira had barely known of its existence, much less thinking it could be the dark god's primary motivation. I would have to question her more closely later, for it appeared the priests of that ancient time had known more about the doings of the Illeniels than their fellow wizards had. "That will deserve a lot of consideration later, anything else?" I asked.

"Well I'm not sure if this is important, but it is certainly interesting. It seems the Iron Brothers keep a secret compound in the woodlands to the northwest," he replied.

Rose spoke up, "How secret?"

"So secret that they're hiding its existence even from the other churches," he answered with a roguish smile.

"How did you find out about it?" I said.

"Purely by accident," he replied. "If I hadn't decided to stay with the Doronites I never would have known a thing. As it was I just happened to hear someone complaining in the dining hall one day and it piqued my interest, after that it was mainly a matter of paying attention."

"Any idea what they use it for?"

"Not a clue," he admitted. "They send a small load of supplies and sundries every few weeks and apparently those chosen for duty there find it exceedingly boring."

I took a deep breath, "Well if that's all your news I suppose I should bring you up to date on matters back in Lancaster."

"Good, I'm tired of wondering what you and Rose have been so tense about," he said mildly.

I glanced at Rose for support but her expression told me that this would be my tale to tell. I took another breath and jumped in headfirst, "Things went badly after I left Penny and Dorian in Lancaster last week. They were ambushed in the guest room they were given. Miriam was stabbed and she and Penny were both abducted." Marc's eyes grew round as I spoke, but he made no move to interrupt.

"Dorian gave chase and saved Miriam. I believe he nearly saved Penny as well, but they were surrounded in the forest by a large group of shiggreth and overwhelmed. He and Penny, along with almost all of the kidnappers are now dead, or worse than dead," I finished.

True to his upbringing my friend kept his calm after I had finished. When he finally spoke it was to ask questions, which I answered as best I could. Over the space of a half an hour I related what had happened after I had found out, omitting my near destruction of everything and focusing on my rage and near murder of the surviving witness instead. I told him about Walter and my thoughts about his possible future usefulness.

When he had run out of questions and I had run out of things to add we both sat silent for a long while. Rose watched us from a short distance away. She had remained quiet the entire time. My guess was that she didn't trust herself to speak on the topic yet.

After some time had passed Marc leaned back in his chair and looked at me, "You know what this means?"

I had some inkling what he would say next, but I simply nodded.

"There is a certain king that needs killing," he supplied.

Rose leaned in, "Yes!" It was the first time she had shown any enthusiasm in the conversation.

I stood up and my nervous energy set me to pacing. "I agree with you, though he isn't the only one, nor should he be the first."

"The shiggreth?" he said questioningly.

I nodded, "They were already on the list but now they will be first. I want to save Edward for last."

"Why?" he asked.

"Because someone is talking to them," Rose interrupted. "They should not have known that the King's operatives would be escaping with fugitives on that particular day, and in that particular place. That means either they have spies in high places or someone has established some sort of alliance with them and is feeding them information, someone close to the King."

"Exactly," I affirmed. "What was a simple war of humanity against the creatures of darkness has now been complicated. Very likely someone on our side has thrown in with the forces of evil. We need to know who before we remove the King from power."

I could see Marc's mind had already caught up with us and he was working ahead to try and figure out the best course of action. "We need someone inside the palace," he said finally.

"What were you saying about being a 'spymaster general'?" I reminded him.

He shook his head, "In this case I'm the wrong choice, even more so than with the clergy I am too well known among the nobility."

Rose agreed with him, "No offence, but even given Marcus' exalted social standing; he was raised as country gentry. This will require someone with an intimate knowledge of the city and the people that call it home, particularly those in the palace."

The two of them exchanged glances. As usual when it came to intrigue they agreed with one another. "You're suggesting that you can find the information we need?" I said looking at Rose.

She smiled in a fashion that reminded me of her usual confidence, "Of course I am. Marcus needs to finish ferretting out the secrets of the priests. I suspect that he may be close to something that may be important."

"Aren't you too well known to sneak into the palace?" I said, bringing up one of the arguments Marc had used to rule himself out.

She raised her eyebrow again, "Why Mordecai, who said anything about sneaking in? Do you have such a low opinion of me? I will discover what we need to know through various contacts. I think it is not too far from the truth if I say that I know absolutely everyone important in this city, and if I don't… I know someone else who does."

A cold shiver went up my spine. Rose could be rather intimidating when she put a little effort into it. Then I realized I was the only one left without an assigned task. "What will I do to keep myself busy in the meantime?" I wondered idly.

Marc gave me a wicked grin, "You should check with my father. It's been a few days; I suspect he's got news by now."

"What makes you say that?" I inquired.

"My father loves to hunt. I dare say he is nearly as knowledgeable in the forest as his master huntsman, William, and William is far from the only hunter in his employ. If he has not managed to trace at least some of them by now I'll eat my hat," he informed me with a certain amount of pride.

"You don't have a hat," I pointed out.

He groaned wearily, "It's a figure of speech. Anyway, you're so used to thinking like a wizard you forget that men are not helpless without magic. He won't have been idle while you were here, but he may need your help when he finds them."

CHAPTER 33

The next morning I returned to Lancaster. We had talked long into the night but in the end we didn't have any better solutions than what we had started with.

Stepping out of the teleportation circle I spotted two men standing guard within the building that held them. They had already taken note of my appearance and were opening their mouths to speak. I was too quick for them however. "You!" I said sharply. "Where is the Duke presently?"

The man looked quite anxious, probably due to my aggressive demeanor. "He should be in the keep your Lordship, taking breakfast, given the hour." I had arrived fairly early.

"Excellent," I replied and turned to head that way.

The man called after me, "He said to tell you that he would like to speak with you as soon as you arrived."

I laughed and kept walking. Entering the keep I headed straight for the great hall. A number of people pointed and began talking as they saw me pass, which gave me the impression I had been the topic of discussion lately, but I didn't bother trying to listen in. When I entered the great hall the effect was entirely the opposite. All conversation died as I made my way to the high table, and silence fell over the room.

James stood as I got close and greeted me with an embrace. As his head came close to mine he spoke quietly, "Where the hell have you been these past two days?"

"I had a wizard to interrogate, people to inform, and information to gather. I take it things have been exciting in my absence?" I didn't bother to keep my voice quiet. The crowd needed something to talk about after all.

The duke sat down again. "Do you think a band of armed men could infiltrate my castle, assault and murder my guests, and then escape without any repercussions?"

"They're already dead," I replied. "Except for the wizard," I added.

James leaned toward me, "And what did you learn from your new guest?"

"That his situation is more complicated than it at first appeared, and our enemies are more powerful than we knew," I said wittily. I had probably spent too much time in Lady Rose's company.

The duke's eyes narrowed, "That is ever the case, but what of the particulars?"

I shook my head negatively, "Not here Your Grace, the matter requires as much tact as dealing with royalty."

James' eyes widened momentarily but he showed no other sign of having understood my meaning. Instead he rapidly switched to his own news and delivered it with his usual enthusiasm, "The news that shiggreth in the hundreds could be roaming my lands with impunity did not sit well with me, nor did it please Master William or my other foresters. Despite the great lengths the enemy went to in order to disguise their trail we believe we have run them aground."

I showed my teeth in an expression that only resembled a smile in the most superficial of ways. "Marc told me you'd find them," I replied.

A shadow crossed James' face so quickly I doubt many would have noticed it, "How is my son?"

"Doing well," I told him. "He has taken to intrigue and subterfuge like a duck to water. At the moment he is engaged in Albamarl, ferreting out secrets for me. More importantly, I think he is recovering from what happened to him."

He nodded, "I want you to tell me in more detail later." I knew he meant his words.

"I will."

"William and I had a devil of a time finding the shiggreth," he said returning to the subject at hand.

"My husband spent more time in the woods than at home after what happened," came the voice of Genevieve from behind me. She had walked up while we talked. I glanced up with an expression of mock surprise. She leaned over and kissed me on the cheek. "Nephew," she said simply.

"Your Grace," I replied. "I hope you can forgive my rudeness the other day."

She raised a hand as if she were shooing a fly away, "Nonsense, I recall no fault on your part."

"Thank you," I told her.

James interrupted, "As I was saying, we searched high and low, but the tracks of so many going in so many directions made it impossible to find them at first."

"So how did you do it?" I asked.

"If it were a cunning beast you would circle the area more widely, until at last you find where the trail emerges, but these were no animals. They are intelligent, and each one took a separate path, even after traveling miles from where they converged. William and I had to divide my lands into sections and assign men to search each of them. Even so nothing was found, until we reached the foothills," he answered.

"I might have thought you would start there, rather than in the forests," I commented.

James sighed, "I had thought it would turn out this way, but I could not leave the forests unexamined. Otherwise we might have left a viper near our bosom while we were searching further afield."

I had to admit he had a point.

"When we started searching the foothills to the east we lost several men," he went on. "I had to increase the size of the search parties to groups of five men each. The next day I lost an entire patrol group and I knew we were getting close."

"They seem pretty bold. Surely they realized that would give away their location," I pondered aloud.

James snorted, "They're desperate and they knew we were drawing close. It was only a matter of time. I mobilized all my armsmen at that point. We swept through the hills leaving no stone unturned in that region."

"When was this?"

"Yesterday," he said with a smile. "We found their hole. There's a cave out there, and they've gone underground. My men have them bottled up now."

"What if they have another exit?" I worried the enemy might circle around and attack Lancaster while he was focused on their 'lair'.

"That thought occurred to me," he said. "I sent a message to you yesterday, asking for men and assistance."

I frowned, "I haven't been home yet, but I'm sure Sir Harold will respond in my stead."

"I received a reply late last night. He promised to be here before noon with as many men as he thought he could safely muster without endangering the defense of Washbrook and Castle Cameron," said the duke.

"Then he is on the road as we speak," I observed. "How soon do you plan to leave?"

"As soon as he arrives."

I rose abruptly, "Then I have some preparations to make."

James chuckled grimly, "You always do… heaven protect us. Best hurry, I won't hold the men up if you haven't returned by the time he gets here."

◆━━◆

Walter looked up as I entered the room where I was keeping him under, 'house' arrest. "How are you feeling?" I asked. He looked tired and he had dark circles under his eyes, but somehow I could tell he was starting to recover.

"Now that the fever is gone much better," he said plainly. "Though I have to admit this necklace makes me feel blind and helpless." He held up the necklace I had used to block his magesight as well as his power.

I had spoken to the guards as well as those in charge of keeping his wound clean while I was gone and they had informed me regarding his condition already. Yesterday the fever from his wound had broken at last, signaling that he would most likely survive. He was still quite weak, though. "Think you can ride?"

He made a face, "It won't be pleasant, but yes."

"How do you feel about the shiggreth?"

"As any decent man would feel, they are an abomination and a threat to all of us," he responded promptly. After a pause he added, "They also scare the living daylights out of me."

"A reasonable response, though I have to say… most decent men don't even know they exist," I sat down next to him so I could see his face more closely as we talked.

He looked at me with anxiety in his face, "You've found them haven't you?"

"James Lancaster has," I informed him. "We ride from his keep in a few hours to burn them out of their nest."

"You know they eat magic as easily as men's souls don't you?" he said nervously.

"I've fought them before," I told him. "I'd like you to see what happens today, and it is entirely possible I might need your help."

He gestured at his wounded leg, "I've just returned from death's door. I'm not sure how much help I will be, especially with this." His hand touched the pendant at his neck.

"My father was friends with your older brother, did you know that?"

He nodded.

"Why didn't you say anything about it?" I said curiously.

"I'm a prisoner. Anything I say will just make it seem as if I'm trying to curry favor. Besides you never knew your father, so there was no way to verify the claim," he answered rationally.

I liked his answer. "If I take that necklace off will you give me your word on something?"

He looked at me suspiciously, "Perhaps, it depends upon what it is. More importantly, of what value is my word to you?"

I wasn't sure how to answer that, but I trusted what Penny had told me. I also found that the more I talked to Walter the less I hated him. He definitely wasn't a man given to violence or aggression. If anything he might even be something of a coward, though I had no way to judge that yet. But I got the impression he was at the very least a man of compassion, a man who had been badly used. "Its value will depend upon how you honor it. Betray me and you will never get another chance," I responded somberly.

"If it conflicts with my need to protect my family I won't give it. If I give it and discover later that my family is jeopardized by my keeping it, I will break it without a moment's thought. Is that the sort of honor you would trust?"

I thought of Cyhan and his unbending oaths. If I had not known him I might have had a different answer, but now I had a wiser view on the matter. "It sounds exactly like the sort of honor I would trust. Help me with this Walter, and if it is possible I will do all I can to help recover your family safely."

He sighed, "Fine. Tell me what you want me to swear to."

"Swear you will not seek to escape or use your power to oppose me. Swear you will follow my orders, except and until they endanger your family. Swear that, and I will remove the necklace."

Walter watched me carefully as I spoke and when I finished he answered, "I so swear." A moment later he added, "I see why the king fears you now."

"What do you mean?"

"If he had been like you he would never have taken my family hostage, nor would he have needed to do so," he explained.

"You don't know me Walter," I replied.

He laughed, "On the contrary I was watching your every move for almost two months. I think I know you fairly well. Your people trust you and your armsmen would walk through fire if you asked them to do so."

His praise was honest but it made me uncomfortable. *And what about my wife?* I thought to myself. *The last part of the fairy tale should have been that my wife was the most beautiful woman in the land and that every man was jealous of our happiness.* I swallowed as a bitter knot rose in my throat.

I ignored his comments and reached over to gently grasp the necklace. With hardly any effort I picked out its voice and in an instant it became a part of me. I pulled it apart as though it were made of soft cheese instead of metal. Once I had it off I put the ends back together and watched the silver chain reform as if it had never parted.

Walter watched with keen interest, "How are you doing that? I can't sense any power being used at all."

"I just listen," I said patiently.

He snorted, "If my wife were here she would say that rules me out as far as being able to do whatever it is you just did."

I laughed politely, but thinking about his wife didn't make me feel any better. Glancing down at the necklace I decided I had better remove the iron sphere just to be safe. The last thing I wanted was an accidental explosion. Repeating my action of a moment ago I separated the iron ball from the silver clasp.

Now that his magesight was restored Walter could sense the power stored within it. "That's what you had set in case I broke the necklace? I doubt there would have been anything left of me. How did you manage to store so much energy in there?"

"That's a conversation for another day," I told him, not wanting to get into the details of how I had rediscovered the art of enchanting. "I'd better get rid of this." I had a chest full of similar explosive iron balls, tucked away, and the pouch at my belt allowed me to safely store and access them without actually carrying them around with me, but I wanted to make one further point while I had Walter's full attention.

With a word I formed a shield around the iron ball and then I redoubled it. Once I felt sure it was strong enough I pulled the glass ball that matched it from my purse and swiftly broke it with a second word. The iron ball exploded silently.

The force of the explosion in my hand was incredible and it came very near to exceeding my ability to contain it in the fist-sized shield I held around it. I was careful to keep my face calm and my features smooth the entire time, but I needn't have worried. Walter's attention was entirely focused upon the roiling sphere of light and flame I held before me. He had leapt back several feet and erected his own shields reflexively. "Sweet Lady protect us!" he yelled and I worried he might hurt himself further trying to move so quickly on his injured leg.

"Sorry, I didn't mean to startle you," I lied. I had definitely meant to startle him. I walked nonchalantly over to the window and then carefully created a small opening on one side of the shield I had around the tightly compressed ball of pure energy and iron fragments. The force vented violently into the air beside the castle and if I hadn't already braced myself the reactionary force might have thrown me back into the room. As it was, I hoped my demonstration had made the desired impression on Walter.

He didn't say anything else, but I could see the wheels turning in his head. I hoped he had gotten my message, which if I had put it into words would have been something like this: *don't even think of crossing me, because if I decide I need to do something about you it won't be any more difficult than it would be for an ordinary person to swat a fly.* Of course the other possibility was that I had just convinced him I was a few cards shy of a full deck. Either way it would serve the same purpose.

Chapter 34

It was late afternoon when we finally rode into the foothills in the eastern part of James's lands. In the distance the Elentir Mountains could be seen rising up on the horizon. Supposedly those mountains had been created long ago, by the first wizard to bear the name Illeniel. What no one really knew was why he had done it. Most people discounted the story as a fairy tale these days, but after my experience nearly destroying Lothion I had come to give the story greater credence.

Walter and I had used the teleportation circles to reach Lancaster quickly and borrowed horses from the duke's stable. Sir Harold had showed up shortly after we arrived, leading a force of some five hundred of my armsmen. Seeing them mustered so quickly and efficiently made me even more aware of how much the war had changed my estate.

It wasn't without irony that I realized I now had more soldiers than my liege, the Duke of Lancaster. Luckily we were friends; otherwise there might have been an issue with that.

I watched Walter carefully, it had taken us a four hour ride to reach the area that James said contained the cave where the shiggreth were hiding, and he looked weary. "How is your leg holding up?" I asked him.

He gave me a smile that only underscored the dark circles under his eyes. "It hurts like hell," he answered honestly.

"We'll be camping here tonight so you'll be able to rest it before we press into the caves tomorrow," I told him.

"A peaceful night sleeping on the ground should do wonders for it," he replied sarcastically. Despite his tone I didn't get the feeling he was really complaining, it was just his way of making conversation.

James and Harold had been discussing the camping plans during the march (most of the soldiers were afoot). As soon as we arrived James sent a detail to relieve the men guarding the cave entrance, while the main body was put to work preparing our field camp. A large area was cleared of the stones and small brush that were ubiquitous here and tents were erected. Latrines were dug and a picket line established around the camp.

All told we had a combined force of some seven hundred men camped there. A group of fifty men were on guard duty at the cave entrance and another hundred were kept active maintaining the pickets around the camp. Although that might sound excessive none of us wanted to have a rude surprise during the night and the shiggreth's particular abilities made them difficult to guard against.

Even with those precautions, I doubted many of us would sleep soundly that night.

⊱━━⊰

Despite my fears I slept hard and I might have had an excellent night's sleep, if it hadn't been for someone kicking me in my bedroll. "What the hell do you want?!" I said, sitting up angrily.

A young soldier was staring down at me, "My Lord, the shiggreth have surrounded us. We are under attack!" His voice was shrill and on the verge of panic.

I bolted up and nearly fell as my feet tangled in the blankets. The soldier was quick though and caught me before I fell. "Thank you," I told him hastily. "Where is Sir Harold?"

"On the eastern side of the camp, the enemy are strongest there, but they have already flanked us on both sides and some have gotten past the lines," he answered.

I cursed silently and stumbled out of the tent, hoping to get a better picture of the camp. All I saw was a madness of chaos and torches. Despite our lanterns and torchlights it was difficult to see more than fifty feet in any direction. Men were running back and forth as messages were relayed and some simply panicked. More than anything we needed light.

I closed my eyes and used my magesight to assess the condition of the camp. I could easily locate our soldiers but the shiggreth were harder, still I had learned to spot them as pockets of 'emptiness'. What I found wasn't encouraging. The eastern line was still strong, largely because that was where Harold was, roving up and down the line. I could see that considerable fighting had already occurred there but he was having moderate success maintaining order.

The western side of our camp was a mess and it was clear that although there were fewer of the undead on that side they would soon overrun the defenders there. *First things first,* I reminded myself. *"Lyet bradek searus ni pyrren!"* I shouted holding my staff out and pointing it at the sky. A blinding streak of white gold shot upward and then formed a great yellow white ball of blazing light several hundred yards above the ground. The overall effect was as if the sun had just come out. Everything was now illuminated by a harsh yellow light.

A cheer went up across the camp for the men knew I was awake now. Looking around I saw Walter standing beside me. "Where did you learn that spell?" he asked. "I've never heard of it before."

I frowned, "I just made it up." I started walking toward the western side of the camp. "Follow me, they need help."

A minute later I had reached the chaos that might be described as our western defensive line. The light did little to allay my fears for beyond the immediate fighting I could see hundreds more pressing forward and all around me men were being dragged down by creatures that stole their strength even as they struggled.

Even as I stood there the men standing in front of me collapsed and five of the undead ran toward me, yet before I could react lightning flashed past my head, branching and forking as it reached out to strike the creatures. Unfortunately the lightning flickered and vanished the moment it reached the shiggreth as their innate ability absorbed the magic powering it.

"They really do eat magic," Walter said behind me.

"That they do," I agreed. It was a lesson Penny and I had learned together one night a year ago, nearly at the cost of our own lives. "You have to use a rune channel," I added lifting my staff to point it at the oncoming creatures. *"Pyrren ni tragen thylen!"*

A blazing cone of fire shot forth from the end and consumed the bodies of the undead nearest us. The flames were so intense that everything they touched was reduced to ash within seconds. Unfortunately more kept coming and I couldn't put the staff down long enough to do what I needed to do. "Here!" I said shoving it into Walter's hands during a brief lull. "You keep 'em off of me for a few minutes. I need to do something."

"I don't know how to use this!" he said anxiously. I could see panic in his eyes.

More of them were running toward us, within seconds we would be overrun and slain if he didn't learn quickly. Standing next to him I reached down with one hand and lifted the end of the staff until it was leveled at the monsters coming for us. I had seen too many battles to panic now. "Alright Walter, just do what I tell you. You can use whatever spell you like, just imagine it flowing through your hands and down the length of the staff, as though it were a pipe, directing your power," I kept my voice calm and steady.

"Any spell?" he said uncertainly.

"Any spell," I replied. "You need to choose quickly though, they're almost to us."

He hesitated and for a moment I thought he was going to freeze, but at the last possible second he came unstuck and his lips began moving. Lightning flared from the end of the staff and struck the oncoming monsters. It branched and forked and before it died more than ten of the shiggreth were lying on the ground, little more than smoking piles of burnt flesh. Walter took a step forward and I could see a look of excitement had replaced his fear.

I put my hand on his shoulder, "Don't move Walter, we're trying to hold a line, not rout them. These things don't rout anyway."

He stopped and nodded, biting his lip as he looked forward.

"Now look behind you quickly, these things have a tendency to sneak up on you and you can't always trust your magesight," I added. He glanced backward but the area behind us was still clear. "Now you burn the next ones that come at us. Just don't lose your head and go looking for them, and remember to check behind us after every other blast."

I watched him for a minute or so, until I was sure he had control of himself and the area around us, and then I reached into my special pouch, the one I had enchanted to open up inside a chest full of dangerous objects. Reaching in I pulled out a handful of dark iron spheres. They gleamed with a dull black luster under the stark light of the artificial sun above us.

I raised the first one to my lips and then blew softly upon it. *"Tielen striltos,"* I said sharply and it went streaking away into the distance. Before it reached its destination I had already brought another to my lips and had sent it following on a slightly different path.

Within seconds the western side of our lines was shaken by a string of powerful explosions as the spheres detonated one after another. I put as much distance as I could between the explosions and the men desperately trying to hold off the undead but it wasn't easy and I was sure that in some cases I had probably killed some of our own men. Again I felt the familiar guilt, though I tried to convince myself that most of those that died would have been killed anyway.

I ran out of iron spheres and reached in to pull out another handful. This time I had more breathing room and I was able to space the explosions further from our own lines. Fire and thunder lit the battlefield as I methodically destroyed everything to the west of our camp out to a distance of two hundred yards. When I stopped at last I could see nothing moving there.

Walter was leaning heavily on my staff when I looked over at him. I took the staff from his hands and pulled one of his arms over my shoulder. "Here lean on me," I said quietly. "We need to go help the other side of the camp."

His gaze was full of weariness as he answered, "I'm starting to think you aren't human."

I half walked and half carried him along with me as I headed toward the area where Harold was still fighting. "Is your leg bothering you?" I asked.

"My leg is fine," he said. "It's my magic, I think I used too much. How is it that you aren't exhausted yet?"

I laughed darkly. "I gave you the hard job. My iron spheres do all the work for me. You had to use a lot more power keeping them away from us." Walter didn't respond but I could tell he didn't entirely believe me.

The other side of the camp was in much better shape but it was beginning to fall apart. Sir Harold stalked up and down the line, stepping in to dismember the undead wherever they overwhelmed the human defenders. Unfortunately the defenders were being overrun in more locations than Harold could be at one time. Looking out beyond the line I could see at least a thousand shiggreth pressing forward.

Since the line on this side was still intact Walter was spared from having to repeat his part with the staff again. Drawing forth more of my iron spheres; I began systematically destroying everything on the eastern side of the camp.

Within a few minutes it was over and I found myself standing alone except for Walter. The soldiers around us were watching me silently, eyes blank from shock and fear. An onslaught of undead monsters followed by an awful lot of fire and explosions seemed to have that effect on most people I had learned.

I glanced around and stared back at the men staring at me. After a moment I grinned and yelled, "And that's what happens when you wake me up in the middle of the gods-be-damned night!"

Silence reigned for awkward seconds around me before finally men began chuckling. Once they started it was infectious and soon most of those that could, were laughing. I headed back to my tent. Harold found me there several minutes later.

"What do we do now?" he asked simply.

"Clear out any bodies inside the camp, ours and theirs. Make sure the men are careful not to touch them directly. They're still dangerous. Set new watches and reform the picket. Once that is done put everyone not on duty back in their bedrolls," I told him.

"Shouldn't we burn the bodies?" he asked worriedly.

I sighed wearily, "Yes, in the morning, not tonight in the dark. That light up there won't burn for more than twenty minutes or so." I pointed upward at the brightly glowing light I had created. I had placed it extremely high to keep the undead from nullifying it, but now that I considered it I realized it was a good idea for any nighttime battle.

"But what about the ones that turn...," he started to ask.

"The men on watch can keep an eye on them. If any of the corpses get up and start walking have them cut them into pieces. We'll burn them in the daytime. The men need sleep." I was already climbing into my bedroll as I relayed my instructions. I was exhausted from my own use of magic, though Walter seemed to be much worse off.

"But..." he protested.

I closed my eyes, "Ask James. Don't wake me up unless we get attacked again." He left after that and I was asleep not long after he had gone.

CHAPTER 35

Irose early the next morning but I had pity on Walter and let him sleep longer. The poor man seemed to have been truly exhausted by his efforts the night before.

I found James and Harold supervising the collection of bodies and body parts. It appeared that neither of them had slept at all after the attack. They both appeared worn and weary.

"How many did we lose?" I asked James.

"Slightly more than a hundred and fifty men," he answered immediately. "They wiped out the men guarding the cave last night before they assaulted the camp."

I grimaced. We couldn't afford to lose men that quickly. The shiggreth could replace their numbers much more easily than we could. "At least there's one bright side," I noted.

"What's that?" asked Harold.

"If they wiped out the detail guarding the cave first then it means they're desperate and that opening is their only means of ingress or egress. If we assume that the ones remaining last night didn't skulk off somewhere then we have most of them cornered," I explained.

"They might have wiped the guard detail out to give us that impression falsely," suggested James.

I sighed, "If they're that clever then we may be in trouble. Let's hope they aren't."

James nodded, but spoke up anyway, "Hoping and wishing are good ways to get men killed."

"You sound a lot like Dorian," I said with a sour grin.

"It's more likely that he sounds like Gram Thornbear, which is where I heard that originally," he corrected me.

Sir Harold spoke up, "Alright, let's assume that they want us to think it is the only entrance. Why would they do it? What are the advantages to them?"

James responded first, "The obvious conclusion would be that all or part of their forces would take us from the rear. Then they could either bring the caverns down and trap us, or slaughter us between them."

"The real question is how many of them are left down there," I pointed out.

"We accounted for over a thousand of the bastards last night," said Harold. "Well Mordecai did anyway," he amended.

"Let's not start counting notches, Harold," I admonished him.

"We can't do anything until tomorrow at least, no matter what we decide," James said, drawing us back to the proper reason for our discussion. "It will take the rest of the day just to collect all of the bodies."

"They need to be burned," I added.

"I agree," he said, "but that will take even more time. Collecting the wood necessary to burn that mountain of flesh will take a lot of men and labor."

"I'm not entirely certain how useful an army will be once we get past the entrance to those caverns," I said at last.

"It isn't as if we can starve them out," James answered bitterly.

That set me to thinking and I put my hand out to forestall further discussion for a moment. "We don't actually know that. In fact, we know next to nothing about them. Those bodies may decay and become useless after a certain period of time, or they may require some form of sustenance."

Harold snorted, "You mean us."

"That might be true, or not. We don't really know," I clarified. "James I'd like you to keep one of the cut up shiggreth bodies quarantined, rather than burning it with the others. We can take it back to Lancaster when we're done. I'd be very curious to know if it will eventually lose its animation, or whether it will decay."

James looked thoughtful. "We need one that hasn't been cut to pieces as well then. They might last longer if they haven't been cut up, if indeed they can starve at all."

Sir Harold spoke up, "This might be beside the point, but how do you plan on capturing a creature whose very touch is anathema to us?"

James smiled, "Ha! We use nets. Once we have one trapped we bind it carefully with ropes. After that we can put it on a litter and drag it back to Lancaster, the dungeon and a couple of guards should be sufficient then."

"Actually I'd like to construct a special holding cell for it James, but we can keep it in your dungeon for a while at least," I added.

"So back to the point, what are we going to do today?" asked Harold.

We all fell silent for a moment, and even the normally decisive duke looked to me first to see what I might say. "Keep most of the men at clean up and burn duty. I'll take Harold and a small contingent into the entrance. If we can clear out whatever defenses they have in there we'll scout a bit further in. If we can't we'll pull back and wait until the clean-up is finished."

Surprisingly they both agreed with me. "How many men?" asked Harold.

"About fifty I think. Make sure they are among the better armored of our men. No one in anything less than full chain, the less exposed skin the better," I told him.

Two hours later we were ready and we were staring into the yawning mouth of the cavern. The entrance was fully fifteen feet in height and more than twice that in width. The morning sun illuminated the first twenty feet or so, but beyond that it was shadowed in darkness. From outside it was impossible to see more than that, if you were relying on normal eyesight.

Thankfully I was not. The contingent assigned with guarding the entrance had pulled back to allow us to enter. They would resume their duty after we were inside. I made note that James had supplied them with onagers and barrels of oil. If the shiggreth tried to break free of the caverns again they were prepared to set fire to the entire cave entrance. I just hoped they didn't panic when we made our exit later.

Harold nudged me, "What do you see?"

I glared at him, "I see a lot more when I'm left undisturbed. Let me finish." Closing my eyes again I resumed my search of the caves. I had already discovered that the main tunnel went back for over a hundred yards, and it was mostly straight from that point. I had difficulty locating the shiggreth along the way, but I could tell that there were quite a few about fifty yards back. They were standing next to some wooden contraptions that looked suspiciously like…

"Ballistae!" I exclaimed.

"They are called 'onagers' your Lordship," Harold corrected me, thinking I was referring to the Duke's catapults.

Harold really got on my nerves sometimes, though he did mean well. "I know that, I'm talking about in the caves."

"What?"

Walter nodded in agreement, "You're right. The shiggreth have ballistae back there. It looks like they are ready to give anyone that enters a greeting with four foot of wood and steel."

I was surprised for a moment. I had never had another wizard around before, but it was nice to have someone else that could share my unique perspective. "I count two of them," I replied.

"I agree," said Walter, "and at least twenty of them hiding in the recesses behind the ballistae."

I could tell there were quite a few back there, but I wasn't quite sure how many there were. It surprised me that he seemed to be able to pick them out more easily. "How far away can you see things with your magesight?" I asked him.

He glanced at me in surprise but he answered readily, "About six hundred yards or so."

That was significantly less than my own range, and yet he was able to perceive the shiggreth more easily. "Interesting," I replied. "I can see further than that, but I can't pick them out well enough to count them in there."

He laughed easily, "It's probably because I'm a Prathion. We're known for being a little different than the other families."

"How so?" I asked.

"Well you have already seen me use my invisibility," he answered. "Or rather you have 'not' seen me while using it."

"I was planning to get you to teach me that," I said.

He shook his head negatively, "I can try, but the odds are you won't be able to manage it. Very few wizards have been able to do it outside of the Prathion family."

"Really?"

"Yeah, the Prathions were famous for their ability to pass unseen, or so I was taught. It's kind of like how the Illeniels were known for their devilish enchanting skills," he explained, "that and their freakish strength."

His off-hand comments were providing me with a window onto a world of lore and common knowledge I had never been fortunate enough to witness. Not for the first time I lamented the fact that I had never known my birth father. I pushed those thoughts aside and returned to the present. "How does your ability to become invisible relate to sensing the shiggreth?"

"Their magic drain ability renders them essentially 'black' to magesight, if you think of magic as a sort of 'color'. My invisibility is different in that it redirects light, and sometimes even magic around me but still I can relate to what they are doing. I suppose I could use my ability to emulate what they are doing, or at least how they appear," he replied.

I was enthralled by his idea. "Show me," I said.

"Alright," he said. "Here, this is what I look like when I become invisible." His visible form vanished but I could still 'see' him in my magesight.

"Shit!" Harold exclaimed. "Warn a fellow before you do that!" I had to laugh at Harold's discomfiture.

Walter's disembodied voice answered, "We've been talking about it all this time. I thought you expected it."

"Don't worry about it," I told him, "please continue."

"This is what it looks like when I become invisible to magesight," he added and his body vanished even to my arcane vision.

"That is why I could not find you when you were spying on me at my home. Why don't you use it all the time?" I asked.

"Because I am currently blind," he said. "When I am invisible I cannot see, but I can still use my magesight. When I do this I can no longer see in any capacity. I am left stumbling along in the darkness with only my sense of touch and my hearing to guide me."

"Can you become visible but remain unseen to magesight?" I queried him.

He paused for a moment. "I don't know," he said at last. "I never thought to try that. I haven't ever really had a reason to do that before."

"Try," I said. A moment later his body reappeared but I still couldn't sense him with my magical vision. "I think you have it right," I told him. "I wonder if they would think you were one of them like that."

He shook his head negatively, "Of course not, this isn't what they look like. It would be more like this."

He did something and I could sense a change. I could still see him with my eyes but he registered differently to my magical senses. He had become more like them, a place that wasn't there, before he hadn't created an empty space. Now he was like a void. "You're right, but I don't understand why."

He released his spell. "Look at me with your eyes and I'll show you why."

I did and nodded at him.

"Ok this is what a normal person looks like," he said, remaining perfectly visible. "Now pretend that visible light is magic, and you are seeing me with your magesight. This is what the shiggreth look like," his face and body turned black.

It wasn't the normal sort of black you might encounter if someone used some dark paint. He was *utterly* black. No light reflected from him at all. It was as if a man shaped hole was standing before me.

"That's what the shiggreth look like to magesight," he explained. "Now this is invisibility." He vanished and now I could see objects behind him.

"I think I understand now," I said slowly. "When you are invisible it's like you are transparent. But the shiggreth aren't like that, magic doesn't pass through them, it's all absorbed."

"Exactly," he agreed.

I looked over the enemy again and now that I understood better what I was seeing with my magesight it was easier to pick them out. It still wasn't easy to count them but I figured I could manage it. Harold broke my concentration with a nudge.

"Excuse me. I know all of this is very interesting but how are we going to get past the ballistae?" he asked and then remembered belatedly to add, "your Lordship."

I smiled at him, "You can handle it for us."

"Pardon?"

"There's only twenty or so guarding the entrance. I've been wanting to see how you fight with the new earth bond and that armor I made for you," I elaborated.

He gaped at me, "Two wizards and fifty men at arms here and you want me to go alone?"

"Be honest," I said, "Do you really think twenty of them will be a problem for you? I saw you fighting more than that last night." *Appeal to his ego first,* I thought to myself.

He sighed in exasperation, "Twenty I can probably handle without issue, but they have *two ballistae* in there!" His voice rose in pitch as he reached the end of the sentence.

I gave him a look that clearly expressed my doubts about his manhood. "I made that armor you're wearing, if I thought something as simple as a ballista could pierce it I'd never ask you to go."

"Surely you jest," he said, staring at me in disbelief.

I ignored him and walked back toward the men, "Someone give me a crossbow." As luck would have it none of them were armed with one, the soldier I asked said something about them not being effective against the undead. Instead he ran off to find one in the supply wagons. Several minutes later he returned with a deadly looking weapon with a steel bow. "Load the bolt and cock it for me if you would," I told him and he did so. Once the bolt was loaded and cocked I gave the command, "Now I'd like you to point it at Sir Harold here and shoot him."

"Excuse me sir?" he said, startled. Harold also jumped at my command.

"It won't hurt him…" I started to explain but then I gave up in exasperation. "Here give me that." I took the weapon from his grasp and pointed it directly at Harold's chest.

To give him credit, even though he thought I was about to execute him he didn't whimper or beg. "Sir I think you should reconsider," he began.

"Nonsense," I replied and I started to pull the trigger, pausing only at the last second. "You there!" I shouted at a soldier standing to one side, "Better move back behind me, this bolt might ricochet." He made haste to do as I said.

Harold stared into my eyes. "You're making a terrible mistake your Lordship," he said in a very reasonable tone.

I laughed, "Best hope I'm not Harold, because otherwise you're out of a job." Then I pulled the trigger and several things happened at once. The bolt itself struck him dead on at point blank range and, as I had predicted, it failed to pierce his armor. Instead it shattered into a dozen pieces. At the same time the force of the blow rocked Harold back and someone shrieked horribly.

Nervous laughter broke out among the men as Harold straightened back up. His eyes were a bit wild around the edges from his near death experience and he kept staring down at the place where the bolt should have pierced his armor. "Holy hell!" he said softly.

I clapped him upon his steel clad shoulder, "See there! I told you it would be fine. I tested that armor many times before I ever gave it to you after all."

"You could have told me that," he suggested with an irritable tone in his voice.

"Someone told me once that a demonstration is worth a thousand words," I told him companionably. "Or perhaps it was pictures? I forget. I think Dorian told me that."

He shook his head, "I really doubt Sir Dorian said anything like that sir."

"You're probably right," I said agreeably. "By the way, why did you shriek like that at the end? You sounded like a little girl." I probably shouldn't have embarrassed him with a remark like that, but I was honestly surprised.

"I think that was Walter, sir," he replied.

Looking around I realized Walter had taken a seat on the ground and was busily fanning his face with his hands. He looked up at me with an expression of weariness. "You are going to give me a heart attack. I am certain of it."

CHAPTER 36

A short time later Harold prepared to enter the lion's den, so to speak, if lions had siege weapons and absolutely no fear of death that is. We were huddled near the entrance, ready to follow him once he had disabled the ballistae, but I really didn't think he would need our help. Unless there were surprises we hadn't foreseen.

"Ready?!" he asked me for the second time. Harold's pupils were dilated and his breath was coming in short bursts. I had never doubted his bravery in any of the battles we had been in before, whether those recently or those of a few months past when Gododdin attacked us, but I worried he might die of adrenalin overdose today. I suppose a heated battle was different than being asked to charge two readied ballistae… alone.

"Yeah, go for it," I encouraged him.

"Now?" he asked, just to be sure.

"Sure, whenever you're ready," I said. "Go massacre them."

"Alright, I'm about to charge," he informed me.

"Godsdamnitt all go!" I yelled at him. I used my voice of command but inwardly I was chuckling at his nervousness. I needn't have worried for he was so charged with energy he didn't disappoint.

Harold took off like an arrow shot from a bow. He leapt over the rock we were crouched behind and sailed a good fifteen feet into the air. Luckily the overhanging lip of the cave ceiling arrested his upward ascent or we might not have heard from him again. Obviously he hadn't quite gotten used to the extra strength he had gained from the earth bond and his nervous enthusiasm had made matters worse. I couldn't help but giggle.

Thankfully he hadn't knocked himself out. The armor was good enough that I doubted he could have killed himself unless he stood still and let them take their time figuring out how to finish him off, but there are always risks in war. He staggered upright and resumed his charge forward into the cave. At this point only a few seconds had passed and the enemy still hadn't reacted to his sudden appearance.

He had covered half the distance to the ballistae before he realized he had dropped his swords when he slammed into the ceiling. As strong as he was I imagined he probably could have made do with rocks or simply pulling them limb from limb, and it certainly would have had an artistic touch but he chose instead to run back for his swords.

Walter piped up in disbelief, "What the hell is he doing?!"

I almost collapsed I was laughing so hard at that point, "He's running back for his swords."

"Why the fuck are you laughing? Are you insane?!" the older wizard yelled at me.

I couldn't answer; I had no air left to me by then. I pointed and tried to say, "Just look at him running," but I couldn't get the words out. The shiggreth had finally realized they were under attack and a massive ballistae bolt shot forth. It grazed Harold's shoulder, knocking him down before it exploded against the rock sheltering us.

Walter ducked down even further, "Holy shit!" he screamed as fragments of rock and wood rained down over us. "He'll be killed!"

I strengthened my shields and peeked back over the top of the rocks. Harold had recovered his swords and was bounding back toward the enemy. The terrain was so rough he probably would have been better off at a fast walk but he was in the throes of adrenaline induced madness now. Miraculously he didn't fall over anything during his second charge.

He reached the second ballista just as it fired at him. This time however he was staring it dead on and his reflexes were beyond human. Stepping right he avoided the massive bolt and bringing one of his enchanted sword blades down he sliced the front end of the massive siege weapon apart. His swing damaged the great bow and the device literally exploded as the massive bow limbs came apart with incredible force.

The first of the two great weapons was nearly reloaded by the time he turned back toward it, but the undead creatures manning it never had a chance. Another swing of his right hand sword and that ballista also fell into ruin. After that it was simply a slaughter as he moved from place to place. Like a whirling dervish he cut the enemy into pieces. With his enhanced strength and impenetrable armor the undead really never had a chance.

I turned to the captain leading the rest of the men in our 'invasion' contingent. "Wait here captain. I'll confirm the entrance is clear before we bring the men in." Standing up I entered the cave with my staff held out before me and my shields readied. Walter followed me in, though I hadn't asked him to come with me.

Harold stood panting near the remains of the siege weapons and their dismembered operators. "Don't say anything," he warned us as we approached.

I gave him one of my winning smiles, "I wouldn't dream of commenting."

"For what it's worth I think he's mad as a hatter," Walter told Harold as he pointed a thumb in my direction.

I couldn't blame him. Recently I had begun to suspect I might be coming unhinged, and losing Penny and Dorian had only driven another nail into the coffin regarding my sanity. I wasn't ready to admit to it yet, though. "Let's clean up the mess and we can bring in the troops. Walter, see if you can spot any more of them waiting in the tunnels further along. I'll dispose of the bodies so they won't have to rest in pieces." My joke elicited a groan from both of them but I assumed it was because of their poor taste.

Pointing my staff downward I spoke a word and began channeling a white hot flame along the length of it. Playing it back and forth I started the rather foul task of incinerating the still moving pieces of our undead foes. The stench of burning bodies was incredibly foul, but unfortunately it wasn't a new smell for me. I had had a lot of experience with it in the aftermath of the battle with the army of Gododdin. The cremation fires then had lasted for more than a week.

As I reached one of the bodies near the ballistae my flames took hold in an unexpected way, blazing up and filling the room with light. The floor was covered in a slick substance that burned, almost as if someone had poured out a barrel of oil. I released my spell but the fire continued to spread across the floor between both of the broken ballistae and then outward in lines, following channels carved into the floor. My eyes grew wide as I realized I had inadvertently set off a trap, just as they had known I would.

"Get down!" I screamed at Harold and Walter as I ran toward them. Confusion was written in their faces as I reached them and they still made no move to do anything. Without time to do anything else I created a shield around the three of us and grabbed them by the shoulders. "Down!" I repeated and thankfully they knelt as I pulled downward on them.

"What's going on?" asked Walter, and then the world exploded. Somehow the bastards had gotten their hands on what I assumed must be quarry powder. The dark grey substance was produced by both the illuminator's guild, which refused to share, as well as by some master stone masons, for use in quarrying rock. The damn stuff was too dangerous to use for much else, though I had heard some talk of incorporating it into siege weapons somehow.

The end result was similar to what would have happened if I had been stupid enough to use my explosive iron spheres, in a cave, under hundreds of tons of stone. The entrance collapsed and although we were rather far back from where the explosion occurred we were struck and nearly buried by a deluge of rock and debris. The noise and vibration were incredible and went on for more than a minute after the explosion itself was done.

When it finished we were cut off from the outside world. My shield had managed to keep us from being buried by the rock but we had several large boulders leaning across the top of it. I was forced to slowly change the size and shape of the shield to allow them to slide to one side. Once the heaviest of the rocks was off of it I was able to release my spell so we could climb out.

Standing amidst the rubble Walter and I surveyed the tons of stone blocking our way out. "That's a lot of rock," I observed.

"It will take forever to get past that, assuming the rest of the ceiling doesn't come down if we try to dig out," Walter added.

Harold spoke up, "I wouldn't mind some light. It's pitch black in here."

Once again I had forgotten that not everyone could see in the dark. It was easier to do with Walter around, since he shared my sensory abilities. *"Lyet,"* I said softly, and a bright light began to emanate from the head of my staff. "Is that better?"

Sir Harold looked around, slowly taking in the scenery, rock, stone and more rock. He whistled, "I do hope you have another trick up your sleeve, Your Excellency."

As it so happened I did have options. One would be to create a teleportation circle that could take us to one of my circles in either Cameron or Lancaster and another would be to attempt simply walking through the stone itself. I wasn't sure if I could manage that with two people, it had been difficult enough with Rose, but I could surely take them one at a time. "I can get us out," I said confidently, "but first I would like to see what else there is down here."

Walter groaned, "I had a feeling you might say that."

We spent several minutes getting a better feel for the layout of the tunnels around us and making sure there were no more of the shiggreth nearby. It appeared that although the caverns branched in several places the offshoots rejoined the main tunnel deeper into the hills. In essence, although it was confusing there weren't too many places to explore along the way.

After a few hundred yards we sensed more of the shiggreth, though. Naturally it was Walter that spotted them first, "There are several hundred in the large cavern ahead," he informed me.

By focusing more carefully I was able to see them as well. The large cavern they occupied was fairly level and had a smooth floor. Compared to the rest of the cave system it definitely gave the impression of having been altered to better accommodate human forms. I looked at my two companions, "I don't really fancy trying to burn them all to ash."

Their reactions were priceless. Walter's eyes bulged as though they might try to escape his head, "But you considered it?" he asked incredulously.

Harold took an entirely different view. Now that he had survived the ballistae he was feeling decidedly more invulnerable. "Perhaps I could manage them…"

"Twenty or thirty perhaps, but more than that I doubt, remember Dorian," I reminded him.

"So you do want to burn them?" Harold replied.

"Oh I'd like to certainly," I answered, "but I worry that using too much fire down here would exhaust the limited supply of fresh air." I had not forgotten using a flash fire to first burn and then suffocate Devon Tremont almost two years ago.

A loud sigh escaped Walter's lips. "Look I hate to be the one to suggest anything to either of you suicidal maniacs but I might have a better idea," he said suddenly.

I looked at him with interest. "I am open to any suggestions."

"Why don't we just walk through them? Our conversation earlier has gotten me thinking I can probably hide all three of us from their senses. We can just walk through them and scout the tunnels beyond. If we don't find anything significant, or any means of escape we could simply leave them down here to rot," he explained.

Walter was an easy man to overlook but his idea was the most reasonable thing I'd heard all day. I wondered if I had underestimated his intelligence. "I like the sound of that," I replied.

Harold wasn't so easily convinced. "You aren't serious are you?" he asked.

Walter nodded and I spoke up, "It sounds worse than it is. There is another tunnel leading away on the far side of this cavern and it appears to be empty. They aren't very tightly packed in there, so if Walter can do as he says we can just walk right past them and see what's down there."

Walter's plan turned out to be more complicated than I had at first realized. We stood close together and joined hands while the older wizard cast his spell. In order to keep us from being visible to the shiggreth he made us invisible to both magic and visible sight, which had the unfortunate side effect of rendering us completely blind. There was no way we could navigate through a crowd like that.

"I don't think I thought this through completely," Walter amended. "Perhaps if we are just invisible to magic and you douse your light Mordecai."

That turned out to be just as bad. Without my light the cavern was pitch black and we were just as blind as before. That's when I had my epiphany. "I think I know why they don't come out during the daytime very often," I said.

"What?" asked Walter.

"The shiggreth," I explained, "in the past they have almost always attacked or been encountered when it is dark. In fact, the only time that I know of them ever appearing during daylight hours was when they ambushed Dorian and Penny."

Harold was more familiar with the shiggreth but he still didn't understand. "I don't see how that tells you anything specific."

I held up my hand. "Let me finish," I told him. "We know they don't have an issue with daylight because they have come out during the day at least once. So why would they generally avoid moving about during the daytime?"

"Because they're creatures of darkness?" said Harold, as if that were reason enough.

"No," I admonished him, "because they don't use light to see, they use magic. In fact, their dead eyes are probably blind to light entirely. They don't avoid daylight, they simply prefer the nighttime because they have an inherent advantage then, because they can see and most humans can't."

"You still haven't made it clear how that helps us," he insisted.

Walter understood though and he began nodding his head rapidly in agreement. "Of course! Keep your staff lit, I'll hide us from magical sight but leave us visible to normal light."

"Will the magic in my staff be a problem?" I asked.

"No," Walter replied, "I can cloak the magic there as easily as that which emanates from our bodies. I just have to let the light pass unimpeded."

Despite being fairly sure we were right those first few moments as we stepped into the open were nerve wracking. I walked in the front holding my staff up to light the way while Walter followed with his hand on my shoulder; Harold followed him in a similar fashion. The experience was surreal, especially since I had never walked invisibly through a room full of people before, much less a room full of undead life draining monsters. I had to keep reminding myself to breathe.

The floor was smooth and free of obstacles but it still took us almost ten minutes to cross the large cavern and reach the other side. Along the way I stared at the faces of the shiggreth, wondering what they thought, or even if they thought. They stood quietly for the most part, not walking or talking to each other, yet they whispered softly to themselves, filling the vaulted spaces with an endless susurration, a sound similar to wind through the leaves of a forest.

By the time we reached the tunnel on the opposite side I was thoroughly disturbed. I wanted to burn them, just to stop the noise. *Surely we don't need air to breathe that badly, right?*

The tunnel we were in now appeared to have formed naturally, but much like the previous cavern it had been smoothed and cleared to some extent, making it much easier to walk without stumbling. That, more than anything, convinced me that there would be something worth finding at the end of it.

After traveling a hundred yards or so Walter spoke up, "I think it might be safe to remove the spell."

"Wait," I cautioned him. "I know it's annoying not being able to sense anything but there may be more of them further ahead."

"We've already demonstrated that we can sense them long before they sense us, otherwise we wouldn't have been able to get as close to the cavern as we did," Walter reasoned with me.

That made perfect sense, but I still had a feeling of trepidation. "Alright, take it down then. We'll examine our surroundings and if we sense any of them close by we'll put it back up," I said in agreement. I was still worried, though.

A moment later he had done so and it was as if I had had a blindfold removed. I had been using my magesight for so long now that not having it had left me feeling blind even though my normal eyes worked fine. I expanded my awareness slowly, feeling the tunnels behind us and making sure that nothing had followed us. I also explored ahead and quickly discovered that the tunnel we were in dead-ended in a fair sized chamber not far from where we were now, perhaps another seventy yards ahead.

As soon as my mind touched that room I knew we had made a mistake. There was a darkness there that lay heavily upon the air. It weighed upon me, and as I saw it I immediately felt it looking back, staring into me in a way that left me feeling vulnerable, as if it could see my innermost thoughts without effort or care.

Simultaneously I saw Walter's face go pale and his eyes widened in shock, he could obviously feel it too. As the moment of recognition passed something drove inward, as whatever we had found sought to enter our minds. Pain shot through my body as I struggled to expel the invader and for a long minute I fought what felt like a losing battle. Walter fell to his knees and Harold looked questioningly at both of us, he was still unaware of the silent assault.

Gritting my teeth I focused and finally managed to speak, *"Cherek Ingak!"* An invisible shield formed around the three of us and suddenly the alien mind was gone. Walter gasped audibly and drew a long breath and I found myself breathing heavily as well.

"What the hell was that?!" exclaimed the older wizard. I could hear a note of panic in his voice but it didn't surprise me since I felt much the same.

"What's wrong?" asked Harold.

"I don't know. There's something down there, something bad," I answered at last.

"That fills me with confidence," Harold commented. If I hadn't known better I might have suspected him of developing a sense of sarcasm, but I quickly dismissed the thought.

"There are three of them," Walter added.

Again he had surprised me with the acuity of his senses. Holding the shield firmly I reexamined the cavern that held… whatever that horrible thing had been. Now that I could see it without being immediately overwhelmed

I saw what he was referring to… there were two large four legged creatures near… whatever it was. The being that had almost overwhelmed us was physically small though it felt quite the opposite to my magesight. All three of the creatures absorbed magic and appeared 'black' to my arcane vision.

Doing his best to remain calm Harold addressed me, "What do you want to do?" I had to admire his reserve. Of course he couldn't sense what we could; if he had he might not have been able to keep his nerve so easily.

Walter spoke first. "We have to go back. We can't stay near it. Once we're safely away from it you can teleport us out of here right?" he said, looking at me with a hint of desperation. "I think it's calling the other shiggreth…," he added.

That made up my mind. Straightening up I looked at both of them, "We have to take care of it quickly, before it can call for assistance."

Walter's mouth fell open, "Excuse me?"

"Get up," I told him. "We have to move now while we still have some small advantage of surprise." *And before I lose my nerve,* I added mentally. I could easily imagine falling into panic, a panic that would end with us screaming in the dark while they hunted us down.

"What did you say?" asked the other wizard incredulously.

CHAPTER 37

I said we're going down that tunnel and get rid of that thing while we still have the initiative," I said with a calm I didn't really feel. "If you don't think you can walk in there with me then you're welcome to remain here," I added. Motioning to Harold we began walking down the tunnel. Every instinct I had was screaming at me to turn around and run the other direction but I had learned the lesson of conquering my fear several times over now. It still didn't make it any easier.

After traveling a short distance I heard Walter running to catch up, though he was now invisible to my magesight. I was slightly relieved to have his company. "I'm coming with you," he said from the dark behind us, "but I'm going to stay invisible. I don't have any way to fight those things without a staff."

I nodded, "That's fine." I had to admit he was right. He was walking into something terrible alongside us, and he had no reasonable way to fight, in many ways that took more courage than what I was doing, depending on how you looked at it. "Let's pick up the pace."

We began moving down the tunnel at a light jog and Harold's armor began an almost musical symphony of sounds as he ran. We definitely wouldn't be surprising anyone. I began casting spells as we ran, leaving glowing balls of light hanging in the air behind us every twenty feet or so.

"What are those for?" asked Walter.

"Once we get down there we'll likely be distracted facing whatever it is in that cavern. You mentioned that you think it's calling for help. If any shiggreth come down the tunnel behind us the lights will start going out, giving us some warning," I replied.

"If you're still fighting that thing there isn't much you'll be able to do about them," he observed.

I opened my pouch and pulled out three of my deadly iron spheres and handed them to Walter. "Use any spell to damage them, or just crush them with something and they'll explode. Hopefully you can bring down the tunnel ceiling without collapsing the entire cavern on us."

He held them in his hand as if they might catch fire at any moment. "You want me to use these after we get inside?"

I shook my head, "No, only if the lights start going out. No sense in risking a cave-in unless we have a reason."

"Why not just toss them in and collapse the ceiling on whatever is in that cavern?" pointed out Harold.

"Three reasons," I replied, "One, I don't think that would kill whatever this is. I strongly suspect it could escape one way or another. Two, I need to know what it is. Leaving now just leaves us with more questions and I'm already drowning in things I don't know." I slowed down since we had reached the entrance to the final cavern, twenty feet or so and we would be inside.

"What's the third reason?" Harold asked.

I paused and glanced in Walter's direction, "This should be good. You can watch from here, just make sure they don't follow us in there if the other shiggreth come running." I looked back at Harold, "I want you to lead the way inside. There are two rather large four legged things in there… try to keep them off of me until I'm done with the little one."

"What's the third reason?!" Harold repeated stubbornly.

I strengthened my shield and lowered my staff in front of me like a spear. "I don't like being afraid of things!" I shouted at him, "Now move your ass!"

Harold had already put his visor down but I heard him laugh inside his helm as he leapt forward. Fear and anxiety had given his voice an edge of hysteria but he didn't give in to it. "Let's make them afraid of us then!" he shouted back.

Harold charged into the cavern as though he was going to meet an army and I followed closely behind him. As I entered I pointed my staff at the ceiling fifty feet above and created a burning orb there to light the room. I could only hope it was high enough that the shiggreth wouldn't be able to quench its light.

Light bloomed in the darkness and the room was filled with brilliant radiance as my spell took hold. Sitting on a carved stone throne at one end of the chamber was what appeared to be a small boy. If he had been alive I would have judged his age at around six or seven based on his size and appearance. Next to him on either side were two enormous bears, and they too were undead. That was a bit of a shock to me since I had never considered that the shiggreth might also be able to convert animals.

Harold's charge came to a faltering halt as we reached the middle of the room and our eyes took in the scene. None of the enemy had moved yet and I was considering my next move when it spoke, "Hello Mordecai."

A shock ran through me as I realized I recognized the creature's face. It was Timothy, the little boy that Father Tonnsdale had murdered back in Lancaster. Penny had been the only one to see him commit the evil deed and the body had vanished inexplicably… until now. "Hello

Timothy," I replied with a confidence I didn't feel. "Or do you have some better name for me to use?"

"Whatever my name was it has long since vanished from the time before I slipped into the void, Timothy will do for our conversation," it replied. Unlike the many shiggreth I had seen before now, this one smiled grotesquely as it spoke, making an effort to project a more human expression. The attempt only made it look more unnerving as there was something subtly off about the facial muscles.

"Very well, Timothy it is," I answered. "How did this happen to you?"

Timothy's eyes glittered in the light, eyes that ignored the brilliant light above, eyes that were obviously blind. "Do you want to know how the child that was called Timothy came to be like this, or how I, the being that resides in this body now, came to be an undying creature of the void?"

The distinction was obvious and yet it hadn't occurred to me before, and the answer to either question would be of interest once I considered it. "Both," I said loudly.

"You are bold to come here demanding answers Mordecai. What would you offer in exchange for that information?" said the undead boy.

"I didn't come to barter. I came to clean this den of the filth residing in it. It is your choice whether you wish to delay that reckoning by answering my questions," I responded.

Timothy laughed… a dry rasping sound that set my teeth on edge. "You make several erroneous assumptions wizard. Your first is that you are capable of threatening me. Your second is that I do not have information more valuable to you than your own life. Your ancestor was similarly ignorant."

The implication that this thing had once spoken to one of my ancestors was unsettling. Even worse, I suspected it was telling the truth, in which case I had to wonder why it was more interested in talking than adding me to its collection of walking corpses. "I have nothing to give. What sort of information would you have that might interest me?"

It smiled again in its disturbing way. "I see you might be civilized. I propose we exchange questions, one for one, until one of us refuses to answer."

I gnawed my lip in uncertainty, but eventually I came to a decision. "Fine, answer my first question and I will exchange questions and answers with you."

"Which part of that question?" it asked me cleverly.

"All of it, in both senses, if you would show good faith in this game," I shot back immediately.

Timothy frowned, "You drive a hard bargain but I will answer, even though that is truly two answers. Timothy, the human boy became this way when Millicenth drew his spirit out and opened the way from the void for me to enter. She did this using the man you know as Father Tonnsdale as her agent, what you would call a 'channeler'." It paused after that, as if unsure how to continue.

The statement that Millicenth, the goddess of the dawn had been directly involved in the recreation of the shiggreth was a shock to me as I had previously assumed it to be the work of Mal'goroth, but I hid my surprise. "And the rest of your answer?" I said prodding it verbally.

"I used my art to hide my spirit in the void, to escape the genocide of your treacherous ancestor. I remained trapped there until Balinthor released us a thousand years or so ago, and then I was trapped again another thousand years or more until Millicenth called me out into this body," it replied carefully.

"For what purpose do you return from that 'void'?" I asked.

"That is a separate question. I believe it is my turn human," Timothy replied. "Have you ever heard of 'Illeniel's Promise'?"

That was simple enough, "No." I followed with the only question that really mattered to me, "Why did you ambush the kidnappers that were sent for my family?"

Its answer was immediate, "To gain favor with the king or a lever against you. Have you fully explored the Illeniel house in Albamarl?"

I answered quickly, "No." The question struck me as odd, for it indicated an unhealthy interest in the Illeniels. Taken with the previous question I couldn't help but wonder what the shiggreth wanted. It made choosing my next question even more difficult. "How does killing my family gain favor with the king?"

Timothy snorted, or tried to; in the end he only succeeded in seeming even more disturbing. "You ask stupid questions human. You squander your information. Killing your family does not help us gain favor with your king, or a lever against you for that matter."

My blood pressure was rising quickly, "Then why did you kill them?!" I shouted.

The monster held up one small boyish hand, "My question mortal, and do not test my patience. Does the phrase 'Illeniel's Doom' mean anything to you?"

I bit down on my anger and forced myself to think. Fear and rage were clouding my mind and I could see that I was missing some obvious conclusions. "Yes, Celior warned me that it would destroy everything. I haven't a clue yet what it is." As I finished answering my mind snapped into motion and I realized I had been a fool. "Where is my wife?"

It smiled wickedly, and for once it got the expression right. "She arrived at Albamarl yesterday. Where she is now I have no way of knowing," the creature paused thoughtfully before continuing, "It seems you do have a brain after all. I had begun to despair of you ever thinking clearly. If Illeniel's Doom was hidden in Albamarl where would you think to look for it?"

My mind was racing at the revelation that Penny was still alive. *I don't know that, he might have been referring to her body,* I corrected myself mentally. Still the implication was that she was alive… as a bargaining piece. *A bargain with whom?* "It would depend upon who last possessed it, otherwise I would have no clue where to start," I said, answering its question. "What bargain did you make with King Edward?" It was a risky question, for it was possible that it had been someone else, in which case I had wasted a turn. If my guess was correct though, it had saved me a question or two.

After an interminable pause the thing spoke, "We offered him your wife and her guardian in exchange for Illeniel's Promise, which you have heard called Illeniel's Doom. Do you think he can deliver upon his end of the bargain?"

"No," I replied honestly, "I doubt he has any idea what or where it may be. Why didn't you seek to deal with me directly?"

The thing that Timothy had become laughed, "Judging by your entry here I doubted we could have a meaningful discussion. The King needed a lever to control you and with it he claimed he could force you to deliver that which we seek." It stared at me for a long minute, "Why did you come here?"

"To destroy you," I said plainly. "Why do you want 'Illeniel's Promise'?"

"To restore my race," it replied simply. "Is there anything we can offer you if you find it?"

A chill raced up my spine before being replaced with a surge of adrenalin. Our conversation was nearly at an end and I could feel the creature's anticipation radiating toward me, an almost palpable hunger. I bared my teeth, "I'd rather be damned than deal with you, nor will you walk free from this place. The shiggreth are not a race, you are a creation, and one that must be undone."

It frowned. "You are wrong mortal. We created ourselves in a last act of desperation. We are the spirits of the She'har." As it spoke it brought up its hand and began weaving signs I could not recognize though I saw the arcane symbols forming in the air.

I was prepared already and pointing my staff at it I spoke, *"Pyrren thylen!"* and a focused line of fire and power struck the abomination before me. It was a spell I had used before, and in combination with my staff it had sliced easily through channelers shields in the past yet this time it scattered and fizzled as it struck the glowing symbols that hung in the air between us. Timothy began laughing as my face registered shock and dismay.

The undead monstrosities beside him had not remained idle; they had leapt forward only to be met by Harold's swords. He ducked a massive sweeping paw from one and removed its foreleg at the shoulder. Spinning back he turned to meet the other but it had moved with unexpected speed and it caught him solidly. This time he was flung like a ragdoll and sent hurtling into the far wall. He struck with a resounding clamor and I wondered if he could recover. At the very least he had to be reeling inside his armor.

I had no time to think however, for the child-like creature I faced was already weaving more signs. The symbols writhed in the air as if they were made of living blue fire. Twisting they stretched toward me rapidly, spreading and seeking to enfold my shield like a net. It stopped them for a moment before I felt them burning inward, eating at the power that I had formed my shield with and causing it to sag. It was an odd sensation, at once similar to the physical touch of the shiggreth and yet this touch ate away at only my magical strength.

I had mere seconds to react. Seeing my failure to harm it directly I changed tactics and turned my power directly upon the ground beneath it, *"Grabol ni'targoth,"* I said quickly, opening a hole in the earth beneath the childlike creature. It was a spell I had used once to incapacitate Cyhan and it worked just as well here as it had then. The undead spellcaster fell into the hole and the magic eating at my shield vanished as it lost its concentration.

I spoke another word to close the hole and trap it within the earth and then I turned my attention to the great bear that was bearing down upon me. *"Pyrren thylen,"* I said again and this time my magical fire tore into its target, slicing the undead beast into two large and smoldering pieces. I felt a surge of exultation as it fell apart and I turned to finish the other monster lumbering toward me on its three remaining legs. Then the light I had conjured above went out and the subterranean chamber was plunged into darkness.

"Did you think I would be so easily trapped?" came Timothy's soft words in my ear as it dropped catlike down from the ceiling above. It had escaped my pit before it closed and it now stood directly behind me, so close I could smell the unnatural state of its flesh. My shield had vanished, utterly absorbed by its close physical presence and now the creature's hand fell upon my bare neck.

The world vanished, replaced by a black void and a dark wind. The wind was hungry and it tore at me, drawing me into the emptiness that stretched before me. I fluttered in that wind, but try as I might I could find no purchase to stop my inexorable slide into oblivion. In the distance I heard Harold's voice screaming something. It was too faint to understand, but I could only assume the bear had found him.

Then the world returned to me in a rush. It was still black to my normal vision, but my magesight could see Harold holding the void wrapped form of a small child, kicking and struggling pathetically in his strong grasp. I scrambled backward across the floor to gain space and then my hand landed upon my staff.

Drawing myself up to my feet I ignored my exhaustion and created a new light above us. The new illumination made it even clearer what had happened. In the darkness Harold had fought and dismembered the remaining bear. One of his swords still lay on the ground near its mutilated hind quarters. Now that he could see again he was preparing to strike the undead child in his vice-like grip with the other sword. It was a sight that made me want to cheer.

Unfortunately the creature that now called itself Timothy had not given up yet. As Harold drew his arm back to slice it in two one of its arms traced more symbols of blue fire and they raced across Harold's enchanted armor, smoking and burning wherever they found a gap that led inward to human flesh. With a scream of pain and anger he threw the small body of our enemy across the cavern to land some twenty feet away. "Damn you!" he screamed in anger. I had to agree with his sentiment.

Raising my staff I sent fire streaming toward it, hoping to burn it to ashes before it could raise another protective barrier. My aim was off however and the thing leapt from the ground with blinding speed before I could strike again. It ran toward me faster than my eyes could track and yet before it could reach me Harold was there, blocking its path and striking out with the one sword that remained to him. His aim was true and one of the thing's arms went flying to the side before it could scramble away.

"Ha!" Harold yelled challengingly. "Not so brave when faced with honest steel are you?"

Honest enchanted steel, I added mentally, but I didn't think it was really appropriate to mention at that point. "Stay close to me, I'll try to burn it from a distance," I told him instead.

The abomination that occupied Timothy's body had had enough. Before I could aim another strike it darted away, fleeing into the tunnel that led back the way we had come.

"Walter!" I yelled in warning, "It's coming from behind you!" A loud explosion answered my cry and a thunderous roar followed. Walter had brought down the tunnel. Dust filled the air and we waited for what seemed an eternity for the rumbling of falling rock to cease.

When the dust had settled the three of us were trapped inside the cavern, with no open route to the surface. The tunnel that Walter had collapsed had been the only way in or out. Thankfully Walter had hidden his presence and the creature had merely run past him. For now, we were alone.

"What now?" Harold asked, breaking the silence that had fallen over us.

I opened my pouch and drew out the silver stylus that was quickly becoming my favorite tool. It would be much easier to create the teleportation circle using it rather than my hands or staff. I held it up dramatically and looked at my tired and emotionally drained companions. Fear is one of the most exhausting emotions. For some reason their weariness sparked my perverse sense of humor. "With this," I began dramatically, "we can cut our way through the rock and take the enemy from behind!" I grinned and waited for their reactions.

Walter couldn't even reply, his jaw simply fell open. Harold was more pragmatic, wiping his sword blades off he sheathed them before commenting… "How did Dorian survive childhood with you?"

I decided to revise my previous estimation of Harold; he was definitely developing a nasty case of sarcasm. "I was joking. Give me half an hour and I'll have us back in Lancaster."

"Why not take us back to the Duke's camp?" asked the burly warrior.

I shrugged, "I can't. There isn't a circle there."

"If you leave a circle here that thing may be able to use it," Walter pointed out.

I opened my magical pouch again and this time I drew a set of two small round objects wrapped together in a small square of paper, one made of glass and the other of iron. "These are a matched set," I told him. "I created a lot of these for the war with Gododdin but I still keep a few handy. They are similar to the necklace I put on you a while back. Smash the glass bead and the iron one explodes. I'll place the iron one near the circle before we teleport away. Once we're safely in Lancaster I'll smash the glass bead and destroy the circle." I smiled smugly; I was rather pleased with myself for thinking up such a neat solution. Honestly though I hadn't thought it up on the spot, I had spent some time considering such problems after some channelers had used one of my previous circles to invade Castle Cameron.

Harold whistled appraisingly, "Dorian was right."

"About what?" I asked.

"He said you were too dangerous to be allowed to run free without a babysitter," he explained.

"Was this when he explained why you were being stuck with guarding me?"

Harold grinned and nodded but Walter interrupted before we could say anything else. "Excuse me…" he said mildly. Once he was sure we had paused he continued, "How many of these explosive devices do you carry about on your person? Aren't you worried you'll trip and blow us all to bits of bone and jam?"

I chuckled at his odd turn of phrase. It was a valid question though, especially since I hadn't shown him my special pouch. I drew it out again and opened the top. Rather than explain I demonstrated by pushing my arm into the bag. Although it appeared to be no more than eight inches deep I was easily able to put my arm into it until my shoulder reached the mouth of the purse. From his perspective it now appeared as if most of my arm had been amputated. "I keep all my dangerous surprises stored far from my person," I informed him.

The look on his face was priceless, but I didn't say anything else. I got busy working on our way out. I didn't think any of us wanted to spend any more time in our subterranean prison.

CHAPTER 38

Cyhan followed the king down a long flight of stairs. He had been summoned late at night but he was used to such odd hours. During his years of service Edward had often needed him to serve in various capacities at times when most common men were long abed. Tonight was unusual in that the King was leading him through a circuitous route. The stairs they were on now led down from the outer palace wall and reached the courtyard near where the infrequently used postern gate stood.

The implication was obvious; Edward planned to meet someone secretly at the gate. Cyhan's presence was purely for protection. If the King had wanted him to serve in a more aggressive role he would have been given more warning and time for preparation.

As they reached the gate the King addressed him, "The ones we will be meeting are dangerous but they should keep to their word unless I am mistaken. They will be bringing hostages, two of them. You merely need to keep them secure until the priests arrive." While he was speaking Cyhan noted that the gate was open and the night duty guards were absent.

The veteran warrior understood immediately. This wasn't the first time he had been asked to perform such a role. The fact that the priests would be arriving to take charge of the prisoners meant that the king wanted these 'guests' kept discretely in a place where none would think to find them. Edward had kept a number of such hostages over the years. What was unusual was the fact that the king had chosen to receive such prisoners without any other guards.

"Your majesty," said Cyhan carefully, "I cannot guarantee your safety and secure the prisoners at the same time by myself."

"We understand that," answered the King. "Just make sure the prisoners are kept safely until the brothers arrive. There will be no treachery tonight."

Other than our own, thought Cyhan. Given the timing he had a good idea who the prisoners might be though it still didn't explain Edward's obsessive need for secrecy. The King had a number of guards that could be trusted in such situations, and in the past he had used them. Something about tonight was different, so different that he needed to hide the details even from his most trusted guards. *Except me, for my oath is my life.*

They waited a short time, less than a quarter of an hour before several heavily cloaked figures entered through the open gate. Between them they had two people, bound and being led on short chains. All in all there were eight of them escorting the two prisoners. The prisoners were also cloaked but their faces were only partly hidden by the deep hoods and Cyhan was fairly certain that his suspicions were correct regarding their identities.

The king stepped forward confidently, "Let me see their faces. I need to be sure they are who you claim them to be."

The voice that answered was a woman's, though her speech was oddly inflected, as if she wasn't used to speaking regularly. "Of course your Majesty, it shall be as you say. We do not wish you to suspect us of any trickery." Despite her strange intonation Cyhan thought she sounded somewhat familiar.

Hands reached up and pulled the prisoner's hoods aside, removing any doubt as to their identities. Standing before them were the Countess di'Cameron and Sir Dorian Thornbear. They appeared unharmed but their eyes were a bit wild around the edges. Penny's gaze immediately locked upon Cyhan. "Snake! I should have known you'd be here serving your…," she said vehemently but she was interrupted by one of her captors.

"Silence," the strange woman's voice broke in as she held up a finger in front of Penny's face. The countess's eyes locked upon that finger as it drew close to her cheek, and a look of intense fear and loathing was evident in her visage. Penny promptly closed her mouth while drawing her head back to avoid her captor's touch.

Dorian struggled beside her, but he was tightly bound and gagged, even so he managed to pull away from those holding him for a moment and struck the woman threatening Penny with his shoulder. She stumbled backward as the two holding his chains pulled and tugged to get him back under control. The motion caused her hood to fall away, and for a moment her face was clearly visible to Cyhan in the dim moonlight. It was Ruth.

A chill passed down his spine. Seeing her there was not unexpected, he had already guessed at the purpose of her mission before she had left. What unnerved him was her expression, or rather her lack of expression. Her eyes passed over him with no hint of recognition. That along with the strangeness of her voice a moment ago told him more than enough. She was no longer the woman he had known.

"Chain them to the post there," said Edward calmly. "I want you gone before the others arrive."

"We have kept our part of the bargain. Do not forget your part, King of Lothion," answered the creature that had once been Ruth.

Edward's eyes narrowed in the darkness. "Do not presume to lecture me. I have not forgotten. Begone lest I lose my temper!"

The shiggreth made no reply and within minutes they were gone, leaving behind their shackled prisoners. Cyhan stood guard silently beside his king while they waited for the priests to arrive. His eyes never left Penny and Dorian's faces but his mind was far away.

My king has made an alliance with the undead, he thought quietly, *and Ruth is now one of them.* Those two facts chased each other in circles within his head and he could find no way to escape the horror they presented. He had gone numb, physically and mentally. Try as he might he could find no meaning or reason in what he had just witnessed. *I have only my oath.*

CHAPTER 39

Our arrival in Lancaster was greeted with some surprise but I didn't have much patience for formalities. I headed for the keep as soon as we arrived, stopping only to ask one question of the guard on duty, "Where is Genevieve now?"

"She's in the study sir," the man answered quickly.

I turned to Walter and Harold, "I will be meeting with the duchess, go ahead and find something to eat but don't go too far. I plan to travel again momentarily."

I ran into Benchley right after entering the main hall. "Your Excellency, it is good to see you again," he said to me in a tone that was genuinely respectful. Since I had been granted the title of count I found I missed his sarcastic tones. *He just isn't the same anymore,* I lamented inwardly.

"Benchley!" I exclaimed. "I'm going to see her Grace but she will need your assistance immediately thereafter. She will want to send several messages. I would appreciate it if you would call for the messengers and tell the head groom to get a fast horse ready."

He gave me a tight lipped smile and walked with me to the study door. "Certainly sir," he replied.

I stopped, "I mean now Benchley. I can let myself in. I don't need you to open the door for me."

He coughed. "Begging your pardon sir but I've already taken care of those things. Do you still wish to open the door for yourself or is there something else you would like me to do?" His hand was already gripping the door handle.

I almost laughed, instead I grinned at him. "You smug bastard, I've missed you."

He gave me a quizzical look, "I never left sir." His tone and expression gave nothing away, but my magesight showed me a distinct flicker of amusement as he answered. *I could study for a hundred years and never attain this man's level of sarcastic excellence,* I reminded myself.

I waved my hand at the door and let him open it for me. I found Genevieve sitting at a desk leaning over a heavy ledger book. She glanced up at me in surprise, "I hadn't expected to see you back so soon. Is James alright?" Her eyes had already taken in the fact that I was alone.

I walked around the desk and held out my hands. She tentatively accepted them and I pulled her gently to her feet before embracing her. "Penny and Dorian are alive," I said softly. It was something I had only learned myself an hour past and the emotion that swept over me as I allowed myself to say the words was overwhelming.

"What?!" she said thrusting me out to arm's length. "Where are they? How did you learn this?"

"They're in Albamarl. The King has them…," I began. It took almost a quarter of an hour to explain the situation and how I had come by the information. The matter was only made more difficult by the fact that I could barely speak due to the storm of emotions that was running through me.

The duchess was patient as I told my story, waiting 'til I had run down before she spoke. "What do you intend to do now?" she asked bluntly when I had finished.

"I need you to send a message to James. He still thinks we're trapped in that cave. He should come back and I will probably need his help soon," I told her.

"And then?"

Frustration boiled up causing me to clench my fists, "I don't know! I want to go to the capital and separate Edward from his entrails!"

Genevieve shook her head, "You know you cannot do that."

"Why not?" I asked. "If he can't speak he can't order their deaths. I simply have to kill him quickly." I knew better but I wasn't in the mood for being rational.

"He has been at this game for much longer than you have been alive. If you kill him they will die, you can count on that Mordecai," she replied sternly.

Helpless anger put tears in my eyes as I looked up at her. "Then what would you advise me to do?"

"You might consider negotiating first. Obviously he will use them as hostages to ensure your cooperation. Depending on his plans for you it may be better to cooperate than risk him harming the two of them," she said slowly.

"No," I said immediately, "Walter took that course and he hasn't seen his family in over four years. Besides, the king doesn't dare kill them. We are at an impasse. If he kills them I will not hesitate to avenge them. Their lives are the only things that shield him."

Genevieve's voice was bitter. "Who said anything about killing? He can do far worse than that, and send you the evidence of their torture to prove his point. This isn't a fairy tale Mordecai. Edward is capable of many fine gradations of cruelty to ensure your compliance."

She was right of course, and her words only gave voice to my deepest fears. Still I couldn't accept things as they were. "He hasn't made his 'acquisition' known to me yet so I at least have some time to think before I have to respond to any demands. How long do you think I have before he reveals his hand to me?"

The duchess had her head down, for she was focusing on writing a letter. "Not long. He will want to solidify his hold upon you as quickly as possible. Most particularly if he already has something in mind he desires to gain from you," she speculated as she wrote.

I straightened up, "I'm going to Albamarl. I don't want to waste what time I have."

She glanced up, "Anything specific you want me to tell James?"

"Stay here and stay ready, if I need him I'll arrive suddenly and probably need to depart again just as quickly," I replied, striding purposefully for the door. I paused with my hand on the knob, "Thank you Genevieve. I'll never be able to say that enough."

Ignoring my words she replied instead, "Don't do anything rash Mordecai. As long as Edward is unaware of your knowledge you are still free to act on your own. Once he communicates with you your every action will be viewed and evaluated carefully, and any consequences will fall upon Dorian and your wife."

◆━━◆

I interrupted Walter and Harold's brief lunch and within a few minutes I had taken us on to my house in Albamarl. I began searching for Marc and Rose as soon as we arrived. I held out little hope of finding either of my two friends in residence but luck was on my side for a change. Marcus was lounging in the downstairs parlor, one leg thrown over the arm of a well cushioned chair. He had a wine bottle in one hand, and another now empty bottle, lay on the floor.

I took one look at him and asked Walter and Harold to give us some privacy. They excused themselves and went looking for the kitchen, most likely to finish the meal I had interrupted in Lancaster. Once they were gone I closed the parlor door.

"You're drunk," I started with a vindictive tone. Marc stared up at me bleary eyed but gave no sign of responding yet so I continued, "Did you even bother trying to discover any information while I was gone? Or did you just spend your time whoring around with priestesses?" My frustration with my situation was definitely spilling over and finding Marcus drunk when I needed him most had pushed me over the edge.

His eyes focused on me finally, "I'm not drunk. I'm a gods-damned heretic!" He held up a sheet of paper and waved it haphazardly in my direction. "See! I have papersh to prove it."

"You're a waste of air is what you are! It isn't as if I have very many friends left. I'm up to my eyeballs in trouble and when I need your help you've gone and pickled what little brains you have left with wine!"

"You think I don't know that?!" yelled Marc. "It should have been me! They were my besht friends! If I had any faith left I'd be praying to thoshe asshole gods to take me instead."

I felt my heart grow cold at his words. "You think I wish you were dead in their place?" I could see the pain in his eyes even as I said the words.

"No idiot! *I* wish I was dead in their place. You need to learn how to lishen better." He stood suddenly and shoved his paper in my direction, "Read thish damnitt."

I plucked the sheet from his hand and then gave him a brisk push, sending him falling backward into the chair he had just risen from. "Sit down before you hurt yourself."

Scanning the page I was surprised to see that it bore a reasonable likeness to Marc's face drawn upon it. The top line read in bold letters, "Warning! This man is no priest of Doron or any of the other shining gods…" It went on to detail his real identity as an ex-priest of Millicenth and a disinherited heir of the duchy of Lancaster. Near the end it labeled him, 'Marcus the Heretic' and included strong instructions to deny him entry to any of the temples of the shining gods.

"How did you manage this?" I asked forgetting my anger.

"They caught me sneaking around in the high priest's shtudy. I was trying to find invoices detailing what they've been shipping to that shecret compound of theirs," he explained with a bit less slur in his voice.

I raised an eyebrow, "I'm surprised you weren't locked up."

"Ha! They might'a tried that but it was jus' the high priest his pox-ridden self that caught me." He punctuated his declaration with a soft belch.

"What did you do?"

He grinned sloppily, "I popped the fat bashtard right in his puffy face. You should have seen how surprished he was!"

"And then?" I prompted.

"He started screeching like a little girl so I hit him again, but he still wouldn't be quiet. I wound up beating him half to death before he finally passed out. For such a weak man he took one hell of a pounding. I hafta' give him that. Anyway, after he finally shut up I had to take my leave suddenly. I was lucky to get out before they sealed the whole damn place." After he finished he began miming the high priest's expression when he surprised him. "Whupsh! Pardon me Father, was that your nose!?"

It might have been funny if he had been sober. "When did all this happen?"

"Yesterday morning... they had those warningsh posted by mid-afternoon," he replied. "I don't think Marissha is going to want to see me anymore—now that she knowsh I'm a heretic." He looked around for his wine bottle but I had already removed it from his vicinity.

"No more of that," I told him, "I need you sober."

"Why?"

"Dorian and Penny are alive," I said abruptly.

His eyes widened and began to well with incipient tears. "Don't do that to me Mort. That's not fair."

"I'm not making jokes you drunken fool. They're alive and somewhere in this city. After you sober up you and Rose are going to help me find them." I leaned in closely and my hand reached into the collar of his shirt. A moment later I had found the necklace I had given him.

"How? I don't understand," he said, trying to shake me off as I unclasped the pendant.

"I'll explain when you wake up. I don't feel like having to repeat myself," I told him as I pulled the chain away and stood back.

His eyes widened as he realized I was about to put him to sleep. "Wait, I have more news. I found their hidden compound. It's several miles..."

"Shibal," I said quietly and he sagged back into the chair. "You can tell me about it when you're sober." After that I called Harold in and with his help we got him upstairs to his room.

Once Marc was safely tucked in Harold spoke, "What was that all about?"

"I need him sober and the best way to manage that is to let him sleep it off. Hopefully Rose will be here by the time he wakes up and I can explain things to both of them at the same time," I said. As we walked back downstairs I could smell something good frying and my stomach began rumbling. It had been quite a while since I had eaten and my last food had been a cold camp breakfast. "What's that smell?" I asked.

"It appears Walter is a passably fair cook," Harold responded. "Once he got a good look at the pantry he decided to throw something together."

My mouth was watering already. I decided to eat first before trying to magically locate Dorian and Penny in the city. I was pretty sure the king would have them kept somewhere far enough away that I wouldn't find them anyway. Still I had to try.

⟢━━⟣

The afternoon passed slowly into dusk. I spent most of that time in a sort of focused meditation as I searched the area within a mile or so of the house. As expected I didn't find any sign of my wife or my friend, but I had to be sure. The city itself covered a much larger area, since it was at least two miles in diameter and simple math dictated that I would have to move at least four or five times to completely cover the area just contained within the outer walls. *The King wouldn't be such a fool as to keep them within the city.*

Rose still hadn't returned by the time the sun had gone down, which left me to believe she probably was staying at her own house again. Unfortunately that simply wouldn't do. I couldn't afford to wait several days for her to check in, and that meant I would have to go out and find her. Normally that wouldn't have been a problem, but considering the fact that I didn't want the King to know I was back in the capital I had to make sure I wasn't seen. Once he knew I was here he would be able to send a summons or message, and my freedom to act would be greatly limited. Until he found me he couldn't effectively leverage my wife and friend against me.

Naturally my house was being watched. I had already spotted the men loitering suspiciously outside with my magesight. The building across the street was also being used. Either that or the people that lived there had developed an intense interest in staring at my house for hours on end.

Luckily I had a secret tool in my arsenal, Walter Prathion, and after some consideration we hatched a plan. I disguised Harold to look like Marcus, since he was still sleeping upstairs. Walter used his talents to make both of us invisible and the two of us slipped out while Harold opened the door and looked out as if he were checking the street. Once we were past him he stepped back in and shut the door. Presumably the King's spies already knew Marc was staying at my address, so we hadn't made his situation any worse.

Rather than take chances Walter kept us unseen while we walked to Rose's home. It was the first time I had ever been invisible while walking through a city and the experience was entirely different from the one I had had underground surrounded by shiggreth. The main difference being since we only needed to be invisible to normal vision we were able to use our magesight. For some reason walking in and around people on the street who didn't even know I was there brought out my inner voyeur.

"You can just go anywhere like this can't you?" I whispered to Walter as we approached Rose's home at last.

"Pretty much," he replied.

After we had reached her door I considered knocking but quickly discarded the idea. Sneaking was simply too much fun. Instead I used my arcane senses to make sure no one was in the vicinity of the door inside the house, and then, with a few words in Lycian I let us in.

"You really know an amazing variety of spells," Walter observed quietly after we were inside. "Where did you learn them all?"

"I got some from a journal I found and the others I just made up, though I did have to study Lycian quite a while before I understood it well enough to really do anything complicated like the door back there," I replied off-handedly.

"You know Lycian?" he asked in a tone of wonder.

I frowned, "I thought it was a requirement of sorts. Isn't it?"

"It's been a dead language for several thousand years and there haven't been more than a handful of wizards for at least six or seven generations. Most of them just passed along what useful spells and phrases they already knew," he replied.

I hadn't considered things in that light before, and frankly I was shocked. "Well I guess if you really needed to do something and you didn't have the words you could just do it without words," I said quietly.

Walter sighed and shrugged his shoulders invisibly, "That's incredibly difficult, not to mention dangerous." He said it as if it weren't really an option.

I decided not to pursue the conversation further. I had done quite a few things without words in the past and while it did take a considerably greater expenditure of energy I hadn't really thought it was dangerous or difficult, just tiring. Somehow I knew Walter would be shocked, and probably disapproving so I figured it wasn't something we needed to discuss.

I had already mentally located Rose so we headed down the hallway and toward the small study where she was currently reading something. As we went I had a sudden thought. "You must be the world's greatest peeping tom," I said to Walter.

He coughed uncomfortably, "Well that is one of the particular uses for my ability."

I nudged him, "I don't mean just 'spying' like you were doing for the King, I mean women, ladies and such."

"I wouldn't do that," he replied.

"You mean you never thought about it?" I asked incredulously. "Are you sure you're feeling well?"

He shook his head, "Well I mean, obviously I've 'considered' it, but I've never abused the ability in that way."

"Bullshit," I declared.

"Look, Mordecai," he began, "you don't honestly expect me to stand here in the hallway and tell the man I was sent to spy upon for several months that I enjoy sneaking around and looking at women undressing and such… do you?"

It took a moment for that to percolate through my head. Eventually it got through to me though, "You pervert! You've peeped at Penny haven't you!?"

If he hadn't been invisible Walter would have been incredibly red. "No! But that is exactly why we are not having this conversation! Rest assured I am a married man and I wouldn't waste my time creeping about and looking in on naked women."

My eyes narrowed, though I wasn't using them anyway. "You haven't seen your wife in four years you said."

Walter finally lost his temper, "Do you realize how stupid you sound!? You're a wizard. It isn't as if you have to be invisible anyway! Hell they don't even have to be naked you moron! Obviously you can simply examine them anytime you want… clothes or no clothes. So why in the hell are you getting worked up over the fact that I can turn invisible?!"

His observations were dead on and I felt a bit sheepish. "You're right Walter. Not that I would do that. I just didn't think it through properly."

Rose spoke up from the study doorway, "As I recall just the other day you were observing our friend Marcus while he was behind closed doors with his lady friend. What was her name? Oh yes, Marissa, that was it!"

I spun about and stared agape at her. "That's not what happened! You told me to check on him!"

She smiled, "I didn't have to try very hard to convince you to do it, now did I? This really isn't fair Mordecai. I'm sure your face must be priceless to look at right now. You may as well make yourselves visible so I can see you."

CHAPTER 40

You don't startle easily do you?" I asked as we sat in her study. I had already taken the opportunity to introduce her to Walter.

Rose laughed, "It is difficult to be startled when the culprits sneaking into your home are having a shouting match in the hall."

"We weren't shouting," I responded while she shook her head in disagreement with me. "Walter, tell her we weren't shouting," I said looking to him for support.

The older wizard shrugged, "Well... we did get rather loud."

"Fine... we got rather loud. That's not why we're here anyway," I said grumpily.

"I'm assuming you noticed the men watching your house," said Rose.

I nodded, "That's why we used Walter's invisibility to arrive here unseen."

"I'm surprised you didn't use a disguise, or just lose them once you were away from your house. Marcus and I have been managing that way for the past few days," she commented.

"I'm afraid that isn't good enough Rose. I can't afford to let the King know that I'm back in the city."

That piqued her interest. "I assume you have some new development to relate," she replied.

"I have good and bad news," I said, unsure how to begin.

She tapped her fingers on the desk. "I've already heard the worst so don't think to spare me."

"Dorian and Penny are alive and probably aren't far from the capital," I said abruptly.

She stood and put her back to us with a speed that surprised me. "Walter would you mind stepping outside," she said carefully.

He rose and headed for the door, "Certainly. I'll wait in the hall."

After he had gone she looked toward me and her appearance shocked me, red eyes and tear stained cheeks where just moments before she had been composed and flawless. "Mordecai, are you sure? If this is some trick I won't be able to handle it."

I shook my head, "I don't have any way to be sure yet Rose. I only found out this morning and the circumstances were unusual, to say the very least." I crossed the room and put my arm around her shoulders.

"You haven't said yet what the bad news is," she said with her head against my chest. Before I could answer I felt her stiffen and she pushed me out to arm's length, "Oh Gods! It's the King isn't it? Edward has them!"

Since I hadn't told her any of the details yet I was rather astonished at her guess. "Yes. How did you figure that out?"

"We already had good evidence he was the one that sent the original abductors to Lancaster. Now you tell me they are alive and I just got news of something unusual that occurred the other night," she answered. "Mordecai, do you have any idea what he wants?"

"Slow down," I told her. "I still don't know what you've learned."

"Why don't you tell me how you discovered that they are alive," she suggested.

"In a moment, first I want to know what you found out about the other night," I countered.

She shrugged, "Not much really, just that the King dismissed the guards at the palace's postern gate for several hours. I had no clue what his reason was, but I knew he had to be meeting someone secretly, or moving something that needed to be kept hidden. Now that you tell me they're alive… you can see how my thoughts lined up."

If I had ever doubted how keenly sharp Rose's mind was I had all the evidence I needed to prove otherwise now. Her mind was a weapon. If we did ever manage to rescue Dorian I almost felt sorry for him. He'd never be able to get anything past her. Good thing he was honest to a fault. "I'm still amazed at your quick wits Rose," I told her.

She was trying to mend her appearance by dabbing at her cheeks with a small cloth she had produced from a drawer in her desk. "Let's hear your story Mordecai," she reminded me but before I could start she crossed over to the door and opened it. "You can come back in Walter, thank you."

I explained our near disastrous exploration of the caves near Lancaster and described our encounter with the creature that now inhabited Timothy's small body. She listened carefully and let me finish before she spoke again.

"Have you spoken with Marcus since you returned to the city?"

I coughed, "He was drunk so we didn't talk much but he should be waking up soon. I put him to sleep to get him to stop drinking so he'd sober up."

She frowned, "He's been sober the last few times I talked to him. Did something happen?"

"Apparently the high priest of the iron god caught him rifling through his papers and after he escaped they figured out his real identity. They've given him a new name," I told her and then went on to describe his encounter.

Rose had her hand in front of her mouth by the time I finished, "That's terrible."

"I rather thought it was funny, though I didn't want to admit it in front of him while he was drunk. I was a bit peeved about that."

"No, Mordecai. I swear sometimes I think you're as dense as Dorian. I'm talking about Marissa," she said the name as if it alone would explain everything.

I stared blankly at her, "What about Marissa?"

She sighed, "He was very taken with her. I think they might have developed some serious feelings."

I couldn't help but laugh, "Are you sure we're talking about the same man? He bedded half the noblewomen near his age and none of them were able to capture his attention for more than a day or two."

Now it was her turn to stare; except her stare was of a much more serious nature.

"Look Rose," I began, "I love him like a brother, but he's an absolute plague on women. I doubt he's even given her a second thought since they chased him out."

"We have too many more important things to talk about right now Mordecai," she said at last. "Let's just leave it at, 'you're an idiot', and move on. And do promise me to treat the subject carefully when you see Marcus later. Can you do that at least?"

Walter started snickering quietly behind his hand at her comment. I gave him a hard look before answering her, "Fine, we'll just leave it at that. Why don't we retire to my house so we can continue this conversation with Marc when he wakes up?"

◆━━◆━━◆

The return trip was equally uneventful though Rose didn't enjoy it much. Since she didn't have the benefit of magesight she was completely blind while we were invisible. For her the experience was essentially identical to being blindfolded and led across the city by hand.

When we reached my door we simply opened it and went inside. To appease the men watching the house I had Harold come back and look out, to give the impression that he had opened the door. After I talked to him though I quickly discovered it didn't matter anymore.

"Is Marc awake?" I asked him as soon as we had gotten inside.

He nodded his head, "Yes, but he's got a hell of a hangover. He's in the kitchen trying to get some food inside him."

I started walking in that direction, "Good, now we can finally get everyone together and see if we can figure something out."

Harold put his hand on my shoulder, "Wait, you might want to read this letter. I think it's urgent."

I frowned at him, "What letter?"

He held up a sealed envelope. Even in the poor light of the entry hallway I could recognize the official seal of the king of Lothion. "How'd you get that?" I asked him with a sinking feeling in my stomach.

"A messenger delivered it after you left," he replied.

"A messenger? Why did you answer the door? What did he say? What did you say!?" I could feel a panic rising quickly from the depths of my stomach.

Harold looked at me oddly and I realized I hadn't given him any explanation regarding my plan to avoid letting the King know of my current location. "He asked if you were present and I told him that you weren't," he answered finally.

I let out a sigh of relief, "Oh thank the gods!" It was a remark of habit but I corrected myself anyway. "Actually damn the gods, but thank goodness you told him that."

Harold smiled, "Don't worry; I told him you would be back and that I would make certain you got the letter today."

I startled Harold by spending the next several minutes practicing my nautical language. In spite of the fact that he was around soldiers most of the time he seemed quite impressed with my extensive vocabulary. When I finally wound down he commented, "I get the feeling that you didn't want me to take mail for you."

That was an understatement but I let it go. "You didn't know. Here, let me read this and I'll explain after." I opened the envelope, fearing the worst. As usual I wasn't disappointed. The letter was addressed to, 'His Excellency the Count di'Cameron' and it didn't waste any verbiage beating around the bush.

His Majesty, King Edward the First requires your presence to discuss matters of great import. Failure to appear will result in grave consequences. As a sign of the nature of these matters we do enclose this token…

The rest of the letter went on to detail the time and place, which happened to be three o'clock tomorrow afternoon. What really got my attention however was the 'token' he had included. It was a small lock of hair, and judging by the color I was sure it was Penny's.

I held it in my hand for long minutes, just staring, until my vision grew blurry and I had trouble seeing. When I could no longer see for tears I brought it to my face in a vain attempt to catch her scent but by then I could hardly breathe through my nose either. Eventually I looked up again, aware at last that I was surrounded.

Everyone in the house stood around me now, in a tight circle and by their faces I could see that I wasn't alone. Marc in particular looked as if he were having almost as bad a time of it as I was. Rose managed to keep her composure this time but there was a look of smoldering anger in her eyes.

Everyone watched me expectantly and the weight of it was almost more than I could bear. I made my way to the kitchen and we all took seats around the table. I handed the letter to Rose first and waited for her to read it. When she was done she passed it to Marc and eventually it made its way completely around the table.

Walter broke the silence first, "So what are you going to do now?"

The question reminded me of another time, another day, when I had been at a similar table with friends and family waiting on me to give them some direction. As I recalled Penny and I had not been on the best of terms then and they'd had to lock us in a room 'til we reconciled before we could decide anything. Thinking of it now it seemed like a fond memory, though I knew that at the time I had been just as desperate.

I reached into my pouch and drew out the letter Penny had left for me, and studied the words she had written. One part in particular stood out in my mind and I found myself rereading it several times:

Do not let this break your spirit. I have seen what will happen if you pay heed to your darker impulses. It is a bleak and empty path, and you will no longer be the man I have loved. There is still hope if you do not despair.

I folded her note and carefully put it away again before I addressed my friends, "First we carefully assess our resources. In this case those would be primarily information, so let's put everything we know on the table."

I made a slow and careful description of the recent events Harold, Walter and I had been through. When I finished I nodded at Rose.

"I haven't very much to add I'm afraid," she said with a graceful tone. "You only left here two days ago and since then I've only had one interesting bit of information come to my attention." She repeated what she had told me regarding the guards at the palace the evening before. Marc paid close attention as she spoke and after she finished I could tell he was ready to begin.

He leaned in toward the table, "As most of you already know I had to leave the temple of the Iron God rather suddenly yesterday." Marcus carefully relayed his tale but when he reached the end of it he caught my eye. "What I haven't had a chance to tell yet… is what I found amidst the high priest's paperwork," he paused dramatically.

"What, damnitt?!" I said impatiently.

"One of the documents on top of his stack detailed a payment received from the royal exchequer. It was for the amount of five hundred gold, but the thing that caught my eye was the fact that no reason for the payment was detailed on the paperwork." He stopped there.

"Is there anything else?" I asked.

He shook his head, "No, but the timing seems… highly congruent."

"The obvious conclusion is that he is paying the Iron Brothers to keep his hostages at that secret compound you mentioned before," said Rose at last.

Marc nodded, "Yes, but it is still a guess. We can't be sure from the little we know."

Walter was fidgeting with anxiety. "Do you think he might be keeping my family there as well?" he asked me suddenly.

"I don't know," I told him, and I didn't. In fact, I knew very little beyond guesswork and suspicion. Glancing around the table I could see everyone waiting on me to announce the next step. The pressure built upon me until it felt like a physical force, bearing down upon my shoulders. Taking a deep breath I stood quickly. "I'm going upstairs. I need to think and I can't do it with everyone staring at me. I'll be back down in a little while," and so saying I left the table.

CHAPTER 41

In the relative silence of my bedroom I stared at the wall where the picture of my mother Elena had been placed. Studying her features I wondered what she would have thought of the situation I was in now. Even more I wondered how she might have judged my actions up until now. *She saved her child while mine has yet to be born and is already in danger,* I thought. I had never known her in life, so even her features were strange to me. I couldn't possibly guess what sort of advice she might have given.

"Think," I said aloud. I had always taken my mind for granted, but now that I needed a truly inspired plan it was coming up empty of solutions. "I have two intelligent and gifted friends," I said to myself, referring to Marc and Rose. "I have a wizard with strong reasons to want me to succeed in liberating the King's hostages and a nearly invincible warrior armed with magical arms and armor. On top of all that I have a strong ally back in Lancaster willing to assist with men and support." I finished listing my assets and considered the goal.

More than anything I wanted Penny and Dorian back, safely and unharmed. Once that was accomplished I could easily dispatch my largest current problem, the King himself. *And civil war be damned,* I thought. Edward had elevated himself to a level of threat such that I no longer considered him to be the lesser of two evils. Another thought occurred to me then, *what about Illeniel's Doom?* That was the true motivator behind the shiggreth making a deal with the King to begin with and I still hadn't begun making a search for it. Hell, I had no idea what it looked like or if it was even a physical object.

"I'll set that aside for now. My only concern at the moment is Penny and Dorian, and once that's taken care of, the King. I can worry about the rest afterward," I said to myself. Pacing the room I enumerated the obstacles to rescuing them. Most importantly I couldn't be entirely sure where they were located. Our best guess lay in the secret compound that the Doronites had. Yet even if we could be sure they were there we didn't have precise directions to find it. Marc's information regarding its location was good but he had never been there.

To make matters worse I had less than twenty four hours. *Roughly twenty one hours now,* I estimated mentally. It was past six o'clock now and my meeting with the King was set for three tomorrow afternoon.

I became still and felt my mind grow calm, filled by a clear silence that brought everything into focus. An idea took shape and I carefully pruned and shaped it until I thought it gave me at least a chance of accomplishing my goal. *I can't be certain of anything, so lacking surety I must simply act decisively,* I thought. Taking a deep breath I went back downstairs.

The others were deep in discussion when I found them. They had moved into the parlor and I could tell by their voices that there was nothing approaching a consensus among them. In fact, they seemed on the verge of an outright argument.

"Well if you have a better damned idea why don't you spit it out *Lady* Rose!" Marc declared, raising his voice and putting an ugly emphasis on her title.

Rose was glaring daggers at him. "It isn't that I mind regicide, you bloodthirsty sot, but it won't solve anything. Even if we managed to kill him the hostages will still die. Edward isn't a fool and I'm certain he has contingencies set up to ensure his revenge in the event of something drastic happening to him." Her voice was level but the words left little doubt she thought Marc was reasoning poorly.

"We could just cooperate," said Walter quietly.

"That's worked out rather well for you all these years hasn't it?" Marcus interjected sarcastically.

I coughed loudly from the doorway to get their attention. None of them heard me. "At least he's thinking of his family's well-being instead of seeking blind vengeance," sniped Rose.

"That's enough!" I barked and this time I got their attention. Walking into the middle of the room I looked around me. "We don't have a lot of time. Marc, you did say you aren't certain of the location of the Doronites secret compound, correct?"

He nodded, "Yes."

"Do you know who would know?"

"The high priest surely, along with the supply master and some of the clergy responsible for rotating there for duty," he responded.

"And which do you think would be easiest for us to lay hands upon?" I asked.

He put a hand to his chin. "None of them really, but the only two I know on sight would be the supply master and the high priest and of the two of them the supply master might be easier. Plus he might not be missed as quickly."

"How long is the trip to reach this place? Or have you heard?"

He frowned, "I'm not certain but based on the few comments I've overheard I would guess about a half a day's travel on horseback."

"Rose, I need a place outside of the city. Something close by where we can move people without being too obvious," I said shifting my attention.

"None of my properties outside of the city are that close," she answered.

"It doesn't have to belong to you," I explained. "I just need something where no one will be watching and we can count on some privacy for a day or so."

She wrinkled her nose. "Would something like a barn be sufficient?"

"That would be perfect. Can you show me where it is?" I asked.

She shook her head, "Not yet, I need to talk to someone first, but I'm sure I can set something up within an hour or two."

I thought for a moment. "That will work. Go now. Don't worry about being seen leaving, just don't let them follow you." I turned back to the others. "I want the rest of you to acquire this supply master from the Doronite temple."

Marc looked concerned, "If we go in there and kidnap him from the midst of their temple it will cause a huge ruckus."

"You know the layout of the temple," I reminded him. "With Walter you can find him without anyone seeing you. Find him and remove him from his bed tonight. If he merely vanishes they won't know enough to suspect what we're doing."

"What will you be doing?" asked Harold suddenly.

I smiled, "I'm going to Lancaster but I'll be back in less than an hour. Once Rose returns I'll go to her house and wait for the rest of you there. After that we'll be moving to this barn or whatever she can find for us."

⊷——⊶

I was back long before Rose was so I started work on another piece of my plan. James had readily agreed to my requests but he had been somewhat surprised when I asked him for two small boxes. I had thought that two small matching boxes would be fairly easy to find but they turned out to be extraordinarily difficult. Genevieve had solved the problem by emptying two of her ring boxes.

I had taken them begrudgingly, since I knew she treasured the boxes, but even after I had told her I would ruin them she insisted. The two boxes were actually smaller than I had planned but they met my most important criteria, they were nearly identical in size and shape, each being three inches square and one inch deep.

Since I wasn't sure how much longer Rose would be I began by using some paper to do calculations and plan out my runes before attempting to do anything to the boxes. I had learned from my prior work that it didn't do to start inscribing runes before I had them exactly planned out.

Rose returned before I had quite finished working out the details, so I had her wait for a few minutes. It would have taken me longer to regain my train of thought if I had tried to stop and start again later. Once I had the runes diagrammed I double checked my notes and put them in my pouch along with the boxes and my stylus.

"Alright, I'm ready to go now," I told her. She had been watching patiently while I worked at the kitchen table.

"I don't suppose you'd like to share the significance of your arcane scribbling?" she said with an anxious tone.

I winked at her. "You'll see," I said with more confidence than I really felt. Picking up my staff I headed for the door.

"Are you worried about being seen leaving?" she asked as I set my hand on the door.

"Not this time," I replied. "In fact, it may be beneficial to have them follow us to your house."

She gave me another of her raised eyebrow looks, "I don't suppose you plan on explaining any of this beforehand do you?"

I gave her a steady look, "Sometimes it's better to act decisively. With some luck and quick action I think we can save them and put Edward in his place, but I won't explain it all now. You will have to trust me."

She nodded thoughtfully, "I like it when you're assertive and confident Mordecai, but I do have one question."

"What is it?" I asked.

"How did you regain your confidence? When you left our little meeting earlier we all thought you had finally cracked under the load, but when you came back downstairs you were commanding and assertive. What set you in motion again?" Her blue eyes were full of curiosity. That and her intelligence were the two things that had always defined Rose in my mind.

I thought about her question seriously for a moment before replying, "I finally realized that no matter what happened I had to do something and the only person that could make those decisions was me."

"I agree, you needed to snap out of your self-recriminating and take action, but why would you say that you are the 'only' one that could make those decisions?"

I blinked, "Because it's my wife and my friend that are being…" Before I could finish her hand came up and I thought for a second she would attempt to strike me. Her eyes were full of fury.

She took a deep breath and settled her hand by her side again. "Sometimes Mordecai, you go from being brilliant to being a moron in the span of two seconds. Don't ever make the mistake of thinking that you are the only one that cares about those two. It's insulting to the rest of us."

I realized the truth of her words even as she said them. "I apologize Rose. That was thoughtless of me. I thought you were about to take a swing at me for a moment there."

"I almost did," she said, "but I remembered your shield. Doubtless I would have only bruised my hand."

I nodded in agreement and then smiled at a sudden thought.

"What was that smile for?" Rose asked as she saw my expression.

I laughed, "I was just thinking that Penny would have taken a shot at me anyway." I opened the door and we both stepped out.

As we made our way toward her house we didn't bother trying to evade the men that followed us even though I could clearly see them with my magesight. Instead we kept up a brisk pace and followed the most direct route. Those following us kept to a respectful distance.

After we reached Lady Rose's home the men following us took up positions to keep an eye on the house. They did their best to remain inconspicuous but since I was already following their movements mentally they didn't really have much chance of hiding from me.

"Do you have a quiet place I can work until Marc and the others get here?" I asked Rose once we were inside.

"You seem very confident they'll actually find the man they need," Rose observed.

I shrugged, "I have other things to worry about. Between the three of them the worst that can happen is they could be discovered and have to fight their way out and with Harold there that wouldn't be a problem."

"Wouldn't that ruin the rest of your plan?"

"Only if their identities are discovered and the news is carried to the palace before tomorrow morning. With Walter there I don't think there's much chance of that happening," I replied.

Her eyes narrowed, "You mean before tomorrow afternoon don't you?"

"No, I mean before three in the morning," I said giving her a tight smile. "I really need to get started. Do you have a place I can work? I only need a desk or table and some quiet."

Rose sighed but led me to her study and gave me the use of her desk. Then she found her maid, Angela, and gave her stern instructions to make sure we weren't disturbed.

"We?" I asked amusedly.

"Yes, I plan on watching you," she answered.

I sat down and drew out the silver stylus and the two boxes. "Suit yourself," I said. "Personally I think you're going to be very bored."

Rose sat down and fixed me in her gaze. "I doubt that. Very little that you do fails to keep me entertained."

I ignored her after that and set about inscribing the two boxes with the rune diagram I had planned out earlier. It was a basic variation on something I had already done so I wasn't worried that it wouldn't work, rather I was more worried I would slip up and have to start over. I didn't have enough time to waste it correcting errors.

Two hours went by and I had nearly finished when I realized I needed something else. I set my stylus aside and glanced around. "Rose…" I began slowly, "do you have any glass beads or cut glass jewels lying around?"

She gave me a funny look, "Do you think noblewomen just keep such things lying about?"

I had encountered the difficulty finding cut glass or beads previously, when I had needed them to make explosive iron balls that I could detonate at a distance. This time I had a different use in mind but I still needed something clear and gem-like. "It doesn't have to be glass per se," I explained, "just something like glass."

"Do you mean something like a gem?" she said with a mischievous grin.

I answered a bit reluctantly, "Well yes, but I wouldn't want something as valuable as that."

"Goodness darling! Why didn't you simply say so? Let me check the cushions over here. I'm sure there must be a few. I'm constantly losing them you see," she said with an air of nonchalance. "Would you prefer a diamond or something with more color?" She rose and pretended to fluff the cushions of one of the chairs in the room.

"Very funny," I replied dryly.

She straightened up. "All jokes aside, I don't have any glass here but I do have a few cut gemstones that might do. If you had to choose between a ruby or a sapphire which would you prefer?"

I stared at her for a moment before answering. "I guess if I had to choose… a ruby. Red would be a better color for this I think. Surely there's something else…" She was gone from the room before I could stop her. *What sort of woman keeps cut gemstones lying about?* I wondered silently.

She returned a minute later carrying a ring and an ornate letter opener. Using the letter opener she bent the soft gold setting as she tried to prize the stone free.

"What ring is that?" I asked in alarm and I felt suddenly foolish for having thought she might actually have loose gemstones in the house. Obviously she would be removing the stone from something else.

She turned her head my way and I noticed she had her tongue sticking from the side of her mouth in a particularly unladylike expression as she concentrated. I had to stifle a laugh. A few seconds later the stone came free and she caught it before it fell to the floor. Placing it in my hand she spoke again, "Will that do?"

I held in my hand what appeared to be a sizable square cut ruby. I didn't know much about stones but I would have guessed it to be at least three or four carats in size. "It should work perfectly. Are you sure?"

Her eyes met mine. "Yes, now finish your work, your work that you have steadfastly refused to explain thus far."

"Your wish is my command," I replied in an overly formal tone. Resuming my seat I held the gem in the palm of my hand and focused my attention firmly upon it, listening until I could hear its voice. Once I had it firmly fixed in my mind I spoke to it and a moment later it split cleanly in two. The division was so perfect it looked as though a master jeweler had cut and polished two separate stones. The two parts were identical and each had a flat side, the side that had been where they were joined.

I placed one on to top of each box, in the middle of the lid and listening more closely to the wood I caused them to sink in a bit, until they were firmly affixed. Sometimes being an archmage had its advantages. Using normal wizardry I would still have needed a separate spell or even mundane glue to join the gems to the boxes. Doing it this way they were joined so perfectly it almost seemed that the gems had grown directly from the wood.

From that point it only took me another half an hour to finish my enchantment. Finally I looked up at Rose, "Do you have a small piece of paper I can use?" As I asked the question I noticed she was no longer watching me. She had been staring at the ring and its empty setting.

"Certainly," she said and moved to open the drawer next to me. I was sitting at a writing desk after all. I immediately felt foolish.

"Where did you get that ring?" I asked her.

She put her hand up to brush her hair back, a gesture I wasn't used to seeing from Rose. She was normally far too poised to fuss with her hair like that. "It was in my jewelry box."

"No, I mean before that. How did it come to you originally?" I clarified though I already knew she was avoiding the question.

"My grandmother gave it to me," she replied smoothly, "as a present when I turned sixteen."

The look on her face gave away more than she intended. "And where did she get it?" I asked.

"My grandfather gave it to her as an anniversary present one year, or so she told me. She's dead now so I can't ask her how long ago it was," she answered. "Is that what you wanted to know?"

I felt terrible for destroying her grandmother's ring. "Rose why?! I could have used something else!"

Before I could continue she put her hand over my mouth. "Don't Mordecai. If there's one thing you need to learn it's that other people have a right to make sacrifices too. My grandmother would have been proud to see her ring used so, and I am more than ready to give it, if it will bring Dorian and Penny back."

I stood carefully and studied the woman in front of me. I had always known Rose was beautiful, but the past few days had shown me the depths of her spirit more clearly than ever before. She was more than simply lovely, she was a creature of compassion and possessed of a nobility of spirit that was seldom seen, in anyone, man or woman. "I can't be certain any of this will work Rose, and if it fails there won't be any second chances."

She never faltered, "I am not a child Mordecai. I know there are no certainties. I know what will happen should things go badly tomorrow." She stared upward at me and for a moment our faces were so close I could feel her breath on my face. A long moment passed before she looked away and I let out a sigh of relief… and to my eternal shame, some regret. "What will you use the paper for?" she asked suddenly, breaking the tension in the air.

"Let me show you," I said and folding the sheet into a small square I opened one box and put it inside. The ruby set in the lid of the other box began to glow with a soft red light.

"What does that mean?"

I pushed the box with the glowing gem toward her. "Open it."

Lifting the lid she looked inside and gasped softly when she saw what was inside. Reaching in, she pulled out the small folded piece of paper. "That's very clever!" she announced. "Does it work both ways?"

I nodded and she placed the paper back in the box she was holding. As soon as she closed the lid the light on its gem went out and the gem on the first box lit up. She opened it and removed the same piece of paper. "So using this you can send messages between the boxes," she observed.

"Yes… and whoever has one of the boxes can tell by the ruby on top whether a new note has been placed inside," I added.

Rose's face grew thoughtful. "What happens if both boxes are opened at the same time? Can you see between them?"

I shook my head negatively. "Only one can be opened at a time. If I had done things differently I could have made something like what you described, which is essentially a portal between places, but it's more difficult. Instead I used a simpler teleportation enchantment. If both boxes were to be opened at the same time it would break this enchantment entirely, so I added another that will lock one lid in place when the other is open." In fact, I was rather proud of myself for finding a novel use for the 'self-locking door' schemata I had read about.

"You plan to use them for passing messages I suppose," Rose surmised sharply and before I could reply I heard a sharp intake of breath. Looking up I saw her mouth had formed a round 'o' and her features were lit with a realization. "That's why you said three in the morning. You can't be in both places at once, so you intend to send them after Dorian and Penny tonight."

I struggled to keep my features calm, which wasn't easy considering the accuracy of Rose's guesses. "You're right," I told her. "I'll send them after Penny and Dorian tonight, so they should reach them before any alarm can be raised. Even if the priests or the King realize what we're about they should be hours ahead of any pursuit or counter-measure."

"You keep saying, 'they'," Rose observed. "Obviously you don't intend to go with them. Do you mean to go to this meeting with the King? Why? Penny and Dorian would be better served if you are there to make sure they are rescued."

"My role is secondary," I answered. "Once I receive the message that they are safe I will visit the King, whether it is time for our meeting or not. Afterward he will no longer be king."

"And if they don't find them? When the King learns of the attack on the Doronite compound he will assume it was you. Do you know what he will do?" she said with an alarmed look on her face.

I winced, "I can't be sure."

Rose glared at me. "He will punish you, through them. Have you considered all the various ways they could be mutilated?" she said in a harsh tone.

"Yes," I replied, "as a matter of fact I have given it a lot of thought. That is the second reason I will be remaining here to meet with the King. If I receive word that Penny and Dorian haven't been found I will make sure he can give no orders of retribution. They may die by some precontrived plan, but they won't be tortured."

Her face was stern but it softened after a moment, "Are you sure?"

"If it were you Rose, what would you want me to do? Wait in fear and submit to the King's demands, or risk everything on the chance of freedom?" I asked seriously.

She paused, thinking and I held my breath until she answered. "I would not wish to be used against my friends and allies," she said finally. "I would rather you took the chance."

"Even if the chance carried a great risk of your death if I failed?"

"Yes."

"Then I have chosen correctly. Until this moment I wasn't entirely sure," I admitted.

Rose stood and held out her hand abruptly. "When did you last eat?" she asked.

That was a good question. "Sometime around noon perhaps?" I said tentatively.

"It's after eight o'clock now, let me feed you while we wait," she suggested. I could only hope she didn't plan on cooking though, her last attempt had almost put me off sausages entirely.

CHAPTER 42

Ineedn't have worried about the food after all. Rose's maid Angela took care of the preparations, which were primarily cold cuts and leftover bread. Even so the food was good.

The others returned while I was still eating but I sensed them long before they reached the door. I stood and rushed to answer it myself, since I doubted Angela would understand opening the door for a group of invisible people. They had arrived cloaked under Walter's spell, and there was an extra person with them… carefully bound.

I poked my head out the door after letting them in, to give the watchers a visible reason for the door having been opened, then I ducked back in. "You found him!" I declared hopefully.

Marc answered first, "Indeed we did. Surely you didn't doubt us?"

I hugged him, partly because I was glad to see him and partly because I regretted my harsh words earlier. "The thought never crossed my mind." Their prisoner had the poor taste to start groaning and trying to shout past his gag at that point. I turned to Walter, "Why didn't you put him to sleep?"

He held up his hands helplessly, "I never learned to do that."

I took him aside and whispered the word quietly in his ear. "Just be careful how you use it," I told him. "My friends wear necklaces to protect them from mental spells but if you don't consciously direct that spell it will affect anyone nearby."

"That spell would have been terribly handy in the temple of Doron just now," he reflected.

I chuckled, "Yes I can't believe you have managed this far in your career without it. It's probably my most used spell. It seems like you have a few holes in your education, and I never had one to begin with. We should probably compare notes in the near future."

Walter gave me an odd look, "I can't believe you trust me like this. I've given you little cause to do so."

I shrugged, "I don't have much choice, besides none of this was really your fault. You just want your family back."

"Do you really think they will be there?" he asked.

"I don't know. If they aren't I hope that they will only suspect me, at least then your family won't face any repercussions," I replied. "Either way, I'll make sure he can give no more orders concerning them."

"What do you mean?"

"Follow me, I need to explain this to everyone before we leave," I said. I led him and the rest into the kitchen. Once they had gathered I spoke up to make sure everyone could hear me clearly. "In a moment Rose will take us outside the city to a quiet building. There I will construct a circle to bring Duke Lancaster and some of his men here to assist you. Then you will ride for the location of the Doronite's hidden compound."

Harold broke in then, "Won't you be coming with us?"

"No," I said immediately, "I will remain here to deal with the King tomorrow once you have rescued our friends."

"The journey is a ten hour ride according to Father Jonas here," said Marc, indicating their prisoner. "How will you know if we find them there or not?"

I brought out the boxes I had enchanted and demonstrated them again as I had for Rose. That won me several whistles of wonder and appreciation. Walter was plainly awed with them and Marc was very vocal in his praise. "You never fail to amaze, my friend," Marc observed.

After a few minutes I had explained to them the basics of the plan and we prepared to exit the house under cover of Walter's invisibility spell. Rose left instructions with Angela to keep lamps burning to give the impression we were still there. Then we left via the garden door and made our way quietly around the house to the street. From there we had a short walk through the streets to the main city gate.

When we reached the gate I had an unexpected surprise. I had forgotten that the portcullis was lowered, sealing the city at night. While I could probably get myself past them, finding a way to do the same for everyone in our party was a daunting task. Walter released the invisibility spell so that everyone could look around once he realized I was no longer leading us forward.

Rose saw the look on my face and laughed, "Don't worry Mordecai; I've already planned for this." She led us to the door that led into the main bailey that protected the gate. It was also the traditional home of the Hightower family, her father's residence. Minutes later she had taken us past her father's guards and down the corridors of the bailey.

Unlike the last time I had come with Penny, we didn't ascend any of the stairs. Instead she took us on a circuitous route that led to a small protected doorway. "What's this?" I asked her. My senses had already confirmed that it led outside the city walls but I had to ask anyway.

"A private door," she answered mildly, "It leads outside the city."

"Wouldn't that compromise the defense of the town during a siege?" I asked.

She laughed, "Hardly. This door is outside the inner portcullis, which is closed, but inside the outer portcullis which is usually open. If this were time of war the outer portcullis would still be open and the gates would be shut. If an invader did penetrate the gates the outer portcullis would be dropped behind him and the murder holes above would ensure he did not live long to regret his mistake. This sally door was built to allow us to clear away the bodies, or to allow quiet egress at night."

Her speech was matter of fact and I was reminded that she had been raised by the family most responsible for protecting the capital in time of war. I decided to stop asking questions and let her lead the way.

Soon enough she was leading us down the dirt lanes that were common in the 'outer' city. Though the city itself officially was bounded by the large stone walls, it was surrounded on most sides by more informal collection of buildings, houses and small businesses. After a short walk she led us to a large wooden building with several large doors big enough to drive a wagon through.

I had expected a warehouse or possibly even a barn but the multiplicity of large doors seemed odd. "What sort of place is this?" I asked.

"A carriage house," she replied amicably. "One of my father's friends operates a business lending carriages for short term use. Most of his customers are visiting nobility that don't maintain a private residence in the city itself," she explained. Reaching into a small purse she withdrew a large brass key and unlocked one of the doors.

Within, the large building was filled with carriages of every size and description, but some of the stalls where they would have parked were empty. Rose indicated one of them with her hand, "Will something like that be sufficient?"

"More than sufficient, thank you Rose," I replied.

"What now?" asked Harold.

"Now you watch and wait for a while. You will know when I'm done," I answered and hefting my staff I walked over to clear away the floor in the stall Rose had chosen for us. Using the staff like a much larger version of the silver stylus I began inscribing symbols on the smooth stone floor with a thin line of fire. The work took me three quarters of an hour before I finished and set the location keys for the circle to match those of a circle I had constructed earlier in Lancaster.

Glancing up I saw the others were silently watching me. "I'll be right back," I informed them and then with a word I vanished, reappearing in Lancaster. I had made arrangements with James on my previous trip and true to his word the Duke was waiting for me when I appeared.

"I had begun to doubt you would come," he told me as I stepped away from the circle.

Clasping his arm at the elbow I clapped his shoulder with my other hand. "You should have known better than that," I replied. Looking around I could see he had twenty men and as many mounts armed and ready to ride. Several men in the rear held the reins for their ten spare mounts.

"Are you sure this will be enough?" James asked me as the men began assembling on the circle for transport to Albamarl.

"If it isn't then an army wouldn't have been sufficient," I said grimly. "If things go as planned even this is probably more than we need." Reaching into my pouch I drew out the small wooden boxes I had enchanted and handed him one of them.

I spent the next several minutes demonstrating and explaining their function to him. Thankfully the Duke was quick witted and had little trouble adapting to new ideas. "Once we've secured the hostages I'll send word immediately," he reassured me.

"Just be sure to take care of yourself James, the future of Lothion will rest on your shoulders," I replied seriously.

A pained look crossed his face. "I don't like this plan of yours Mordecai. You do not have the power to force this and you cannot be sure of enough support. Without that it will mean war, and war of the worst sort, with brother fighting brother. I am tempted to refuse."

I'd had enough of self-doubt and striving to appease those who had done nothing but attempt to manipulate me and my anger showed as I answered, "You have no choice James Lancaster. I have been pushed and prodded 'til my back is to the wall. They will accept this or I will make them regret ever choosing to cross me."

James stared into my eyes as if seeking assurance but whether he found it I couldn't tell. He nodded and looked away while I returned to transporting his men and horses back to Albamarl.

Rose and I watched them ride from the carriage house and into the dark night. The road they followed went westward but soon they would be leaving it and taking what amounted to little more than a goat trail into the wilderness to the northwest. Riding in semi-darkness, even with an experienced guide and a wizard to light their way, I worried that they might easily lose the path and wander aimlessly. Anything that delayed their arrival might doom my plan, or at the very least drive me to unfortunate decisions, decisions with irrevocable consequences.

"It's just you and me now," Rose said as we stood in the darkened building. "When will you act?"

"As soon as I receive word that they have our friends safe," I responded, tapping the box I held in my hands.

"What do we do tonight?"

"The theory is that we get a good night's rest, but somehow I doubt it will be easy," I replied. "Do you mind sleeping at Castle Cameron tonight?"

"Why there?" she asked.

"Without Walter it won't be easy to get back into your house or mine unobserved. We can take this circle back to Lancaster and then from there we can go to Castle Cameron easily enough. Tomorrow we can teleport from there back to my house when we receive word," I explained. "Tonight we can enjoy good food and be among friends at least."

CHAPTER 43

That night proved every bit as difficult to get through as I had expected. I tossed and turned for most of it, and slept fitfully for the rest. During the night I woke constantly and found myself staring at the small wooden box sitting on my bedside table. Each time I thought I had seen a flicker of light coming from the ruby embedded in its lid and each time I discovered it was just a figment fabricated by my sleeping mind.

Morning found me sitting on the divan, dressed and awake, watching the box from across the room. Given the time they had ridden out of Albamarl I was expecting a note from James at any moment, yet the ruby on the lid stubbornly refused to light up.

"Come in," I said loudly in the direction of the bedroom door. Rose was standing on the other side about to knock but I had already sensed her approach. She opened the door and glanced inside.

"Any word yet?" she asked anxiously. Despite the early hour she was already dressed in an elegant gown and her hair was a delicate mixture of braids arranged to restrain the rest of her free flowing hair. I couldn't imagine how she had contrived that miracle. Penny was altogether more practical when it came to morning hair—as long as it was tied up and out of her way, she was happy.

"No," I said abruptly. "Why are you dressed like that?" My mood was sour or I wouldn't ordinarily have been so rude.

If I offended her she showed no sign. "I'm nervous, and when that happens my first instinct is to do this," she gestured at her gown and hair. "I blame it on my upbringing."

I was tempted to ask her about the weaponry she had strapped to her thigh and hidden in her bodice, not to mention the steel spike nestled amid her braids but I kept my silence. If I gave away my knowledge of those things it might lead to an unfortunate conversation regarding what else I was capable of glimpsing.

"Have you eaten?" I asked.

She shrugged, "My stomach is full of butterflies. I haven't tried to put anything in it yet." She examined me carefully for a moment before speaking again, "Are you planning to meet the King dressed like that?"

The question nearly made me laugh, "Why does it matter? I'm going to kill him when I see him… one way or another."

She bit her lip, showing a hint of delicate white teeth. "Because I'm going with you and I won't be seen being escorted by a lout in a stained linen tunic and patched leather boots."

That got my attention and my eyes lit upon her. "You aren't going with me."

Rose's eyes sparkled as she sensed a challenge. "How well did that work when you told Penny that?"

She had me there. Most of those occasions had ended with her coming with me anyway. "Doesn't matter," I replied crossly, "you aren't my wife." I stood up to keep her from looking down on me.

She didn't back away from the challenge; instead she stepped into my personal space and stood just inches from my face. "Your wife isn't here and until you get her back I'm in charge of taking care of you." A strange urge to strangle her swept over me but I restrained myself. I could see her nostrils flaring as she breathed and I felt my face flush. The tension I was feeling wasn't just anger and if I'd laid hands upon her it wouldn't have ended in a fight. It would have been far worse.

"Fine," I said stepping away from her, seeking cooler air to calm my emotions. "I won't be held responsible if something happens to you there. I can't guarantee your safety."

"I didn't ask you to," she replied calmly. "Why don't you see about a bath while I look through your clothes," she added with a serenity that belied the anger she had shown only a moment before.

I left and went looking for Joe McDaniels. By the time I had found him I had made up my mind to follow her advice and take a bath. It had been days already and I was starting to smell.

Rather than have the copper tub taken to my room, as Penny and I had normally done I used the communal baths in the barracks. Given my state of mind and the hormones that had been flying through the air already this morning it seemed the safest option. Thankfully Joe didn't ask why I suddenly wanted to bathe there; he simply showed me where the towels and other things were located.

Normally baths were taken in the evening so there weren't any other bathers present, but then neither were the fires lit so I had to make do with cold water. That actually suited me even more than I cared to admit.

When I finally returned to my room I was in a much better frame of mind. The first things I saw upon entering were the clothes Rose had laid out for me upon the bed. I ignored them and checked the wooden box, but the light still wasn't lit.

Returning my attention to the clothes I couldn't help but admire her choices. Grey trousers matched with black boots and a sable trimmed doublet. Gold accents marked the doublet itself as well as the cloak she had set beside it. I wondered if any of it would fit, but I needn't have worried. Though I hadn't ever worn the clothes before, Penny had had them made by the same tailor that made my more usual wardrobe items. Knowing Penny, she and Rose had probably discussed all of it before she had ever commissioned them to be made. The two of them had been thick as thieves when it came to my wardrobe over the past year.

Joe appeared after I had dressed. "You need to eat something," he said as soon as I opened the door.

"I don't think so."

"Nothing heavy… just a bit of porridge," he insisted. "You'll need it later."

I didn't have the heart to argue so I let him have a small bowl brought up to me. It wasn't easy to start, but once the first few bites had gone down I discovered I was ravenous. I finished the portion and gave serious consideration to asking for more.

Rose arrived before I could send for him. "You look much better," she commented dryly.

"I feel better, thank you. Though I think I must look a fool in these clothes."

She smiled, "You look dashing."

"Isn't the hero supposed to wear white?" I said questioningly.

"You aren't quite that good," she replied. "You're planning to commit regicide. Dorian might be good enough for white, but I'm afraid the best you should wear would be shades of grey."

Her words stung a bit but I shrugged the feeling aside. "These clothes are mostly black," I noted.

"It looks better than all grey." Looking at me she frowned. "Stop pouting. I told you once before, you're the right man for this task. There are some things that require shades of grey."

I opened my mouth to speak but she put her finger on my lips. "Close your eyes and be silent for a moment Mordecai," she said gently. Something in her tone struck a note within me, and I did as she bade. Stepping forward she planted a quick kiss on my cheek, which surprised me, and then she wrapped her arms around me.

"You're a decent man Mordecai, not a perfect one, but better than most. I love you almost as much as I do Dorian, and I love Penelope just as much. You have to promise me one thing today." She stepped back and I opened my eyes.

"What?" I asked suspiciously.

She sighed, "So cynical at such a young age. I want you to promise me, for Penelope's sake, that whatever happens, you will try to survive… no foolish sacrifices."

I was tempted to remind her that she was only a year older but it seemed a crass thing to say. "I cannot do that," I said instead. "As you told me just last night, I have learned that we each have a right to make our own sacrifices. I cannot make any promises when there is so much that is uncertain…" I paused without finishing. From the corner of my eye I could see a red glow had appeared on the small box near the bed.

Forgetting everything else I strode quickly to the side table and opened the lid. Inside was a small slip of paper. Carefully unfolding it I found it carried a message written in James' neat hand:

We have safely recovered Walter's wife and young son. Of Penny, Dorian, and his older daughter we could find no sign. There were no survivors among the priests. No witnesses to our attack either. We have searched the area to no avail and are now returning to Albamarl.

I am truly sorry, Mordecai.

James

A cold calm washed over me and I let Rose take the note from numb fingers. Walking over to my writing desk I quickly penned a response:

Wait for me at the carriage house tonight. If I do not appear by morning ride for Lancaster and prepare for war.

Mordecai

I could have embellished the note in any number of ways, but I didn't. My heart was too cold to care anymore. Closing the box I handed it to Rose. If any further messages were to be sent she would have to be the one to manage it. Walking to the corner I belted on my enchanted pouch and lifted my staff. Then I headed for the door… the time for waiting was over.

CHAPTER 44

The palace gates rose up before me in the afternoon sun and the guards standing beside them were blissfully unaware that today was the day their world would change. My walk from my house in the city to this point had been mundane. Rose and I had garnered quite a few looks given our extravagant clothing. In most cases people wearing such clothes would be inside a carriage, or be riding at the very least. We simply strolled.

I didn't care if we drew attention anyway. *I'm dressed for the funeral,* I thought to myself. Considering it in that light it was everyone else who was underdressed. I suppressed a chuckle at that thought.

Rose glanced over at me, "Everything alright?" Her features displayed nothing of her nervousness, but my senses could pick up her racing heartbeat.

"No," I told her truthfully. "I doubt things will ever be alright again. Not for us, in any case, or anyone close to us." I was referring of course, to Dorian and Penny.

The guards watched us approach with curious eyes. They had already recognized us but I doubt they had expected me to appear dressed for a high society function in the middle of the afternoon. One of them addressed me as we drew close, "Pardon me your lordship, may I ask you your name and reason for seeking entry to the palace today?" The man's tone was formal and very deferential.

"You already know my name," I replied. "And very likely you know to expect me."

He bowed his head respectfully, "Yes, Your Excellency, the questions are mandatory. Please pardon me if they seem strange."

For a moment I felt sorry for him. Neither of these men had done anything to deserve the chaos my presence would visit upon their lives today. "What's your name?" I asked him suddenly.

"Nathaniel, your Lordship."

"Nathaniel, do you have family in the city?"

"Yes sir," he answered, giving me an odd look.

I met his eyes and tried to convey my seriousness. "You should take the day off and stay with them. No one will miss you here. You might consider telling the other servants and guardsmen within the same thing."

His face took on a look of disbelief so I left him and walked onward. He and his fellow guardsman rushed to open the door before I reached it. Rose and I resumed our leisurely walk after they had it open, but one of them called out behind us, "Let me call an escort for you your Lordship."

I ignored him and we kept going. I remembered the way perfectly well. As we went I warned everyone we met as I had the first guard. I hoped they would listen and pass the word along. Despite my reputation I had a feeling most of them would stay at their jobs but there wasn't much I could do about it. *Hopefully things won't get that out of hand,* I thought. In truth I didn't care anymore. My warning was a habit of kindness rather than a genuine desire to help them.

As we progressed toward the audience chamber I could feel a heavy foreboding in the air. My senses were alert and focused but I could find no cause for the feeling. Surprisingly many of the people in the near vicinity were already making their way out of the palace proper but I could find no reason for my sense of dread.

When we reached the final doors leading into the throne room I was surprised to find Adam, the servant who had greeted me on my first stay at the palace. He was waiting by the doors. Adam bowed perfunctorily and moved to open them for us but I motioned to him to stand away.

"Don't you wish to enter Lord Cameron?" he asked.

I could sense two figures within and it was easy enough to identify them. The first was Edward, and the second was his ever loyal servant Cyhan. "Thank you Adam, but no, I prefer to open these doors myself."

Something about my expression must have warned him because he backed rapidly away from the heavy double doors. "You should probably give yourself the day off Adam," I told him and then I faced the doors.

The moment had arrived and I felt Rose's hand tighten on my arm. Lifting my staff straight up I brought it down to strike the iron shod heel hard against the stone floor. *"Borok Ingak!"* The words rolled out from me like a breaking wave and shattered the massive double doors. The room within was showered with flying splinters and bits of wood. When the dust settled the only thing left of the doors within the frame were the iron hinges that had held them there.

Stepping forward Rose and I entered the room. I was mildly disappointed to see Edward sitting calmly on his throne rather than cowering. *I suppose some things are too much to hope for,* I reminded myself.

The room itself was impressive for its size. It was much larger than the small informal meeting room that James and I had met the King in a few times previously. This was a room used for state functions and as such it had a high vaulted ceiling, rising up some forty feet above our heads. It stretched thirty yards or more from side to side and the distance from the doors I had just destroyed to the throne at the opposite end of the room was at least thirty yards as well. Long rows of benches were arranged between here and there, to allow the nobility and clergy ample seating during major court events. There were two exits, aside from the way we had entered, in the form of two normal size doors leading from each of the two corners of the room behind the throne.

The throne was positioned atop the dais at the far end and Edward seemed quite composed as we neared it. If my destructive entrance bothered him he didn't show it. He smiled as we approached. "Ahh! My dear Count di'Cameron, we are pleased indeed to see you this day."

I stopped before reaching the dais and addressed him from some twenty feet away. "The feeling is not mutual."

"You seem out of sorts Mordecai and you have arrived almost two hours early for your audience. Perhaps you have received some distressing news this morning?"

I ignored his goading. "Let's dispense with the games Edward. You have one opportunity if you wish to live through the rest of this day and that is to deliver my wife, Penelope Illeniel and her guard Sir Dorian Thornbear to me now, safe and unharmed."

His eyebrows shot up in mock surprise. "Bold words from such a young man, are you certain you have thought this through properly Mordecai? You really shouldn't threaten the man that holds your wife and unborn child's lives in his hands."

My eyes narrowed at his words. "And you shouldn't attempt to use hostages against a man who can kill you on a whim," I replied.

The King laughed as he answered, "If I die you will never see them alive. You can count on that! Do you understand? You're playing at games you are ill-equipped for, boy."

"Your threats do not hold power when those you threaten no longer fear you," I replied.

"Careful child, your words here will determine the fate of your loved ones," he said sternly but I could detect a flicker of uncertainty in his eyes. He was beginning to realize I had moved beyond the point of being coerced.

"That is the first and most basic lie used by the corrupt to assert their will via threats and extortion. I will not accept responsibility for your actions. If I cannot stop you from harming them I will at least make certain you never repeat your evil deeds against others," I declared.

Edward sneered, "Such noble words from a man who is dooming his wife and child to death at the hands of another."

"Your twisted delusions have made you incapable of ruling. I doubt now that you ever understood the nature of a ruler's power," I answered, deliberately goading him.

"You seek to lecture me on the basis of power? I rule by the divine right of kings. None of your feeble words can change that and your 'magic' is insufficient in the face of the power of a nation," he replied.

"That is where you are mistaken. The 'divine right of kings' is a farce. A wise man taught me the true source of a ruler's power," I said remembering Dorian's words from the past. "It lies in the people that serve him. The strength of his people is a gift that a true king must cherish and nurture, and in that you have failed. None of this would have been necessary Edward, but for your constant failure. Failure to put your people first, both during the war with Gododdin and again when you forsook the people to make a deal with the shiggreth. And for what? The chance to coerce and control me? If you had been a good king I would have served you without coercion."

As I spoke I could feel Cyhan's eyes boring into me. Rose was watching me as well, and I had a feeling there were others, though my mind could not find them. There was another presence in the room, and it lay heavy upon the air, like a great power held in check.

Edward had to know by now that I wasn't bluffing. I had come to kill him. Yet he still showed no fear. "You fool!" he shouted at me. "You spout that tired old philosophy at me and yet it still isn't true! My power is from the 'consent of the governed'? Lies! My power is granted me by the gods themselves!"

I had had enough. My decision had been made before I entered the room and our conversation had merely served to reaffirm his madness. Lifting my hand I held a small pebble on my palm. I had picked it up from the road during our walk to the palace. "This stone will be your end Edward. I would not waste anything more on you now, and in truth even this is more than you are worth." Raising it to my lips I blew upon it and said the words that would send it hurtling with lethal speed at the King, *"Tielen striltos."*

A flash of golden light, visible only to my arcane senses, flared near the King, and my stone struck an invisible shield in front of him. Where before he had stood alone with only Cyhan beside him, there were now two more figures. The golden glow emanated from a young woman and I could feel the shield she had erected around herself and Edward. She was either a wizard or a channeler. Cyhan still had made no effort to move. He was still and silent.

"Where did they come from?" Rose asked beside me.

"I don't know, but it appears that Edward has reinforcements. You should leave now Rose," I told her. "This isn't going to be pretty."

She spat at the ground in the most unladylike gesture I had ever seen from her. "I'll be damned first."

The woman standing beside Edward was slender, with light brown hair and fair skin. Examining her more closely I realized she was hardly a woman at all, but rather a tall teenager, still gangly and awkward. She was dressed richly in a dress made of golden satin but her face gave away her lack of experience.

The second figure was that of a well-built man, tall and perfectly formed. He kept his face hidden in the deep recesses of a hooded cloak but there was a sense about him, an air of menace I couldn't yet define.

"Who is the girl Edward?" I asked casually.

He smiled, "Allow me to introduce Elaine Prathion. I suspect you may have met her father already, have you not?"

I winced inwardly. Now I knew why Walter's daughter hadn't been there when they liberated the rest of his family. I ignored the King and addressed her directly, "Elaine, listen to me. This man has no hold upon you, not any longer. Your father helped your mother and brother escape early this morning."

Her eyes were slightly unfocused as she stared back at me and I could hear Edward's laughter as she replied, "Celior has told me of you. You are a pestilence that will bring the destruction of the world if you are left to fester unchecked. I serve the true King, Edward, for he has been ordained by the gods to lead us through these dark times."

Stretching out her hand she said something I couldn't hear and a searing beam of light lanced from her hand toward me. Unconsciously I strengthened my shield but I needn't have worried. Although her power was strong it was nowhere near enough to penetrate my defenses.

"Elaine, stop, you have to believe me. This man has been using you to control your father for years." I pleaded with her, hoping she would hear me.

"She will not listen to you," said Edward looking past her. "She listens only to me, and her god."

"Very well then," I replied and raising my staff I threw my power against her shield in a manner meant not to pierce but to crush. My aim was to overwhelm her so quickly that she collapsed from the strain rather than die trying to match me.

For a moment it appeared my plan would work. Her shield buckled and her hair flew back as she fell to one knee under the sudden strain. My respect for her grew however as she stabilized her shield and slowly stood back up despite the pressure. I could see the muscles in her jaw clenching and sweat was beading on her brow but she wouldn't surrender easily. Clearly she was stronger than her father.

I briefly considered using my staff to focus a line of fire that would slice through her shield, but I knew that would be instantly fatal and I really didn't want to kill Walter's daughter. My hesitation cost me precious seconds however and she regained the initiative. Gesturing at the ceiling above she made a pulling motion with her hand and I looked up to see part of the ceiling collapsing inward; tons of granite were falling toward my head.

Trying to stop that much stone with just my shield would probably have been immediately fatal and even if I succeeded it would certainly render me unconscious. Instead I spoke and gestured at the floor around myself and Rose. The giant blocks that made up the floor swung up and over us to form a shallow arch. I had positioned them to brace each other and I added my shield to help hold them in place.

Thankfully the massive bulk of granite absorbed much of the impact, and my shield managed the rest. Without waiting for the dust to clear I located Elaine with my mind and tried a spell I had once used with great effect against Cyhan, *"Grabol ni'targoth."* A hole opened in the stone beneath the teenage girl and suddenly bereft of support she fell, losing her grasp on the shield around her at the same time.

With another word I sealed her within the stone. I was careful to avoid injuring her and I knew the tactic wouldn't hold her for long. Crawling forward I drew Rose with me until we were free of the massive pile of stone rubble that had fallen over us. "Is she dead?" Rose asked as we emerged.

"I'm trying not to kill her."

"Fool!" she shouted, "This is your only chance to kill the King. If you play nice that girl will kill us and then Penny and Dorian will die for nothing!"

I ignored her and focused on Elaine. An explosion of rock told me she had escaped from my stony prison but she vanished as she emerged. She had taken refuge in the Prathion's famous invisibility, a few months prior I might have been helpless to predict her movements, but having known Walter I knew a lot more about the ability now. If she was invisible to the eyes she couldn't see, if she was invisible to magesight she couldn't sense anything magically, and if she was invisible to both she was effectively blind.

She wasn't deaf however.

"Thank you Elaine!" I shouted at the air. "Now I can finish what I started with the King." Raising my staff I sent a massive bolt of force hurtling through the air.

She reappeared instantly, dropping the invisibility and throwing a shield up in front of the defenseless king. My attack hadn't been directed at the King however, I had aimed it at the area where she had vanished. Knowing she was blind I had figured she wouldn't go very far so I had kept my attack broad and unfocused, and the bludgeoning force of it swept her unprotected form across the floor. She struck the wall with a resounding 'crack' and slid unconscious to the floor. I worried that despite my efforts I might have killed her anyway.

Straightening up I began walking toward the King. "I was already angry, but every time I think you can't sink any lower you find new ways to surprise me," I said as I approached him. "Using children to fight your battles is about as low as a human being can get." Hefting my staff like a spear I gripped it in the middle and swept my hand from the tip of the iron shod heel and out into the air. *"Thylen ingak ni'lyet,"* I said, and a three foot blade of pure shimmering force appeared from the end.

Edward flinched back as I swung it back toward him and he cried out in fear, "Celior defend me!" He flung his hands up as if to ward the blow but I knew the blade would slice through flesh and bone until it had cleaved entirely through his rotten heart. Victory, bitter though it might be, was mine.

There was no way I could have anticipated how mistaken I was.

The cloaked man drew back his hood and the golden locks of his hair fell free as a luminescent radiance filled the air. Before then I had felt a fearful hint of an unknown presence; I now found myself overwhelmed by the stranger's sheer blinding power. The very air had become heavy with it, and though I struggled, I could not move to finish my blow, so heavy was his crushing presence.

Knees buckling I fell to the floor, genuflecting despite myself. The stranger's features were so bright I was forced to bow my head to shield my eyes from the light and I knew without doubt that I was in the physical presence of one of the shining gods. The experience was different than when I had faced the gods before. In the past they had been channeled, limited by their human vessels. Now I stood before Celior himself, and there was no limit to his power.

A voice so beautiful that it drove my heart to tears spoke, "Only now do you understand the folly of your ways Mordecai."

I struggled to clear my mind. I still held my shield tightly about myself but Celior's power seemed to bleed through it like contagion, seeping into me despite my best efforts. Gritting my teeth I contracted my shield and put everything I had into sealing my mind. *You may take my body you bastard but you will never have me!*

Celior laughed. "Look Edward! It thinks it can defy me! You are an insect mortal, your death will mean nothing to me and yet I will relish your despair."

With my mind clear I found myself able to stand again, though it still felt as if I had a giant standing upon my shoulders. Drawing myself up I looked to Edward in desperation, "What have you done?"

The King however was lost in a fit of divine ecstasy. He was kneeling with his head raised and a look of frenzied euphoria on his face. A few feet behind him Cyhan still stood but his expression was even more fearful to me… tears streaked his cheeks and his eyes held a look of sorrow so profound I wondered if he were even the same man I had known.

At my side Rose was still on her knees and her face was drawn in an expression of pain. My eyes met hers for a moment and I could feel her terror and despair. What we faced now was beyond human comprehension.

I seemed to be the only one left in the room that retained a modicum of sanity. Celior's presence had deprived them of their reason as well as their dignity.

The shining god spoke again, "My arrival is not by your rightful king's doing, but rather by the hand of that sweet girl, who shall be revered above all women." Celior's hand swept out to point at Elaine's unconscious form and he began to laugh. "She was so desperate. Her imprisonment led her to despair of ever finding freedom, or safety for her family. Without the guidance of her father she called to me and offered me passage here, to your world, if only I would grant her justice!"

My tongue finally found its will and I slowly ground out a reply, "You're no better than Edward."

Celior smiled and the beauty of his face seemed to light the room. "Is that what you think?" The god turned and addressed the King, "Rise o' King, I would seek your counsel!"

Edward stood slowly. "What would you have of me?"

"This man will die, but he must suffer first. Tell me how you would increase his anguish."

Edward smiled, "His wife and friend lie below the palace, in a hidden vault, bring them here and let them watch."

Celior looked at Cyhan, "Fetch them here mortal."

I struggled to move, to do anything, but it was all I could do to remain standing. It took everything I had just to keep my mind clear and I was barely succeeding at that. Try as I might the only freedom left to me was the power of speech. "You'll regret this Celior," I said slowly.

The god laughed. "Do you think that I will suffer the same fate as Balinthor? He was tired and sick by the time he was called to this plane, thanks to your ancestor. The destruction of the She'Har was his undoing long before Moira Centyr was." Taking notice of Lady Rose the god gestured in her direction, "Come here child."

Like a twisted imitation of a marionette Rose stood and walked haltingly to stand before the golden perfection that was Celior. "You have sinned against me child," said the god, and tears began flowing freely down Rose's cheeks. Leaning down Celior kissed her slowly. Rose's body jerked as if she had been shocked for a moment and then she began to writhe sinuously in his grasp.

The god pulled away from her causing Rose to cry out in anguish at the sudden loss. "That is the bliss you might have had," he told her and then twisting her thick black tresses in his hand he lifted her from the ground by her hair. "This is what you will receive instead," he intoned cruelly as she cried out in pain.

"Stop it!" I screamed.

"Or what?" asked the god, sneering in my direction.

"Put her down," came a gravelly voice that I nevertheless recognized. Dorian Thornbear stood in one of the corner doorways behind the throne. Cyhan and Penny were close behind him. Impossibly he wore the armor I had made for him, though I couldn't imagine Edward would have been foolish enough to leave him with it.

CHAPTER 45

Dorian repeated himself again, "Put her down or I'll cut your fucking head from your shoulders." He held one of the enchanted swords I had given him.

Celior looked at him in amazement. "A stoic? How unusual. Do you think you can save this woman? Here, I didn't really want her anyway." Using a slow sweeping movement the god threw Rose at Edward and the two of them went down in a pile of tangled limbs. Several torn locks of her hair hung loosely from Celior's fingers. Glancing at the hair the deity began to laugh.

Screaming in rage Dorian charged at the mocking god. He moved with speed and his size along with the shining armor he wore made Celior seem small in comparison.

The god didn't bother trying to dodge or avoid him. With one arm he caught Dorian, grasping his armor at the gorget that protected Dorian's throat. Despite Dorian's incredible momentum Celior was not moved at all, and even his hair hung calmly about him. Lifting he drew Dorian up, until his feet dangled above the floor. "You amuse me greatly, but you must not die yet little warrior."

As he found himself rising above the floor Dorian swept his sword up and across, attempting to cut Celior's arm from his shoulder. His heart pounded with the strength of the earth and when his blade struck the god's arm it made a sound as if a massive gong had been struck. The sword shattered as though it was made of glass and fragments of steel flew in every direction.

In a movement that seemed almost languid the shining god threw Dorian across the room. My friend's armored body struck the wall so hard that it bowed outward and the stones cracked, and then he fell to the floor unmoving.

While Celior's attention had been on Dorian the pressure on the rest of us lessened. Hearing a cry of pain I saw Rose rise from the dais holding a bloody dagger. Edward lay bleeding beneath her.

Turning his attention back to us the pressure increased again and Rose's knees buckled. Kneeling in the King's blood she still laughed. "You cannot have everything," she said in a voice so soft it was almost inaudible.

Around the room everyone was on their knees again, including Penny and Cyhan now. My eyes sought Penny's and for a moment we were together again, despite the intervening distance. In Penelope's haggard face I could see fear and exhaustion, along with worry, probably for me. Still I felt a tiny flower of hope blossom in my chest at the sight of her.

The god's attention was fully on Rose now and holding up his hand a tiny ball of flame flickered into life above it. "You have displeased me child. I think perhaps you should burn first." With a twist of his hand he casually tossed the flame at her.

Drawing on reserves I hadn't known were there I somehow erected a shield before her, sending the flame sliding away to one side where it flickered and died. The god laughed and looked at me. "You amaze me wizard. I thought you had reached your limit."

The continual strain of shielding my mind against his power had left me weary and I found myself wishing for a clever response. The best I could manage was, "That just shows your ignorance."

Celior frowned and holding his hand out toward me he said, "Learn humility." Then he turned his palm toward the floor as if pressing downward.

The pressure on my shield and mind increased several fold and I collapsed. Pain shot through me as my shield vanished. Drawing inward I tried to protect my mind but Celior's will shot through me and it felt as though knives were stabbing into my skull. Blood began to drip from my eyes and I could hear myself screaming.

My entire world dissolved into agony and I felt my sense of self slipping away. In my desperation to escape the pain my body curled into a ball on the ground while my fingers clutched at the hard floor. *The stone!* That single thought permeated my being and gained focus as I sought to preserve what was left of my sanity. Remembering the stone Moira had once given me to shape, I struggled to emulate it. Surrendering my humanity I tried to become the stone… for stones feel no pain.

Still the sharp barbs of Celior's thoughts wrapped around my tortured mind and even through my misery I could hear his voice, echoing in my mind, "Did you think you had the power to protect yourself tiny mortal? I let you believe so only to increase your shame and suffering."

I was utterly blinded by the agony, and yet somehow I could hear. A sharp cry rang out, and I recognized Rose's voice. It was followed by an anguished yell and then Celior spoke again, "You seek to hinder me by killing your King? Watch and know despair." After an unknowable pause he spoke again, "Rise Edward, King of Lothion, your wounds were not fatal."

"Mort! Mort! Can you hear me?" Penny's voice was next to my ear and somehow I knew she was stroking my brow, though I couldn't feel it. The only sensation left to my body at that point was ceaseless burning pain.

My deepest desire was to answer her, but I couldn't. Instead I focused on the only thing that seemed to give me surcease from Celior's torment, the image of the stone I held in my mind.

My focus increased and the wracking agony lessened as I felt my conscious mind harden. At last I was able to open my eyes again and I saw Penelope leaning protectively over me. Over her shoulder I glimpsed the angry god approaching.

"Do you think to protect him woman? He is of no use to you anymore. I will make his death long and painful. You should worry more for yourself," Celior announced with a grin that would have made children laugh at the beauty of it.

"His dying breath is worth more than your entire being!" Penny screamed in defiance as she drew me close, cradling me beneath her. Her tears fell on my face and I struggled to speak, but my mouth still would not cooperate.

At last the pain was gone, along with my vision of the world around me. I saw and felt nothing. In peaceful bliss I relaxed and deep below I could hear the steady beat of the earth. Closer and yet more faintly I heard a single perfect voice, "I will rip your cursed child from your womb and crush it before your eyes."

"No," I said simply and I began to sit up. The pressure against my mind was still there, but it was no longer beyond my ability to stop. Something had changed inside, and a new strength had emerged, drawn primarily from the pulsing heart of the world. Looking around myself with new eyes I took in the room with a clarity that came from a calm center. I had found my balance, and in that timeless instant I saw everything.

Dorian and Elaine were both still unconscious, their bodies collapsed near the wall to one side of the room.

Rose lay face down near the throne, a still spreading pool of blood fanning outward from beneath her. Edward stood over her now, a bloody dagger in hand and a smile upon his face. His grey hair was gone and he looked younger than I remembered. Last of all, I spotted Cyhan, crouched near the doorway, still holding a sword though he seemed powerless to move.

Most importantly the shining god was reaching down, though his movement seemed terribly slow. Penelope's face was still above me, framed by loose strands of soft brown hair, shining golden with Celior's light behind her. Her eyes were on mine and in that moment something passed between us, a type of communication that was ineffable. Apologies and regrets were forgotten and meaningless, for our hearts had found each other once again.

Celior's hand was over her head, and his fingers were beginning to clench inward, to grasp her by the hair when finally the universe snapped back into motion. Without conscious thought I drew deeply upon the power beneath me while reaching up to meet the god's greedy hand with my own, *"Na'Pyrren Ingak mai Lathos"* It was the spell I had created to harden and strengthen my hands when working with the hot metal of the forge.

Our hands entwined for a moment and I felt the immensity of Celior's unwitting strength, but I didn't care. Clenching my hand into a fist the shining god's bones broke, snapping like dry twigs under my fingers. Staring into the brilliant blue eyes of the god I spoke, "You will never touch her."

Celior screamed and drew back as I released his hand but he recovered his composure within seconds. "I am done playing with you wizard," and so saying he held up his hand, flexing it, as if to demonstrate that it had already healed.

Raising my staff I created a new shield around the two of us. Using my newfound strength I imbued it with so much power that blue sparks sizzled and spat around the edges. My instincts were screaming at me to find some way to get Penny and our unborn child away, but I knew there was no escaping the monstrous deity that stood before us.

Luminescent tendrils of power were beginning to test the boundaries of my new shield but I ignored them and looked back, into Penny's dark brown eyes. There were dark circles under them and her body had swelled even more with her pregnancy, but gazing at her all I could see was the girl that had run with me through the open fields of our childhood summers. The word love simply wasn't enough to describe what she meant to me. Gazing into those eyes I saw my future, and the proof of it was growing in her belly. I wanted nothing more than to hold her and forget the nightmare around us.

I opened my mouth and said, "You are such an asshole."

Her expression faltered, "What?"

"Was that really the best message you could leave me? I thought you were dead!" I said angrily.

Disbelief marched across her face, "I couldn't say more! I didn't know what might affect your fate."

"Fuck fate! Fate is a goddamned whore! She changes her mind more frequently than that fickle bitch Lady Luck! Next time, you tell me the truth and consequences be damned!" I shouted.

Penelope's face twisted into an expression that was a mixture of irony, humor and worry. "There may not be a next time, this was as far as my vision got; the rest is up to you."

Now it was my turn to be incredulous. All the suffering and fear I had been through, and this was the extent of her vision? "If we make it home alive we are going to have a serious talk," I said and turned my attention back to the angry god.

In the short time I had ignored him Celior had changed. He had grown several feet in height and golden mists wreathed the ground about his feet. His overall luminosity had increased as well, making it almost painful to look at him. *This isn't looking good,* I thought to myself.

Across the room, Cyhan was kneeling over Rose and from his awkward motions I could tell he was having difficulty moving. Celior's presence was like an iron weight and without powerful protection I doubted any normal human could move. Reaching down Cyhan pulled the necklace from around Rose's limp form and settled it over his own head. His movements became considerably quicker after that. *Is he just seeking to escape?* I wondered. Dorian couldn't possibly have appeared with his arms and armor by chance. "Take them and get out!" I yelled at him as loudly as I could, gesturing at Rose and then Elaine. I would have liked Dorian safe as well, but there was no way Cyhan could have carried them all and at least Dorian was armored.

Celior smiled chillingly, "Save your breath mortal. I will only hunt them down once I am finished with you." Reaching out, his hand pressed against my shield causing brilliant sparks to fly. "Your shield has improved. I might have to exert myself slightly to break something like that," mused the shining deity, "though I know an easier way."

I hardly liked the sound of that. Glancing backward I noticed one of the giant stones from the ceiling lay beside Penny and me, forming a natural barrier. "Get behind the stone Penny," I ordered quietly. Turning back to Celior I tried to buy some time. "I'm done listening to your pathetic childish threats," I said loudly.

The god laughed, "One small taste of the earth and you think you have a chance, I begin to doubt your intelligence Mordecai."

For a moment I doubted my resolve. Obviously bear-baiting an angry god wasn't among the smartest things I had ever decided to do. *Stupid never dies,* I thought inwardly, and then I replied, "Intelligence is overrated. I don't need wits to see that you are nothing, despite your power. You are a parasite, a plague upon humanity, a figment of some man's demented dream, drawing your sustenance from the hearts and souls of those who mistakenly worship you."

As I spoke Celior's face went from amused to thunderous and I put even more power into my shield. Whatever was coming would be bad. "I will show you the folly of your fool's tongue," the god replied and then I discovered my error.

A flash of light illuminated the room and for a split second it was as though the sun had touched the earth. It centered upon Celior and so intense were those rays that everything they touched burned and turned instantly to ash. The cloth furnishings in the room burned so rapidly they didn't even have time to catch fire. Even the very stones smoked where that awful light played across them. My shield, on the other hand, was transparent, for light had never been a danger.

Staring up at Celior my skin and clothing crisped and vanished almost instantly from the half of my body facing him. My eyes shriveled and burned so quickly it was a mercy to no longer have to see the light. A scream rose in my throat but failed to escape for the pain had taken my breath away. As quickly as the light had appeared it vanished.

In its wake I was left a smoking ruin. The outer layer of clothing, skin and fat on the side of my body that faced the shining god was gone. If it hadn't been for the cauterization that occurred simultaneously I might have bled to death, but instead I was left in a horror of agony and pain. Collapsing to the ground I knew I was dying already, but it might take hours unless Celior decided to hurry it along.

"Mort? What was that flash? I can't see anything!" That was Penny's voice. Though my eyes were gone I could still see her with my magesight, shielded by the lee of the stone. "Are you alright?" she asked.

Oddly enough the pain faded. *Most of the nerve endings are gone,* I mused. "It's alright," I tried to answer her but though my voice worked my ruined lips made the words sound almost foreign.

"Now you more closely resembled the blind worm you truly are," said Celior mockingly, "when your whore's sight returns she may thank me for improving your appearance."

Anger was all I had left to drive me, that and a stubborn desire to somehow save my wife and child. The drumbeat of the earth quickened in response and I sought refuge in its rhythm and solace in its rage. "I don't need eyes to see your ugliness Celior," I answered and then I began to stand once more.

Something struck the back of my head like the blow of a forge hammer, sending me back down against the stone floor. *Moira, help me!* I cried mentally. Somehow I began rising to my feet again, though another hammer blow sent me reeling to one side. Celior was battering me with his fists now.

I can do nothing against the might of a god Mordecai, came Moira's words in my mind.

Another strike sent me flying across the room to strike the wall, and yet again I started to rise up. *Not me! Hide Penny. Take her away, through the stones if you must. Save her!* My attention was fully engaged by Celior's fists then.

Though his blows struck ever harder they seemed to hurt less. I was larger now, though Celior had kept pace with my growth. At a guess we both towered a full twenty feet above the floor now.

"You should stay down," Celior's voice told me. "You only delay the inevitable."

His next blow swung toward my head but I was ready for him and this time I brought up my own arm to block it. Before he recovered I drove my other fist into his stomach. Without realizing it my hands had grown massive stony spikes and they pierced the shining god's belly, spilling blood that looked like liquid gold upon the ground. "I am so tired of hearing that," I replied in a voice that was reminiscent of the grating of two massive stones. "You'd think you would find some original threats during your eons of immortality."

Celior stumbled back and then tried to counterattack. Ignoring his strikes I grabbed his head as he leaned in, and jerking it downward I brought my massive stony knee up to meet it. With a crack like the sound of thunder I felt the bones in the shining god's face break. Drawing his head back I repeated the motion, pulverizing what was left of Celior's beautiful face. Then I reached down and grasped the limp god by the legs and swung him bodily into the wall.

Unfortunately I lost my grip on him at that point and he flew from my grasp. Despite the grievous injuries he recovered faster than I could reach him and leaping upward fiery wings sprung from his back. Several desperate wing beats sent him soaring above my head and through the ruined ceiling of the palace. *That was not in the damn rulebook!* I thought, cursing him mentally.

Taking advantage of my brief respite I scanned the area for my friends. Only Dorian was near, still lying unconscious in the stone rubble of one wall. Cyhan was almost out of the palace now, carrying Rose over one shoulder and Elaine over the other. Of Penny I could find no trace and I took that as a good sign.

I decided to get some fresh air. Raising my fist I demolished one wall and pushed my way through the rubble until I stood in one of the palace's inner courtyards. Given the relative size of the dollhouse I was destroying I must have stood over forty feet tall at that point. As soon as I emerged from the fallen stone and timbers I discovered what Celior had been up to. A searing beam of pure sunlight bore down on me, burning into my stone skin.

Above me the god flew on his flaming wings, like some grotesque parody of a phoenix. He kept the light focused upon me and parts of my body began sloughing away like bubbling magma. Even in my rocky form I began to experience a sensation that my human self might have labeled pain and I tried to shield myself with my arms to no avail.

Drawing upon my magic I sent a bolt of pure force at my antagonist but the distance and his maneuverability made it impossible to hit him. "Fool!" Celior screamed down at me. "Your power cannot last, but mine is eternal."

I was beginning to think he might have a point. As his assault continued it was becoming more and more difficult to reconstruct my body and even my thoughts were growing sluggish. The more power I drew from the earth the less I cared. I was beginning to forget myself. *If I could just get my hands on that glowing bastard,* I thought desperately.

A shadow crossed the sun and in the distance I saw something impossible. It was too far for my magesight, but my stony eyes could see what appeared to be a huge bird diving from the sky, down toward Celior. Apparently the god sensed something as well, for he broke off his laughter and glanced up and behind himself in alarm. His measured wing beats became frantic strokes as he tried to gain speed and altitude, but it was far too late. The bird… no it was a dragon, had far too much speed already from its dive.

It struck him with such force that they both plummeted from the sky and Celior was driven into the street beside the palace. The ground shook and the dragon tore at the god's body, ripping into his belly. For a moment I was still, staring on in complete shock. *Could that be Gareth Gaelyn?* According to the story Moira had told me dragons were the stuff of myth and fairy tale. The only one that had ever existed was the result of an archmage gone mad and that was over a thousand years ago. He had also slaughtered his own people.

The dragon was at least a hundred feet in length from nose to tail and armored in glistening grey-black scales. His body was sleek and streamlined yet as he moved I could see powerful muscles rippling under his skin. The dragon's wings were folded tightly against his body now that he was down on the ground, but they had been vast when they were unfurled a moment before. He held Celior with his jaws and two powerful forelimbs while his rear legs clawed and tore at the shining god.

Not knowing what else to do I started running to reach them, at least I tried to run. I quickly discovered that my size prohibited such activities and I was forced to proceed at a hurried lumbering gait. I still covered much more ground than I could have in my normal human form.

Even as I neared them Celior recovered his balance and twisted free of the dragon's grip. Rolling, the two of them fought on the ground like two drunken brawlers. *If drunks had scales, wings, and glowed...* I thought. Celior had the advantage now, using the weight of his body to press the dragon into the crater they had formed while his hands attempted to rip the beast's head from its neck. The deity's wounds had already vanished and his beauty was horrible to watch as he began to exert himself, pulling the dragon's head inexorably upward.

How do you kill something that heals instantly? I wondered. My anger had faded somewhat, slowly being replaced by fear. Despite everything, Celior seemed more powerful than ever and there were no signs of him weakening.

I had little time for thinking, since it appeared my only ally was about to lose his head. Diving into the fray I wrapped the shining god in my arms and squeezed. Laughing, Celior began glowing brighter than the sun and I felt my body beginning to melt and sag where it touched him. I couldn't afford to let him get airborne again, so I did the opposite.

"Let's see how you like the center of my power," I ground out between granite teeth and I redoubled my efforts. Contracting my arms I felt his back break and the god twisted in pain. Stretching outward with my thoughts I let my body sink downward, into the ground, dragging the struggling deity with me. *Sorry Penny,* I thought with regret. *I couldn't keep that promise Rose wanted me to make for you.*

Ever deeper we went and still I clutched Celior tightly. I could feel him weakening now, or perhaps it was just my growing strength, but I was able to encase him in the massive stone coffin that my body had become for him. Moira Centyr had defeated Balinthor this way, I remembered. She had drawn him down and when her power had been great enough she had crushed him to death. The resulting explosion had changed the face of the earth and created a new sea.

That will kill everyone above for tens of miles, came Moira's voice in my mind.

How close is Penny? I asked.

What of your other friends? What of the people? she answered.

I felt a sense of anguish and desperation. *I can't have everything,* I replied.

You cannot do this, not here.

Then I'll move him, I said mentally.

There is a better way, she replied and then her mind touched mine and showed me.

Descending deeper I moved down beneath the crust of the world, into a realm of extreme heat and pressures. There I began crushing Celior, until his size was what it had been when I first saw him. Pushing further I compressed him until he had become nothing more than a brilliantly glowing sphere about two inches across. I reached within my massive rocky body and drew forth a power that was intensely concentrated and began weaving it in deep red lines around the trapped god. *The blood of the earth,* I thought to myself, for blood was the closest thing I could think to the appearance of that power.

Using my memory of the stasis enchantment and something akin to intuition I wove a series of runes that would lock the god's twisted mind into a timeless and unchanging state. When I had finished he no longer struggled against his gem-like form but still his power was so great that it warped even time around it, causing energy to bleed outward. Drawing upon my strength I encased his enchanted form with a dense crystal that would absorb his power as it leaked out.

I'll have to make sure the power is used or drained away regularly, I thought. Otherwise the giant diamond would eventually explode with a force that would make my iron bombs seem paltry in comparison. *And the malign being within would be free again,* I mentally added.

When I had finished I spent long minutes resting. The deep earth was comfortable and now that I no longer had to struggle against my foe it soothed my ragged emotions. My pains began ebbing away. My body no longer had any distinct margin or border and the deep drumming of the earth drew my tired spirit out. *I should sleep,* came a thought I hardly recognized as my own any longer.

Mordecai, no! Wake up! You must return. Don't give up now. Moira Centyr's voice nagged at my consciousness.

More from irritation than any desire to please her I lifted myself up through the dark layers of earth and stone until I once again lay upon the street in Albamarl. The dragon still lay nearby, bleeding and nursing a terrible wound to its neck. The sight of it roused my mind and brought back thoughts of my humanity.

Lifting my massive stone form I moved carefully closer to the dragon, unsure what it might do. "Can you understand me?" I said in a voice so deep and booming it surprised me.

Its eyes opened and fixed on me with a look of such intelligence I could not help but think it understood my language. Its mouth opened for a second but no sound emerged and a look of what I thought must be frustration passed across its strange reptilian features. "Are you Gareth Gaelyn?" I asked, thinking it might be able to nod or respond in some other way.

Before my eyes the creature began to shrink and its flesh flowed like water reshaping itself into something far different and much smaller. Seconds later I found myself staring down at a bizarre looking man. His skin held a strange lustrous tint and his eyes were slitted like those of a cat… or a dragon. Utterly naked he had no evidence of external genitalia and his belly was covered in large scales much like those of a snake.

Looking down at himself he cursed, "This isn't right." He seemed surprised when he heard the words emerge from his mouth.

I repeated my question, "Are you Gareth Gaelyn?"

Staring upward he answered, "I think I used to be, but I am unsure. I was human once."

"Why did you help me?"

"I heard the earth rouse itself a few days ago. I came to find the reason, and to feed," he said in slow and oddly accented words. "The shining god reminded me of my crime and my shame."

His words made me anxious, particularly his mention of 'feeding'. I wondered if he might repeat his first slaughter of the men he had meant to save. Before I could put my fears into words he spoke again, "Are you a wizard?"

"I am," I replied simply, not knowing what more to add.

"That form is dangerous. More so even than mine, it will eat at your mind," he said somberly.

His words reminded me that I still had not resumed my original flesh and blood body. Closing my great stone eyes I remembered Moira's lesson and visualized myself as I had been before. The memory of my burns flitted through my mind for a second and I stopped, that thought had come close to killing me. Clearing my thoughts again I remembered myself as I had been before the burning light, healthy and whole.

When I opened my eyes again I saw the world in more normal hues and standing in front of me was Gareth Gaelyn. He was close enough now I could see how thoroughly reptilian he looked in every particular. "I think I still have my mind intact," I told him.

He smiled oddly, showing rows of needle sharp teeth. "You think so, but each time you leave bits of yourself behind. Small things you don't even notice. And you bring new things back without realizing it."

"Will you return to the world of men?" I asked him.

He shook his head, "This is as close as I can come to your form now. The very thought of going further repulses me."

"Then why did you take this form?" I asked, gesturing at his humanoid body.

"I'm not sure," he said carefully. "I think just to warn you, and to thank you for helping me settle my debt."

"Debt?"

"I failed to stop Balinthor, but I think today has settled the score," he replied walking away from me.

"Where are you going?"

"To feed," he replied.

"On what?" I asked.

He glanced back and showed me his teeth, "Whatever I find, human. My debt is settled and I must eat." Saying that he began changing again and moments later the dragon was back.

"Take care where you find your meals dragon!" I shouted as he began to beat his wings. "If I find you eating humans I will not stand idly by."

I watched him fly away through the long afternoon sunlight. The palace nearby was ruined. Walking back into it I decided to find my friends, or whatever was left of them.

CHAPTER 46

Now that I was of a more modest size the damage done to the palace was much more apparent. Large swaths of the complex had been utterly ruined. Rubble and wreckage were strewn about willy-nilly… as if two titans had run amok with giant hammers. The destruction was far from complete however, for at least three quarters of the place remained untouched.

In places I found perfectly sound areas bordered by sections where even the stones had been crushed into gravel. If I hadn't known the cause I might have thought some bizarre earthquake followed by a tornado had done the damage, but even that explanation wouldn't have been sufficient.

As I walked (and sometimes picked my way) through the palace, I searched with my mind for my companions. Scanning the undamaged areas I found Rose and Elaine had been laid side by side on a bed in one of the guest suites. Frighteningly a section less than twenty yards from them had been crushed and it appeared that mere chance had saved the two unconscious women.

Dorian still lay where I had last seen him, in the now collapsed main throne room. He was partly buried under stone and rubble but I could tell he was still breathing so I decided to check on the two ladies first. The last time I had seen Rose she had been bleeding profusely from some sort of wound. I found no sign of Penny.

Moira, where is Penny? I asked mentally as I headed for the room where Rose and Elaine lay.

She is with me. Fear not, she is safe, came the reply.

Bring her to me, I commanded.

Moira's answer had a strange feel to it when she responded, as though strong emotions were overwhelming her thoughts. *Not yet, we are… talking. I will bring her back when she is ready.*

That was interesting, and it did little to relieve my anxiety. Pressing onward I found the room that Rose was in, I needed to make sure she wasn't dying before I addressed anything else. I found her lying on a large bed where it appeared she had been hastily dumped. Her arms and legs were askew and by their unnatural positions I didn't think she had moved at all since Cyhan had presumably left her there. That didn't bode well, normally even unconscious people move a bit.

Elaine was curled up at the foot of the bed and a cursory examination showed she had nothing more wrong with her than a large goose egg on the back of her head, along with an assortment of scratches. I passed over her immediately and set my hand over Rose's forehead.

Her skin was cold but not clammy for she wasn't sweating, in fact it felt remarkably similar to what I would have expected from a corpse but I could tell her heart was still beating. Her gown had been ripped and a large wadded up ball of the fabric had been tied against her abdomen. Even so blood had seeped through the material and the bed beneath her was soaked with it. *Shit!* I thought and immediately I focused my senses on her wound.

She had been stabbed and likely with a very sharp blade, for her assailant had ripped the blade out with a slashing motion rather than simply withdrawing it. Cyhan had probably had to tuck her innards back in before binding her wound. I had no more time for thought, forgetting my weariness I began sealing arteries and torn vessels, knitting everything back together as quickly as possible before she could lose any more blood.

Unlike the terrible wound Penny had suffered once this one was much simpler and I was able to effectively repair the injuries without trying to work from the inside as I had done before. The biggest problem was loss of blood; she had lost so much of it that I feared her body might shut down from that simple lack. Her heart was beating at an incredible rate trying to make up for the paucity of blood.

I glanced down at the brilliant golden stone I held in my hand and wished I could heal the way the gods were able to. I had seen them heal far worse and yet I struggled with something as simple as a mere shortage of blood. In desperation I briefly considered connecting her blood vessels with those of the girl next to her and trying to share some of Elaine's blood between them.

More likely you'll kill both of them, I chided myself. I didn't know enough to try something like that. Instead I found a pitcher of clean water and used my magic to coerce it through the air and then slip it through her mouth and down her throat. I filled her stomach halfway and stopped, and then I stood back and wiped my forehead. I could only hope that it would help.

A wave of fatigue washed over me and I knew I couldn't keep going for much longer. I needed rest like a starving man needs food. I ignored the impulse to lie down on the floor and instead I moved Elaine close beside Rose, arranging her so that she might help keep the other woman warm and then I wrapped them both gently in the large comforter that lay underneath them.

Closing my eyes I fought the urge to sleep and sent my mind outward again. Briefly I checked on Dorian… he was still breathing steadily and his heartbeat was strong so I moved on. Searching the grounds I finally found the man

I was searching for, Edward, King of Lothion. *Soon to be the late-King,* I added mentally.

He had had plenty of time to escape, but for the stone column that had fallen and pinned him beneath a pile of rubble. Moving steadily through the palace and across torn gardens I drew closer and I could tell that his left leg had been crushed. I had trouble imagining a better man to suffer such misfortune. As I neared him I felt Cyhan approaching from a different direction and I paused to wait for his arrival.

He saw me standing amid the rubble and changed direction to meet me. I called out to him when he was close, "Thank you."

Cyhan frowned, "What's that for?"

"You freed Penny and Dorian didn't you? I'm fairly certain Edward wouldn't have had him locked up with his armor and weapons," I said as if it were a matter of plain fact. "I also appreciate your help getting Rose and the girl out of there," I added.

The older warrior's eyes appraised me silently but he only grunted and gave a small nod. "Have you found the King?" he asked, ignoring my gratitude.

"He's close by," I said guardedly. I still had doubts regarding Cyhan's motivations. "First I'd like to know where you and I stand."

A ripple went through the big man's shoulders as his muscles twitched. "Twenty years ago I gave my oaths to the king and I have not yet broken them. So long as that remains true the only thing that can change between us is either your death or my own."

I felt a surge of anger at the other man's irrational behavior. Clinging to his outdated vows he wouldn't be satisfied 'til one of us was dead, even though he obviously no longer believed in the reasons behind those vows.

"Why don't we just settle things now then," I ground out. "I'm sick of waiting for you to try and kill me."

Cyhan glanced at me and then looked away, scanning the area for some sign of Edward. "I'm not a fool, nor do I plan to issue a challenge and face you in some knightly bout. My only chance of killing you will be when you are either unconscious or badly wounded. Pray I do not find you so. Where is the King?"

"What's to stop me from just killing you now then?" I said bitterly.

The large man spun around and glared at me as if I had just caught fire. His eyes were lit with fury. "You should have done that long before now!" he almost shouted, spitting the words from his mouth as if they had left a bad taste there. "Since you won't, why don't you tell me where my King is."

I fought down the impulse to give the other man what he so obviously desired… a quick death. Taking a deep breath I answered him, "I want to talk to him first. You can see him after that."

"Then hurry, I grow impatient," Cyhan replied.

I bit my tongue rather than reply and began walking to the north. Crossing a ruined garden and stepping over a fallen wall I found the large stone pillar that had fallen upon the king of Lothion. Edward was lying quietly near the base, wedged between the stone column and a heavy bench that had kept the massive weight from completely crushing his lower body. He was losing blood slowly for the heavy weight had effectively compressed his torn blood vessels. It would take him hours to die, unless he was healed.

Watching me approach he gave me a pained smile. "Count di'Cameron, it is a pleasure to see you again. Have you come to finish your business or just gloat over an old man?"

I had no intention of healing him. After a long pause I spoke, "Time will finish our business. I merely wanted to ask your advice regarding the succession."

"A cruel reply, Mordecai, you would let me bleed to death while in considerable pain. Why should I give you advice? The world is done with me." There was a tone of resignation in his voice.

Leaning down I touched his throat and uttered a few words quietly. Standing straight again I disguised myself as the King and answered him in his own voice, "If you care about Lothion you should want her ruler to act wisely."

His eyes went wide and anger grew in his features. "It appears you have no need of my advice if you simply intend to usurp my place," he said acrimoniously.

I resumed my normal features and voice. "This kingdom will go on without you Edward, and someday they will remember you as a wise ruler. Your life is ebbing away as we speak and I will not heal you. Given the choice you should do what you can to prevent a civil war… if you love your people at all."

"I badly underestimated you, young Illeniel, but I do not care one whit for those I leave behind. I will help you only on one condition… that you give me a swift end afterwards," he responded with pain in his voice.

"That I will not do, but your servant is close at hand. If you advise me well I will let him see you and perhaps he will grant your wish," I answered.

"Very well," he replied, "What would you know?"

"Who is next in line for the throne?"

A choked laugh escaped the dying monarch, "You really didn't prepare for this did you? You should have known that already. My second cousin, Brian Southwell, the Earl of the Eastern March is next in line since I have no surviving children of my own."

"I had not planned to kill you until a few days ago Edward. This is your own doing," I said. I was surprised that such a minor noble was his heir. I had thought one of the members of the greater families, such as Tremont or Lancaster would have been more closely related. I learned later that the royal family had avoided matches with the more powerful noble houses to avoid giving them more influence. "I'm afraid that the Earl simply won't do," I added.

Edward smiled wickedly, "Then you must kill him and dozens of others besides him if you wish to clear your path to the throne."

I stared down at him without compassion. "I do not intend to take the throne; I will install James Lancaster in your place."

"His claim is little better than your own. If you want him as king you will have to issue a royal decree naming him as my heir and simultaneously declaiming the rights of more than a dozen men that would come before him. You would then have to have me die, or rather give the appearance I had died recently if you are still deceiving people with my likeness." He paused for a moment as a sharp pain stole his breath away. "Once you have my doppelganger die, the noble houses will revolt and it will take a bloody war to enforce your decree making James king."

"What if you abdicate?" I suggested. "I could have you retire due to declining health and advise the new king from your sickbed. After a year or two you could pass away quietly in your sleep."

Edward's face grew thoughtful. "That might work, though I doubt I would ever have thought of it. Such a peaceful solution makes me wonder whether you have the mettle to rule at all. I think I agree with you, James is a better choice. You are too soft to govern."

"You've earned your reward," I said suddenly, not bothering to acknowledge his backhanded insult. Turning away I walked back toward where Cyhan stood and beckoned for him to approach. As he passed me I warned him, "He will not leave this place alive."

Cyhan paused and then responded, "I cannot allow you to harm him." He had misunderstood the meaning of my words.

I simply shook my head, "You'll understand when you see him."

The veteran moved past me and found his king lying where I had left him. I gave him plenty of space but I stayed close enough to hear their words.

"You again," said Edward as he registered Cyhan's face.

"Your Majesty," answered Cyhan kneeling and bowing his head.

"Ever the faithful lapdog aren't you?" said the King, insulting his guardian even as his own face twisted with pain. "Do me one last service and finish me," he said after a moment.

The man who had spent his life training Anath'Meridum and then royal guardsmen and assassins answered in a voice that could have been cut from solid granite, "I am sworn to preserve your life sire. I cannot do that."

Edward's face clouded with anger, "You are sworn to obey me! Do as your king commands!"

Cyhan's voice remained neutral, "My oath to protect your person supersedes my oath of obedience your Majesty."

The King's voice grew desperate for his pain was unbearable. "Cyhan, please, do not leave me like this! Cut me loose from this agony! I would be done with the world."

The warrior's face remained still but his tone became sympathetic, "Release me from my oaths your Majesty."

"Just kill me damnitt!"

"I cannot. Dissolve my oaths your Majesty… release me," Cyhan replied softly.

"Very well, I absolve you of your duties and release you from your oaths. Now please, for the love of whatever gods are left, stop this pain!" cried the dying king.

Cyhan laughed and stood looking down on the man he had served for so long. "I would sooner give mercy to a dog," he said with disdain, and then he spat upon his former master. "You are not worth the effort to lift my sword and cut out your black heart." Bringing his foot down the big man stepped on the King's hand and ground the bones into the hard earth until the older man began screaming.

Sickened, I wanted to look away but I forced myself to watch.

The large warrior left him then and marched toward me, ignoring Edward's pitiful cries. "Let's get some air," he said as he drew near. "Listening to him disgusts me."

I followed him a good hundred yards until we could no longer hear the sounds of the King's suffering and then he turned back toward me and drew his sword. I drew back reflexively and readied my shield. I hadn't expected him to attack me after everything that had occurred, but I supposed that recent events might have unhinged his mind. I was utterly surprised and confused when instead of attacking the massive warrior instead went down on one knee and held up his sword, hilt first.

"I have spent my life serving a worthless master and bound by vows that I believed were worthwhile. Now I am free and I find that my life has been wasted," he said in a voice that was filled with emotion. This was a side of

Cyhan I had never seen, or even suspected. As I looked down on his face I saw there were tears welling in his eyes. "I have watched you Mordecai Illeniel and I know your heart. I cannot live as other men do for I have been bound by honor and vows my entire life. If you will have me, I will serve you for whatever remains of my life, in the hope that I can atone for the wrongs I have been forced to witness and commit."

A sadness and deep melancholy came over me as I looked on this man who even now could not live free. "I do not want your service Cyhan. You deserve to live your own life."

"You will have it or I will die here. I will not live otherwise," he answered determinedly.

"Very well," I said at last. Taking his sword I thrust it into the ground and placed his hands over the hilt before covering them with my own. Looking into his eyes I spoke, "I Mordecai Illeniel do take you into my service. Will you swear to serve and protect me as your solemn duty?"

"I will."

"I would have you take service as one of the Knights of the Stone, an order sworn to protect the people and serve the greater good. Will you accept a place among them?" I asked formally.

"I will if you so wish," he replied.

"I do," I answered. "I have one last oath I would have from you before I will accept you fully."

"I am willing," he responded.

"Will you swear to listen to your own conscience? Should fate and events conspire to such an extent that your past vows no longer make sense in the face of the present, I would have you swear to act according to your best judgment, rather than blindly follow your oaths."

He paused for a moment before replying, "I will gladly swear it."

"As your lord I have certain duties and responsibilities on your behalf and I shall endeavor to remain worthy of your service. We will hold your knighting in a few weeks once Sir Dorian is well enough to attend," I told him. "Now get up, I get uncomfortable when people kneel for too long," I added with a smile.

Cyhan stood and sheathed his sword. "If you don't mind I'd like to wait here until it's over." Although he didn't elaborate I knew he meant Edward's dying.

I nodded. "Meet me at my house in the city when it is done," I said and then I left him there. I wanted to check on Rose and then I needed to find Penny.

CHAPTER 47

Rose's condition hadn't changed much when I returned though she seemed warmer. Elaine still lay beside her, but her eyes were now open and she watched me silently as I checked on Rose.

Eventually her curiosity won out and she spoke before I did. "How did I get here?" she asked.

"I tricked you into making a mistake and then I threw you against a stone wall. I'm surprised you're awake already," I answered mildly. "Do you remember the fight?"

She shook her head negatively and after some questioning I discovered that she had no memory of the events that had occurred since she had summoned the shining god, something that had apparently happened the day before. Ironically, she had been praying to Celior to kill the King when he had offered to do more for her if she would help him cross the world bridge.

I ended our conversation as quickly as I could. "I need to find my wife and help a friend. I want you to stay here and keep Lady Rose warm until I send someone for you. Will you do that?" I asked.

She readily agreed and I went back to the throne room, or what was left of it. When I arrived I found Dorian conscious but unable to dig his way free of the rubble. I couldn't examine his body through the enchanted armor that encased him but I suspected he had some serious injuries.

Struggling with fatigue I began carefully moving the large stones and granite blocks that had him trapped. It would have been easier to 'listen' to the stones and extract him in the same way I had carried Rose through the ground once before but I had no desire to risk any further use of those abilities that day. I was still feeling rather strange after my experiences within the bosom of the earth.

Dorian gritted his teeth when I finally pulled him free. "Damn that hurts!" he declared through clenched teeth.

"How badly are you injured?" I asked him.

"I feel like everything is broken but somehow everything still seems to work," he replied.

"Let me get the armor off so I can examine you," I said quickly.

He pushed my hands aside with surprising strength, "I can walk. Once you take this armor off I'm not sure how bad it will be but it won't be pretty and I probably won't be able to move around much after that. Let me help while I can. Have you found Penny?"

I shook my head, "She's safe but I'm not sure where. I need to find her." I didn't bother explaining that she was with Moira.

"Then why are you here?!" he exclaimed.

I almost laughed at his reaction. It was typical of him. "Let me show you where Rose is before I abandon you. She's badly wounded."

That got his attention and it was several minutes before I could explain well enough to reassure him that she wasn't about to expire instantly. I led him to where Cyhan had left her and explained why she had a teenager bundled up with her. Someday I felt sure Dorian would eventually come to expect weird things to occur around me, but it didn't seem to have happened yet.

"Stay here with them," I said, to which he rolled his eyes. Obviously I didn't need to tell him that. "Cyhan is nearby and I'll have him come help you later when he's done," I said and surprisingly he simply nodded. I couldn't help but wonder what had transpired between the two warriors before Dorian had appeared in the throne room armed and armored.

Walking out I turned my thoughts outward and called to Moira again. *I need to see Penny. Where are you?*

After a long pause I heard her reply, *she is with me beside the great stone.*

What stone?

The stone I created before my final battle against Balinthor. It is near the palace on the east side, she replied.

I remembered the place. *Why there?*

When she answered I could detect a poignant feeling to her thoughts, *I sought to protect your child. There is no safer place in Lothion.*

Obviously she wasn't remembering my house. The enchantments there made it by far the most impregnable location in the capital. As I considered those things I hadn't meant to broadcast my thoughts, but Moira heard me anyway.

No, she countered, *there is no place safer than this. Even the gods could not enter here against my wishes.* There was a note of pride in her reply and a hint of something else, a feeling that seemed almost maternal.

My curiosity was fully engaged now and despite my bone weary state I hurried to reach the place she had named. I found them both, as she had said, standing beside the great stone that thrust up from the bedrock beside the palace. There was no sign of any door or entrance and I had never considered that there might be anything inside the colossal monolith before, but now I wondered.

Ignoring my inner questions I headed straight for Penelope. Considering my last words to her, she had a look of some apprehension on her face as I walked steadily toward her. "I did the best I could…" she began but I put a hand over her mouth and pulled her into a fierce embrace.

Her belly was larger than I remembered and before I knew what had happened I found myself sobbing as I held her. My emotions were so great that it took a short while before I realized that our awkward embrace was being shaken by Penelope's cries as well. It was the sort of moment that normally would only occur behind closed doors, but both of us had been through too much to worry about such things today.

Eventually we both calmed down and began to collect our thoughts. Looking around I realized Moira Centyr was gone already. "Did she take you inside the stone?" I asked. Despite my emotions I was curious what she had seen there. My magesight showed nothing but a solid rock with no hollows or inner chambers.

Penny nodded and then kissed me, which effectively ended our conversation for a minute or so. Holding her now, I felt fresh tears forming. "I thought I'd never see you again," I said softly, when I was able to break away from her lips at last.

"About the note," she replied, "I didn't think I could put anything more there…"

"Let's worry about that later," I interrupted. "What was inside the stone?"

"You have too much to deal with. We can talk about that in a day or two," she said with an odd look in her eyes.

I found the lack of details maddening. "Look Penny, I've had about all I can take of cryptic messages and hidden meanings. If you discovered something strange or important in there I need to know what it is!" Stress and weariness led me to raise my voice more than I might have normally.

"Mort, stop," she said calmly. "This isn't anything like that. Nothing bad, nothing serious or dangerous, we just talked, woman to woman."

"And what did you say?"

"Tomorrow," she insisted. "I can see Lord Hightower leading the city guard up the streets. You need to deal with him and explain what happened. We can discuss family matters later." She ran her hand over her belly and I was even more mystified than before.

I assumed the face of King Edward and spent the rest of the afternoon giving orders and generally making an ass of myself. Under my direction I had some of the rubble cleared away and Lord Hightower took charge of his daughter and Elaine. He moved them to his own residence to have them looked after. Dorian steadfastly refused to be separated from Lady Rose, so in the end Lord Hightower allowed him to 'guest' in the Hightower residence as well.

Cyhan was nowhere to be found and he had taken the King's body with him, or hidden it somewhere. I was grateful for his quick thinking, for once Hightower arrived the palace was swarming with activity and I had no further chances to sneak away from my new role as King of Lothion.

It looked as though I would be unable to meet James at the carriage house but luckily I still had the wooden message box, so I sent him a short note detailing the recent events and requesting they meet me at the palace.

My official story was that the Count di'Cameron had been summoned for an audience when the dragon attacked and partially destroyed the palace. I had no particular explanation for the shining god but I discovered quickly enough that few people questioned the king. I told a harrowing tale involving magic and the timely intervention of one very heroic wizard, Mordecai Illeniel. By the time I had finished my tale I was quite impressed and almost wished I could meet this amazing hero, for certainly I bore no resemblance to him.

When James and the others arrived that evening I had them brought in to one of the private guest suites (the royal chambers were partly demolished and unsuitable for visitors). Once I was sure that there were no eavesdroppers I dropped my disguise and addressed them as myself.

Because of his magesight my change in appearance was no surprise to Walter, but the others were still a bit shocked. "Damn Mordecai! Give us some warning next time!" said James.

I wanted to laugh but I was too tired to find the energy. "I did warn you as I recall."

He snorted, "I mean, right before, that was hours ago. A man needs a chance to prepare himself."

I wondered at the quirks of a man who had been unfazed by an evil wizard possessed by one of the dark gods assaulting his home, yet who found my sudden change of appearance unsettling. I passed over his remark and went on, "I am about as bone weary as a man can get. If you don't mind I'll get to the details before I collapse."

After my transformation my physical body had emerged unharmed, but my mind was beyond tired. The sensation was similar to having stayed up three or four days without sleep and I was beginning to see double. "Let me tell you what occurred on our end first then," replied James and he began to describe their raid on the Doronite compound.

It had started well, as they had easily gotten inside with the aid of Walter's invisibility. When they reached the area where the hostages were being held things got a bit out of hand. Harold had tripped and alerted one of the door guards, partly because he couldn't see while invisible. Fearing the worst he had slain the guard and an alarm went up.

The Duke's men outside were waiting for a problem such as that and had been given orders. When the cries rang out they stormed the small collection of buildings and the fighting turned bloody. Meanwhile Walter and Harold had secured Walter's wife and son, but they found no sign of his daughter. The older wizard's wife was named Rebecca, and some of the guards had played a cruel prank upon her, telling her that her daughter had been slain.

Neither she nor Walter had known the truth of the matter, and her husband reacted rather badly. Despite James' efforts to calm his men they had taken no prisoners, or more precisely, Walter had not. He had even gone after the few that escaped into the forest, though he wouldn't say what he had done to them.

I had a very good idea what the other man had been feeling. "I have excellent news for you Walter. Your daughter was here, though she gave me a bit of a hard time about being rescued."

"What?!" he managed to say, before he lost the use of his voice. The news overwhelmed him to such a degree that it was some time before I could finish my story and we all got a bit misty eyed.

Then I explained what had happened in the palace, though I abbreviated the story as much as possible. Still, much of the tale was outlandish so I had to repeat some parts several times. Near the end I pulled out the glowing stone that held Celior, "Here, this is it. Now do you see?"

Harold had asked me one too many times what the stone looked like.

As I drew the stone out it filled the room with a soft golden light that pulsed gently. Its presence in the room left no doubt in anyone's mind that it was indeed a living thing, even if it did appear to be just a glowing rock. "What are you going to do with it?" Harold asked.

I rubbed my short beard, "I have no earthly idea. I will have to find some use for it though; otherwise it will eventually destroy itself and free Celior. We can worry about that later. First on my list of priorities is getting some rest."

I had already shown Walter the spell for imitating the King's voice, as well as demonstrating it for him. He had known how to disguise his appearance beforehand so that wasn't a problem. I could see he was reluctant now when I mentioned him taking my place as Edward. After a moment I realized why. "You haven't seen your daughter yet!" I exclaimed, "…or spent any time with your wife and son. I'm sorry Walter! I didn't think."

He shook his head, "No Mordecai, you've done enough for me today. I don't mind this duty if it will help keep the kingdom in one piece."

I started to argue with him, for I couldn't stand the thought of him being separated from them any longer. It had been four years for him already. "Let me handle today and you can take over for a week or so after that," I replied. "I'll just sit down and rest my eyes for a few minutes and I'll be right as rain."

Needless to say… I didn't wake up again anytime soon.

EPILOGUE

I woke in bed several days later. I might have slept longer but for the loud snoring in my ear. Penny lay beside me and her pregnancy had done nothing to diminish her nighttime noise, quite the opposite actually. I smiled and watched her for a while. Finding her beside me was the best thing to have happened to me since she had been kidnapped.

Using my fingers I lifted a stray piece of her hair away from her mouth and nose. I tried to do it without disturbing her but her eyes opened anyway. She had become a light sleeper as her belly had grown.

We spent a long time there, simply watching each other in the dim light. I could have stayed that way for years, but for the urgent call of Mother Nature. When I returned from the privies I found Penny sitting up and waiting for me.

"I thought you would never wake up," she said as I climbed into the bed beside her.

I leaned in and smelled her hair. Something about Penelope's scent had always captivated me. It was a smell of warmth, affection, and home. "I thought I might never see you again, and for a while I thought you were dead," I replied.

"About that Mort," she began but I shushed her with my hand.

"I was under a bit more stress than usual when I saw you yesterday. Don't apologize, you did what you thought best and it worked out in the end," I told her. "I'd rather apologize to you Penny. I failed you terribly, and I've done nothing but struggle with that knowledge every day since I found out what had happened to you."

She leaned over awkwardly (her belly made it difficult), and kissed me quickly. "I know that's what you felt, but it isn't the truth. No one person can ever be prepared for everything."

"Do you want to talk about it? What happened after they took you...," I asked. I feared the story she might have to tell for the guilt it might leave me with, but I had to know nonetheless.

Penny looked down at her hands, "It wasn't pleasant but nothing happened that you should worry over. I'll get past it."

Something in her features pulled at my heart. "I'll worry anyway. Did they hurt you?"

"The King or the undead?" she replied with a bitter voice.

"Either."

"While we were with the shiggreth there was no respite, no privacy, no comfort, and no warmth, but they did not hurt me," she answered slowly. "They wanted us for hostages, but they kept us like animals."

A dozen questions ran through my mind but I kept my tongue and waited, watching her carefully. Penny looked away before she spoke again.

"We were fed well enough, but they took Dorian's armor and clothes from him. He was badly bruised and battered beneath it, with blisters where it had pinched and chafed. I had to bathe him with what water they would bring me and eventually I managed to convince one of them to give us a blanket," Penny stopped and looked down, letting her hair cover her face.

A new fear replaced the ones I had held before, a fear not of abuse but of solace. Alone for so long I began to realize the toll her isolation might have taken… and the ways she might have held it at bay. Yet I could no more voice those fears than I could have deliberately hurt her in any other way, but the seed of doubt was there now. I had been tempted as well, though my situation had been far easier to bear.

"It was cold at night, especially when we were in the caves. They fed us nothing but meat and water. We had no fire and so we slept huddled together. Occasionally they approached us, but Dorian wouldn't let them near me, though if they had wanted they could have slain us both very easily by then. When they eventually brought us to the King it was a relief. His men clothed us and gave us both privacy and warm rooms. It was almost like being a guest of the King again," she finished.

I stroked her hair. "I suppose that is one thing I cannot lay blame on the King for… he did treat his hostages well," I said at last.

Penny glanced up at me with wet eyes, "Mordecai… I need to talk to you… about Dorian."

Closing my own eyes I summoned up all the strength I could muster before opening them again. "Penelope, I love you. Whatever happened I will not feel differently or lay blame upon you," I answered with honest eyes and a liar's heart. I knew that deep down it would bother me and it might take years to completely accept it. Still I knew I could not honestly blame her.

"Hey!" she said loudly, snapping her fingers in front of me. "Don't ever think that again. Nothing of the sort happened! Are you listening Mort?"

Something like relief washed over me. "I just want you to understand that I love you, no matter what."

She glared at me suspiciously and then her face softened. "You are right to worry. They kept us like caged animals and we had only each other for support. I was tempted Mort, sorely tempted, I will not lie. We slept together for warmth only, but I do not know if Dorian will ever get over his shame."

I understood immediately. Dorian was the one man I would trust more than any other in that situation, but the toll upon his self-image might be too much for him. He held impossible ideals for himself and even having resisted temptation the reality of his own human frailty might have undermined his sense of self-worth. "I'll talk to him," I replied.

"No!" she said, alarmed. "He'd die of shame if he knew I had told you this."

I shook my head. "He'll die of guilt if I don't. I know Dorian. He won't be able to live with himself until he has confessed every sin that he didn't actually commit, both to you and me," I told her. Then I had a sudden realization, "Oh damn!" He would also want to confess to Rose. I trusted her reaction but things might get terribly awkward before it was all said and done.

"What?" asked Penny.

"Rose," I said simply.

Penny shrugged, "I think you're underestimating her."

"Maybe you're right," I agreed. "She is a woman of rare talents."

Penny gave me a discerning stare, "Something happened."

I stared back, "Nothing. You have my word on it."

Her features relaxed, "What was that look then?"

"Rose and I both suffered a tragedy at the same time, so I got to see her at her worst. There were some temptations… but mostly I just gained respect for her character. You are still the only woman for me my dear," I said truthfully.

Penelope's face contained a mixture of warring emotions, or so I thought. Eventually she leaned over and kissed me quickly. "I have to go."

Confused I asked, "What?"

My bewilderment set her to laughing, "Nothing serious, I believe you… it's my bladder. I think it's the size of a pea these days. Honestly, I can't go more than ten minutes without having to find a chamber pot or run to the privies."

I laughed as well. Marriage was nothing like I had expected a year ago, instead it was different, better in some ways and simply weirder in others.

The weeks went on and things settled down. Walter and I took turns playing King and keeping the kingdom running, though he took the larger portion of the job. James was kind enough to stay near and lend his advice on policy matters. His newfound closeness to the King was the source of a number of new rumors but none of them amounted to much. A few weeks after the 'incident' at the palace Edward suddenly decided it was time to clear up the matter of his succession.

Cyhan had hidden the King's body and I used the 'stasis' enchantment I had found to preserve his corpse until we would need it at a later date. I was quite grateful for his quick thinking… otherwise we might have had to find a body and then arrange some sort of disfiguring accident or fire. In either case there would have been rumors.

A proclamation was made and a document drawn up, setting out in clear language that James Lancaster was to be the next king. This created an uproar among the gentry, but most of the nobility were wise enough to avoid antagonizing King Edward… at least while he was still alive.

A month later he abdicated in favor of James, though Edward was kind enough to stay in the capital to provide advice and counsel to the new king. He also made it quite clear that it was fully his intention to make certain that James held the throne. There were numerous grumbles among the landed nobles but none were made within hearing of the King, present or past.

⟢———⟣

The summer had faded and autumn was beginning to make itself known. The leaves had yet to turn but there was a crispness in the air that hinted at the coming cold of winter. The mood in Albamarl had become rather festive as people began to anticipate the final harvest and the end of another year's labors.

Penelope had ripened to a fullness that I had trouble believing and I had grown nervous with anticipation. I was also afraid she might fall every time she took to her feet.

We were sitting in the parlor on one of my days 'off' from playing the retired king and Penny was watching the fire when she suddenly rose from her chair. "Mordecai," she said.

I was already up and across the room. The midwife had told me she was due in just a week or so and since then I had been unable to relax. "Let me help you," I offered.

"I'm not dying you know," she said irritably, "just pregnant."

"I know," I said for what was probably the twentieth time.

"I need to show you something," she told me. "My time is soon and I need to talk to you beforehand."

"Why don't you sit down and let me fetch whatever it is you need?" I suggested.

The look she gave me was anything but grateful. "I want to show you what is in the stone," she explained.

"Oh," I said with remarkable wit. "Wait… what stone?"

She graced me with an expression of deep sympathy, such as one might bestow upon a very dim but well-loved child. "For all your cleverness you really do have the memory of a turnip sometimes Mort," she answered. "Moira's stone… the great stone," she added to clarify.

I couldn't understand her change of heart. "After months making me wait and putting me off, you suddenly want to show me… now?" I asked.

She nodded.

"You make no sense. Your water could break any day now. I don't know if it's even safe for you to leave the house. What if something happened?" I told her sensibly. "Why not wait 'til after the baby comes?" I suggested.

Penny laughed, "The baby won't just fall out right after my water breaks you know. There would be plenty of time to get home and call for Sarah." Sarah was the name of our midwife, a woman of towering confidence and experience. Penelope gave me a more serious look, "Besides, there is a very good reason why we need to go now… before I deliver."

An hour later we had reached the great stone. As always it stood forebodingly over the road near the east side of the palace. Nothing had changed.

"Should I call Moira to open it for us?" I asked.

Penny shook her head negatively and approached the stone. "She said to show you this spot." Her hand rested upon the stone in a place roughly three feet from the ground. The stone was discolored there, a slightly different shade of grey than the rest.

I examined the area closely but I could detect nothing. No sign of magic or anything else, other than rough grey stone. "There's nothing here."

"You have to say the password," Penny told me.

"And that is?"

"It's your name… just your first name," she replied. "She told me that she set the password a thousand years ago, Mort, just before she fought Balinthor."

"Then why would she choose my name… oh!" I had just remembered that the man she had loved then bore the same first name as I did. Leaning closely I placed my hand over the spot and spoke, "Mordecai."

Runes appeared, lightly etched in the stone around my hand. They were delicate and only visible to my magesight but I recognized the pattern. It was similar to the one in my house, the pattern that guarded the secret room in the library, shielding it from magesight. *It must work in a similar manner to Walter's invisibility when he uses it just to avoid magical detection,* I thought.

I put the thought aside for later and used my hand to activate the runes. A modest doorway appeared in the rock near where I stood. The door itself was solid stone but even as I watched the massive granite door slid away into the interior of the great monolith, leaving an open passageway. Penelope stepped forward and led me inside.

Having entered, my mind immediately began to explore the interior, for it became visible to my magesight once I was past the outer enchantment. The corridor led ahead for almost ten yards before ending in a small chamber, one that was devoid of any furniture or adornment, save for a strange object in the center. My arcane senses could make little of it other than its strange egg-like shape, that and the fact that it glowed intensely with powerful magic.

Penny spoke as we walked down the tight hallway, "Moira built this place to guard something precious to her. It was the last and greatest of her tasks before she sacrificed herself to defeat Balinthor."

The sense of anticipation built until at last we emerged into the chamber and I could look upon the thing it held with my own eyes. The room was dark but for the glow of the enchantment around the pedestal in the center of the room. *"Lyet,"* I said softly, creating a gentle glow above my head.

Now that my normal eyes could see it was plain what was there. A stone pedestal rose up and held a wooden cradle. The entirety of it was wrapped within a powerful stasis field enchantment. The runes were inscribed carefully around the entire pedestal, sealing the cradle and its occupant within a pocket of frozen time.

I stared at Penny in wonder, awe, and with a considerable amount of trepidation. "Is that what I think it is?"

Penny's eyes were brimming with tears, "No Mordecai, not 'it', *she*. This is Moira's daughter."

To say I was shocked was an understatement. Flabbergasted might have been a better term, if I had been capable of speech. "How...?"

"She held off facing Balinthor until she delivered her child. That is why she didn't help Gareth fight him previously... she was pregnant. She built this place to protect her child and waited... until she could place her child safely here... before she attempted to defeat the dark god," she elaborated.

A number of things began to fall into place within my mind. Moira's secret purpose, her occasional willful initiative, and now that I thought about it… even her very existence. "She created a copy of herself, not to protect her knowledge, but to protect her baby," I said aloud. "But she's hidden it for so long… why tell us now, and why did she tell you first?" As I spoke my mind raced ahead while my eyes slid downward from Penelope's sad eyes to her heavy belly.

"Her daughter is a newborn, Mort. She needs a mother… and a father. You already bear the same name her father had." Penny rested a hand atop her bulging abdomen. "We can raise them as twins, brother and sister."

I looked down on the small infant, partly shrouded by the glow of the enchantment. My vision was blurry though I wasn't entirely sure why. Reaching up I found that my cheeks were wet. "Let me remove this enchantment," I said suddenly.

"No Mort!" Penny said grabbing my arm. "You silly goose, you have to wait 'til I give birth!"

I was fairly disoriented. "Why?" I asked without thinking.

Penny placed my hand on her chest. "So I can feed her… babies get hungry."

I left my hand there. It was a good place and I was in need of comfort. I couldn't help but find some irony in her reply however. I had spent half my life thinking of bosoms, and yet the first time they were the answer to a question I failed to consider them.

Penny pulled my hand away at last, "You'll have to behave yourself more once the children get older."

Children, I thought, and the room swayed around me.

⟶⬥⟵

Edward died later that week. The story that was told was that he died quietly in his sleep. I had planned to wait a few more months… but I had a feeling I would have my hands full soon. One child was scary enough, but two… twins, that would be a monumental task. I wasn't quite sure I would be up to it, and only time would tell what sort of children Matthew and Moira would be.

The Story Continues In:

The God-Stone War

Stay up to date with my releases by signing up for my
newsletter at:

Magebornbooks.com

Books by Michael G. Manning:

Mageborn:
The Blacksmith's Son
The Line of Illeniel
The Archmage Unbound
The God-Stone War
The Final Redemption

Embers of Illeniel (a prequel series):
The Mountains Rise
The Silent Tempest
Betrayer's Bane

Champions of the Dawning Dragons:
Thornbear
Centyr Dominance
Demonhome

The Riven Gates:
Mordecai
The Severed Realm (coming summer 2018)
More to be announced

Standalone Novels:
Thomas